D1800140
9780434418275

# DORIS LESLIE

# Notorious Lady

*The Life and Times of the*
*Countess of Blessington*

---

HEINEMANN : LONDON

William Heinemann Ltd
15 Queen Street, Mayfair, London WiX 8BE

LONDON MELBOURNE TORONTO
JOHANNESBURG AUCKLAND

First published 1976
© Doris Leslie 1976

434 41827 7

Printed in Great Britain by Cox & Wyman Ltd
London, Fakenham and Reading

*Notorious Lady*

BOOKS BY
# DORIS LESLIE

## Novels

FULL FLAVOUR
FAIR COMPANY
CONCORD IN JEOPARDY
ANOTHER CYNTHIA
HOUSE IN THE DUST
FOLLY'S END
THE PEVERILLS
PERIDOT FLIGHT
AS THE TREE FALLS
PARAGON STREET
THE MARRIAGE OF MARTHA TODD
A YOUNG WIVES' TALE
THE DRAGON'S HEAD
CALL BACK YESTERDAY

## Biographical Studies

ROYAL WILLIAM: *Life of William IV*
POLONAISE: *A Romance of Chopin*
WREATH FOR ARABELLA: *Life of Lady Arabella Stuart*
THAT ENCHANTRESS: *Life of Abigail Hill, Lady Masham*
THE GREAT CORINTHIAN: *Portrait of the Prince Regent*
A TOAST TO LADY MARY: *Life of Lady Mary Wortley
Montagu*
THE PERFECT WIFE: *Life of Mary Anne Disraeli
Viscountess Beaconsfield*
I RETURN: *The Story of François Villon*
THIS FOR CAROLINE: *Life of Lady Caroline Lamb*
THE SCEPTRE AND THE ROSE: *Marriage of Charles II
and Catherine of Braganza*
THE REBEL PRINCESS: *Life of Sophia Dorothea,
Princess of Celle*
THE DESERT QUEEN: *Life and Travels of
Lady Hester Stanhope*
THE INCREDIBLE DUCHESS: *Life and Times of
Elizabeth Chudleigh*
NOTORIOUS LADY: *Life and Times of
the Countess of Blessington*

# CONTENTS


| | | |
|---|---|---|
| Foreword | | *page* vii |
| Part One | Wednesday's Child | 3 |
| Part Two | The Circus | 69 |
| Part Three | Scandal | 141 |
| Part Four | The Broken Mirror | 189 |
| Afterword | | 271 |

# FOREWORD

In this life of Margaret, Lady Blessington, I have adhered strictly to fact. No character is fictitious and much of the dialogue is taken from her journals and her 'Thought Book', as she named the diary she kept at night.

Of her wretched childhood we know little more than that, having been born on a Wednesday, according to the old nursery rhyme, she was 'full of woe'. We have no actual record of the dialogue during the scenes of her early years, as it was not until after her marriage to Blessington that she kept a diary of her travels, her 'Idlers in France and Italy'.

Although in the first few decades of the nineteenth century she became well known for her salons and her intimacy with important men in politics, the arts and literature, many of whom have become immortal, she was shunned by the women of society because of the scandals attached to her name. These may have had little if any foundation, but certain it is that her disastrous first marriage, when sold by her scoundrel of a father to a sadistic brute, resulted in an abnormal frigidity that repelled any advance of sexual intercourse from those men who desired her. It was not without reason that a contemporary chronicler said of her that 'she won all mens' hearts, who had never a heart to return'.

She has become known to later generations, not as a novelist, for such of her works that have endured are mediocre, but for her *Conversations of Lord Byron*. These again were condemned by her enemies either by the men she repulsed or the women who envied her popularity with their menfolk, as a 'tissue of lies' or 'entirely her own invention'. Yet there is no doubt that she did reproduce with accuracy much of Byron's words and character and has given us a more faithful portrait of the poet than have many who attempted to do so.

None the less, despite the animadversion her name aroused among the women of her time and age, she, from an obscure and unhappy youth, became one of the most famous, or infamous, women of her day whose name has been coupled with that of d'Orsay he, who as the last of the dandies, has been better known to posterity than she, either as 'Sally' Power, or Margaret, Countess of Blessington.

A bibliography of authorities consulted will be found at the end of the book.

DORIS LESLIE

# PART ONE

## *Wednesday's Child*

ONE

It had rained heavily overnight; the lawn held pools of water reflecting the sullen November sky and the wind-swept branches of the almost barren trees . . . 'Throwing their arms about,' she whispered, 'as if afraid the wind will hurt them.' She knew all of hurt when she happened to be within reach of her father in one of his savage drink-sodden tempers. Not that she could have known him for drunk since, on the few occasions she with her sister and brothers had been taken to Mass, she had come to regard her father as God the Father who could do no wrong, least of all to be drunk like some of the squireen neighbours who came to dine and play at cards till dawning, to keep one awake all hours. So that she must say *mea culpa mea maxima culpa*, which meant, as explained by Miss Dwyer, that she had sinned exceedingly and must ask God the Father (her father?) to forgive her, *libera nos a malo*, which Miss Dwyer said was to deliver us (or me?) from evil.

But more than her father's rageful fist, which she could dodge if careful, did it hurt to hear her brother Michael laugh to see her cringe in fear of a blow, glad it was not him to be damned to hell for being what she was and what he wasn't . . . 'And what am I?' she would ask him, wiping a furtive tear (never let him see her cry – to laugh the more). 'What you are,' he jeered, 'is the ugly duckling, as Papa calls you.'

Ugly. Yes, that's what she was and why Michael and young Robert jibed at her and her sister Ellen pulled her straight, dark hair. Ellen's hair wasn't mousey nor straight; hers was all goldy curls, her cheeks pink, not 'peaked and pasty-faced,' as Michael would taunt her. And her mother would look at her to scold: 'Turning up your nose at good food. Don't like this and can't eat that, little misery. No wonder Miss Dwyer thinks we starve you. Interfering old cat...'

Miss Dwyer, who last year had found her lying in the woods on the wet moss shaken with sobs, less for the pain of her bruises than for having deserved, if she did deserve, Papa's anger and his kick – yes, a kick this time – on her bottom for getting in his way when he was in haste to the privy where she could hear him being sick. And Miss Dwyer who had seen her lying face downward had called to her:

'Why, Sally – Sally Power, is it? What do you here, lying in the wet?'

She had been made to get up and brought home by Miss Dwyer in her pony-trap, she having been to the village and back through the bridle-path of the woods – Lord Donough-more's woods, but he gave right of way to Miss Dwyer and Papa, 'Beau' Power, as Papa was known. Why 'Beau?' (which Sally always believed meant the bow of a ribbon until Miss Dwyer began to teach her French).

'She should not be allowed out, lying in the woods after the rains to give her the rheumatics,' Miss Dwyer had told Mama, 'especially with these marauding rebels hereabout. And what is that nasty bruise under her eye?'

'She must have fallen,' Mama had said. 'She is always falling. Such a puny little thing. Wonder 'tis we reared her.'

And on this shivering sun-lost day with winter hard on autumn's heels, Sally recalled how Miss Dwyer had been given reluctant permission from Mama to teach her how to read and write, for until then she had learned no more than the alphabet and part of the Mass. The boys had some schooling from the priest, but Sally, Mama told Miss Dwyer, was 'so sickly, always having colds and kept in bed not to give it to the others. Never well enough to take lessons had she the wit to learn them which she has not, at all.'

4

But she did learn them under Miss Dwyer's tuition and was taught to spell her name, her baptismal name of Margaret after her patron saint, although she had been called Sally as long as she could remember.

'Too stupid and ugly to be called after a saint,' her brother Michael teased her.

Kneeling there on the window seat looking out on the sodden lawn where the slow death fall of yellow leaves lay like newly minted pennies among the last of summer's rose petals scattered from the drenched flower beds: How long, she asked herself, must I live so unkindly? . . . A strange thought for a six-year-old, yet not so strange for one who had never known love from either parent, and none to care for her save Miss Dwyer, whom her father, that blackguardly handsome rake 'Beau' Power, called, 'a poker-stiff virgin of fifty who for want of a man needs must take a hot brick to her bed to warm her!'

Edmund Power, a vulgar, swaggering boozer had, in a series of drinking bouts, attracted the attention of Lord Donoughmore, the local representative of the Castle party. He was ever on the watch for some suitable bullying type to hunt the rebels swarming all over Tipperary. To relieve himself of the ruthless persecution deemed necessary to deal with malcontents, Donoughmore approached Power, who had recently moved his family from the village of Knockbrit where Sally was born, to the county town of Clonmel.

There Power had joined a firm of corn-chandlers where, for his conviviality allied to a ribald sense of humour, he became popular among other topers and neighbouring squires, to his undoing.

While still living in her native village near Cashel, Sally had come under the protection of Miss Dwyer and it was a bitter grief to the forlorn, lonely child when the family removed to Clonmel.

No sooner had Donoughmore decided to make use of

Power for his own ends, than he raked him in for the uncongenial job that should have been authority's devoir: systematic terrorism against the rebels. Thus, with a flattering amiability that appealed to Power's respect for a title, and even the hint of one for himself should he serve the Castle party well, Donoughmore, representing the Viceregal Court, offered him a magistracy.

The offer was instantly accepted: and as the new magistrate heading a troop of dragoons but with no definite assurance of a stipend nor any guarantee of further honour, 'Beau' Power embarked on a country-wide campaign to bring the poverty-stricken rebels to their knees or, with threats, to the gallows.

On that day in November 1797 when we first met Sally bemoaning her 'unkindly' fate, she and the rest of Power's brood had been moved from Knockbrit near Cashel to the house in Clonmel only the week before: a sorry day for Sally, snatched from the one and only friend she had ever known.

Miss Dwyer, despite her 'poker-stiff' exterior, sustained within her spinsterish flat bosom a secret longing, less for a man to her bed than for a child to care for and mother. In this lost frustrated little one she had found compensation for her own virginal frustration.

Sad indeed for Sally was the parting with Miss Dwyer, the only soul who had ever shown her kindness, but a kindness that never bordered upon sentimentality. No. Miss Dwyer could not shed her protective façade more than could a snail shed its shell to reveal its inner self. Brusque, forthright, she bade the tearful Sally:

'Give over snivelling, my dear. You will not be forgotten in my prayers for your well-being, and the hope that you will continue in your studies, and in particular that which I have taught you of botany. Do you remember what the Good Book says of the flowers of the fields – the lilies? What did Solomon say of them? Solomon who was – what was he?'

6

'A king and – the cleverest man who ever lived,' piped Sally.

'The wisest man. And what of the lilies, the flowers of the fields?'

'They tile not —'

'Toil not,' corrected Miss Dwyer, 'meaning they do not labour for their living, yet Solomon in all his glory was – what?'

'Not,' hesitated Sally, 'dressed like them.'

'That is near enough.' Then seeing Sally's mouth pucker and her eyes overflowing, 'Clonmel,' Miss Dwyer reminded her, 'is not too far for me to come and visit your mama and you, once in a while.'

'You will? Oh, Miss Dwyer, if you will!'

'I make no promises but we will see. So goodbye and,' Miss Dwyer stiffly bent to bestow a kiss on the child's forehead 'and – God bless you.'

Nor, maybe, were Sally's the only tear-moist eyes.

The departure of the Power family from Knockbrit was an occasion of rejoicing for Sally's brothers and sister Ellen, excited at the prospect of living in a town, for they had only known village life and the isolated solitude in one of the most beautiful counties in Ireland.

Not so Sally; to her this parting from the dour Miss Dwyer was a bitter grief; she whose outward stern austerity concealed, as the child's instinct sensed, a warmth and kindliness that she had never received from those nearest her.

During the drive to Clonmel, the county town of Tipperary, Mrs Power, harassed with the upheaval of the move and another pregnancy, her almost perennial state during eight years of a miserable marriage, had vented her exasperation on Sally, still heart-brokenly 'snivelling' in a corner of the tumble-down carriage, hired, since Power had drunk the wherewithal to own one.

'Stop that whining, can't you!' cried the mother, 'stop it,

little misery!' Nor could a series of alternate cuffs, buffetings and pinches administered throughout the remainder of the journey, result in more than temporarily halting Sally's tears.

The arrival at their new home was greeted with boisterous jubilance from the other children, while Sally stood disconsolately apart clutching something hidden under her cloak. Michael, seeing a suspicious bulge that she endeavoured to conceal, pounced on her with derisive whoops to drag forth a bunch of withered flowers she had brought with her as a memento of the country lanes and hedgerows that, under Miss Dwyer's guidance, she had come to know and love.

'Look here! Look what she's got here!' shouted Michael. 'A lot o'stinkin' weeds.'

'For mercy's sake!' exclaimed her mother, who, between the bustle and hustle of removal, the placing of furniture, much of which had been brought the day before, and a week's packing of baggage amid the incessant clamour of her offspring, had come to the end of her tether. 'To bring that rubbish into the house!'

' 'Tis the flowers o' the fields when Sol'man in all his glory was'n dressed,' whimpered Sally.

'I'll give you glory!' With another cuff on the weeping Sally's head, Mrs Power tossed the cherished if withered gatherings out of the window. 'I've had more than enough of you!' her mother wrathfully exploded. 'Taking your tales to that Miss Dwyer and telling lies about your father and me.'

'I never – I didn't,' sobbed Sally, 'tell tales and no lies, at all.'

'Yes, you did – you do!' Michael formed a ring with the rest of the children to surround her, echoing their mother in a chant of: 'Little misery, tell-tale *liar*!' . . .

Who to see the scorned neglected child, the Ugly Duckling of Beau Power's handsome brood, could have guessed at the brilliant future destined for her, to dazzle the social world of London with her beauty and wit, 'to win all men's hearts', as was said of her, 'she who had never a heart to return!'

That heart, bruised, battered and unmended, was to be replaced by an artificial replica of the heart of Sally Power: 'The most gorgeous Lady Blessington' as one of her chroniclers named her.

*　　*　　*

Edmund (Beau) Power was mightily pleased with himself and his new magisterial appointment. Having swallowed, in equal quantities, the flattery and liberal wine with which his noble patron plied him, he and his riproaring dragoons scoured the country from dusk to dawn hunting the rebels.

The Beau's elevation from an out-of-pocket, out-at-elbows drunk with not an acre of land nor a pound in his purse that was not owed to a dozen or more creditors, aroused much bibulous mirth among his cronies in the taverns with punning allusions to 'Power's rise to power', and, as was added by some who had reason for envy, 'Power's rise — to fall!' Little could he know, so puffed up was he by his change of circumstance, that this prophecy made over the tankards would, some few years hence, be catastrophically fulfilled.

In the meantime Power, well content with his promotion, continued assiduously to hunt the desperate rebels unaware he was heading for disaster that would rebound not only on himself but upon Sally, his innocent young daughter.

Until the removal from Knockbrit and the idle, *laisser-faire* existence Power had enjoyed, as a more or less devout Catholic he had sympathized with the rebels and their grievances. But now that he had gone over to the enemy, Lord Donoughmore, representative of Castle rule, he brought upon himself much hostility from those with whom he had been wont to fraternize.

Clonmel, indeed almost the whole of Tipperary, was

known to be strongly opposed to Viceregal authority, while Power's ruthless persecution of the rebels, the capture and beating up of many who had been his friends, resulted in vengeful attacks upon his property or such of it that his small income from a firm of corn-chandlers, enabled him to reclaim a modicum of his acreage at Knockbrit.

A few months after the removal to Clonmel, Power had acquired a granary which besides the slight income derived from the corn-chandlers' business had brought him some little profit. But while he rampaged through the country-side chasing miscreants, whatever yield his granary could afford him went into the tills of the taverns where he and his dragoons would halt in their pursuit of fugitives.

Power's 'rise to power' had not given his wife much relief from her perpetual household problems of making frayed ends meet with insufficient means to provide for her young, though Sally still exasperated her mother by her want of appetite.

'A skinny bit of rag and bone,' Ellen Power would complain to her husband, contrasting the pale, frail, unattractive 'little misery' with the rest of her healthy boisterous brood. 'However did I come by so unaccountable sullen a brat, a changeling! I'd lay my life on't that one o' the Green People came in the night of my labour to carry her off and misplace her, unless I did not know I'd conceived her with you for my sins.'

Ellen Power, descended remotely from the Earls of Desmond and more immediately from the Catholic family of Sheehy, lacked nothing of Irish folk lore; and it is likely that her connections with the Desmonds and Sheehys may have induced Power to woo and, unhappily for Ellen, to win her, he who had no ancestral peerage, no reputable county family of whom he could boast.

On a night in the new year of 1798, Sally, who shared a bed in an attic with her younger sister Ellen, was awakened by a formidable commotion in the courtyard below. Through the casement, for which Mrs Power had not yet bought a curtain, could be seen a reddening sky – 'Sure, 'tis as if,' said Sally when, for want of better audience, she did sometimes talk to herself, ' 'twas a sunset in the middle o' the night.'

Ellen turned, muttering in her sleep with a somnolent kick. She was given to kicking while she slept, pushing Sally to the edge of the bed, in danger of tumbling out of it; on this occasion she did tumble out of it and landed on the floor. Picking herself up, she went over to the window uncertain if the terrifying sight that met her eyes were a nightmarish dream. The granary hard by the house was ablaze. Flames soared skyward amid clouds of smoke. The attic casement was half open, and smoke drifted into the room causing Sally chokingly to cough. No dream was this, and no need to pinch herself to know that she had wakened to horrific reality.

Down in the courtyard hordes of men were crowded, bearing torches, yelling execrations at one figure in night-shirt and nightcap whom she recognized as her father; and above the shouting mob she heard his voice ring out: 'You devils! I'll see you hanged for this!'

Then from among that seething throng come from all parts of the county, another figure fought his way fore-most, raising a fist to smite the air and fling back at Power: 'You! To talk o' hangin', bad cess to ye – divil's kin that ye are! To turn coat an' hunt them what ye swore to befriend! What roight ahve such as you to do us wrong! Be damned to you and them that persecute us, run us to earth loike the foxes – them that ahve holes but we have none, turned from our doors, our homes ravaged – our pigs stole from us, our potato crops ruined, trampled under the feet of your —'

His voice was strangled in his throat at the sound of a shot and then a cry from him of 'Break! Break!' followed by a general stampede. The raiders, pursued by Power's dragoons who had seen from their quarters the fiery sky

and the columns of smoke, fled helter-skelter seeking escape
from capture, if not from death.

It is not known if many were caught on that particular
night or thereafter, but certain it is that if one or none
suffered the ultimate penance as threatened by Power when
his granary was burnt, his persecution of the rebels continued with renewed brutality.

For several years he and his dragoons pursued their ruthless activities – presumably to maintain law and order, and,
as far as Power was concerned, in the hope of recognition
from the Viceregal Court for services rendered.

That he had at last received an invitation to visit Dublin
and be presented to the Viceroy gave him ambitiously to
hope. He saw himself with a medal on his chest kneeling in
homage to his Sovereign's deputy, and a lump sum endowed
with gratitude for his unfailing loyalty. Alas for his hopes!
Beau Power, apart from a chilly acknowledgement of his
bowed head, was offered nothing more tangible than a brief
sub-royal handshake; no reward either financial or honourable. Viceregal hospitality went no farther than a presenta-
tion once in two or three years. No favour, no coveted
honour came his way and, dismayingly, no cash as had been
hinted by his patron, Lord Donoughmore, who, since
Power's initial promotion to a magistracy, had completely
ignored his existence. The counties of Tipperary and Water-
ford, where he had hunted the peasantry and the anti-
Castle rebels causing untold hardships, destruction, the
confiscation of their meagre properties and the continued
vandalism, in the name of loyalty to his King and Country,
lost him many of his friends. These were the neighbouring
squires and officers from the local garrison with whom he
had used to drink deep, play high, and entertain throughout
each uproarious night.

During those few years things went from bad to worse
for Power, no longer the 'Beau'. He had considerably
coarsened, was bloated from drink; and his less disreputable
neighbours, notwithstanding that he represented Castle

rule, ostracized him. His house at Clonmel had become a nightly saturnalia where he and his cronies would drink themselves paralytic, to be lugged back to bed by their servants. Although he was still nominally a magistrate this did not enhance his prestige with the county while he continued ruthlessly to harry the rebels, devastating their crops, maiming their cattle, seeking vengeance in reprisal for the damage to his property and fostering hatred to create continuous revolt over which Power had little or no control.

His leisure hours, which were invariably almost half his days and all his nights when not chasing rebels, he spent with his rowdy companions, while his wife, cowed into submission by her violent-tempered husband, had developed into a timid, negative nonentity who, seeking any roof but her own, would leave him to his orgies and take herself and her young daughters to a neighbour's house for shelter. None was particularly eager to receive her for the name of Power stank through Tipperary, but rather than endure the orgiastic revelry at home she sought whatever alternative was offered her no matter how unwelcome her reception.

In this riotous atmosphere dominated by its tyrannical, bullying master, Sally, who should still have been in the schoolroom, was forced to meet and mingle with her father's rowdy visitors.

And as she grew from bud to blossom, the pale weakling unwanted child was, in her early teens, as a flower late in blooming, so that her father, in or out of his cups, came to realize his 'Ugly Duckling' might be less of a liability than a profitable asset. She and her younger sister Ellen, although not such a surprise in her development since she had always been a pretty, attractive little girl, were both commanded to attend their father's table and, against their mother's feeble protest, presented to his neighbours and the officers from the garrison.

It did not escape Power's bleary eye that of his two young daughters Sally engaged the attention of one who was not too drunk to see, for as he told the gratified father: 'This girl of yours is a pleasing little piece, and looks to be a beauty were she grown.' For Sally, late in flowering, was still breastless as a boy and this for some of them enhanced her charm.

'And why,' asked another, 'have you kept her shut away from us so long?'

It required no astute perception among the officers to see that the child Sally, if dumb and painfully shy, being more frightened than flattered by their attention, since most of them were anything but sober, was 'something worth having!' as they put it to themselves and laid wagers on which one would have her first.

But her father was not to let her go – 'rented out', as in assumed indignation, he gave it to all and sundry who might bid for her. 'Nor is she for sale, and if any one of you thinks that either of my daughters can be offered at a price, you'll have to meet me at sword or pistol point.'

A righteous enough reasoning, though Power had it well in mind that Sally was indeed for sale 'at a price' but, be it understood, only as an honourable wife and not, as parental wrath defined it between hiccups – 'not as you – you who dare to con – contemplate so dish-grashe – outra-jous – hic – unpar'nable, so mon – hic – monstrous crim'nal —' the string of adjectives was inexhaustible while his temper, whether natural or assumed, mounted violently to assert magisterial judgement upon the guests around his board who were – 'If offishers,' he thundered, 'no gen'le-men.' To be dealt with, so their host implied, as it behoved him as a Justice of the Peace.

This threat to deal with those of his company who had cast lecherous eyes upon Sally had the desired effect of striking a bargain to obtain her at an 'honourable' price; and an offer was forthcoming from one Captain Maurice St Leger Farmer. He had been in the running with a brother officer of his regiment, the 47th Foot, a Captain Murray. Of these two gentlemen James Murray was in earnest to woo and if possible to carry off the prize who promised, were she 'grown', to be an ornament to his bed and board. Sally, for her part, as she put it to her sister Ellen, some eighteen months her junior:

'I'd liefer be married to Captain Murray than to Captain Farmer, for he don't pinch my bottom like does Captain Farmer, and he caught me and kissed me with his tongue in my mouth . . .'

'Ooh!' exclaimed Ellen, 'if he did that to me I'd scratch his eyes out!'

'I might have done that too,' said Sally, 'had I not seen Papa making faces at me and he hissed in my ear so's the gentlemen wouldn't hear that I must be polite to his friends and 'specially Captain Farmer as he had made him an offer.'

'An offer?' repeated Ellen round-eyed. 'What for?'

'For me,' Sally told her with ever so little a smirk.

'For you?' echoed Ellen, parrot-wise.

'Yes, for me. He wants to marry me.'

'Marry you?' gasped Ellen. 'For why?'

'For why any man – any gentleman – would want to marry someone, I suppose.'

'You mean – what do you mean?'

'I don't know, at all,' confessed Sally, 'unless – f'rinstance – Why did Papa marry Mama? I know he is what was called "Beau" which Miss Dwyer told me means beautiful in French. Perhaps because he was beautiful *then* is why Mama married him.'

'Men aren't beautiful. 'Tis ladies who are beautiful,' said the literal Ellen. 'Leastways some of them, not any as I can see around Clonmel. And as for Papa he couldn't ever have been anything but what he is – fat as a pig and red as a turkey cock when he's not sickly with his drink.'

'Miss Dwyer,' mused Sally, her eyes suspiciously brightening, 'is a great loss to me all these years.'

'All these years?' came the inevitable repetition. 'You speak as you was fifty.'

'Wish I was,' sighed Sally. 'Then I shouldn't have so long to live.'

'Don't you want long to live?' pursued Ellen.

'No. Why should I when everyone hates me?' Sally was stating a fact upon which she had often brooded, but without prejudice or malice aforethought. 'Everyone, that's to say except Miss Dwyer when I was very young – hates me or hated me then.'

'Hated you then? I didn't hate you then,' Ellen said equably, 'and I don't hate you now. I hate Papa but we all hate him.'

'Yes.' Sally's nod was doubtful. 'But we ought not to hate him. We should honour our father and mother as the Commandments tell us.'

Ellen sniffed.

'Our father don't honour us. The Bible says not to spare the rod meaning they can go on beating us – or you – as much as they like.'

Although Sally accepted this as incontrovertible she felt justified in modifying it with the reminder that:

'He doesn't beat me as much as he did, now that Captain Farmer has made an offer for me. He used to knock me about because I was so ugly.'

Ellen regarded her judicially.

'You aren't so ugly as you was. You're not so skinny and your face is fatter which makes you not so peaky – or beaky,' she giggled, 'like a duck.'

Sally shook her head.

'Ugly or not I can't think why Captain Farmer should want to marry me. I don't want to marry anyone, least of all him.'

'Will you,' asked Ellen, 'have to sleep in a bed with him?'

'I don't know. Why should married people have to sleep in one bed? It's bad enough sleeping with you, the way you kick in your sleep. I hope if I have to sleep with Captain Farmer that he won't kick in *his* sleep.'

'Perhaps,' said Ellen, 'it will be a larger bed than ours. What do you suppose he'll do to you when you sleep with him?'

Sally flushed hotly. It was a question she had often asked herself, for, strange though it might seem in view of these children's upbringing and their father's debaucheries, he had contrived to keep his young teenage daughters as innocently ignorant of the facts of life as if they were walled up in a convent instead of in a stew. Drunkenness, which they had come to believe was a gentlemanly habit, held no shock for them. And Power much preferred the society of men to that of women whom he despised and for whom he had no use except on extra-marital and libidinous occasions.

While the sisters were thus engaged in the momentous discussion of the disposal of Sally, a still more momentous discussion was taking place between their father and Captain Farmer.

This centred upon the price demanded by Power for the purchase of his daughter – 'to be settled,' he insisted, 'upon me rather than on her as a minor, so that she be safe-guarded from your possession of whatever sum shall be agreed. The law being what it is,' he magisterially pro-nounced, 'a husband is entitled not only to full possession of his wife but of all her worldly wealth which, as the mar-riage service gives it in your Protestant Church – and I presume you'll marry her in your English Church – that's to say if I consent to part with this –' he manufactured a throaty sob – 'most loved of all my children —'

'Come to the point. Come on!' impatiently urged Farmer. 'What's this worldly wealth with which *I* endow her – *she* doesn't endow me – what's it worth to you?'

' 'Tis worth to me —' said Power who, having divided the better part of two bottles between his guest and himself and been at it on and off from dawn that morning, was feeling the effects of it; yet he could keep his head suffi-ciently to 'Come on' and to the point – 'It-it'sh worth to me,' he drained the last of the flagon of wine and screwed an eye at the dregs, 'to lose her and br-break me ha-heart —' the dregs were beginning to discomfort his speech – 'Whether it be a penny or a per-pound or fi-five hundred poun's – cash down, I'd be the loser – either way!'

'Five hundred! God's truth!' declared Farmer, 'not on your life! I'd pay half that for a doxy. Two fifty to wive her and take it or leave it.'

'Goddamme!' expostulated Power. 'Do you think I'd sell my girl to you as you'd buy a bawd from a brothel! 'Tis no *sale*! I'm safeguard-hic-ing my daughter that I may keep her portion in good hands – *my* hands that you don't lay *your* hands on't! Five hundred or nothing. Here's Murray would take her without a rag to her back.'

'She'd want neither rag nor shift to her back,' chuckled Farmer, 'were she mine. I'll lay she'll strip as neat as a new penny which is all you'd get from Murray. He hasn't a groat to his name beyond his pay.'

'Five hundred – cash down,' growled Power, sticking to his point, 'and dirt cheap at the price for a virgin.'

Farmer got up from his chair where he lounged with his empty glass in his hand, and lifting the flagon that Power had drained, 'Dead,' he muttered. 'Get another. Say three fifty and that's my limit.'

'Make it guineas.'

Power, though fuddled, had sense enough to see that three hundred odd guineas cash down would cover his immediate debts and silence his wine merchant who had handed him a writ to be paid within seven days or else — He did not relish the notion of fighting it out before a brother Justice of the Peace.

As for Farmer, three hundred and fifty guineas was easy money for him who had ten times that amount per annum, and he bethought him that when he tired of his own particular methods of deflowering a virgin, he could leave her planted wherever he might be stationed and go his ways with his regiment at home or abroad. The encumbrance of a woman other than for temporary enjoyment could be got for far less than the sum he was paying as the rapist of a wife.

Had this reasoning been imparted to Power, his greed for money and the less pressing of his debts paid off, he might have reconsidered the striking of a bargain with the sale of Sally to such a one as Farmer; but he did not envisage the possibility of the suffering to which his young daughter was compulsorily committed.

So the bargain was struck, the wedding day fixed, the marriage hastened and with scantiest ceremony performed in the presence only of the bride's parents; and Sally Power became Margaret Farmer.

She was just fifteen years old.

*   *   *

So this, she said, is marriage, but she did not say it aloud. All spoken words had died when on her wedding night she had died a little death.

Bruised, broken, bleeding, she lay inert, exhausted in the bed where she had been flung when he had done with her.

The white bridal gown her mother had cut up and made to fit her from her own wedding dress of some eighteen years before was heaped on the floor with the under-garments he had torn from her. . . . She shuddered and retched, sick at heart and stomach as memory revived these awful hours of the night when he had dragged her to bed.

He had gone, left her at day-break in that bed of torture, to go, he said, on duty at the barracks. He had brought her to the house he rented furnished on the outskirts of the town. He had taken her there with her mother to see it during the brief betrothal when he had comported himself with the conventional decorum of a prospective bride-groom. To the child he had bought on which to glut his sexual aberrations, he had presented himself as a kind if

elderly lover. No; not a lover, for, 'He is,' she confided to
Ellen, 'more like a sort of – uncle. Except that he touches
me rudely and kisses me good morning or goodnight when
he comes to visit, in that nasty way I told you about –
which I s'pose an uncle wouldn't do.'

He had been careful to satisfy Power that he would at
least fulfil his part of the bargain by treating his girl as wife
and not as harlot.

And while Sally, or Margaret as she must now be named,
watched a sun-shaft probe a chink in the drawn curtain, and
saw by the faint glow of light the rod that stood against
the wall . . . 'Spare the rod, and spoil . . .' the thought
stabbed her and caused an hysterical choke of laughter.
Strange that she could laugh even while the weals on her
back cut her as if with knives as she turned on her front to
ease the pain of it. But what – *what*, she moaned within
her, have I done to be beaten and worse than any of my
father's thrashings – he never used a rod. 'Mother of God,'
she whispered, 'have pity on me, save me from this beast –
he is sure no man, unless run mad . . . And as he kept on
saying that this dreadful cruelty is love . . . Love! How can
he love me to do these awful things to me?' And then when
all was over the way he took and fondled her with caresses
and his nasty way of kissing her, and then to empty a bottle
of wine on her naked, battered body and drink it as it
dripped down to . . . No, no! she screamed within her, I
can't bear it . . . let me die! . . .

She buried her face in the pillow, God help her! What to
do? Where to go? Escape – yes, but how and to whom? Not
to her father, not back to that dreaded house where, save for
Ellen, she had lived all these years friendless and unloved.
Unwanted. But nothing, not the home that had never been
a home could be worse than this . . .

Came a knock at the door. She raised herself on an elbow.
'Who is it?' Fearfully, in case he had returned from duty.

The maid entered. 'What would you be wanting for your
breakfast, ma'am? Will I be bringing it ye here?' A rosy

20

cheeked buxom girl whom she had not seen the night before
. . . 'Ma'am!' So she was 'ma'am' now. Married. No longer
'miss'.

'The Cap'n sends you these, ma'am.'

A bunch of roses and carnations tied with a blue ribbon
and a note enclosed. 'To my darling little wife from her
devoted St Leger Maurice.'

St Leger . . . ! A saint's name for one who could be no
saint. One of Satan's devils more like. As if flowers could
atone for what he had done to his 'darling little wife'!
Again that mirthless laughter shook her, and stifling the
surge of threatened hysteria she said: 'Thank you. Please to
put them in a vase of water.'

'And for your breakfast what'll ye be wanting?'

'Nothing, no . . . Not to eat. Just a cup of tea.'

Later when her parched mouth had been refreshed with
a hot drink that burnt her tongue, she managed to dress
herself, having bathed her face and hands from the jug of
warm water brought by the maid. Wincing at the touch of
clothes against her broken skin she put on one of her old
dresses unpacked from the luggage she had brought from
home and went downstairs to what she presumed was the
parlour. They had come from her father's house in Clonmel
on the previous day where they had been given a wedding
breakfast. There, both Power and Farmer had drunk their
fill until nightfall. The bridegroom had then taken his bride
away and to their bed where he had asserted his nuptial
rights – and wrongs.

What can be told of a child's suffering, the misery and
horror of the next few months as wife of a man who, she
slowly came to realize, must be insane if any such excuse
for his brutality could be found? Haunted daily by fear of
his return from barracks, not more than two or three times
a week, she must submit to her husband's abnormal demands of her tortured young body. Even had she been able
to find one in whom she could confide and seek advice how

to escape from the hell of this marriage (that was no marriage but a systematic maltreatment of a helpless child at the mercy of a sadistic brute), it is unlikely she would have been believed.

Married to a Protestant, in the Church of England, and, although baptized in the Roman Church, she had little or no Catholic upbringing, so knew no priest of whom she could ask aid. Nor is it likely that Farmer's unnatural impulses to obtain satisfaction could have been influenced by knowledge of the Marquis de Sade who has lent his name to the dictionaries of the world as descriptive of the sadism which this unfortunate child endured during her first disastrous marriage.

During her lonely walks in the country around Clonmel her bewildered and agonizing thoughts found a certain consolatory enjoyment in the beauty of nature that, fostered by Miss Dwyer, had lain dormant until now when she was bereft of her sister Ellen's companionship. And even though teased and harassed by her brothers, she had never been left entirely alone.

It may be that this enforced solitude by day and the constant fear of dreadful nights contributed to the moulding of her character that, in after years, would render her the more provocative to all men whose passions she evoked and to which she was unable to respond. She must for ever remain cold, desirable, desired, but desirous, never . . .

On these walks in a land of endless enchantment where the very air is colourful; where silver, gold, or grey and green – but always green – absorbed the eye with beauty and the heart with fleeting gratitude, those moments of magic might erase from memory, if only for a brief pause in time, the awfulness of that which life and marriage had done to her. Such moments must have enlarged her vision to an awareness of potentialities which she could not then have realized; yet it could have expanded her chrysalis emergence from child to girl, from girl to woman of whom it was said: 'Hers was a life diffusing happiness, her kindness instinct yet ardent as though it had been passion and, above all women of her time, she fascinated . . .'*

If she diffused happiness it must have been her chameleon-like quality that in later years could adapt itself not only to circumstance and environment but to those about her, seeking in dissimulation to expunge from unforgotten corridors of memory and horrors experienced as a child-wife.

It was on a day in the spring of the year when she became Margaret Farmer that she wandered along the twisting lanes beyond Clonmel between ragged walls of stone that belted a huddle of small fields, spreading green aprons to the bogs where, as if risen from those darkly glittering waters, the mountains shouldered the sky wrapped in mantles of lilac mist. Then, as she halted to pluck from the grass-verged hedgerows a handful of starry primroses and shy half-hidden violets, she heard the sound of approaching hooves. A couple of horsemen rounded a bend in the lane; the foremost of these reined in his horse, his companion trotted on and halted a few yards ahead. The first rider lifted his hat and greeted her with:

'Miss Power, Sally Power, is it?'

'Yes . . . no,' she stammered, wondering who he could be. One of her father's visitors she supposed; she could not remember all of those who came to dine and drink before she had been taken from her father's house by Farmer. 'I was Sally – Margaret – Power, but I am married now.'

'Married! And not yet out of the schoolroom?'

'No, sir,' she replied in the soft Irish accent which remained with her throughout her life, 'I was never at school, at all.'

'And who did you marry? Anyone I know?'

She hesitated before answering scarcely above a whisper:

'Sure, sir, it was – is Captain Farmer.'

'What! Farmer of the 47th?'

* Lady Wilde, mother of Oscar Wilde.

She nodded, unwilling to admit it to this gentleman whose tone betokened disparagement.

'I had no idea,' said he, 'that Farmer had got himself married.' His eyes raked her slender form from head to foot, noting the tremble of her ripe under-lip and the young lost look of the small pale face – too pale? – with its delicate bone structure of chin and jaw. He vaguely remembered having seen her at Power's orgies which he had seldom attended and recollected his surprise that the child, as she was (and still is, he told himself), should have been brought into such company. Not that he ever heard her speak, nor that any one of Power's boon companions had seemed to notice her.

Mounting to the saddle: 'I hope,' he replaced his hat, 'that we shall meet again at your father's house.'

'Yes, sir . . . I . . . do not often see my father. He is a magistrate and has much to do with his . . . his business, and my hus . . . Captain Farmer is engaged on duty with his regiment most days and,' (thankfully) 'most nights.'

'Yes, he would be. Almost all the men stationed here are expecting daily orders to be sent on active service against the French. Napoleon's armies are camped at Boulogne and we need all we can muster to hold back invasion.'

This was news to Sally, who knew little or nothing of the war with France and the indomitable yellow dwarf with a giant's stride who had already conquered half Europe and whose only enemy to be feared was Great Britain.

But the information casually imparted by this civil-spoken gentleman, a stranger to her though not to her father or 'her hus' – Captain Farmer, gave her a sudden heartening hope. If That Man, as to herself she always alluded to Farmer, should be sent to fight the French he might be killed in battle.

'Will you, sir,' she asked less timidly now with the knowledge that he to whom she was bound body, if not soul, might be in danger of his life, 'will you be sent to fight the French?'

'No, not yet, nor do I live in Ireland. I live in England and my regiment is temporarily stationed here. Goodbye.' He stretched a hand to her. 'Or let us say *au revoir*.'

He rode off to join his companion who, with his horse, was showing impatience.

Much to her disappointment the 47th Foot stationed at Clonmel had so far received no orders to join the forces already sent to the Kentish and South coasts to combat Napoleon's threatened invasion. So Sally must continue to suffer Farmer's connubial rights on the three or four nights a week he spent at the house. For the rest of his time he remained at barracks or elsewhere.

She had seen nothing of her father since her marriage, nor did her mother visit her more than on one or two occasions as the Powers possessed no conveyance and it was too far for her to walk back and forth to her daughter's temporary home, as Mrs Power was again pregnant. However Ellen did manage to walk over to see her sister whenever she could get away; and she was the only one in whom Sally could confide, although she did not divulge to Ellen all that she endured, partly from shame but also from a certain sense of loyalty to That Man whose name she bore. Yet enough had been told to make Ellen believe that Farmer was 'unkind' to her as Sally, with tactful understatement, suggested.

'In what way is he unkind to you?' Ellen wished to know. 'Does he beat you like Papa used to?'

'Well,' (it was going to be difficult to explain) 'not quite like Papa used to – beat me. It's – different.'

'How different?'

'He's not so . . . he doesn't get into such tempers as Papa did.'

'Then why does he beat you if he's not in a temper?'

'It may be,' said Sally desperately, 'a *sort* of temper. I suppose he is so used to shouting orders to his men that he doesn't like not being able to . . . to shout orders at me.'

'So he beats you instead. Do you like him?' persisted Ellen.

This she could answer and did, emphatically.

'I hate him! I never wanted to marry him. Papa and he arranged it all between them. I had nothing to do with it.'

'Looks like you had everything to do with it.'

'Not at my age. I'm too young to be able to choose who I could marry or not.'

'I don't see why you are too young to choose who to marry. If you had refused to marry him they couldn't have *made* you.'

'They can make us do anything while we are what they call minors – that's to say not twenty-one.'

'But even if you aren't twenty-one you could escape – run away from him, couldn't you?'

'Where could I run to? Papa wouldn't have me back home.'

Ellen eyed her critically.

'You look more peaked than you did before you married him. You are too thin. Do you get enough to eat?'

'As much as I want. I don't want to eat,' declared Sally fiercely. 'I wish I was dead.'

'Sure,' was the dispassionate reply, 'I'd never want to be married if marriage does that to you. I'd put an end to it meself.'

As marriage had done that to Sally, or Mrs Margaret Farmer, she decided to summon courage for herself to put an end to it, and confronted her husband, a Goliath to her David, with a stone of defiance slung at him.

'You! You cruel monster!' We may believe words tumbled out of her uninhibited by fear, long stored, now overcome by her longing to be done with the agony of marriage.

Shades of Miss Dwyer, who had instilled into her a few crumbs of learning, recurred to tell him, her little body quivering with surprise at her own temerity:

'Sure to God you're as bad or worse than the Roman

Emperors, Caligula who tortured people – his slaves for his pleasure, or Nero who murdered his wife – he kicked her to death – and you'd beat me or kick *me* to death for your pleasure, you wicked, *wicked* man – if you dared, but you daresn't or you'd hang. Only you won't have the chance to beat me to death for I'm going. I'm going to leave you . . . You can't keep me here by force. My father is a magistrate and I'll tell him what you've done to me. I'll tell him – I'll tell them all! I'll tell your Colonel. I'll tell him you're mad. You *must* be mad – you beast, you! To do what you do to me!'

If this child, his innocent victim, had suddenly sprouted horns and a tail, Farmer could not have been more shocked. An unexpected personality was at large in his house. Come from God alone knew where, the devil if he could credit such a being, to rob him of his absolute faith and dominant belief in himself and his autocracy. And now – this chit, this puny midget for whom he had paid more than he would pay for a thoroughbred mare – yes, he *must* have been mad to take *her* on, and that she should accost him with abuse and threats – 'Be damned to you,' he shouted. 'I'll have the hide off you for this!'

And seizing her by the arm he dragged her to him, his rage in ascendance above the astonishment that she should have attempted this incredible revolt. To *leave* him, forsooth! 'I'll beat you within an inch of your bloody life, you brat! You can go – and welcome! I'm off to the Curragh and as for you —'

And this time in real fury, not lust, he thrashed her with a whip and let her go.

Escape! That was her one objective. She had threatened to go and he had told her to go having beaten her black and blue. But where and to whom could she go? Miss Dwyer? Yet she had not seen Miss Dwyer more than twice in these three or four years, nor had she heard from her of late. She knew her mother had disapproved of Miss Dwyer's interest in her and that she discouraged any further intimacy from 'that interfering old cat!' . . . Miss Dwyer, Sally thought fearfully, must have left Knockbrit or – might be dead. As for returning to her father's house, much as she disliked the idea of that, it looked to be the only alternative, although she knew she would have to explain why she had left Farmer and probably suffer more beatings, though none so bad as all she had endured with That Man.

None the less she would have to wait her moment. Farmer, as he said, would be off to the Curragh so that he would not often be at Clonmel and with any luck he would be sent to join the fighting forces in France – or somewhere. In the meantime she would not risk remaining in his house as his wife or – his slave, on the chance that he would be sent to the war and, pray God, be killed.

There was only one resident servant in the house, a man of all work, gardener, stable hand, sixtyish, deaf, which was all to the good as she intended to make her getaway at night when she was less likely to be missed, seen or heard by the woman who came only daily for the housework. Since the cataclysmic day of her defiance Farmer had not been back to the house, but she dared not stay upon her going lest he should return from the Curragh.

She waited for a moonless night; it was pitch dark, no stars, heavily clouded and a slight drizzling rain. The old man had gone early to his bed; she crept up to his attic room and heard him snoring. She then packed a hand bag with immediate necessities of clothing should she be turned from her father's house, and without more delay or hesitation let herself out at the back door. These outskirts of Clonmel were chiefly open country with few houses and these mostly labourers' cottages belonging to farmers or the owners of neighbouring estates. She would be unlikely to meet anyone on her way, or if so would not be recognized in the dark and her hooded cloak. Her feet squelched in the mud of the road as she ran to be away faster from that

'place of hell' as to herself she named the house where she
had suffered to the end of her endurance.

She came into the poorly lighted streets of the town
and, breathless with her hurry, she reached her father's
house. It stood back from the street screened by high
hedges, but she saw that the windows of the ground floor
showed uncurtained lights. Treading carefully lest her steps
be heard she came to the front door, which was ajar.

From the sounds within of loud laughter and men's
rowdy voices, she gathered that her father entertained.
This was an unhoped for lucky chance since it dispensed
with the necessity of announcing her return with possible
immediate eviction and the command to go back whence
she had come. She could now slip in unnoticed and up to
the attic she had shared with Ellen.

The noise and bawling from the dining-room pursued
her, but the rest of the house was quiet and, undiscovered,
she reached the room where Ellen slept. There in the dark
she undressed. Ellen still slept soundly but, as Sally crept
into bed beside her she woke, startled, and cried out in
alarm. Her mouth was immediately covered.

'Quiet,' whispered Sally. 'It's me. I've come back.'

TWO

For the next two or three years the life of this wretched brutalized child can only be guessed; yet we know that when she made her escape from Farmer, Power vented the full force of a drunken rage upon her for having dared to leave the man to whom for his greed she had been sold. As for the money he gained from that disgraceful transaction, it had all been spent in those three months of the marriage. Power's affairs had gone from bad to worse thanks to his patron, Lord Donoughmore, who had hastened his ruin by persuading him to launch a newspaper purporting to implement the interest of the Castle. Always ready to feather his grubby nest with whatever he could gather to line it, he plunged the small remainder of his capital into this venture.

With the publication of the paper, Power, as its nominal proprietor, looked for further preferment from the Vice-regal Court which of late had shown him a rather less chill reception than formerly for he had kept cold sober on days preceding his presentations; but no sooner had the paper appeared than Nemesis followed. It was found to contain a serious libel against certain persons to whom Donoughmore owed a grudge.

The fat was in the fire, and the fire burnt to bring all Power's hopes for elevation to ashes. Donoughmore, who had so treacherously made him his scapegoat, denied having any knowledge of the libel and the whole prosecution of the case fell upon the luckless Power.

Left to foot the bill of costs and having lost what little capital he possessed invested in 'that damnable paper' he raged, he managed to scrape up enough from his share in the corn-chandler's business temporarily to stave off the most pressing of his creditors, but nothing sufficient to cover his surplus debts.

And now the house at Clonmel and its master were shunned by all respectable and respected neighbours, his only visitors a few of the officers who came to drink and play at cards and lose more often than not, to Power who was less scrupulous than he might be with an ace or two up his sleeve.

Among the young men from the garrison who came to make passes at their host's attractive young daughters was Lt-Colonel Viscount Mountjoy who paid the girls some but not any significant attention. Whatever Power's failings, he would not tolerate an approach to either of his daughters other than with intent to marriage. Having done so well with Sally whom he had put up for sale and made a good profit financially therefrom no matter that the bargain as far as Sally was concerned had ended in disaster – he would never allow Ellen to be given away without hand-some compensation unless it were to Mountjoy, who was not only a peer but one of considerable wealth. He, how-ever, showed little desire for more than a passing flirtation with either of them, and none of those who came from the garrison could afford to buy and keep a mistress much less a wife.

Before very long Power's unsavoury reputation became a byword in the district. Thus the few who came from the barracks thought it expedient to keep away save for an odd man or two who, having recently arrived at the garrison, had not yet been warned by the commanding officer that Power's house must be out of bounds.

Apart from the hell of her marriage Sally suffered with almost equal wretchedness her life in her father's house. Ellen was her one solace; but, while Ellen came in for their father's drunken tempers, his rageful grievances were directed chiefly against the wife of the man to whom he had sold her and, since she had left him, there appeared to be no chance of Farmer taking her back nor that Power, as he had hoped, might have touched him for a loan to a part settlement of his debts.

Both Power's teenage daughters held out against his hated presence and his violent abuse, but it was Ellen whom he regarded as a possible asset. Sally, already married, was no use to him; she could not be sold again in lawful wedlock. Yet, if an offer for Ellen under any condition other than marriage came along, he was now so heavily embarrassed he would not refuse it. Unfortunately no offer for Ellen did come along.

Sally had been two years under her father's roof during which time some of the neighbours, having taken pity on Power's young daughters and shocked at the scenes they must have witnessed, would invite them to their houses as formerly they had invited their mother; but not any more. Mrs Power, poor soul, had degenerated into a slavish slut unable to put up a fight for herself or her girls against her husband's ill treatment and mode of life.

It must have been at a kindly neighbour's house that Sally became acquainted with a Captain Thomas Jenkins of the 11th Light Dragoons. This was not the first time they had met for he was the young man who, while out riding, had spoken to her on one of her solitary walks when she lived with Farmer as his wife.

Because Power had made it his business to know that Jenkins was a man of means with an estate in Hampshire and had only been stationed with his regiment at Clonmel, he encouraged Jenkins' visits to the house. Had this eligible young man any serious motive in his frequent attendance at Power's noisy dining-table and cardroom with intent to acquiring a wife, any such proposition was out of the question concerning Sally, yet Power could still hope that Jenkins might have honourable intentions toward Ellen. But he soon discovered Ellen was not in the running, and Jenkins, if not in love with Sally, was greatly attracted to her. Already, although unconsciously, she had begun to wield that fatal fascination for men which throughout her life would render her desired, yet never, to her cost, desirous. Since all physical response had been killed in her as result of her infamous marriage, it may be that her very unawareness of her own potentialities, that elusive charm, less actual beauty than beauty's emanation, was the secret of her attraction. That she could have developed into so well-favoured a young girl was a continuous surprise to her father who thought to make good use of her while these lads from the garrison were around, especially this Jenkins, since Sally might, he hoped, be widowed if Farmer were at the fighting front.

'This Jenkins' was a pleasant-mannered young Englishman, well-bred and well-to-do, the only son of parents now dead. He certainly enjoyed the company of the Power girls, in particular of Sally. True he knew her to be the wife of Farmer and that they were separated, though he knew nothing of the facts that had driven her to leave her husband.

Having seen enough of the unhappiness Sally and her sister underwent in their miserable home life, Jenkins did all he could to mitigate their wretched circumstances, and that is why, we may presume, he became so frequent a visitor to the house which most of his fellow officers avoided. They naturally suspected his ulterior motive to be amatory, either for one or both Power's girls, but they were wrong. Jenkins was quixotically concerned on behalf of 'that drunken sot's' daughters and intended in any way possible to help them.

How exactly he could further his intent he had no definite plan until opportunity arose which proved to be a godsend to Sally and a crowning disaster to Power.

It was a stormy October night on one of his expeditions in pursuit of rebels when Power, leading his dragoons, fell foul of a boy carrying a lanthorn that in the dark looked to be a torch. He also carried a bucket of milk on the way back

to his mother's cottage from the farm where he had been
sent to fetch it.

Power, riding ahead of his men, could not see the contents of the bucket; there had been repeated cases of arson,
the burning of haystacks and crops, since the destruction
of his granary some years before. On that occasion squibs
had been found in buckets after the rounding up of the
remaining marauders. Power immediately suspected that
this boy with his bucket was bent on mischief, the emissary
of the very rebels he and his dragoons were chasing.

He vociferously commanded him to halt and the boy, in
desperate fright and completely innocent of rebellion,
attempted to explain in answer to Power's demand as to the
whereabouts of the fugitives that: 'Oi know nought of 'em.
Oi seen none – ha' been to the farm —'

Power, believing the worst of him, roared: 'You lying
cub! Stand and deliver your bucket or – I'll shoot!'

In pitiable fright, the boy – a child, no more than ten –
made a dash for the hedge, jumped it, and hared across the
field hanging on to the precious bucket for his mother who,
unlike some of her less starved neighbours, possessed
neither goat nor donkey to supply her with milk.

Power, probably the worse for drink, put his horse to the
hedge, cleared it and yelled: 'Halt – or I'll fire!' The boy, still
running, may or may not have heard him. Then Power, as
good as his word, fired. The boy fell . . .

'The pistol inadvertently went off,' was Power's explanation when the boy, covered in blood, had been brought to
Clonmel Gaol, and died within an hour.

Useless for Power to declare this shocking incident was
accidental, and that he had believed the boy's protests as
having no knowledge of the fugitives' whereabouts. But he
admitted to dismounting from his horse to examine the
bucket which the lad asserted was only carrying milk, for
he remembered that when his granary was destroyed by
fire squibs had been found in buckets, so he had to ascertain

there was no danger in the bucket carried by the boy . . . In vain. Power had enemies enough to warrant an arrest.

He was accused of murder and imprisoned, awaiting his trial, but insufficient evidence resulted in an acquittal.

None the less it was the ruin of Power. All hope of Castle favour crumbled to dust. His one-time patron, Lord Donoughmore, furious that he had chosen so discreditable an agent as magistrate, told him plainly he had no further use for him in any capacity whatsoever.

He appealed to Donoughmore for reconsideration, to give him one more chance to vindicate himself, although he knew that insufficient evidence could not remove suspicion; but for all his grovelling he was given no mercy. Donough-more refused to see him or to hear his pleas for help and justice.

And now shattered by this unkindest stroke of fate, Power's savage disappointment was turned against his wife and daughters, in particular the girl, the cast-off wife of his one-time friend as he had thought Farmer to be. He had hoped to touch him for more than the few hundreds gained by the sale of Sally. He remembered how Farmer, in company with others of the fellows from the garrison, had sought his board and the green baize in the days when he had been in favour with the Viceregal Court and now — sunk to nothing. Disgraced. Ruined.

Talk gave it that Farmer had been discharged from his regiment for having drawn his sword against a superior officer in one of his frenzied rages, and that he had gone to India in the service of the East India Company. So Farmer, his wealthy son-in-law, was lost to him as well as to his daughter. She, he told himself, had been instrumental in this ultimate calamity. 'Yes,' he thundered. 'You! But for you, who deserted your husband and came whining back to me — as if I'd ever want to see you or keep you here, feeding you, housing you, when I'd gotten you a loving husband and a man of means to keep you in every comfort, you bitch! I'll hide the skin off your back for this!'

The very words used by her 'loving' husband when she had dared defy him.

Suiting action to words her father took hold of her arm, and raising his fist battered her head and face to draw blood; she struggled free and turned on him.

'If I were to tell Lord Donoughmore what you've done to me, he'd send you back to prison. You're a brute! A devil! I'll leave you and beg in the streets rather than stay here with you to be so abused and – and beaten as I was with him – that madman you made me marry. I've suffered all my life with you! But no worse than what I suffered with him. I'll never – *never* go back to him and I won't stay here, I won't! I'll – I'll leave you. I'll go now!'

With which she turned and ran from the room, slamming the door behind her.

This threat from her, as when she dared defy Farmer, first astonished then alarmed her father. That one so timidly submissive, afraid to offer the least rebellion against his omnipotence, should assert herself with such audacious temerity sent him furiously to recall her.

'Come back, you fool!' Then, instead of bringing this recalcitrant to heel with more physical assault, he changed his tactics, mindful of her threatened report to Donoughmore, who already held enough against him, not only for depriving him of his magistracy but to bring about another trial if sufficient proof should yet be found . . . 'God damn her,' he swore to himself. 'Never run the risk of all *that* again!' . . . And to her, his voice wheedling as he followed her up the staircase:

'Come here, my girl. I didn't mean to hurt you. I lost me temper. I've had so much trouble – am quite beside meself. You've no idea – God send you never will – what it is to be misjudged and falsely accused of a heinous crime. I —' dramatically he smote his chest, standing there on the stairs while she paused on the landing looking down at him. 'I was innocent – I swear it – of that which they so maliciously accused me. Have pity on your injured father. You see him here a ruined man through no fault of his own – ruined by those he so faithfully served!'

The sight of him disgusted her, his mouth sagging, his drink-tainted breath pervading the air, his mouth fallen apart with spittle on his lips; but, though she had cause enough to seek vengeance for all she had borne uncomplainingly from him, she came slowly down the stairs to take his hand.

'Papa, you need have no fear that I'll tell anyone,' her words dwindled, 'what you – you have done – to me. Only I'll have to leave you. I'm sorry I ever came back here. But I'll have to go.'

'To hell with you, then!' His temper rising again, he roared at her. 'Go! You've been more trouble to me than you're worth. And now there's none who'll take you off my hands. I can't afford to keep you so – get out – go!'

She would have got out there and then had she known *where* to go. She had none to whom she could turn – unless – Yes! She might go for a governess! The limited tuition given by Miss Dwyer had supplied her with interest enough to rummage among her father's books in the room he called his 'study' during this few years' interim after leaving Knockbrit. Time was when, as a youth, he had read and imbibed some learning from the parish priest, for in those days he had been a devout Catholic, and even had thought of the priesthood as urged by his confessor. But drink and greedy ambition had lost him his faith and brought him to these lowest depths. Yet the remnants of learning, dust-covered, forgotten, provided Sally with God-sent oblivion in dwelling upon the past and present literary masters.

In this way did she come across a newly arrived poet, Thomas Moore, writing under the pseudonym of 'Thomas Little'. Born in Dublin the son of a grocer he, at five and twenty, had already made his mark and came to be known as the Bard of Erin. His patron was none less than the Prince of Wales.

Having abandoned his pseudonym after the publication

of *The Poetic Works of the Late Thomas Little*, a jibe at the dubious reception accorded to those pretty erotics that delighted the Prince and the Carlton House set but shocked his more envious critics, he became even more widely read under his own name.

Little did Sally guess that in some not far future this same Thomas Moore would be numbered among her most intimate friends.

No sooner had she been summarily dismissed by her irate father than she decided she would no longer stand upon the order of her going but would go. At once. Panting with her hurry up four flights of stairs she burst in upon Ellen in the attic room they still shared, more dingy and shabbier than ever, for Ellen Power had neither the heart nor the wherewithal to keep her house in order since Power's disgrace. They could afford no servants and the two elder girls were called upon to do the household chores.

'Godsakes!' cried Ellen swinging round as Sally entered. She had been making the bed. 'What've you done to your face?'

Her nose was swollen, oozing blood; there was a darkening bruise under her eye.

'My face?' She put a hand up to it. 'Oh,' (indifferently) 'nothing.'

'But you're bleeding. You look awful.'

'Papa,' Sally said, 'was in one of his fits.' She went over to a cupboard, opened it, stood a while in thought.

'I can't take much,' she murmured, 'as I don't know where I'm going. I'll have to get a room at an inn somewhere. I've got two pounds saved from what Farmer used to allow me. Pity I didn't take the rings and brooch he gave me. I could have sold them.'

'What are you saying?' demanded Ellen. 'Sold what? Going where?'

'I don't know where except that I'm not staying here to be beaten and yelled at by our father in or out of drink. I can't help feeling sorry for all he's been through, only there *are* limits.' She left the cupboard to examine her face in an old cracked mirror on the wall. 'What has he done to my nose, then? Sure, 'tis broke.'

'So he's been at you again, has he? You'd have done better to have stayed with Farmer,' Ellen told her. 'He wouldn't have knocked you about as Papa does. He's much worse with you than with me or Mary Ann. The worst he's ever done to me is to hit me, but not to make me bleed.'

'Farmer did other things worse than this.' She touched her nose.

'What other things?'

'Listen.' She went to the door. 'That's Mama calling me. Go tell her I've gone out.'

'Why should I? She'll know you aren't out. Better see what she wants.'

Sally shrugged a shoulder, 'I suppose so . . .' And at the door she called to her mother: 'Yes, Mama?'

'Come down, Sally. I want you to go to the grocer for a pound of butter and cheese. Be quick. I'm right out of both, and some flour.'

Armed with a shopping basket, her mother's purse, and wrapped in a warm cloak, for it was bitterly cold that windy March day, she went on her errand thinking: I don't have to go *now* – not in this weather. But go I will. He can't keep me here for ever . . .

Having finished with the grocer she walked on out of the town. She never tired of her solitary walks in the lovely country around Clonmel. It was market day; and the towns-folk were busy in the square at their stalls offering their goods in a cacophany of cries:

'Hot 'taters!' 'Prime fat bacon!' 'Pickled oysters!' 'Pigs' trotters!' And a tinker with his cart and a patient over-burdened donkey while the tinker belaboured him shouting: 'Frypans! Kettles, all for twopence – good as new!' And a hawker, slung around with the corpses of rabbits crying: 'Coney skins!' or 'Bobbins for your hair, miss,' to Sally, or 'A pair o' fine singin' glasses.' And a merry-andrew with a tumbling aged dwarf attached to a cord on his wrist; and a large hump-backed man with three cages of birds, a moulting terrified canary and, to Sally's horror, a robin and a lark. So small their imprisonment they had barely room to perch, no bird seed, no water. 'O, God!' cried Sally, and flew at him. 'Caged birds, wild birds! You beast! Cruel *beast*!'

Undismayed by this offensive, the birdmonger soothingly replied: 'No woild birds be they, missy. Born an' bred in me own av'ary. Crucify me if Oi lie to ye!'

'Liar! I *would* crucify you had I a tree to hang you on! You swine! Brute – beast!'

And seizing the cage that housed the robin, for one look at the lark had told her he was all but dead, the only escape for him, she wrenched the cage from the man's arm. It came away easily enough for it was loosely tied by a string; and taking to her heels she made off with it.

Heedless of the yells and imprecations hurled after her, she ran out of the square pursued by the man and up the steep cobbled street that led from the town. Once beyond pursuit and capture, for she was swift and slight and the man, with his hump, stout and heavy, she came to the grass verge of a wood. Clambering over a stile she jumped down, unfastened the cage and lifted the robin out of it. She felt its tiny heartbeats against her hand. 'My darling,' she whispered, 'who was it – what poet said that *you* – a robin redbreast in a cage puts all heaven in a rage? Heaven won't rage for you, now, my love.'

She opened her hand. The robin turned his head weakly to gaze up at her for a split second, then with a feeble flutter of his wings he spread them – was away.

She watched his flight, still feeble at first and then, gaining strength, he was up and up, high above the trees – 'to Heaven,' she said, 'where you belong.'

She went back over the stile into the lane, and suddenly realized that she had dropped her basket with the purchases she had made at the grocer's. While she ran off with the

robin, forcing a way through the crowd, the basket had
either been snatched from her or – what to *do*? How explain to her mother that she had lost the butter, cheese and
flour . . . More trouble brewing, more paternal wrath and
wailings from Mama. She dared not go back to face her
mother without her purchases, paid for and – no purse,
although it had contained only three halfpennies in change.
She was in two minds whether or not to make her escape
now – not wait for a more opportune day, only that the
precious two pounds she had saved lay hidden in a drawer
in her attic room. She would have to return to the house to
fetch that, and the few clothes to take with her.

All this time she was on her way home, skirting the
square to avoid the marketeers and, taking back streets, she
passed the garrison from which the officers, or some of
them, had used to visit her father's house. Not of late. He
had been shunned by almost all of them except one or two,
among them Captain Jenkins.

He had shown her marked attention and had on one
occasion told her: 'I know you are unhappy here in your
father's house, and although there can be no question of
marrying you as you are still Farmer's wife, I have great
regard for you and am concerned that you are submitted to
what I know to be your father's —' he hesitated before
substituting for the word 'cruelty' 'your father's somewhat
too strict surveillance. If there is anything I can do to
alleviate your present circumstances, pray do not hesitate
to call upon me.'

Reporting this suggestion of the captain's to Ellen, 'What
he is telling you,' she said, 'is that he wants to take you for
his fancy piece.'

Sally rounded on her sharply. 'Yes, you *would* think the
worst, you would! He's kind. He knows – everyone knows
how Papa treats me and that I was bought like a slave by
Farmer.'

'Maybe Jenkins wants to buy you,' Ellen said calmly. 'Not
that I'd meself want to be bought to live with him, married

or slave or not. He's too English. So poker stiff and no fun or jollifying in him like some of the others. The Irish officers don't speak with their voices coming out o' the backs o' their throats nor look at a girl as if she were the Virgin Mary – not to be touched.'

'Better that than how Farmer touched me when he was courting – and afterwards,' Sally replied.

And, as she wended homeward brooding on the misfortune of having lost or been thieved of her basket and its contents, she remembered that conversation with Captain Jenkins and was not a little startled to hear her name called as she passed the barrack gates.

'Mrs Farmer!'

She wheeled round.

'Why, Captain Jenkins – I —'

Confused at his sudden appearance at that moment as if risen from her thought of him (and subsequent events made her believe that it must have been fate rather than accident), 'I – I didn't – see you,' she stammered.

'I had intended,' said he, 'to have visited your father this evening.' And then, anxiously, gazing at her more closely, 'Are you hurt? You look as if —'

She interrupted. 'I – fell and – knocked my face.'

'How – or where,' he asked, 'did you fall? You have a nasty bruise over your eye and your nose is —'

Again she interposed. 'I fell in the – the market square. And I've lost my basket with the groceries my mother sent me to buy.'

'That,' he sedately replied, 'is very distressing. But you are some distance from the square. Can I accompany you back that we may search for the basket?'

'I think – I don't think we could find it in such a crowd and it may have been snatched from me when I – I fell.'

'We can but try. At any rate let me walk with you through the square to your home where your mother can attend to that bruise.'

Likely, she said, she'd attend to it. She didn't even notice it nor my nose when she gave me two shillings for the grocer . . . But this she did not say aloud; what she did say, meekly was:

'Sure, I'm much obliged, sir.'

So together they went toward the square, but with some distance yet to go, she stopped.

'Captain Jenkins, I told you a lie. I – I did not fall. My father —' No, she could not speak of it to him. Loyalty forbade it.

He spoke for her.

'Your father,' he said quietly, 'has been maltreating you?'

She shook her head.

'No, sir. Not that. I —' she covered her face. 'I cannot tell against my father.'

He took her hand in his and drew her to him.

'There is no need to tell. I know how your father in his . . . insobriety and his passionate tempers is not responsible for what he says or does. But such irresponsibility is dangerous to those who have been placed in their care.'

'It was of my own accord,' she told him, 'that I left my hus – Captain Farmer, and he – my father took me back.'

They were standing in the public way. Some of the marketeers were passing, women driving their laden carts, men carrying heavy packages; the swarming crowds had diminished but those who were homeward bound at this end of the town thronged the road.

'Come away,' he urged. 'Come with me. I cannot take you back to barracks but I beg – please believe I mean this – that you will let me care for you. Protect you. Were you free to be my wife I would be honoured, but as you are not free – yet, and until such time, if ever, let me offer you a home and my protection – nothing more,' he added hurriedly as she started from him, her eyes wide with fear and mistrust. 'Pray do not for one moment imagine I would take advantage of your – your unhappy circumstances. But I cannot – I dare not for my own peace of mind leave

you to the – the vagaries of your father who I have reason
to believe is out of *his* mind!'

Although still mistrustful, the possibility of freedom
from that which he with careful understatement had called
her father's 'vagaries', was not to be dismissed too hastily,
she faltered:

'Sir, I – I thank you for your – your consideration of my
– yes, I am unhappy living there at home. My father does
resent that I left my – my husband. He has had so much
trouble, as you know – has lost almost all his property . . .
But how can I go away with you, if that is what you mean?
It would only bring more trouble to my father, sure, he's
had enough. That awful trial, and imprisonment . . . How
can I bring more misery to him by – what you suggest?
'T'would be best I leave him to earn my own living rather
than go with you – unmarried.'

The March winds were now less boisterous and a light
breeze like a mischievous urchin played with the straw and
refuse in the gutter. Her hood had fallen off and lay about
her shoulders held by its cord. Stray wisps of hair drifted
across her forehead. 'You,' he breathed the words, 'are too
lovely, too frail, to be submitted to all that I know you
have endured both under your father's roof and with —' he
paused, 'with Farmer. But I have had news he is returning
from India, and he has the right to claim you.'

'No!' She released her hand from his. Fear and horror
drained from her face the flush caused by this more personal
approach than he had ever made to her. 'Coming back?
How do you know? *I* didn't know. I have heard nothing of
him since I left him.'

One of the men in his regiment, he told her, had heard of
his impending return from India. 'So please,' his words were
hurried, losing the somewhat stilted manner of speaking
that she and Ellen had disparaged as 'English coming from
the back of his throat' . . . 'I beg you will let me take you
away from here to an aunt of mine in Dublin. She is married
to an Irishman. My aunt will welcome you, and from there

44

I can take you to my place in Hampshire. I am not required to remain here with the 11th indefinitely, and there is no question of our being sent out at present. Sir John Moore has sufficient fighting force without drawing on the home front. We stand by until we are wanted. In the meantime I must return to England and attend to my own home front but you shall not go alone into the world to earn a living. So,' his voice strengthened, 'come with me. Come to my home which will be *your* home where you will be safe and cared for – loved, for I – I do love you, Sally, as a man should love his – wife. Come with me now!'

The surprise and shock of this singular announcement deprived her of what little breath was left to her, that when regained was poured forth in torrential negation.

'No! Oh, *no!* How could I go home and tell them that I am to go away with you? I must – I tell you I *must* go tell me mother I've been thieved of – or dropped me basket in the square. 'Twas the robin – I saved him from the cage and he came after me. Imagine! That beast of a man selling wild birds. It was then I dropped me basket or someone snatched it from me and butter so hard to come by and her purse and the cheese and she waiting for the groceries, it only had three ha'pence left in it but I'll get another beating from me father if I go back without me basket and you to be taking me away. Oh, no! No, never!'

At this coherent speech which Jenkins may have found somewhat difficult to interpret, a smile of rare humour crossed his elderly young face.

'I will buy your mother more groceries,' he said, 'and a basket, and a purse with three halfpennies in it and then —'

'No,' she cried again cutting him short. 'Me mother'll know 'tis not her basket and how am I t'explain that I've the money to buy what I've lost?'

'Leave that to me,' he said. 'Leave all to me. I will see your father and there will be no more beatings.'

She did leave all to him, and thus it came about that for a second time she left her father's house in company with one who, if not her husband, was prepared to give her everything except his name.

What may have passed between Power and Jenkins to enable her to leave under his protection is not known; but it is possible that a financial understanding was arranged, in that no opposition had been raised by her father to rid himself of this burdensome Sally.

*    *    *

So now two years after her marriage to Farmer we find her established at Jenkins' house in Hampshire. We have her word as related to her biographer and friend, R. R. Madden, that she was treated with the utmost consideration and kindness by him in this sylvan retreat from which she seldom stirred beyond the grounds and the park. In those equivocal circumstances she was happy for the first time in her life.

'Neither wife nor mistress,' as later she confided to her sister Ellen; yet if this were so it inevitably aroused much curiosity and comment concerning the actual relationship between a man and a young attractive woman whose husband had deserted her or she had deserted him. None could ever be sure upon that point, but it was generally assumed that she must have been the mistress of Jenkins since rumour gave it there were orgies at the manor house where the officers of Jenkins' regiment were invited to see the lovely lady clothed and, if not in her right mind, stark naked and dancing on the table amid hilarious applause.

Such rumours spread around gained credulity – a rolling stone to gather no moss more than venomous spite from the jealous mouths of women less fortunate to come under the protection of so eligible a bachelor as Jenkins.

That he would have countenanced any such performances as ill-natured gossip had retailed concerning Sally's conduct is unlikely, and completely at variance with what was known of the puritanical Jenkins.

Sally was always reticent regarding those four or five

years in Hampshire, yet from what has been reconstructed to do with the revolting experience of those few weeks when married to Farmer it can be assumed, judging by later developments, that when Jenkins saved her from a wretched existence with her father he might have thought to possess, if not a wife, a charming young mistress. She for her part, out of gratitude, may have complied with his desire, if indeed he did desire her physically. The general impression of his intimate friends, no women (he had never been a womanizer), was that he preferred the companionship of his beautiful acquisition out of his bed rather than in it.

Before long it became known that not only did they inhabit separate sleeping rooms in his house, but that he found contentment enough in her receptive mind that responded as a delicate instrument to his exploration of her naïve intelligence without more personal approach.

He had a well-filled instructive library inherited from his father, along with the rest of his property and, although he had not hitherto evinced much interest in the many volumes, some of which were rare first editions, since his army service had taken up the years of his earlier twenties, he now shared with her the delight of browsing among the works of past masters of literature.

If Jenkins found their relationship to be less amorous than platonic, he seemed content to leave it at that, for it was evident she found his attempt at sexual intercourse abhorrent to her and that if she did oblige him it could only have been from a sense of duty. Nevertheless her life with Jenkins in his bachelor establishment brought a widespread denigration of her name that branded her the mistress of Jenkins and a willing participant in the debaucheries that were supposed to have taken place at his house. Yet it is difficult to credit that during her few years of intimacy with Jenkins, who had instituted himself her guardian and protector as if she were legally his ward until she came of

age, she would have shared in the bawdy revelries purported to have been sponsored by Jenkins, nor that she
lent herself and her body for his guests' enjoyment; yet
rumour persisted. There were those good ladies of the
county whose malicious criticism bred from jealous rivalry
labelled her a harlot *de luxe*. And later, when she came to
London under the protection of yet another man who
wished to marry her but could not while she was still the
wife of Farmer, there were women whose morals were
none too impeccable and who ostracized her as if con-
taminated by her very presence.

She had left Ireland comparatively uneducated and with
only the seeds of learning implanted by the excellent Miss
Dwyer, who had found in the neglected child an eager
appetite as of a fledgling for the food its mother bird
offered. The sparse knowledge thus imbibed by the receptive Sally was to yield a fruitful harvest in after years.

While in that Hampshire solitude she cultivated her
interest in reading; spent long hours devouring the works
from the library at the house in which, if not its mistress,
she was the honoured, and not dishonoured, guest. There
were a number of drawings and caricatures collected by
Jenkins' father and attributed to Raphael. It is unlikely she
would have passed a weekend as hostess to the friends of
the captain discussing, as we are assured she did, the merits
of Raphael or the works of seventeenth- or eighteenth-
century masters of literature, were she entertaining, either
dressed or undressed in the manner of a *fille de joie*. Later to
be recognized as one of the most widely read and knowledgeable women of her day, could she in her girlhood have
indulged in bouts of debauchery in a disorderly house as
evil gossip alleged?

Unfortunately she never lived down the discreditable
inference of compulsive wantonness ascribed to her past,
even when launched upon her brilliant future in which the
Ugly Duckling was turned into a Swan.

*   *   *

The year 1813 was one of great excitement and hopeful anticipation of an end to the war against the self-styled Emperor of France, he who had conquered almost the whole of Europe. Yet the eclipse of Napoleon, who for fifteen years had engaged Great Britain and her allies in a devastating conflict, was not thought by some to be the last of him. While rejoicing in his fall there were those who could not believe that Elba must be the end of one whom they had thought to be unconquerable. There were some in the corridors of power who did not feel so easy, in that far from treating him as a captured war criminal they had made him master of an island in the Mediterranean. There, it was said, he had been studying his miniature kingdom to decide where he might build fortifications and thus enable himself and his faithful adherents in France to manoeuvre his escape. In Paris, on his journey to his island, he had been welcomed with the enthusiasm accorded to a conquering hero, even by enemy sovereigns.

But it was still to be an anxious time for Britain. Nor was the peaceful life that Sally passed with Jenkins free from anxiety. She was for ever haunted by the fear that Farmer would return to claim her. She did not know, nor could Jenkins ascertain, if he had come back from India – or not. And apart from this perpetual suspense was the fear that Jenkins whom she had come to love, not as a lover but as the best of friends, and in truth her protector from the miseries she had suffered in her former life, might be called to rejoin his regiment. During the Peninsular crisis our armies, although victorious under the command of Lord Wellington, had been outnumbered by the French more than ten to one, and who could tell if war with France was finally over despite the capture of Napoleon? Even those in touch with the men of Government might doubt the ultimate annihilation of an obscure little Corporal in the French army who had become one of the greatest military geniuses the world had ever known.

It was in the spring of the New Year 1814 that to the

quiet undisturbed house on the fringe of the New Forest came a visitor to spend a day or two with Jenkins.

This was Lord Mountjoy, one of the officers who had frequented Power's house during the unhappy years Sally spent under her father's roof. He had been a Lt-Colonel in the Irish Militia and was welcomed by Power with effusion on account of his wealth and his peerage. Sally had seen him only once or twice if forced to put in an appearance at the table when Power entertained his bibulous company, so she did not recognize Mountjoy when Jenkins presented her to him; but Mountjoy recognized her and, raising a quizzing glass to his eye, exclaimed: 'As I live, is it not Mrs Farmer, the young girl who was a wife and no wife to Farmer of the – damme which was it – the 11th Light Dragoons?'

'No, not the 11th of ours,' it was Jenkins who answered, 'thank God!'

Sally said, flushing hotly: 'My husband was of the 47th Foot.'

'Was? Then he – was he killed on active service?'

'I – I do not know,' she replied, the flush fading.

'He was never on active service with our army,' Jenkins supplemented hastily. 'Got himself into trouble and went to India. Whether he has ever come back we have not heard.'

The glass dropped from Mountjoy's eye.

'I see,' was all he had to say to that, but thought: So that's it, is it? Farmer was always a bad lot. Which led him to hope that if Jenkins possessed this lovely young creature, he himself might not be out of the running were she disposed to pick – and choose.

At the time of Mountjoy's first visit to Jenkins he was in his thirties, very good-looking and of an engaging personality with an income of thirty thousand a year. He had come into his father's viscountcy and fortune while still a boy at Eton; from there to Christ Church, and on leaving the university he launched forth on a life of luxurious extravagance. Nothing of a rake despite his wealth, his

50

tastes ran less to wine and women than to the arts and literature. Not particularly knowledgeable in his cursory study of the masters of the Renaissance, he had become acquainted with most of the English painters of his day, wrote a little, read a lot, especially the latest craze in poets, Byron; but his chief passion was for the theatre. He assiduously attended the opening nights of a new play when in London, was himself an enthusiastic amateur actor and had built his own playhouse in his country estate in Ireland.

Of him it was said he cared more for men than for women, was easily gullible and generous to folly. To any who came to him with a hard luck story he would hold out a helping hand. Some time at the end of the eighteenth century, while still a youth in full enjoyment of his money, he became friendly with an officer of the name of Browne, married to a beautiful wife. This Browne was a young man of equally good looks if not the good fortune of Mountjoy. And when his regiment was ordered out to fight the French he appealed to Mountjoy to care for his wife and to be, in fact, her guardian, since she had none to look after her and was but a young girl in her teens. And, he might have added, since he had not cash enough to supply her with the luxuries she demanded, he hoped that, were he to be killed on active service, Mountjoy would marry her and she would then be well secured for the rest of her life.

When Mrs Browne had lived for a year or two under the guardianship of Mountjoy with no news of her husband whether alive or dead, it was assumed that Browne had been killed in action. Mountjoy, having zealously fulfilled his guardianship of the attractive Mrs Browne, became the father of her two children. She had no child by her lawful husband.

Then, after the birth of the second of these two, Mount-joy who, despite his life as a carefree dilettante, was possessed of a troublesome conscience, decided that he should marry Browne's widow and give his name to his two illegitimate children for the sake of their future.

The widow, delighted at the prospect of being the wife of so wealthy a peer, readily consented to his suggestion. They married privately and in haste; with ample time, if they wished, to repent at leisure.

No time nor need for repentance. The first months of their marriage went as merrily as the absent wedding bells, for none except two witnesses had attended that very quiet marriage in the parish church of Mountjoy's country seat. What then must have been their consternation when suddenly, without any warning, the defunct major arrived at the bridal couple's home!

Far less concerned was he than those on whom he had so catastrophically descended and with the utmost affability accepted the manner in which Mountjoy had fulfilled his guardianship. Browne, having escaped serious injury in the war, now temporarily over with Napoleon safely islanded, he found himself as sadly out of pocket as he was out-at-elbows.

Mountjoy, whose conscience again nagged him with the reminder that his two 'bastards' must for ever go nameless, offered Browne a substantial gift if he would take leave of his lawful wife and allow her to remain in name if not in fact Lady Mountjoy. To this arrangement Browne, who may have returned to claim her with just this end in view did, after tactful hesitation, agree.

Accordingly he resigned her to the care of his friend who would resume his guardianship of her – for a consideration. Exactly how considerate Mountjoy had been is not precisely known but it was estimated in the region of five figures.

The major, evincing every sympathy for the predicament in which his untimely reappearance had placed Mountjoy and his lady who, through no fault of her own had lived, as she tearfully told him, 'in sin' with the man she believed to be her husband, Browne departed and left the happy pair in flagrant delight.

Yet Mountjoy's goodnatured *laissez-faire* philosophy could not lightly accept the conditions which still must leave his two children with no name, and their mother his mistress. He therefore felt that his first marriage to her, performed in good faith, had not been sufficiently substantiated, and although by a second ceremony she could be guilty of bigamy in the eyes of the law and that of his troublesome conscience, he felt it his duty to take her to 'wife' again.

So off to another parish church they went and were duly remarried before witnesses and by another clergyman. Yet it happened that fate had one more trick to play them, for within a year of that second 'marriage' reliable news came to them that the husband of Mrs Browne, *alias* Lady Mountjoy, was dead indeed!

With immense relief and heartfelt gratitude to the gods of fortune, Mountjoy for the third time took the now indubitably widowed Mrs Browne as his lawful wife.

Telling all this to Jenkins and Sally at dinner on the occasion of his first visit to his friend, 'How happy was I,' said he, 'to have taken my dear wife to the altar for the third time and *that* time to make her lawfully mine. But alas!' dramatically he sighed and mustered tears; he could never avoid histrionics when telling the tale of his three marriages to an appreciative audience, though Sally was less appreciative than Jenkins. She, having learned life the hard way from her tenderest years, had lost not only desire for the love of man for woman, but the emotional sentiment of such love. So Jenkins, himself a sentimentalist or as unwillingly he proved himself to be the dispassionate guardian of Sally, was extremely touched by what Mountjoy had to say, while she, unobserved by either of the men, was in the giggles.

'Yes,' Mountjoy continued, 'I was the fool of fortune or *mis*fortune! My wife – my true and legal wife, mine for the third time married to me and having borne me two more children and these legitimate and one my heir, within three years she was taken from me.' Another deeper sigh; another tear rolled from his eye, disposed of by a silken, coroneted handkerchief.

'Taken,' echoed Jenkins. 'You mean her former husband returned to take her? Not dead as presumed to be?'

'Oh no, God be thanked, *no*! Not another *revenant*, as I thought was Browne when first returned from a supposed grave in the Peninsula or somewhere. No, not that, but taken where she belonged – to her eternal life to dwell in everlasting lo–lo-love, wor-world without end!' And into that silken handkerchief he sobbed.

'How very sad,' murmured Sally, suppressing again that undesirable giggle.

'Too, too, tragic,' replied Jenkins, almost as tearful at hearing this tale of woe as was Mountjoy in recounting it.

'Taken,' brokenly repeated Mountjoy, 'to that everlasting life where there is no more sorrow and no ler-ler-loss.'

Sally was to learn when she came to know him better that Mountjoy was given to repetition, not always in precisely the same words but with the same meaning.

'Left desolate. My loss was irreparable. Two – no, four children motherless and I – wifeless after three times married to the one woman in my life.' (More resort to the handkerchief.) 'The house I had bought for her in London, Seamore Place, I vacated. Too large and too empty – of *her*. No mother for my motherless four. And I – her widow – widower – left alone . . . So I brought her to Ireland. She lies in my family vault in my house near Dublin. I had the pall made in France and sent over here. Gold embroidered. Cloth of gold em-embroidered in forget-me-nots . . . A great company of mourners attended the ceremony and my poor little motherless ones – four of them – my heir led by me, a rosary in black. Forgive me —' his voice cracked. 'It is two years ago but it seems like yesterday.'

'Time heals,' was Jenkins' platitudinous offer of comfort, 'as God has ordained it.'

'Yes, my *only* comfort,' assented the lachrymal Mountjoy, 'if time *can* heal.'

Sally rose from the table.

'If you will excuse me,' she curtsied to the gentlemen, 'I will leave you to your madeira wine.' . . . And as she might have added inly, to your pathos or your – bathos. Sure to goodness if ever I am called to wed again, which should be never, for Farmer will outlive me as the wicked flourish like the bay tree, I'd liefer marry a wife-beater than a weeping-willow widower. I must be hard as nails to find him to be laughed at in his sorrow, God forgive me . . .

For four years Sally enjoyed a life of luxury and ease under the protection of Jenkins, the recipient of his lavish generosity, gifts of jewels, trinkets, and an ample personal allowance. Nominal mistress of his house and if not mistress of him she was presumed so to be by his immediate family of sisters and other near relatives. They greatly disapproved of what they regarded as an immoral relationship with 'that woman', and deliberately shunned all contact with her. They were doubtless in part responsible for the tales spread about the neighbourhood of the debaucheries and disgraceful misbehaviour of Thomas's 'demi-rep' as they were pleased to call her – 'dancing in a state of nudity before his brother officers – too shocking!' And to be shockingly retailed far beyond rural Hampshire to besmirch the name of Margaret Farmer long after she could lay claim to it.

But as neither wife nor mistress, which for her was a much happier state in the present than her experience of marriage had been in the past, she did not forget her sisters, Ellen and Mary Ann. It is likely that some of the money Jenkins had placed at her disposal was sent to buy her sisters presents of gowns, hats, furbelows, that their penurious father denied them. And often Ellen and Mary Ann, the

youngest sister twelve years junior to Sally, were invited to
stay at the manor house where Jenkins entertained his men
friends, never women, for none would visit him while
shamelessly he 'lived in sin' with a mistress.

'I am damned to everlasting by the good ladies of the
county,' Sally told Ellen on one of her bi-yearly visits.

'Do you mind that they lift their noses at sight of you as
if you was a smell?' asked Ellen.

'Mind? Why should I mind? What I saw of the Jenkins
family, his sour three old maid sisters, he being the only son
and younger than they are, I wouldn't want them to know
me nor I them. In any case they don't have a sight or smell
of me for I keep to myself here in the grounds and the park
and the woods where I ride without a groom. He has given
me a lovely little horse – and no one comes into the woods
which are his private property, for they'd be trespassing.'

'As you are his private property too,' Ellen reminded
her.

'I'm no man's property,' she retorted, 'I'm a free agent, to
stay or to go – if I want to.'

'Where would you go? You haven't any money of your
own. How would you live?'

'On my wits and the little I have saved from the allowance he gives me and I could write for the ladies' magazine
– or write books. I *can* write. I've always known I could
write. You remember how I used to make up stories to tell
you and the boys. And I could earn enough to keep me if I
ceased to be,' she laughed, 'a kept woman.'

'Don't you want to be married again?' persisted Ellen,
'that is, if Farmer were dead?'

'Which he isn't, not that I've heard, and he might come
back any day and drag me from Jenkins by force. And if he
*were* dead, which I profoundly pray he is – I wouldn't
marry again. Once bitten – and I *have* been bitten too, down
to the bone – twice shy.'

'I'd want to be married,' Ellen said dolefully, 'bitten or
not. What chance do I ever get of meeting a man who'd

56

want to marry *me* – the daughter of Power, ex-jailbird, tried for murder.'

'And acquitted,' put in Sally.

'But nobody believes that he *didn't* shoot that boy, and his name,' continued Ellen with uncommon energy, 'stinks to high heaven throughout Tipperary and as far as Dublin. And what of Mary Ann? She's only a bit younger than when you was married.'

'We'll have to see about Mary Ann when we've seen about you,' Sally told her. 'I noticed that Mr Home Purves at dinner last evening didn't take his eyes off you.'

'*One* eye, the other squints. But I'd be twice shy about taking him even if he didn't bite! He has pimples and a shock of red hair and he's a Scot.'

'The Scots are every bit as good if not better than the Irish, and we're all Celts so we're the same race.'

'The Irish wouldn't think so.'

'And,' pursued Sally, 'he's the son of a baronet.'

'Which would make no odds with me. Besides,' said Ellen placidly, 'he hasn't asked me yet and so far has got no nearer than looking at me – with one eye and the other staring at the ceiling.'

'Well, he has only been here twenty-four hours,' said Sally. 'Wait till he's been here a week.'

So Ellen did wait till Mr Home Purves had been there a week, at the end of which time he made her a proposal which, as reported to Sally, must have gone something in this wise.

'Miss Ellen, I would do me the honour – I mean would you do *me* the honour – if you could – I am entirely – yours if that's to say – if you could think of being a wife, I mean – my wife – to marry, that's to say —'

'I was hard put to it,' so Ellen recounted, 'not to explode holding myself in while he let himself out with one eye on me and the other round the corner.'

'Are you going to take him or not?' demanded Sally.

'I suppose I must – if Jenkins thinks it worth my while.'

'He's obviously not worth your *wiles* for you've done all you can to discourage him. But Jenkins says he can keep you well enough.'

'If as well as he keeps you I shouldn't object!'

Sally had asked Jenkins, when informed of the intentions of Mr Home Purves, as to his position. 'For she must on no account go back to Clonmel. If this Mr Home Purves should see Papa and our awful home the match would be off. What do you know of him?'

'Enough to recommend him as a husband for Ellen. He has money sufficient for her needs, is a good officer, or was, in the war, and he may be called upon again for active service. While Bonaparte marks time upon his island he can be planning any day to escape – at least that's what he thinks, and what he *thinks* – he does. A pity,' reflected Jenkins, 'that he is against us and not for us as he is the greatest general we, or all Europe, will ever see.'

'How dare you say so!' cried Sally. 'What of Lord Wellington? How can that little yellow horror who may be some good in leadership – that I'll grant him – with his *grande armée* and they almost as brave fighters as ours to follow him across Europe to be – defeated!'

'He may yet be *un*defeated,' Jenkins said.

'I don't want to listen to such pro-Boney talk!' she flared. 'You, an officer in the King's army to say such things. I've heard some of your friends from your regiment incline that way. I suppose they imagine they are being intelligent and tolerant and Christian – to love their enemy. Would you and they have been so Christian and loving if Boney had invaded us as he has invaded and trampled down thousands of innocent people and made his Corsican peasant brothers Kings! And had half a dozen mistresses and got rid of the one he married. Josephine – the *Empress* Josephine! – a Creole, half Negress – in order to marry Marie Louise, Princess of Austria, and she deserted him when he was falling! Don't talk to me of Bonaparte! I want to talk of my sister Ellen. Do you think she can be happy with this Scot?'

'As happy with him,' Jenkins said, 'as any woman can be who marries without love, which is why,' he put an arm around her, 'I would not ask you to marry me even were you free, for I am well aware you don't love me.'

'I *like* you more than any man I have ever known,' she told him, disengaging.

'That is not saying much, since what man other than Farmer have you known intimately?'

She gave a slight shudder.

'I don't want to know any man — intimately.'

'Not even myself — if you were ever able to know me — intimately? And even if so, you wouldn't, or couldn't love me, could you? There's as much difference between liking and loving — I mean the love of man for woman, as there is in liking and *dis*liking.'

'You have given me,' she said warmly, 'the only happiness I have ever had in all my life. I can never be grateful enough to you for that.'

'For which,' he returned, 'I should be grateful for even such small mercy.'

Steering carefully away from that more personal approach, 'If Ellen accepts this Home Purves,' she said, 'I won't let her go back to Clonmel to be married. So if you have no objection — may I let her stay her until the wedding so's she can be married from here in the parish church?'

As Jenkins had no objection, nor ever would object to anything Sally asked him or wished for, all was satisfactorily arranged.

The marriage took place in the village church, and the bridal pair went off happily, as far as the bridegroom was concerned, for their honeymoon to Scotland.

Soon after Ellen had been dealt with in marriage to her Scot, Lord Mountjoy paid another visit to the Jenkins *ménage à deux*. He had recently acquired the Earldom of

Blessington. Whether it were a title bestowed on his ancestor, the Bishop of Armagh, during the mid-sixteenth century and revived by Mountjoy in either a financial or political interest is not clear. None the less it was much to the interest of Sally, or Margaret as henceforth she would be known, since Viscount Mountjoy, Earl of Blessington, on his second visit had evinced his undisguised admiration for young Mrs Farmer.

In confidences exchanged or perhaps extracted between himself and Jenkins, Blessington had ascertained that the enchanting Mrs Farmer was neither wife nor mistress but – 'My ward,' Jenkins assured him. 'I rescued her from an unhappy home and a still more unhappy and undesirable marriage, and although she had fled from her husband she lived in mortal fear that he would come back to claim her. We do not know his whereabouts, if he is dead or alive, so we cannot find evidence for a divorce. But if he is not dead,' Jenkins said grimly, 'he ought to be.'

'I know something of this Farmer,' Blessington remembered. 'When I was in the Militia at the Curragh it was said of him he was subject to fits of insanity and that there was an inherent tendency to madness.'

'I also understood as much,' Jenkins told him, 'which is why I took charge of this young girl, who had been forced into that marriage with a brute of a husband when she was barely fifteen.' Then forestalling Blessington's next remark, 'Do you,' he said bluntly, 'want to take her under *your* protection?'

'I want to marry her,' said Blessington; and despite his thirty odd years his fair boyish face blushed like a girl's. 'I think she would make me an admirable wife, she has excellent qualities, is well fitted to be my countess.' His newly acquired earldom was still a novelty of paramount importance to himself. 'I find we have many tastes in common. Her interests in art and literature are similar to mine, she is very well read and a great judge of art, is interested in drama too. She admires the same actors and

60

actresses as I do, Mrs Siddons, Kemble – she is a really informative judge of the arts. I would like to take her to Italy to see the Italian masters, she can converse so intelligently on Raphael, those drawings your father left to you – we both agree about Raphael. So, if you have no objection – if she agrees to my proposal, that is if or when she is free or a widow, if she would take me on the same understanding as yourself – that is if you would not object?'

The repetitive recital terminated in a blushful query.

'It is not for me to object,' Jenkins said coldly, 'she is of age and her own mistress.'

'Not yours – I mean —' suggested Blessington, the blush deepening.

'Not mine,' came the emphatic denial. 'She is and always has been my ward and I her guardian.'

'As I would wish to be. Do you think – do you suppose,' Blessington asked anxiously, 'that I would have a chance?'

'As much chance as I had,' Jenkins said shortly; and added after a pause: 'She made it clear from the first that she owed me gratitude, but as for anything else —' he shrugged – 'I think all desire for love of man for woman was killed in her by that brute of a husband while she was yet a child.'

'If not in love with you, as I presume you were with her,' Blessington dived a hand into a pocket and produced a jewelled snuffbox. Delicately inhaling a pinch, he offered it to Jenkins who declined with a shake of his head. 'And as I think,' Blessington went on, 'you were or are still in love with her or you would not have taken her under your protection in the hope, perhaps, of a more intimate relationship, as I,' he floundered, 'would take her under mine also in the hope of – of marriage – that is if you have no objection.'

'I have told you,' Jenkins stonily replied, 'that I have no objection. Any objection must rest with her.'

'Yes, of course.' Blessington replaced the snuffbox and rising from where he sat, held out his hand. 'It is very generous of you, very generous indeed. If she will take me on the same understanding as she took you, or rather as you took her – I'll try my luck anyway.'

In silence Jenkins accepted the proffered hand, his long face grown longer while the face of Blessington broadened with pleasurable anticipation.

That on this second visit to Jenkins he did take advantage of his host's 'no objection' to his proposal to Sally is certain; that she agreed to his terms, or her own, is not so certain. She may have kept him in suspense for a week or more before she could bring herself to make a decision which would mean a complete break from a life that had given her, as she told Jenkins, 'the only happiness she had ever known' in exchange for a life, that when discussing Blessington's proposal with her 'guardian' – 'is a choice between the devil I know and the devil I don't'.

'Have I been your devil?' He took her by the arms drawing her to him. 'Has your life been so hellish, then, with me?'

'It has been heaven,' she was tearful. 'I came from hell to you and you have been an angel to me. Do you want Blessington to have me?' she asked urgently. 'Don't you *mind* if I go to him and leave you?'

'I only want what you would wish – your happiness.'

'But I have been happy here with you.'

'If never leaving this house, its grounds and the estate for years can be for your happiness, then stay with me. But it must be of your wish, not mine, if,' he said earnestly, 'you consider that, even were you to remain married, *legally* married to Farmer, Blessington as your protector could give you more than I could ever give. He is a man of far greater wealth and position than I. Do you not realize what such wealth could mean to you? The world could be yours.'

'My oyster, in fact?'

'Your oyster with a priceless pearl in it – money.'

'He wants to marry me,' she drew away from him, 'but

how can he? There's no evidence for divorce and I don't know if Farmer is alive or dead, but,' she clasped her hands, looking down, 'I admit – I do admit it – that I would like to be a countess. At least I would not be despised, regarded by the women hereabouts as if I were a – a leper or worse – your whore!'

'Let them dare!' he burst forth. But she:

'They do dare and you can't prevent it. I am not your wife and I live here with you, if not as your mistress, to them and to all intent, I am! They are not to know how good you are to me and how – how ungrateful I have been to you to deny you your rights.'

'You have denied me nothing.' He took her hands in his, 'I have no rights, for I have asked – have wished for nothing that you could not give me with yourself of your free will. I understand that what I would have had from you no other man can have – unless he be content to take without response.'

She tiptoed to throw her arms about his neck.

'Oh, you are too good! I have been so selfish – so cruelly ungrateful.'

'You have said,' he gently removed her arms, 'that you can never be grateful enough to me. It is just that I – I do not want gratitude. I wanted only mutual desire, and as that is lacking – so be it. As Blessington wants what I have wanted and not had, then go to him and my blessing goes with you both.'

*　　*　　*

The agreement between Blessington and Jenkins for the disposal of Sally was no less a material transaction than that enacted by her father between himself and Farmer, except that this had no immediate concern with marriage. That there was, however, an agreement between Blessington and Jenkins on the assumption that should Mrs Margaret Farmer become a widow or secure a divorce from her husband she would be the wife of the Earl of Blessington. He installed her in a house of her own in London and undertook all possible means to secure her freedom by divorce.

That Jenkins seems to have raised no objection to handing over to Blessington his ward, or whatever had been their relationship and without any obvious reluctance, points to the suggestion of her contemporaries that the future Countess of Blessington was devoid of all sexual impulse. 'That strange riddle of a woman', as was said of her by another man who had aspired and failed to engage more than her platonic interest in his companionship.

And so it came about that the suggestion of expenses incurred by Captain Jenkins during his protectorate would include the many gifts of jewels and other valuables bestowed upon his ward.

The sum offered and accepted was, we understand, in the region of ten thousand pounds. On these terms Blessington became the owner or proprietor and hopefully expectant husband of Mrs Margaret Farmer.

So for the second time Sally was sold by one man to another. There seem to have been no regrets on either side; in fact the arrangement was greatly to Sally's advantage for not only was she the mistress of her own house, an elegant establishment in Manchester Square, London, she was no man's mistress. Blessington treated her with the utmost courtesy and correctness, never visiting her alone, providing her with an elderly chaperone and conducting himself as any suitor for a lady's hand in marriage, yet with no evident impatience to consummate his suit. When his courtship terminated at the altar it is possible that, like his predecessor Jenkins, he was less desirous of normal lovemaking than in the possession – as of a rare piece of furniture or any other *pièce de résistance* – of a beautiful young woman who could enhance his taste for the arts and share his enjoyment in them.

No sooner had he settled her in London than Blessington

took steps to investigate the possibilities of divorce. But legal action had not progressed to any satisfactory conclusion when fortunate news halted the proceedings.

Farmer, as had been discovered after his return from India, had made no effort to reclaim his wife. He had degenerated into a hopeless drunkard, always in debt, surrounded only by fellow debtors and worthless adventurers. He was in and out of debtors' prison, and on one night when more than usually convivial with his carousing debtor friends, he paid a visit to the Fleet, where prisoners were permitted to receive guests. Farmer, then released from his detention, had managed to obtain an appointment in the service of the Spanish patriots and by way of celebration he brought with him several bottles of rum. These distributed among his cronies, in conjunction with what they had already imbibed, rendered the lot of them, including Farmer, mad drunk.

His ruffianly companions wished him to stay the night with them there in the Fleet, but although far gone in drink he had sense enough to remember he must report to his employers early in the morning. It was already dawn.

As he made for the door two of them, forestalling his intent, promptly locked and bolted it, forbidding him to go. Farmer, furious, weaved an unsteady way to the window, flung it open and, confronting them all, threatened to jump from it if they refused to let him out.

A chorus of drunken laughter and derisive jeers met his demand, whereupon, in order to show them he meant what he said, he scrambled out on to the ledge of the window, where he stayed arguing and, dangerously swaying, repeated his threat to throw himself down unless they unlocked the door and let him go. Of course he meant nothing of the sort; he was far too enamoured of his life deliberately to end it, but as he stood there on the narrow ledge threatening and arguing by turns, accompanied by the roars from the bibulous company of 'Go on, then – jump! Go on! Wager a pony to one you won't –' he suddenly lost his balance and, franctically, with nerveless fingers clutching at the ledge, he fell.

There came a terrified silence from the awed and shock-sobered company, crowding to see where a head had been, saw nothing, followed by a sickening thud. And no sound more than the frightened breath of those craning necks to look over and see, on the stones below, a scattering of blood and brains.

Even as Sally for her second time had been sold to a man, so did Blessington find, for his second time, the woman he had chosen was at last a widow and free to be his wife.

PART TWO

*The Circus*

# THREE

On 16 February 1818, by special licence at the church in Bryanston Square, London, Margaret Farmer was married to the Earl of Blessington. He had gained the desire of his heart, and she not only a coronet but the change of her Christian name of Margaret to 'Marguerite' at her lord's request. 'For you are like a flower,' he rhapsodically exclaimed as they drove from the church to the splendid house he had bought for her in St James's Square.

It is not known if that night of the wedding their union was consummated then – or if ever. Always reticent regarding her marriage even when the wife of an adoring husband, so did she keep her silence concerning the marital revulsions endured with Farmer, apart from a hint at his brutality. Yet from subsequent events and in the light of what Jenkins had revealed to him, Blessington may have realized that in winning a wife he forfeited the enjoyment of a mistress.

But it might appear he obtained a certain compensation for any lack of sexual satisfaction in her ready response to his interest in the arts, literature and, in particular, the poets. Byron, was then in high ascendence, and Blessington well acquainted with him although his wife had yet to meet him. As a poet he was less a favourite of hers than Herrick, born almost two hundred years earlier, and as Sally – No! We must remember her now as Marguerite – was fond of quoting:

> Love of itself's too sweet
> The best of all
> Is when love's honey has a taste of gall.

If Blessington found it so, he seemed content to taste the honey of her love even were it tempered with a taste of gall.

As for her, the transformation from rural Hampshire to this astonishing new life, surrounded by every luxury that money could buy, was as exciting as it was unbelievable. And, if Blessington desired the complete fulfilment of his connubial rights he, never exigent, seemed to be satisfied with an enchanting wife of whom he could be equally as proud as of his peerage.

While the house in St James's Square was undergoing its final costly embellishments he determined to introduce this latest of his treasures to his friends and family in Dublin.

The day after the wedding the bridal pair departed for their honeymoon in Ireland. He had a house in Henrietta Street, Dublin, the same house to which a few years before he had brought the body of his thrice-married first wife to lie in state in the magnificent drawing-room. There, to a large concourse of guests, he presented his second wife.

He robed her in a glory of silver and gold brocade, and effected a dramatic entrance to the expectant company. The doors were flung open by powdered footmen in scarlet and elaborate trappings, and he with his bride stood poised on the threshold amid loud applause and a buzz of admiration for the Earl's delight.

Perhaps not quite so delighted was his young Countess with the rapturous reception accorded her during that visit to his Dublin home. The lavish entertainments, banquets, parties, that her lord gave in her honour, as if she were the wife of the Viceroy at the Castle instead of Sally Power, as she could not help but feel herself still to be, the Cinderella who, on the stroke of midnight during these festal occasions must return to her rags from these riches, to find it all a dream.

It may have been an uncomfortable awakening after the glamour and novelty of the honeymoon subsided, for when introduced to his sister and to his stepmother, Lady Mount-

70

joy, who also had a house in Dublin, she found the reception offered by her husband's relatives far from the warmth with which his friends had received her; it was, in fact, distinctly cold.

Lady Mountjoy, second wife of Blessington's father, the first Viscount Mountjoy, had taken charge of the Earl's two legitimate children, a girl, Lady Harriet Gardiner, and his heir, Viscount Mountjoy. Nor did her ladyship intend to hand over these two children to the care of her stepson's wife. Gossip concerning the now well-established Countess of Blessington had reached the ears of the Dowager Lady Mountjoy and Miss Gardiner, her stepdaughter. The eccentric behaviour of Blessington in giving a house in London to a woman already married to another man, and treating her with the same regard and courteous attention he would have bestowed upon a girl were she his virginal betrothed, was bad enough. But that she had been living with a man in England and was, no doubt, his mistress (for all that he purported to have been her guardian) was too shockingly worse . . . 'Guardian, indeed!' snorted the irate Dowager. 'Guardian to a woman well over twenty-one and married to a rascal of a husband, a notorious scoundrel in and out of prison. And now to have captured Blessington before, if you please, the first husband, this Farmer, killed himself in a drunken brawl. How can Blessington dare presume that I should receive such a creature as my step-daughter-in-law – or out-of-law for that matter! Foh! Disgraceful! Never.' Emphatically did the dowager stress it. '*Never* will I receive her to contaminate my innocent young stepdaughter.' (Miss Gardiner was neither innocent nor young in her late thirties and, as current talk described it, 'very much on the shelf'.)

Small wonder, then, that Margaret Blessington felt herself still to be the spurned, unwanted Sally Power when confronted with such undisguised hostility from her husband's nearest relatives. So when Blessington asked if

she would like to see his estate in County Tyrone, she joy-
fully assented.

On his house, Mountjoy Forest, he had spent a fortune
in improving a vast gloomy mansion into something re-
sembling a miniature Versailles. He had extended a wing of
it to build a theatre. Here be brought players from Dublin
and a few from London to perform. Some of the plays he
wrote himself and played the leading parts.

The Dowager Lady Mountjoy had lived there before all
this rebuilding took place, but when her stepson was surrounded with 'strolling players and mountebanks', as she
disgustedly described them, she removed herself and Miss
Gardiner to Dublin, taking with her the late Lady Mountjoy's two legitimate children. The other two, Blessington's
'byblows' as the Dowager called them, he had placed in
charge of his late wife's relatives and saw to it they should
be provided with everything his two lawful offspring
enjoyed.

Generous to folly, it was not surprising he should be
easily beguiled into parting with largesse to any of his boon
companions who sponged on him with hard-luck tales, or to
his theatrical friends whom he paid to act in the plays he
produced at Mountjoy Forest.

But the improvements of the Great House at Mountjoy
were still unfinished when he decided to turn his attention
to a smaller place on his estate that had been his father's
hunting box. An extension must be added to make of
the parlour a drawing-room forty feet long and twenty
wide with an elaborate Italian ceiling, marble columns,
niches, statues, bronzes. If the House, the larger building,
resembled a miniature Versailles, the 'Cottage' (nothing
of a cottage), Blessington modelled on his one visit to
Carlton House.

His lady's private sitting-room was converted into a
boudoir and hung with crimson velvet curtains fringed with
gold, and the furnishings of the entire 'Cottage', as Blessington insisted on euphemistically naming it, surpassed

anything with which the Earl had filled his houses in London and Dublin.

Yet while his wife appreciated and was grateful for all the money spent on her it also evoked that bewildering sense of unreality as if it must be a dream and she were still the Ugly Duckling, Sally Power. During the hours of complete awareness of this extraordinary change in her life, she was conscious of regret that, for all its splendour, she would rather it had come to her in London. She wished now she could live in the magnificent house he had bought for her in St James's Square and be received in fashionable society as the Countess of Blessington. She began to dread that Mountjoy might be her permanent home, and she must live in Ireland that held such hateful memories despite the beauty of the land she had known and loved as a child. But here in rural Tyrone with no neighbours other than Blessington's tenants, ignored by his relatives, she felt herself to be completely isolated. She knew his family looked upon her as an 'abandoned woman, the mistress of one man while she was married to another and had been the mistress of this present husband whom she had captured and forced into marriage with her, the daughter of a drunkard, jail-bird, murderer, thief'. . . . The litany was inexhaustible and would continue to be retailed from one woman to another while she remained in Ireland.

Little could she have guessed that similar reports would follow her when, after tactful persuasion, she managed to induce Blessington to take her to London. 'Just once or twice a year during the summer season,' was her plea; determining that it would not be once or twice a year but all the year round – for ever.

It was not going to be easy and required all her tact to make him see that: 'You are wasting your great gifts here buried in the heart of Ireland, lovely though it is. You must let the world know you and all that you can give them. You could build your own theatre, produce your own plays, *write* your plays there as well as act in them as you do here. Or politics! You could be a great force in politics. Look at Wellington! From an ordinary and quite unimportant young officer to be the victor general of Waterloo – he too is Irish and see where *he* has ended. And he will be Prime Minister, I wouldn't wonder. And so could you be – mark my words!'

Greatly flattered, he did mark her words; with the result that she and their entourage set sail for Liverpool. She was never to return again to Mountjoy.

St James's Square at the height of the season in the year 1818 . . . To the unknown and unknowable, to the dregs of humanity swarming like beetles disturbed by a light in the dark cellars of their hovels, come from the stews of St Giles or the brothels of Old Drury, to them these stately mansions overlooking the gardens of the Square presented a wondrous glimpse of a world as far removed from theirs as heaven is from hell.

They were drawn from their underworld by distant sounds magnetic, as might have been played by a Pied Piper to a troop of joyous laughing children, though no joy nor laughter came from those tatterdemalion hordes who stood gaping up at the lighted windows of the houses where the Great Ones dwelt in Olympian splendour. But they who had been born into stark poverty and ignorance of anything save hunger and who lacked the bare necessities of life, knew nothing of the champions of Reform fighting for them and all other dispossessed. Nor could the unhappy sisters of the light-hearted, carefree women who danced in those houses of splendour – the lost ones come from their haunts in the gutter with the paint dried on their sunken cheeks, grown too old for their faded wares to whet the appetites of chance custom, they could not know or had forgotten a God of love who seemingly had forgotten them.

On a night in June of that year, at one of the Blessingtons' lavish parties, a company of notabilities thronged the staircase to be received by their beautiful hostess and affable, smiling host. Among the many celebrated men of letters, artists and distinguished politicians, there lacked but one interest: an absence of women in that preponderance of men who mounted the marble staircase at St James's Square. Women, yes, a few, but none of the same class distinction as were the absent wives of the men. Some well-known actresses were there and society courtesans, or ladies received only *sub rosa* by certain royal princes, yet of her sister peeresses Sally-Marguerite-Countess of Blessington could number none her friend.

From the first when launched upon society by her husband it was evident to her – if not to him, so dazzled was he by the sensation his wife had caused among his male satellites – that the women of his circle were not prepared to receive her, nor to accept invitations to her magnificent dinners and conversazioni where the men who gathered round her paid homage to her beauty. Not so their wives. Yet, while they who frequented Carlton House dared not disdain the favourites of His Royal Highness, the Great Corinthian, since Royal favourites were beyond reproach, . . . but *she*! 'A *no*body, a common Irish peasant . . . or, if not a peasant, something worse. Who knew *what* she had been but everyone knew what her father was! . . .'

Thus the condemnatory gossip over teacups in the drawing-rooms of Belgravia and Mayfair. These good ladies, one and all, were horrified to have thrust upon them by Blessington, that eccentric but most wealthy of peers and the most eligible too, having at last become a widower . . . who had been married *three* times to the same wife, hee-hee —! . . . 'But only once legally married to her who had so conveniently died having borne him two legitimate children and two others . . .' And then to have snatched Blessington from their own daughters of marriageable age – yes! Snatched him and married him, the fool! And she already the kept woman of another man tucked away in the country – somewhere. Yes, Jenkins, and he gave out he was her guardian and she his ward, and married to some scoundrel of a drunken beast imprisoned in the Fleet and killed by falling out of a window which gave Blessington – or rather gave *her* – the chance to snaffle him! . . .'

Talk from the Dowager in Dublin had been wafted across the Irish Sea carried by visitors to the Viceregal Court for the edification of ladies in London.

The gossips were enchanted and could never have enough of it. 'Blessington brought her here —' '*Brought*, my dear? No! *Bought* her from this man in Hampshire – Jenkins, was it? And gave her a house in Manchester Square while waiting for her to divorce her husband – Farmer?' . . . 'Yes Farmer, courtmartialled wasn't he? But she was spared divorce for *he* could have divorced *her* had he not got himself killed, and here she is and here we are but not to be saddled with *her*. Never! . . .'

One and all agreed that the 'Blessington woman' must be cut. Dead . . .

It was an increasingly sore point with them that the men of their circle, whether their husbands or eligible bachelors, sought the society of 'that Woman' to pass an evening in her house, or her 'salon' as she called her drawing-room, where she entertained (heaven dared not guess how!), rather than spend their more tedious but irreproachable time with them.

Had Blessington been less foolishly absorbed in his volatile existence, he might have realized the humiliation suffered by his wife. A dilettante in all aspects of the finer arts but without any particular talent he filled his house with men of similar tastes who could entertain him with superficially brilliant conversation, while the only women who cared to visit the Countess of Blessington were those equally shunned by society.

But it could never enter his mind that she, possessed of every luxury, surrounded by his admiring friends, must make a valiant pretence of indifference to the slights of her

feminine competitors. Before long this indifference to her
social outlawry became so entirely a habit that it was no
longer a pretence. She accepted it as her way of life, and in
compensation for her ostracism she was imbued with the
desire to shine as the hostess *par excellence* to the distinguished company of men who flocked to the house in St
James's Square. Politics, literature, paintings and painters
were discussed with intimate knowledge in surroundings
that, despite their elaborate appointments, were neither
formal nor ostentatious. It was here that the former Sally
Farmer, protected by Jenkins, taught by him to appreciate
the influence of the individual in a selective community
did, as Lady Blessington, turn to good account her association with men of the world. She had learned to listen with
receptive eagerness to the opinions and discussions of the
latest newcomer in literature, politics, art. And so, from
their joint efforts, the Blessingtons' dinners and soirées
were the most popular *rendezvous* for men of distinction in
London.

The catalogue of celebrities who signed the visitors' book
which her ladyship had placed in the entrance hall presented by a flunkey to each of the elegants who came or
went, were, among others: Lords Palmerston, Grey, Castle-
reagh and Messrs Canning, Erskine, Brougham (later Lord
Brougham) who was to defend the cruelly maligned Princess Caroline of Wales in the divorce case brought by her
husband against her after he became King. Among writers
and artists could have been found Thomas Moore, Wilkie,
Varley, Lawrence and many others. One of them, Joseph
Jekyll, mentions a dinner he attended at the 'gallant Blessington's house . . . He gave us a banquet last week composed
of *beaux esprit*. Miladi is a beauty . . . She keeps an album
and desires all her literary friends to write in it and per-
petuate their autographs . . .'

During the early years of his marriage, despite his
Marguerite's persuasive enticement of a brilliant future in
politics, drama, the arts or whatever, in order to bring him

and herself to London, 'the gallant' Blessington did not care
to take any prominent part in public life. Certain of his
contemporary journalists and columnists, and one of the
lesser women novelists writing under a man's pseudonym
as Sydney Morgan, represented him as 'stage struck to the
point of lunacy . . . the genius of fools . . .'

But for all the malicious spite levelled at him by both
women and men who had not won his favour to grace his
table at 11 St James's Square, Blessington was no fool; too
easily duped, maybe, and full of good intentions, frenetic-
ally engrossed in a dozen worthy causes, not the least of
them Reform and Catholic Emancipation . . . If fate had
decided that he would not inherit a fortune, or only a
Fortunatus purse which due to his reckless extravagance
was found to have a hole in its bottom; or had he married
for passionate love of the woman whom he took unto
himself to add to his collection of exquisite objets d'art,
regarding her as a beautiful toy; or if he had been less of a
dilettante and a man of more positive parts, his life and
hers might have been different . . . But why speculate?
He was moulded in a cast by a purposeful nature, and as
one of his satirists quick to pounce on his smallest possible
squint, for which he favoured a quizzing glass, denounced
him for a futile Whig in the high Tory paper, *John Bull*:

> Blessinton (*sic*) hath a beaming eye
> But no one knows on whom it beameth
> Right and left it seems to fly
> But who it looks at no one dreameth.

Yet criticism, whether favourable or not, was directed
more at his lady than at 'Blessinton' (the G was often
deliberately omitted, suggesting his somewhat affected
drawl, still in vogue a century later in the reign of the
Seventh Edward). She came in for more than her share of
attack both from women and men who may have aspired to
but received no invitations to her soirées.

We have heard how the battered child-wife of Farmer when she fled for safety to her father's house – a case of out of the frying pan into the fire – took from Power's dusty bookshelves the poem of the then not so well known young Thomas Moore. He, like his immortal contemporary, woke one morning to find himself famous, yet unlike Byron he was not born of the aristocracy but of a Dublin grocer, which may have accounted for his ridiculous tuft-hunting, a lion cub among the lions. While the Countess of Blessington received him at her parties and admired his work she would at the same time tease him for his snobbery.

'You and I are both from the Emerald Isle, but I am not so green as you for I don't care a row of beans that I have a handle to my name . . .' Yet if truth, which she was not always particular to tell, were told, she cared more than an acre of beans for the handle to her name and to be addressed as 'my lady', and carry a coronet upon her lovely head. But Tom Moore had his *tu quoque* retort ready to dart at her in one of his diaries – they all kept diaries, she had hers too – in which he returns her jibe with:

'Today I called on Lady Blessington, who is growing very absurd . . .' Which, if that were the worst he could say of her, fell flat when repeated in the clubs of St James's and Almack's where he, the grocer's son, the latest fashionable poet was welcomed as one of the *élite* where she, if grown 'absurd', could never be accepted.

It may have been whispered in clubland, a merest hint to make more eager the hope of conquest for some who might be in the running for her favour, that whatever were Blessington's hopes as a husband had not yet been fulfilled . . . 'He is *un triste* Pygmalion', was the verdict of a young Parisian recently arrived who spoke a mixture of French and broken English. The son of a distinguished general in the Army of Napoleon who had been ennobled by the Emperor, although not of the *ancien régime*, he was a very beautiful young man, just twenty.

'He? Why should he be a Pygmalion, triste or not?' was

the amused reply from the redoubtable Lady Holland who had taken him under her ample wing so soon as he set his immaculate foot in London society. 'He did not mould her from clay, although she may be cold as marble. He met and knew her in England.'

'Veritably, Madame, c'est ça,' agreed the young Comte d'Orsay, 'and the one difference between the true Pygmalion and milord is that he can never bring his belle statue to life.'

'Maybe not,' laughed the lady with smiling spite, 'since so many others have tried and, if not *all* have failed, she has the advantage of choice!'

'And to affamer – make hungry where she will *not* satisfy,' was Alfred d'Orsay's answer to that. He had been tutored in Paris by a Frenchman who had taken a degree in English at the Sorbonne.

Lady Holland's reputation was not of the most impeccable since before her marriage to Lord Holland she had committed the unforgivable sin of being found out in adultery as the divorced wife of Sir Geoffrey Webster; nor did her elopement with Lord Holland mitigate the scandal among ladies of the highest *ton*. Others, however, whose own indiscretions would hardly bear investigation, and who refused to know Lady Blessington, could readily excuse Lady Holland her fall from grace that they might be received at the dinners and soirées held by the chatelaine of Holland House.

Her eccentricities had won recognition in highest circles. Nor was she selective in the company she kept. Her odd behaviour and loud-voiced questionable language, gave lion hunters the chance to meet other big game stalkers in the chase to run to earth the latest quarry.

Margaret, who although received by the doyenne of Holland House had suffered not a little from that lady's rudeness and sarcasm, was determined to ensnare the exquisite young d'Orsay whose remarkable good looks and charming manners had captured all feminine hunters of big game.

Before 'Miladi' met him at Holland House she had heard of him from Sir Thomas Lawrence, then at the height of his career, had asked 'the Blessington' to sit to him for her portrait. It caused a sensation when exhibited in the Royal Academy and brought eulogies from the more articulate of the critics and as the father of Coventry Patmore said: 'I have seen no other so striking an instance of the inferiority of art to nature as in this celebrated portrait of Lady Blessington. As the original stood before it she fairly killed the copy . . .' For she and her lord had gone to see it at the private view. And while she sat to Lawrence, he had talked of 'this remarkably handsome young d'Orsay whom I have met at Lady Holland's and am yearning to paint his head . . .'

Whether he did paint his head or not is uncertain for if so we have no record of it as we have of the lovely portrait of Lady Blessington.

It is now that the life-long association between Alfred d'Orsay and Margaret Blessington begins, and within a few months we see the anonymous publication of her first literary effort, a series of four essays: *The Magic Lantern* that she described as from *Scenes in the Metropolis*.

Her acquaintance with men of letters, fostered by her husband who himself a few years later published an historical romance entitled *De Vavasour*, may have started her career as a popular writer, if not one of distinction. But if the subjects of her essays were trivial they contained interest in her observance of social life.

Naturally her observations, both shrewd and slily satirical of easily recognizable persons in her descriptive backgrounds of 'the Metropolis' confined to her own territory of Belgravia and Mayfair, aroused indignant repercussions from the women and some of the men whom she had naughtily caricatured, although there was insufficient evidence for libel. None the less revenge, if sought, was fairly satisfied by malicious reports spread around her name as the mistress of d'Orsay, who was reputed to be as madly in love with her as she with him. This, like similar gossip that had followed her from Ireland and had never ceased to pursue her in London, was grossly exaggerated or conjectural. On the contrary, it was not the Lady 'madly in love' with this remarkably handsome youth, but the Lord who had fallen victim to the dandiacal d'Orsay's charm. Blessington, whose physical possession of his wife had suffered disappointment in his marriage, found ample compensation in his affection for and ultimate sexual enjoyment of the bi-sexual d'Orsay. Nor is it likely, however much he may have admired and loved the boy as in a Theocritan idyll, that he would have been disposed to share his 'Marguerite' with any man or youth who might desire the favour of her ultimate concession. Blessington was not a complaisant dupe to allow himself to be cuckolded; and, although malicious gossip ran riot it might never have resolved the truth of the Blessington d'Orsay trinity. As for Margaret, although attracted to this adorable Adonis, she did not, in any physical sense, love him. It is fairly certain, in view of the damage done to her in her puberty by Farmer, that the thought of sexual intimacy still filled her with horror.

Even had she been able to overcome the repugnance that had developed into an abnormal revulsion to the union of marriage, she was too fond of Blessington and grateful for his generosity to jeopardize the luxurious life and social position as his Countess to betray him with any man, least of all a youth who had the face of a girl under the chestnut beard portrayed by the many artists who painted and drew him. A singular ménage indeed, and one in which d'Orsay could adjust himself with elegant ease. He had benefited by a wealthy grandmother's endowment but had little money of his own; and his grandmother could not afford interminably to provide for the boy she had fostered.

D'Orsay's mother was the daughter of an Italian

adventuress by the Duke of Wurtemburg. Her beauty secured her some prominence as a dancer and she married one of the corps de ballet. The daughter born to her by the Duke of Wurtemburg became the wife of General d'Orsay and the mother of Alfred; but his grandmother, Anne Franchi, the dancer, after living under the protection of various men of high or low degree, had eventually married again, whether having obtained a divorce or been widowed is not known. Yet before her second marriage she had become the mistress of an enormously wealthy nabob, a Belgian of English origin and a member of the East India Company: one Quintin Craufurd.

He brought her to Paris, where his wealth enabled him to gain entry to the Court of Marie Antoinette; for the French, in particular the Queen's Court, were not critical of a *liaison* that did not necessarily entail marriage.

During the Revolution of the 1790s Craufurd quixotically involved himself in the plot to smuggle the King and Queen from France which ended so tragically at Varennes. Anne Franchi, his all but wife, remained faithful to Craufurd when, as a result of this attempt to aid the King and Queen, he escaped the revolutionary tribunal, and became an *émigré*. Although much of his wealth had been dissipated when peace was signed at Amiens, all persons who had taken part in royalist activities returned to Paris.

After many years of unmarried state, Anne Franchi, known for so long and accepted as 'Madame Craufurd', was at last the legal wife of Quintin Craufurd; and Madame's grandson, born of her daughter by the Duke of Wurtemburg, was Alfred d'Orsay.

The d'Orsay family, although of some distinction, was of moderate means, but Quintin Craufurd had become a man of wealth again due to his negotiations with the British Government in India and at the same time had made good business deals in property appertaining to the Bonapartes. He died in 1819 when his wife's grandson, Alfred, was eighteen years old.

With Craufurd's return to Paris after his marriage he and his wife again figured in the highest Parisian society. Consequently her grandchildren (General d'Orsay also had a daughter a year or two younger than Alfred and just as beautiful) passed their childhood and adolescence with their grandmother to enjoy the extravagant luxuries that their father, the General, could never have been able to afford. It would seem that their mother had surrendered the sole charge of her children to their wealthy grandmother, Madame Craufurd.

Alfred's sister Ida at seventeen married the Duc de Guiche, heir to the Duc de Gramont. It was she who brought her brother to London.

His entrée to London society was sensational; and no sooner did he become the darling of *le beau monde* than the word 'dandy' was coined and attributed to him. Baudelaire fifty years later defined dandyism as: 'Not so much an exaggerated sense of fine clothes and material comfort . . . as primarily the desire to be individually original.'

Original he was, in his point device attention to sartorial finesse. Only the young Disraeli would capture the feminine hearts of the *ton* by a similar defiance of men's fashions. But Disraeli's début was yet to come.

It is not surprising therefore that both the Blessingtons should fall under the spell of the irresistible Alfred, half girl, half Ganymede. Yet if Margaret regarded him more as a beloved young son or brother, her husband's infatuation may have been induced by his obsession for objets d'art and his love of the theatre and of all things theatrical, of which d'Orsay was a shining example.

Before long it became apparent to those, ready to discuss and delight in any shred of scandal, that this exquisite youth was not only an inmate of the house in St James's Square, but the lover of its mistress. They were mistaken. Yet his influence with both the Blessingtons was paramount, as with his doting grandmother, who could deny him nothing. So had he asked the favour of the Countess he might not have been refused; but there is ample evidence, whatever gossip or rumour spread to the contrary, that any favour bestowed on him was from the husband, not the wife, as ultimately proven in the Will of the Earl of Blessington.

It was on a morning in the summer of 1822 shortly after the publication of Miladi's first attempt as an author that d'Orsay called upon his friends after his ride in the Row, where he had attracted the usual attention, not only for his splendid horsemanship but for his startlingly outré apparel.

When he halted to address one of the women in her carriage who had beckoned him to stay his horse, he was also accosted by a fellow rider, John Galt, the novelist, an habitué of the Blessingtons' soirées and one of her lady-ship's devoted admirers.

'Are you off to the "Blessings"?' Galt enquired, knowing he would certainly go there straight from the Row.

'Yes, and you too?'

'No, not I. There is something of a rumpus going on there today which I may have started.'

'Rumpus?' The word was new to the Parisian's English vocabulary.

'You will hear all about it,' remarked Galt with a grin. 'As did I, and have answered her not unnatural complaint in a letter she will, or should, receive this morning.'

D'Orsay, baring his head to the lady in the carriage who had ordered her coachman to stop, addressed her:

'More lovely than ever, Miladi Cork.'

She was the well-known septuagenarian hostess, a toast of the past remarkable in her day for her beauty, her wit, and caustic tongue. If the beauty were somewhat faded, the rose of her cheeks and the gold of her hair not now guiltless of her maid's artifice, the wit and caustic tongue remained and were perhaps advantaged by the passage of years. She was also noted for her disregard of the reputa-tions of others, either women or men, for whom she had a *tendresse;* one of these and a favourite of hers was 'the Blessin' ', as she invariably named her.

The indefatigable Captain Gronow, whose reminiscences of five decades have left us memorable, if not always charitable, portraits of the persons he had met and known, and among them the venerable Countess of Cork who lived in Old Burlington Street, where she entertained persons of all nations and, according to Gronow, even savages from 'the Isles of the Pacific'. In fact, as he and others described her and Lady Holland, they were the two most fashionable lion-hunters of their time. She also appeared to have a peculiar ignorance of the laws of *meum* and *tuum* and would attempt to lay her hands upon any article of value she had seen and coveted, never mind in whose house or wherever. On discovery the lady would apologetically return any misappropriation with the invariable excuse of: 'My usual absent-mindedness'.

'What's this you say of a rumpus between the Blessins'?' she demanded, blowing a kiss from her small gloved fingers to d'Orsay, as bowing low from the saddle he said:

'A t'ousand pardons, Madame, that I cannot stay and feast my eyes upon your beauty, for I have an appointment *immédiatement.*'

'For a more luscious feast than I can provide? Go then, and enjoy it – and her.'

The faintest blush pinkened all of Alfred's delicate skin as, bowing again, he murmured: 'No feast so tempting nor so appétissante as you could offer, were I so favoured, Madame.' And saying that he cantered off.

'Pretty boy,' laughed the lady, diminutive in the cushioned upholstery of her immense barouche. 'And he can turn a pretty speech. His grandmother, Craufurd, may have taught him her trade, for she had a flourishing trade during and after the Revolution in the capture of hearts. Queen of Hearts, some of them called her, and as in my young time I heard of her in Paris. So the Blessins are having their first rumpus and all on account of you?'

'If it were so I'd go hang myself on yonder oak,' Galt replied. 'Yet I have reason to think the Countess is determined not to go to Ireland with the Earl, and I sympathize with her for I know how much she prefers London to the outposts of Mountjoy Forest.'

'We all know that. Ireland has no happy memories for her. I am surprised he wants to return to Ireland, but not surprised that she refuses to go with him. I expect she will win, she always does win, even to the publication of that amusing book, scratching at all of us with her velvet claws. I suppose Blessinton paid to have it published.'

And before Galt could refute that remark, for he knew the satirical trifle had been well received by its publisher who had commissioned other volumes to follow it, the lady, raising a quizzing glass to survey passers-by, exclaimed: 'I declare! Is not that Rosina Bulwer on the arm of a glowering young man – her husband, isn't he? Or ought to be for they are for ever quarrelling. Quite the coming novelist to put *your* nose, Galt, still more out of joint.'

It was Galt's turn to blush, for his nose – a sore point with him – was just a trifle crooked and gave to his long narrow face a whimsical twist; but the lady, without pausing to hear his comment on her last remark, announced with her usual irrelevance: 'Albert, my grey parrot, has laid an egg. I have had him fifty years, he is sixty if a day – his language is atrocious and so embarrassing. He told Lord Palmerston to "go to hell, you old" — No! I cannot repeat it and I have always thought him a cock. The sailor I bought him from – a brother of one of my footmen – taught him to swear and he never told me he was a hen so new I must call him Alberta. Come to dinner this evening and tell me more of the Blessingtons' rumpus.' And to the coachman: 'Drive on.'

The 'more' Galt had to tell of the Blessingtons' rumpus must have been more than he could possibly have known. It was not he but Alfred who, without waiting to change from his riding kit, had hurried to the house in St James's Square.

His arrival interrupted the reading of a letter written by Galt some few days before. With the letter in her hand Margaret rose to greet him.

'Alfred! In the nick of time. I have just had this –' she waved the letter at him – 'from Galt. My Blessing is furious with me but I am determined not to go because – But you must hear Galt's letter.'

'My angel!' protested her 'Blessing'. 'How can you say such a thing? I am not and never have been furious with you, only it is necessary that I go to Mountjoy to attend to the estate. My agent,' he explained to d'Orsay, 'has left me without a word of warning – just left me and no one to look after the estate. He just goes without a word. Simply wrote "I am leaving" and I pay him twice what I paid his predecessor. So, as he has gone, I shall *have* to go and see to the place which is falling to rack and ruin – so you must see —' he rambled repetitively on until:

'Rubbish!' his 'angel' cut in with. 'There is no rack or ruin at Mountjoy and never will be unless you drag me there by force – which will be *my* ruin!'

She placed a hand to her head, and to Alfred who was looking from one to the other in some bewilderment: 'I am ill,' she said, 'suffering from sleeplessness – driven distracted with the thought of Ireland; for, once there, Blessington will never come back.'

'That is entirely wrong and you know it!' Blessington's round good-humoured face darkened as he paced the room and halted in front of her where she sat and was turning over the pages of the letter.

'Listen, Alfred, to what Galt, who utterly sympathizes with me, has to say . . . "I was so impressed with the repugnance which your ladyship feels at the idea of going to Ireland —" ' she looked up – 'that was when he dined with us a week or two ago – Where was I? M–m-m – "led me to think that some other cause at the moment tended to lend the energy of its effect to the expression of your reluctance —" '

'He always writes,' broke in Blessington, 'as if he were delivering a sermon – so long-winded.'

'Is it possible!' exclaimed d'Orsay who had understood little of the 'sermon', 'that miladi is not well? But my dear milord, if our adored lady is malade you surely would not wish her to – s'engager – to a journey formidable to Ireland. That wet climate!' He shuddered. 'It is also bad enough here en Angleterre when the rains fall and to ride in the route du roi, or as you call the Rotten Row – is to ride in – how you say? a svamp.'

'Swamp,' corrected the Earl, still darkening.

'Bogs,' said Margaret, grimacing. 'Ireland, and especially Mountjoy, is full of bogs.'

'Bugs!' Alfred knew that word from his experience of inns when travelling across the Alps to Austria and he retreated in terror. 'Sûrement, milord would not wish miladi to meet with les – mon dieu! – pas les punaises!'

Blessington, who knew more French than d'Orsay knew of English burst into a roar of laughter. 'Not bugs! *Bogs*, for which Ireland is noted.'

'Ah, I comprehend. It is the svamp as in here in England. But écoute, mon cher milord, I have to visit *ma* grand'mere, Madame Craufurd, in Paris. She write me it is too long she has not seen me, and entreat that I come now to Paris.'

'Not to live there?' cried Blessington, alarmed. 'I thought you had decided to settle in England – to make your home here – with me – with us. I mean —' he coloured hotly, 'that you will *live* here.'

'But yes, I do – I will live here.' He went over to take the hand of Lord Blessington beseechingly held out to him, and turning it over he dropped a kiss in its palm. 'Do you t'ink I leave you and —' he turned to her still silently reading the letter, 'and ma chère miladi – never! No! Jamais de la vie!' (with exaggerated vehemence) '*Mais* – as I must go to Paris why do you not go with me and voyage through ma belle

France to – Avignon!' He withdrew his hand from Blessington who seemed reluctant to let it go. And kissing his finger tips, he repeated: 'Avignon! They say to see Naples and die, but me, I say see Avignon and – live! So you meet with me in Paris, yes? And we voyage to Italy en route through the sout' of France. Ah, c'est si belle! And madame who is not well now will be bien heureuse – more beautiful in the warm sun and the glorious blue of the Méditerranée. Yes? So you will come – come with me and we go all t'ree together, isn't it?'

It was.

# FOUR

With the change in her position as Countess of Blessington, she who had been Sally Power was not forgetful of her family's misfortunes. The ruin that had overtaken her worthless father necessitated his removal from the house at Clonmel to Dublin with his wife and children. There they continued to live in poverty since Power had no means of earning a living nor the desire to do so.

It is typical of Margaret's generosity of spirit that she nurtured no grievance against the father who had caused her such suffering while she lived under his roof, and all the misery she endured as the wife of the man to whom his ruthless greed had sold her. She knew that her father had nothing left from his share in the corn-merchant's business which had vanished with the rest of his property, and that he had run through every penny of the money he took from Jenkins when he handed her over to him, so she saw to it her father should not want while she could provide for him and her mother and their youngest daughter, Mary Ann. When she married Blessington she increased the quarterly allowance she had sent to her father while she was under Jenkins' protection and continued to do so for the remainder of his life. Of her two brothers, Michael and Robert, the former, a ne'er-do-well, had gone his own disreputable way, but she would have helped him also had she known where to find him, only he seemed to have vanished, gone abroad or to prison or, as she would tell her husband – 'to hell where, if he follows in our father's footsteps, he will end' . . . As for Robert, a more likely and likeable lad, she arranged for him to be assistant agent to the Mountjoy estates; and with the departure of Blessington's chief agent,

Robert took over the entire management of all Blessington's property in Ireland and married a good little wife.

So much for the brothers.

Mary Ann, her young sister, also benefited from her marriage to Blessington, for Margaret, having won her point in persuading her husband to take an indefinite holiday on the Continent to which, as with all her requests, he complaisantly agreed, and arranged that Mary Ann should go with them. She, more than twelve years younger than her eldest sister, was 'a shy, demure little primrose of a girl', as described by one Charles Mathews, a young protégé of Blessington's who joined their party at Genoa.

In the August of 1822 the Blessingtons with Mary Ann (renamed Marianne which her sister thought was more *distingué*) left for France with a retinue of servants, flunkeys, carriages, wagon-loads of baggage, a cavalcade that evoked the wonder of the natives when they arrived at Rouen en route for St-Germain-en-Laye. In the diary Margaret kept daily during their travels, she writes glowingly of the forest of St-Germain and declares she could walk for hours 'through its stately avenues where the glittering pageants of olden times were held'; and she reflects on 'the same blue sky that looks down on the gigantic trees . . . the same air rustles their leaves, the same greensward offers a carpet to the feet . . .'

One cannot but wonder how she became so popular a writer if she presents these gushful effusions in all her novels.

They stayed only two days in St-Germain, which Blessington found less delightful than did his 'Marguerite'. He was anxious to get on to Paris where they were to meet d'Orsay. Yet her enthusiasm for the little town and the forest with its 'gigantic trees' may have been a premonition that she would return there many years later never to leave it again . . .

* * * * *

Their arrival in Paris created a similar stir to that with which their extravagant cortège had astonished the natives of St-Germain. To be sure, Parisians were not unaccustomed to seeing the comings and goings of *le beau monde* with servants and carriages and wagon-loads of baggage, but onlookers in the streets, as the procession passed on its way to the hotel, commented it would seem as if a regiment was *en route* to a war; and another, a journalist for one of the English newspapers who had heard of the coming of Lord and Lady Blessington, named it with jovial sarcasm: 'the Blessington Circus'; the name stuck. None, since the arrival of Byron some three years before on his way to Italy, had seen the like of it. But the 'Blessington Circus' far surpassed Byron's cavalcade with its retinue of servants, various travelling carriages loaded with bedding, chaises longues, flunkeys, coaches, horses and shining trappings which might have been a royal procession.

Her diary records this *embarras de richesses* as: 'The chains which luxury forges for votaries'; yet she admits she 'would not care to renounce her barouche with its double spring sleeping arrangement, her bookcase and innumerable other little comforts' . . . Did she recall the comfortless bed she shared with Ellen in that dingy attic room at Clonmel where luxuries such as these were unheard of? How could she, Sally Power, abused, unwanted, scorned, that 'wretched little misery', believe she would ever drive in a splendid carriage dressed like a duchess and almost second in rank to one!

After a brief stay in Paris the 'Blessington Circus' in all its splendour of scarlet liveries, gilded trappings, horses, coaches, their painted panels bearing coroneted crests, the Lady reclining on her satin cushions with Mary Ann, the 'primrose of a girl', beside her, and the Lord Bountiful-Blessington riding an equally splendid horse, the Circus clattered through the Faubourg St Denis to Fontainebleau and thence to Geneva.

A week in Geneva, then on to Berne, Zurich, Lucerne . . .

The Lady is ecstatic. The Lord is treated to rhapsodic descriptions of 'the glorious Alps, the wondrous blue sky, the lake like a gigantic sapphire' (the word gigantic is much favoured both in her vocabulary and her journal) – 'a sapphire set at the foot of a mountain of pearl . . .' Her Lord is less impressed. He has seen it all before as a youth on the Grand Tour and is blasé, restless, impatient to be gone from a sapphire lake and mountains of pearl to Avignon where he would again meet d'Orsay, whom he had seen for only a brief moment or two in Paris at a crowded reception given by his grandmother, Madame Craufurd, where the whole Circus and its Lady were too tired after their journey from St-Germain to wish for anything but bed. . . . Yet her rhapsodies subside when they travelled on to Vienne. The cleanliness of the Swiss hostelries had not prepared her for the discomfort of the inn that the Earl's courier had reserved for them, even though he had bespoken almost the entire house for his lord and lady and their retinue.

'Dirt!' she declared. 'Dirty!' turning up her impertinent tip-tilted nose for which in her childhood she had been teased. 'And,' she continued, 'the food is atrocious.' This an injustice to the cuisine provided by the ex-imperial chef of the late Emperor of France whom milord had engaged while in Paris, and who had brought with him his own cooking utensils and his scullion to clean them.

If it ever crossed the mind of his wife that the Fortunatus purse of her lord might not have been so bottomless as she believed she did not air her thoughts; she had developed the same *laissez faire* attitude to life as her husband, in that he cared nothing for the morrow, sufficient for the day. Blessington, however, having had as much as he could stand of the day, now looked to the morrow, his impatience increasing to move on to Avignon and d'Orsay.

So, after a week or two, enjoying the fresh air and unaccustomed exercise, Margaret took long daily walks to reduce what she dismayingly saw in her mirror to be a certain redundancy of – plumpness, that in contrast to the fragile 'primrose' prettiness of 'Marianne' she seemed to appear as a full blown rose about to shed its petals. This would never do. She must eat less of the imperial chef's superb cuisine and was not sorry to fall in with Blessington's wish to move on to Avignon.

In November of that year, three months after they had left London, the Circus arrived at Avignon and were met by a joyful Count d'Orsay, henceforth to become a permanent member of the Blessington household. Her ladyship's diary is discretion itself concerning that singular trinity and her husband's infatuation for this beautiful boy, no less than d'Orsay's infatuation for her.

They remained in Avignon from November until the following February.

Avignon! . . .

With d'Orsay as guide conducting his Lord and his Lady, he conjured for her visions of Petrarch and Laura. If he hoped that his passion for the only woman he had ever in his pampered youth desired would be returned, he hoped in vain. His Lady continued to regard him as an adored and adoring young brother. Nor did she fail indulgently to see that he identified himself with the handsome young poet known to be an *arbiter elegantiarum*, delighting in fine clothes, and who first sighted his Laura whom he had married – 'In this very church!' declared d'Orsay, kindling enthusiastic response from the Lady and glum looks from the Lord at the attention bestowed upon his wife to the neglect of himself who, with Marianne, trailed behind the pair of them as they crossed the ancient bridge: 'Where,' d'Orsay told her, 'Petrarch and Laura looked down as we do now upon the river Rhone, so fast it flows, isn't it?' . . . And then to the fountain of Vaucluse, which Petrarch had made famous in one of his poems. 'I tell you, did I not? See Avignon and – live? Yes! To live again in the love of Petrarch and his Laura . . .'

At which milord is in the sulks and Mary Ann, demure, down-glancing, in the giggles.

We find this youngest Power girl, for all her modest simplicity, is not unobservant; nor do we think her as enraptured as her sister with Avignon, Petrarch, Laura, and still less with Gédéon Gaspard Alfred de Grimaud, Count d'Orsay et due Saint-Empire, as he flourished his name in the register of l'Hôtel de l'Europe on arrival at Avignon where, under his, she modestly inscribed her own name of Mary Ann Power.

With the coming of d'Orsay it was a ceaseless round of festivities. The cousins of Gédéon Gaspard Alfred, etc, the Duc and Duchess de Caderousse Grammont, had a château near Avignon and entertained the Blessingtons lavishly at balls, banquets, dinners, routs, and were entertained in their turn at l'Hôtel de l'Europe.

The de Grammonts were enchanted with 'Marguerite' and she no less with them; her diary notes that she is charmed with the waltz as danced in France, 'which loses,' she says, 'its objectionable familiarity by the manner in which it is performed. The gentleman does not clasp his partner round the waist with a freedom repugnant to the modesty and the *ceinture* of the lady . . . but her assists her movements without incommoding her delicacy or her draperies . . . Although no advocate of this exotic dance, as seen here it could not offend the most fastidious eye.'

We may wonder if the lady had not cast her fastidious eye on the possible publication of this diary* that she hoped might dispel the rumours spread about her during her sojourn in Hampshire with Jenkins when (as Sally Farmer) she is alleged to have performed in some such 'exotic' dance with or without her draperies.

D'Orsay would have lingered longer at Avignon, but the lady was anxious to move on to Italy notwithstanding the rapturous reception accorded her by the Duc and his Duchesse, in flattering contrast to the manner in which the ladies of London had received her. Milord may not have been quite so delighted with Avignon nor with the atten-

* *The Idler in France.*

96

tions showered upon la belle Comtesse Marguerite by the Duc de Grammont, which caused some disquiet to d'Orsay; not a little also to milord to see his pretty protégé sulking in a corner of the ducal salon, biting his delicate nails and glowering at the Duc who partnered miladi in the so very decorous valse as danced in France without incommoding her delicacy. And when the violins, the harp and harpsichord ceased seductively to play, to see monsieur le Duc accompany miladi to the terrace there to remain – *ciel!* – *pendant une heure* in the moonlight! . . . Monsieur le Comte may not then have wished to linger longer in Avignon, despite its amorous association with Petrarch and his Laura that he dared believe had awakened an equally amorous response in his lady.

The departure from Avignon of the Blessington Circus may have aroused as much excitement and interest among the townsfolk as if the restored Bourbon King of France were terminating a royal visit. La belle Comtesse Marguerite and her sister, la petite mademoiselle Marianne, were loaded with gifts from monsieur le Duc, trinkets, masses of flowers, baubles, perfumes, and for mademoiselle a large box of bonbons. The retiring, shy, almost speechless Mary Ann, who knew no French, was thought to have been still in the schoolroom, perhaps by insinuation of miladi, since were the youngest Miss Power's age to be confessed as twenty-one it would not have required much mathematical deduction to discover miladi in her thirties. She had been wont to say, when she renounced her twenties, that no woman over thirty should admit her age, for: 'A woman is as old as she looks and a man as old as he feels!'

Blessington may have thought to dispel any misapprehension with regard to *his* age which he was not anxious to admit as nearing forty, when he chose to ride a favourite horse, Mameluke, in preference to the cushioned carriage with Marguerite and Marianne. So did they journey through the South of France, and only out of consideration for Mameluke did he call a halt to the whole retinue at Nice for two weeks. Then on to Mentone where Blessington, still anxious to spare Mameluke, decided to take the Corniche road to Ventimiglia on mules. This caused a complete disruption in the travelling arrangements of the Circus. Superfluous servants were dismissed; the luxurious sleeping carriages and all unwanted accessories sold for less than a quarter their cost; and when miladi objected, not only to the loss of her sleeping carriage but that she too must take the road to Italy on a mule, Blessington, for once unheedful of her wishes, over-ruled her, especially as d'Orsay expressed himself delighted with the novelty of riding muleback and what Alfred desired he must have. Mameluke, always adoringly pampered, joined the cavalcade led by his own particular groom, and despite her ladyship's complaints of the discomfort entailed in riding a mule that she must lie in a bed face downward for a week, they came at last to Genoa . . .

Genoa la Superba, beautiful gateway to Italy! . . .

For six months since she had left London Margaret with pleasurable anticipation had awaited her visit to that city, justly called 'The Proud'; and, 'Desirous as I am to see Genoa the Superb', she records, 'I confess that its being the residence of Lord Byron gives it still greater attraction for me . . .' On the evening of their arrival, where Blessington had reserved hotel apartments for her and their suite, she gives this entry in that day's journal:

'Am I indeed in the same town as Byron? And tomorrow I may perhaps behold him!' To which she adds a rider: 'I hope he is not *fat* . . .' For so Moore, who had met him in Venice, cattily described him to her. None the less imagination prompted by hearsay of him who had been worshipped by women – and Caroline Lamb – she visualized an even more glamorous replica of d'Orsay.

When, retiring on the third of March 1823, she tested the featherdown of her bed she found for the first time since she had dismounted from her mule on the journey though France and Italy, that she can thankfully sleep face upwards, her last entry in that day's journal is: 'Well, well, tomorrow I may see what he is like!'

*　　*　　*

Tomorrow and tomorrow, a succession of tomorrows when disappointment wars with hero-worship as recorded after their first meeting: 'He is witty, sarcastic, and lively enough for the author of Beppo and Don Juan, but he does not look like my preconceived notion of the poet . . .'

We may guess what her preconceived notion of the poet had been, and can well understand the shock she sustained when with Mary Ann, Blessington and the ubiquitous d'Orsay, she was driven to the Casa Saluzzo where Byron temporarily resided.

Blessington sent in his card while Margaret and Mary Ann waited in the carriage:

'I wonder,' ventured Mary Ann, 'if Lord Byron is as handsome as people say he is, but I expect he is getting old now, for he has been famous as long as I can remember.'

'Which is not very long,' she was told, 'for he is only a young man in his —' she hesitated, 'about a year older than I.'

'I see, but,' Mary Ann demurely folded her little pink gloved hands in her lap, looking down at them, 'that doesn't make him young, does it, as you are thirty – something, aren't you?'

'We do not discuss ages,' retorted Margaret sharply, resisting a regrettable urge to administer assault on the pretty, downcast face of Mary Ann. 'For,' as she had on one or two occasions mentioned to her 'Blessing', 'there is about Marianne a certain – I am loth to describe it as – slyness, yet I think she is far less simple than one is led to believe.'

To which her 'Blessing' had replied: 'I think you misjudge her. I know she seems much younger than her years, but, as for sly, she is, I am sure, innocent of subterfuge. She hardly ever opens her mouth.'

'Yes, and when she does – at least to me – she speaks as if with an *arrière pensée*. I repeat she is sly. Still, I hope to find her a good husband on our travels, for it is not right she should live with our father, although she has always been his favourite – that is to say, he doesn't ill-treat her.'

It was at this moment that Margaret, recalling this conversation with her husband, heard footsteps on the flag-stones of the courtyard, and Mary Ann said in a whisper:

'Here is Lord Byron. He looks —'

But how he looked her sister did not hear, or did not wish to hear, for that first sight of him, whom rumour had led Sally Power, Margaret Farmer and 'Marguerite' Blessington to picture an Adonis, is noted in her diary, not inappropriately dated the first of April:

'I have seen Lord Byron and am disappointed.'

The man who came limping across the courtyard to the carriage accompanied by Blessington was rather less than medium height, hatless, the wisps of his auburn greyish hair hung over his cravat. He was not in the least fat, for which she felt relieved, and might have preferred him plumper. He was so thin that his clothes hung on him like a sack. Accustomed to the exquisite dandified d'Orsay in suits of many colours, it shocked her not a little to find him untidy, a bow loosely tied with ends fallen over an open-throated shirt, none too spotlessly white.

But his low-pitched seductive voice when he addressed her somewhat atoned for his appearance.

'You must have thought me *un sauvage* and ill-bred, as I am reported to be, for allowing your ladyship to wait at my gate for a quarter of an hour before inviting you to honour me by entering my house. I beg you will pardon my rudeness.'

He bowed profusely to her ladyship and somewhat less profusely to Mary Ann before he lent a hand to each to help them from the carriage. It was evident he thought Mary Ann, in a bonnet wreathed with rosebuds and a high-waisted muslin with a blue ribbon sash, to be the mere child as Margaret had dressed her.

'Your ladyship's daughter, I presume,' said Byron.

'No,' the lady flushed, 'I have no daughter. Marianne is my young sister.'

'My sister-in-law, Miss Power,' put in Blessington after an awkward pause. 'My daughter, Harriet Gardiner, is in Ireland but I expect to have her with us when we return to London.'

Then the four of them led by Byron were escorted to his study. This overlooked the garden with lawns like green velvet fringed with box hedges carved in the shapes of birds and beasts interspersed with flagstoned paths and parterres of flowers.

'*Bella, bella Italia!*' ecstatically exclaimed 'Marguerite' gazing rapturously out of the window . . . 'Our visit was a long one,' she records after that first meeting with Byron, and gives her ample opportunity to write glowing descriptions of Genoa. 'Nothing could be more beautiful were it not for one blemish. I refer to the bold and bleak range of the Apennines that form its background . . . On looking at the Apennines I am reminded of Rogers' lines in the "Pleasures of Memory":

> "'Tis distance lends enchantment to the view
> And robes the mountains in her azure blue"

'For this chain of mountains so beautifully blue in the distance are, when seen near, of a cold greyish tint and have a cheerless frowning aspect. It is not mountains alone to which distance lends charms, it gives a halo to anticipated happiness that reality dissolves . . .'

Which seems to express disillusion in her preconceived notion of Byron, for the next day she is censorious of the 'perfect abandon with which Byron discussed recent acquaintances that even friends would think too delicate for discussion . . .' Also she disapproves of 'the pleasure he takes in censuring England and its customs'.

She may have wondered if he discussed her with 'perfect abandon' to his friends, which is not unlikely since a letter to one of them, Lady Hardy, written a few weeks after the arrival of the Blessingtons at Genoa, tells her:

'Our Irish Aspasia has been a mistress of some kind or other before she espoused the Earl of Blessington. But her slightest acquaintance with me was of the most decorous description.' This could have been an understatement if we are to believe in the sincerity of her journal that gives numerous accounts* of how Byron conducts her on various excursions to see places of interest in the surrounding villages, she riding Mameluke and he on his horse sometimes accompanied by d'Orsay (not Blessington). Of him his correspondent learns that his 'Irish Aspasia, poor woman, seemed deranged almost to *ennui* with her Lord and is a little sick of her Parisian Paladin also, although why I could not perceive, for he is not only remarkably handsome but certainly clever and apparently amiable . . .'

Which may have partly accounted for miladi's criticism of Byron, since his attention to her 'Parisian Paladin' far exceeded his attention to herself.

However, we have her opinion of Byron which makes no attempt to disguise the disappointment and irritation he caused her, for: 'I never met anyone,' she writes, 'with so decided a taste for aristocracy as Lord Byron.' In fact she finds him a snob and pridefully aware of his rank as a member of the House of Lords. None the less, few of his fellow peers could forget his memorable maiden speech in which he declared the sufferings of the working men as 'liable to conviction of the capital crime of poverty'. This won him the whole-hearted approval of the highest Whig circles preceding, within a few days of that speech, the publication of the first Cantos of *Childe Harold's Pilgrimage* which raised him to his pinnacle of fame.

* *The Idler in Italy.*

But Miladi is not prepared to judge him on his literary value, for it seems he has not fallen victim to her charms as have so many other men; so she enlarges on his 'taste for the aristocracy' by deriding his bed at Genoa as: 'The most gaudy and vulgar thing! Its curtains in the worst possible taste, his carriages and liveries in the same bad taste . . .'

Reading between the lines of her diary we may believe Byron to be more interested in the Blessingtons' travelling companion than in the Lady. In a letter to Thomas Moore he writes: 'He has all the air of *Cupidon déchainé*, and is one of the few specimens I have seen of the ideal Frenchman before the Revolution.'

Byron is evidently much intrigued with these new arrivals to Genoa, where he tells them he has 'lived like a recluse,' which is belied by the fact that his mistress, Contessa Teresa Guiccioli who, married at sixteen, deserted an elderly husband to follow Byron, and had apartments in the Casa Saluzzo with her father and young brother. In his letters to his various friends he is insistent on his disinclination 'to philander with miladi', and hints at her absorption with her 'Parisian appendage'; and while allowing that 'miladi is very pretty', he suggests 'Madame la Comtesse G. is seized with a furious fit of Italian jealousy . . . God he knows she has paid me the greatest compliment for what little communication I had with this new goddess of Discord is literally *literary*, and besides I would much rather fall into the sea than in love . . .'

If he does not find this 'Irish Aspasia' so desirable as do many of her admirers, the gossipy letters he writes to his intimates may be intended to deny a warmer interest on her than he felt. Instead he pays effusive tribute to Lord Blessington.

'I never saw the milk of human kindness overflow in any nature in so great a degree as in Lord Blessington's. I used, before I knew him, to think Shelley was the most amiable person I ever knew. I assure you I have thought better of mankind since I have known him intimately . . .'

This recorded by the Lady in *Conversations of Lord Byron*, if reliant upon memory, may be a trifle exaggerated. Yet there is no mistaking that he finds d'Orsay irresistible.

'The Parisian appendage' was now a continuous guest at the Casa Saluzzo and he drew a flattering portrait of Byron, which was graciously received as another example of the enchanting d'Orsay's versatility.

During these first weeks in Genoa which filled pages of Lady Blessington's journals, subsequently published as *The Idler in Italy*, Blessington is given little or no prominence. He figures only in the background of the diaries, which are concerned mainly with her vivid impressions of Genoa, the English and Italian notabilities to whom Byron had introduced her, and of course, the ubiquitous d'Orsay. Of Mary Ann we hear nothing and presume she is called upon to accompany her brother-in-law on drives to the town, or to sit in the garden and listen to his recital of a drama he has begun to write and never finishes. But we hear *ad lib* of her sister's excursions with Byron to places of interest, art galleries, the opera, and daily rides on 'her favourite horse, Mameluke', which she has appropriated to herself despite her 'Blessing's' mildest objection for, as he repeatedly told her:

'I cherish Mameluke. I had hoped to bring him back to England. Byron wants to buy him but of course I wouldn't sell him. I love him far too much to part with him.'

'You surely do not contemplate taking that dear creature back to England,' objected Marguerite, his 'Little Flower' who on Italian food and liberal spaghetti was now in full bloom. 'Remember that dreadful crossing from Dover to Calais – how we suffered from sea-sickness. Would you allow Mameluke, our dear dumb friend, to suffer that misery?'

'I will never part with him,' protested her 'Blessing'. 'He is a treasure beyond compare. I should have thought him too mettlesome for you to ride and certainly too much for Byron with his lame leg.'

'Foot,' she corrected. 'And it is hardly noticeable that it is slightly different from the other.'

'It is what they call a club foot. As for selling Mameluke,' Blessington dared to venture, 'I would as soon sell him as sell my own son. Indeed I love him as if he were Mountjoy.'

'Whom you have scarcely seen more than half a dozen times since your first wife died,' he was somewhat unkindly reminded, 'and you left him and his two sisters to the care of your stepmother. And not only does Lady Mountjoy foster your own two legitimate children, but also the other two, a boy and girl. Had I been fortunate enough to have borne you a boy or a girl I doubt if Lady Mountjoy would have received them as she does your four, two of whom are illegitimate.'

'My stepmother,' Blessington tearfully recalled, mentally adding: Surely his Little Flower should not begrudge his beloved deceased, a mother's – no, a *step*mother's care of my darlings.

She was tapping an impatient toe on the Aubusson – Blessington had brought with him to the hotels he commandeered certain luxurious appointments and furnishings – 'My stepmother,' he continued, 'believed as I have told you that sad *histoire* of how we, my dear late wife and I thought her husband to be dead and how he returned—'

'Yes, as you have told me – a hundred times.'

'And the shock of finding we were *not* man and wife save in the sight of God,' a handkerchief was here produced to mop a brimming eye, 'is ever present with me.'

She forbore to pursue this sorrowful '*histoire*' further which she had heard if not a hundred almost half as many times before; and as always she humoured him, for to her he was less an irresponsible husband than, despite his eight and thirty years to her unconfessed thirty-three, he as d'Orsay was a much loved son. Her maternal instinct never permitted fruition, was somewhat compensated in her love for Blessington which only she and he could know had never in marriage been fulfilled. For that she felt herself to blame, or rather the circumstance of her first initiation in a sexual intimacy that had left the stain of it upon her life as the mark of Cain upon a soul . . . Even as she loved her husband, so did she love d'Orsay; yet none, not even those who knew her best, especially Byron, would believe that her 'Parisian appendage' had never been her lover. If Blessington credited this, he may not have cared deeply enough to demand proof of it since his own love for d'Orsay was even more to him than his love for her or his horse.

Then, in the midst of the colourful pageant presented by Margaret in her journal, full of emotional rapture at the beauties of Genoa with Byron and d'Orsay ever in the foreground, her 'Blessing' is suddenly highlighted, or rather overshadowed by a tragedy that allows him now the centre of the stage.

No presentiment of catastrophe had occurred to him while he sunned himself in the garden of the hotel where he had engaged almost the entire building for himself, his wife and his entourage; or swinging in a hammock between two cypresses he would read to Mary Ann excerpts from a book he was writing, which although of little quality was ultimately published entitled *De Vavasour*. But if he were content to let matters of graver import or forebodings pass unheeded, his wife, who possessed a Celtic strain and believed in omens and superstitions, records how: 'A presentiment of evil seized me when I saw a courier, his steed covered with foam and himself with dust arrived at our inn . . .'

The news, that had taken more than two weeks to come from Ireland, announced the sudden death of Luke Wellington Gardiner, Viscount Mountjoy, aged ten years, only son and heir of the Earl of Blessington.

Shattered by shock, the grief-stricken father shrank beneath the blow, nor could his wife's efforts to comfort him lighten the darkness that clouded his hitherto carefree existence.

'My son, my only son, my heir!' was his repetitive cry.

Huddled in a chair, a soaked handkerchief to his streaming eyes, he turned from her who strove 'to find words,' she wrote, 'that seem to me so cold and valueless that they falter on my tongue . . .'

But if her tongue faltered in words to console him, it was d'Orsay who, always with an eye to the main chance, succeeded where she had failed. Blessington, already dazzled by this beautiful youth, now became utterly enslaved by him. The shadow that enveloped this amiable cuckold, as his world thought him to be, was to spread and enshroud the life of her who had believed herself his closest and dearest, to share with him whatever might be of good or evil . . . Was it merely a trick of fate, or thoughtless misplaced confidence, that against his better judgement he should choose one so mentally inferior to her, his wife, philosopher and guide? . . .

'My son, my only son and heir!' The constant repetition did not help to increase the ready sympathy she offered. 'I am lost. My peerage dies with me. Extinct. I had hopes of Mountjoy succeeding me, and of his heirs to my name and now . . .'

Yes, what now? . . .

'Time heals' . . . The familiar cliché offered to console the sorrow-laden lends to a majority its soothing anodyne; but for the few to whom their loss is irreparable, their life broken, bereft of cherished love, there is no solace, no balm laid to an unhealed wound.

Yet Blessington, having wept himself dry amid repeated bemoanings for the extinction of his earldom and the death of his heir was, after a week or two, sufficiently recovered to think how he could best provide for his remaining offspring: two girls and a boy.

'Alas!' he sighed to the sympathetic d'Orsay, 'He, my son Charles, although flesh of my flesh, is not my heir as he was born out of wedlock to my beloved first wife, only – I assure you – *only* on the assumption that she was the widow of her husband killed in the war – and to find that she was still his wife! He was not killed! . . . And then,' the handkerchief came again in evidence to wipe his eyes . . . 'And then to find she had a husband living . . . Think of that! The shock! . . . Of my two daughters, Harriet is legitimately mine, her sister two years older, they are but ten . . . or is it eleven? Or maybe one or other is twelve, I forget. My son, Charles, born also in my full belief that he was my rightful heir as he is older than my beloved Mountjoy', (more tears) 'I will insist he takes the name of Gardiner, and the courtesy title of the Honourable Charles Gardiner. Likewise will I give a courtesy title to Mary to be the Lady Mary Gardiner; but Harriet, she *is* lawfully Lady Harriet Gardiner, and so . . .' The handkerchief was returned to his pocket and replaced by a gold snuff box. 'And so,' continued Blessington, inhaling a pinch of spicy bergamot, 'in order that my three remaining children, my two daughters and my son may benefit by whatever wealth I may have left to me, I have decided —' he laid a hand on the exquisite Alfred's velvet sleeve, 'it is my wish – I pray you, my dear – my *dear*est friend not to take this amiss – that you will marry one or other of my daughters that they may be well endowed; for as you know, or may not know, under the law of England a wife's money is, upon her marriage, held by her husband . . . You see?'

D'Orsay saw, and with what little breath he had left to him from this staggering announcement while unimaginable vistas of riches swam before him, he said:

'Mon ami.' A strangled sob tore at his throat; he too had a flair for dramatics, and was ready with his tearful answer, 'Cher ami, mais! Naturellement I am overwhelmed with the honneur you bestow on me to offer your daughter to my care. Assuredly I will be —' His voice dwindled. 'Mais! Words are not enough to tell you how much I will guard her – with my life!'

And only he parenthesized: *Et aussi avec des millions de francs! Nom de nom! Combien de francs ou de Louis d'Or?*

'I trust you,' said Blessington brokenly, 'as I could never trust any other man because I know you to be worthy of my trust. As I explained to you, under the existing law of England a wife cannot claim her marriage settlement or any monies bequeathed to her – all goes to her husband, and should she marry a man unworthy of my trust I dare not contemplate what might ensue. He could fritter it away, but you would not. You would dispose of all she might have had for her benefit – and for yours, too, of course. So after careful thought I have decided,' continued Blessington, with a faraway look over d'Orsay's immaculate shoulder, 'I have decided to make a codicil to my Will that my houses in Dublin and London and the whole of my estates, my English and Irish properties, shall be settled on you, (repetitively) on condition, my dear friend and almost brother as if you were David to my Jonathan.'

At which to hide his elation at this munificent offer his 'almost brother', with a care for his mascarad eyelashes, did, in his turn, apply an elaborately embroidered handkerchief to his eyes, murmuring: 'You are plein de cœur, mon adoré!'

'So I have decided,' repeated Blessington for the third time, 'that you will take one or other of my daughters, preferably Harriet, the younger of the two, who is – as I have said – legitimate – not that it would make any difference, as it is unlikely an heir will be born to me now, since my wife, although I adore her, is not – not responsive to, er, to the, er, intimacy of marriage. She is too spiritual, tu comprends?'

Having got this out, Blessington took another pinch of snuff, his face suffused with a reddening flush.

'Précisément.' D'Orsay's delicately pencilled eyebrows rose to the curled fringe upon his forehead. 'Je comprend. C'est – she is plus comme la déesse Diane une désse chaste, isn't it? Plus spirituelle qu'une Aphrodite. Yes?'

'Yes,' agreed Blessington, with a look ceilingward as if to a celestial being, 'she is not of this world – worldly. She is unconcerned with the material or physical. Her mind is centred on higher things.'

Apparently too moved to speak, d'Orsay, concealing his delight at the prospect of an endowment which, in his pecuniary state represented a king's ransom, raised Blessington's hand to his lips leaving a faint trace of red upon it from the cupid's bow of his mouth.

'I will never fail your trust, mon cher ami. Your daughter, my wife, will be guarded and loved pour la vie durant – for ever ...'

Thus the tragedy of Mountjoy's death if tragedy for Blessington, soon to be forgotten, had far-reaching results to affect all those concerned. For the consequence of this unnatural marriage arranged between d'Orsay and a child of eleven was destined to bring to Lady Blessington not only more hostility nurtured against her by her husband's step-mother and sister but, as a stone flung into a pond that widens its ripples to a distant bank, so did the spread of scandal against her leave its stain upon her life.

No sooner had Blessington made known to d'Orsay his intention to give him his daughter Harriet in marriage with all benefit to him, than he at once imparted his intent to his wife.

'I know you will agree, my love, that I should entrust my girl to Alfred, that she is guarded from importunate adventurers because if I were to predecease her marriage to some unknown fortune hunter, as a married woman is not entitled to any money that may be hers by right – most unjust – so,' he rambled on, 'I think it best I provide for Harriet and the other two children for what is the best for *them*. I am making a codicil to my Will that Charles shall have an income when he comes of age and Alfred is to be his guardian and my executor with a thousand a year – for Charles not for Alfred, for he will have it at such time as Alfred shall think proper and then Mary who will be known as the Lady Mary which she isn't but as a compli-mentary title so that she will not be thought to be born out of wedlock and Harriet, my one surviving child – legitimate child – but wait —'

Having got that out, which offered some difficulty for him to say and for her to understand it, he produced a draft of the codical that he read to her before sending it to his lawyer.

The codicil allowed his wife an annuity of three thousand pounds but d'Orsay was principal legatee since Blessington had decided to confer his wealth upon him rather than the child Harriet, d'Orsay's future wife.*

If Margaret objected to this appalling injustice in not reversing the order of the codical in her favour as principal legatee, she offered no outward demur, but she did insist on one stipulation: that the marriage must not be consummated for at least four years.

This precaution, doubtless prompted by the memory of what she had suffered in her own too early marriage, gave further rise to venomous gossip from those who chose to believe she had cunningly sought to secure a fortune for her lover.

That a woman of her intelligence would have attempted such a clumsy device as to persuade her husband to so unjust an alteration of his Will in favour of a man he was supposed not only to have accepted as his wife's lover ('And his too!' sniggered the blades of St James's), but also to marry him to his child daughter is as incredible as it is absurd. For what woman in her senses would have induced her husband to make a codicil to his Will allowing his wife but a moiety of his fortune while endowing her lover with almost the whole of it? Yet that is precisely what he did, and went one better when within three months he made an entirely new Will, which retained the main points of the original codical, but reduced his wife's annuity to two thousand instead of three thousand.

Unfortunately in her agreement to her husband's codicil,

* The Married Woman's Property Act that allowed a wife benefit of her property did not become law until 1883.

which she still believed would allow her three thousand a year, she failed to foresee that when d'Orsay eventually became the husband of Harriet Gardiner the scandal-mongers would pounce upon a strategem that savoured gloatingly of something unspeakable, in that Blessington's wife had agreed to what they believed was an incestuous marriage between her lover and the child, her stepdaughter.

As for d'Orsay it mattered nothing to him how the Will might be misconstrued to his Lady's disadvantage; her reputation had long been ruined by her previous association with Jenkins. Nor did he care if he were thought to be a participant in so shameful a scheme. His fortune was secure for the rest of his life, and if any blame were attached to anyone it would be to damage – her.

*　　*　　*

Three months after the Blessington Circus had halted at Genoa they were again on the move. If Byron had not prepared for his journey to Greece it was likely that the lady would have prolonged her visit to Genoa. Byron, however, now short of ready cash for the Grecian pilgrimage, had sold his yacht *Bolivar* to Lord Blessington, for considerably more than it had cost him. He also managed to purchase from the lady her 'favourite horse, Mameluke . . . To no-one else would I have resigned him . . .' she confides to her diary. 'My groom is in despair at my parting with him . . .' As so no doubt was Blessington to whom the horse, her 'favourite horse', belonged; but as usual his wife had her way, and Mameluke was sold to Byron – 'Given away,' muttered Blessington, who would as soon have sold his son as his beloved Mameluke.

It is during the time spent at Genoa that the diaries of the Countess of Blessington were written, from which the *Conversations of Byron* were conceived, and when ultimately published set all the salons buzzing with even more scandal to blacken the already tarnished name of Lady Blessington . . .

The final farewells between the Blessingtons and Byron lacked nothing of the theatricality so dear to Lord Blessington and, as she indicated in 'The Idler', Lady Blessington did not over-estimate the weakness of the man in the greatness of the poet, since Byron was also inclined to dramatize himself and his emotions. We are told that at this last meeting he wept; Blessington wept, d'Orsay wept, or may have manufactured tears insufficient to spoil his eyelashes; Lady Blessington remained calm, although she admits she is 'overwhelmed with sadness that made me forget the many defects which had often disenchanted me . . .'

Byron brought with him a heterogeneous distribution of farewell gifts. The Earl received a book, we are not told the title, but Lady Blessington also received a book, an Armenian grammar with his autograph and his scribbled notes. Whether she had any use for an Armenian grammar is unlikely as she had no intention of visiting Armenia. D'Orsay was favoured with a bronze bust of the poet that would have been more acceptable to the lady than a grammar in an unknown language. Then Byron, having offered his gifts, asked if he might beg a token from the Countess as a keepsake. She drew a ring from her finger and placed it on his. In return he gave her a pin from his flowing tie, but the next morning he wrote a note asking if he could have it back and offered her a chain instead. As she had gold chains galore set with gems, she was not overjoyed at relinquishing the poet's jewelled tie pin. D'Orsay at the same time received a ring of no intrinsic value but was formed, Byron fatuously told him, from volcanic lava 'adapted to the fire of his youth and character'.

And with more tears, more repetitive declaration from Blessington that 'he with whom we have had the great privilege of friendship here in Genoa will be greatly missed', the Circus surrounded the poet's departure. Mounted on Mameluke and followed by carriages and wagons laden with furniture, books, cages of love birds and hampers of food off he went. They watched him go.

So ended that highlighted interlude as described by *The Idler* in her journal at Genoa. Whether entirely factual or not, she has bequeathed to the world so revealing a portrait of the poet in those intimate *Conversations*, that, as one critic writes: 'It does more to illustrate the mental and moral character of him than all the lives of Byron put together'.

That night of his parting with the Countess of Blessington could she as Sally Power, battered child, battered wife, brutalized and later scorned, maligned as a promiscuous 'kept woman', have dreamed that on this second of June 1823 she would write in her diary:

'Poor Byron! I will not allow myself to think we have met for the last time . . .' Is this another proof of her own presentiments in that she says she is also 'infected with his superstitious forebodings' that he may never return to Genoa?

And closing the book in its red morocco cover which she kept locked with a small gold key, she sat gazing out of the window at the moon-drenched garden of the hotel that overlooked the velvet lawn, the cypresses and silvered tideless sea lying at the feet of the mountains swathed in lilac mists of evening. And as she watched night fall upon the gracious palaces of Genoa the Proud, she recalled what he had told her of the city's ancient history, of the Crusaders who sailed from her port in the year 1095 to the very gates of Jerusalem to fight the Saracen for the Love of Christ. He told her of Columbus who wrote from Seville before he sailed for what was to be his last voyage:

'Although my body is here, my heart is always with you . . .' Did she read into those quoted lines an illusion to herself? . . . From between the covers of her journal she took a folded paper. On this he had written an impromptu when he had taken her to see a derelict villa, Il Paradiso, near to his Casa Saluzzo, which he said if redecorated might suit her to buy and live there at intervals, and he wrote:

Beneath Blessington's eyes
The reclaimed Paradise
Should be free as the former from evil
For if the new Eve
For an apple should grieve
What mortal would not play the Devil?

A smile came upon her lips followed by a sigh. She replaced the paper and closed the book. 'As I close,' she whispered, 'an unforgotten episode, I think we shall never meet again.'

They never did.

# FIVE

With Byron gone there was no reason for the Blessington's eyes to dwell longer on 'The reclaimed Paradise', as the poet extravagantly described her Genoese interlude. She now lost no time in assembling her caravan to take the road southward through Italy. Her diaries, bereft of the companionship of him who from her jotted notes had produced the famous *Conversations*, revert chiefly to sight-seeing and gossip concerning local customs, women's clothes, and brief scenic descriptions. But Florence brings pages of enthusiasm for 'the grandeur and beauties of a town that surpasses all expectations'.

She 'saunters' through the galleries, she 'wanders' through the streets; she has tourist's knowledge of the history of this most beautiful of Europe's cities, but closer intimacy with those immortal figures risen from the past evades her. The lofty splendour of the Palazzo Vecchio towering above the crowded Piazza where the tormented, self-condemned, self-murdered Savonarola was hunted to his awful death, passed unmentioned; and when visiting the magnificent church of Santa Maria Novella she gives not a word to that loveliest of treasure houses and its piazza where Boccaccio herded his band of laughing girls and young man to escape with him from the plague for the safety of Settignano.

Nor do we hear of the church's exquisite frescoes that Ghirlandajo has left upon the walls to trace those who lived in the Flower City and loved and fought and died for all posterity; the Medici, Lorenzo the Magnificent, and the girls and youths who followed in their steps and are as fresh as the colours from the magic brush that remain unscathed by the passing of centuries. But she is meticulous in her exploration of the galleries, and names those works of the masters that focus her attention, preferring Canova's Venus in the Pitti Palace to the Venus de Medici. 'I never see a female statue of his [Canova's] without being reminded of his first triumph having been executed in butter!'

It is evident that she has studied assiduously from the guide books and far back as when she browsed among the volumes in Jenkins' library, for she is well instructed concerning the famous families of Florence who have left their mark upon the stones and portals of their palaces. Yet one feels, on reading her impressions, that had Byron been there her enthusiasm would have been more emotional than instructive. Of d'Orsay we hear nothing, but it is certain she did not explore the city, its churches and galleries alone. She may have dragged Mary Ann along, who would almost as certainly have been as unimpressed as she was bored.

She is not awed by Michelangelo but is struck with the resemblance of some of Titian's work to that of Thomas Lawrence who we know painted her portrait. He should have been flattered. She is immensely excited to see the Raphael, having first heard of him when she was living with Jenkins, but she obviously prefers the fleshly attraction of Rubens' bosomy women to the tender loveliness of Botticelli's Virgins, or the Tuscan primitives to which she gives no second glance.

So after three weeks in Firenze she and her entourage leave by way of Siena for Rome.

Rome! She waxes sentimental at her first sight of the 'Eternal City', as she never fails to name it, notwithstanding, as she says, 'she would forbear to indulge in the enthusiasm peculiar to female travellers'; yet she confesses she cannot suppress 'the expressions of delight that rose to my lips . . .' But finding the hotel does not offer the service

and amenities she demanded, she decided to curtail her visit
to a few days. However she managed to see the museum of
the Vatican by torchlight and the Colosseum by moonlight
that evoked verses from Byron's fourth Canto of *Childe
Harold,* which affords her 'a better notion of the Colosseum
in those exquisite lines than all who have written of it
before or since'.

So short a stay gave her little opportunity to explore
Rome more extensively, but the increasing heat, and the
'dread of malaria dinned into my ears' as the diary records,
'has driven me away . . .' And so to Naples.

Her journal tells us that when she arrived there at even-
tide 'before I seek my pillow I must note down the journey
of today . . .'

She sought more than her pillow; she was immersed in
the classical associations which she had studied en route and
found 'immortalized the scene where Ulysses met the
daughter of the King of Brundisium, when Naples burst
upon us from the steep hill above the Campo Santo. Never
did aught so bright and dazzling meet my eyes!'

Something almost as dazzling as the combustion that
'burst' upon her at this point in her narrative, halted her
pen and spilled a blot of ink on the silken counterpane
where with her diary propped on her knees she wrote that
day's entry, dated July 17th 1823.

Her husband bearing a lamp flashed its lights upon her,
exclaiming:

'What! not asleep? I thought to have found you in darkness and sleeping long before this.'

'Which,' she answered snappily, 'is why you came to
wake me?'

'I didn't intend to wake you, but hearing no sound and
as I thought you slept, I came to see if I had left my snuff
box here when I bade you goodnight. My gold snuff box.
The others have not yet been unpacked. Still writing?'

'I was.' She closed the diary. 'But my train of thought has
left me. I believed you were in bed.'

'I could not rest. These damn mosquitoes have bitten me all over and he heat is worse here than in Rome. I cannot stay here.' He lowered himself on to the bed.

She said, 'Please! You are on my feet.' He moved himself.

'Forgive me . . . Your darling little feet . . . But what I wanted to tell you – I can't stay here, not now. I have to go to London to the Lords. The Catholic Emancipation Act is coming up again and I must be there. The Upper House will have to pass it, although it may not go through yet, but I should be there for the debate.'

She closed her diary.

'You have never been an orthodox Catholic, nor, I fear, have I. So why this sudden interest?'

'Not sudden. I may have lapsed – for my sins – in not attending Mass with the regularity that I should have done and I admit I have sinned. I must confess and ask for Absolution. You too, my dearest, you did not go to Mass in those beautiful churches in Florence.'

'I did, if Mass was being said when I visited them. So you go to London? When?'

'Tomorrow, if my man can muster my bags and baggage at short notice – I shall take only him and two carriages, and then —'

'Does Alfred,' she interrupted, 'go with you?'

'No, he begged to accompany me but I would not wish to leave you here alone.'

'I would not be alone with a dozen servants and Marianne.'

'Alfred will stay with you and I must hasten away to be back again soon – in good time, because —' he moved himself nearer avoiding her feet, 'do you remember that palazzo we passed before we entered Naples? It is high on a hill and you said what a beautiful view it would have of the bay?'

'Well, what of it?'

'I have made inquiries here and it is to rent from Prince Belvedere. If we were to take a lease of it you could have it for your winter quarters and need not suffer the fog and damp of London.'

The candle at her bedside had burnt low in its socket. She said: 'The hour is late. I cannot now discuss whether I want to leave Naples for London in the spring and take up my winter quarters here, and back and forth – it would entail weeks of travelling. So, please – you go to bed.' She nestled down in her pillows. 'Take the lamp. Goodnight.'

True to his word, many times repeated before he made his arrangements for leaving Naples, not on the morrow but in the next week, he set off after having arranged to rent Prince Belvedere's palace, with which his wife was delighted. She saw in this grandeur much that she would enlarge and a few things with which she would dispense. Blessington left her to make her own alterations and arrived in London at the beginning of August. But he stayed only one night in St James's Square and was off at once to Ireland, and did not attend the Lords.

On his way to Mountjoy through Dublin he called upon an old friend whom he had known in the days when he collected actors to play in his theatre. This was one Charles Mathews, now retired from the stage. He introduced Blessington to his son Charles, a handsome boy of twenty who had just completed his articles as an architect.

With his usual impetuosity Blessington, on the journey from Naples, had dreamed up the idea of a castle built on the site of some ruins in the grounds at Mountjoy where once a monastery had stood. When Charles Mathews showed Blessington his son's drawings that had gained him his finals as a fully fledged architect, Blessington at once decided that this beautiful young man had been sent to him by Providence. A reward for having confessed to his sins of absence from Mass. Also young Mathews compensated somewhat for the loss of d'Orsay's companionship. This attractive youngster found instant favour with Blessington and, after a week or two when Mathews had submitted the plans of the castle at Mountjoy for his patron's approval,

Blessington proposed an immediate return to Naples for his wife to see the plans of yet another home for her in Ireland, forgetful of her determination never again to live in that land of hateful memories.

Mathews' parents were delighted at the opportunity offered to their budding young architect to be taken under the patronage of one so influential and so well able to pay substantially for his work; and in September the two of them set forth on their journey to Italy.

Charles Mathews, following the fashion of the day among the more leisured classes, kept a journal of his travels and his visit to Naples. This gives a more intimate portrait of Lord Blessington than the cursory allusions his wife allows him in her diaries.

They passed through Switzerland en route for Naples and during a few days at Geneva they ran into Margaret's sister Ellen who had married Home Purves. Now the mother of five children, she had parted from her husband after a marriage that proved to be a failure. With her was the Rt Hon. Charles Manners Sutton, Speaker of the House of Commons, and an acquaintance of Blessington who hailed the pair of them with exuberant welcome and at once invited them to accompany him to Naples.

Ellen's girlish prettiness had blossomed into beauty, and, if she lacked the culture of her sister, she could respond, as the unfortunate Sally Power never could, to the desires of men. It was evident to Blessington that Manners Sutton, a widower and also the father of a family, was more than a convenient escort for Ellen in her travels abroad. Blessington, an incurable romantic believed, not incorrectly, that Ellen and Manners Sutton were lovers. So by mutual agreement they and their respective families joined forces with Blessington and travelled on through Switzerland to Naples.

It was for Ellen a happy chance encounter with Blessington who indulgently sponsored her relationship with Manners Sutton by offering to lend them when they returned to London his house in St James's Square until such time as they could find a home of their own. Perhaps this generous offer decided Ellen not to go to Naples but to return to London from Milan; or it may be she feared a rival in Sally, having learned how every man with whom she came in contact fell victim to her charms, which Ellen knew might eclipse her own.

Mathews gives an amusing account of his journey to Naples with Blessington and how, owing to heavy floods and the overflow of the river, they had to halt at the little town of Borghetto. They were incarcerated, he writes, in a 'wretched hut called an inn, with bare walls, no sashes to the windows, and the intrusion of any stray pigs that happened to pass the doors which had no fastenings . . .'

He also tells us how Blessington accommodated himself to this 'wretched hut', with a truckle bed in a corner, the society of stray pigs that appeared to be as friendly as they were inquisitive, as well they might be to see the gentleman seated upright in his bed wearing a large flannel night cap, a shawl round his shoulders, a brocaded dressing-gown flung across a broken-backed chair and a rickety table at his side bearing his breakfast tray on which the food ('quite awfully inedible') was served in silver dishes unpacked from his baggage. Cut-glass bottles and silver-backed brushes from his dressing-case kept company on the floor with papers strewn about, discarded manuscripts of the novel he was writing, amid amiable visiting pigs.

Blessington may have enjoyed these unconventional conditions that regressed him to the buoyant, care-free happy-go-lucky young Mountjoy who had recently acquired an earldom and a fortune, and opened house in Ireland to his boon companions from the Dublin and London stage, of whom Mathews' father had been one. Those days of fun and jollifications in the green room of his own theatre were long past, but, as young Mathews gives him to us at this wayside inn, we can believe that in this short interlude he was very different from the nondescript Earl who was known merely as 'the husband of his Countess'.

In Naples, loaded with gifts for his Lady and Mary Ann and, of course, extravagantly for d'Orsay, he is scarcely to be recognized by Mathews as the laughing, untidy, fun-loving companion who could feed stray pigs from silver dishes, while sitting up in bed writing a novel, which, when published as *De Vavasour*, received very poor reviews.

In her husband's absence Lady Blessington had been putting her new palatial house in order. Mathews was greatly impressed with what he calls 'the perfection of an Italian palace with its exquisite frescoes, marbles, arcades and terraces adorned with orange trees and pome-granates . . .' No less enthusiastic is the Lady of the Palace Belvedere (with which her husband had nothing to do except pay for it) and an abundance, as catalogued by her, of 'rarest porcelain, rock crystals, malachite and agate orna-ments, marble tables, consoles, curtains, carpets . . .' There was no end to it.

While Blessington dutifully admired he may have been slightly apprehensive as to the cost of all this 'aspect of English elegance', as recorded by his Lady, 'allied to Italian grandeur'. But when his steward presented him with an enormous bill he sent it to his banker and thought no more about it.

Mathews was delighted with everything, including d'Orsay, in whom he immediately found a congenial friend. He enthusiastically described him in a letter to his mother as 'the model of all that could be conceived of noble demeanour and youthful candour with a gaiety of heart and cheerfulness that spread happiness on all around him'.

If d'Orsay had also found in Mathews a similar 'model of noble demeanour', he may have wished that his patron's protégé had been a little less attractive, both to the lord and the lady.

Yet although Mathews found d'Orsay to be all he could desire in this youth even more delectable than himself, there came a day when these two friends fell out of the love they swore for each other.

We know that Blessington had bought Byron's yacht, *Bolivar*. It was docked in Naples harbour, but never used for any purpose more than to provide the Earl with cruises round the coast, and one day when the heat had become really too much for the palazzo's hostess and her guests who rested in the shuttered shade of the rooms, Blessington decided to take a trip to Castelmare.

None was willing to accompany him. D'Orsay, half asleep on a couch, declared it too dreadfully hot to risk being becalmed in the middle of the Mediterranean. Mathews, profuse in apologies, begged to be excused as he had further plans he was drawing for the Mountjoy castle. Then Blessington losing patience with the pair of them ragefully rounded on Mathews:

'As for your *plans*, Alfred says you carry your sketch book with you everywhere you go and never a drawing in it!'

This tactless remark brought Mathews to turn sharply upon the reclining Alfred.

'I have to thank you, Count d'Orsay, for giving Lord Blessington so generous an account of my diligence!'

'*Comment?*' demanded d'Orsay, reddening under his rouge.

'You heard. Unless you don't understand English. I said I am obliged to you for bringing your tittle-tattle – your *cancans* as you call it – to our host to make mischief. How typical of you French, who eat snails and frogs in preference to good honest English beef steak!'

Whereupon Blessington, foreseeing a formidable row, made himself scarce, leaving his lady to deal with the belligerents – but to no purpose. Her attempt to make them see reason served only to make them see red. She too left them to it and as she hurried from the room heard d'Orsay spring up from the couch to come out with:

'*Voyez-vous!*' And snatching the sketch book from Mathews he tore out a blank page and shoved it under his adversary's nose.

'You call me – menteur – a liar!' shouted d'Orsay.

'I did not call you a liar but if the cap fits – I said you —'

'You said as good or as bad – the cap *sur la tête. Parbleu!* (bursting into voluble French) *Vous êtes un mauvais blagueur comme tout les godans! Je voudrais bien vous casser la tête et vous jeter par la fenêtre!*'

'You threaten to punch my head!' Mathews in his turn shouted. 'Come on then – but not with your fist. We godons as you froggies call us, fight as gentlemen. I'll thank you, Count d'Orsay, to name your seconds and a meeting place tomorrow morning!'

'*Certainement! Voulez-vous les sabres ou les pistolets?*'

As Mathews, having fenced with d'Orsay, knew himself to be no swordsman whereas d'Orsay was an adept, he chose pistols. Each bowed coldly to the other and went to seek their seconds. D'Orsay approached Blessington who naturally refused to act for him since he was host to both. Mathews had lately formed a friendship with a medical student, one Madden,* who willingly agreed to act as second; but Blessington, having refused to act for d'Orsay persuaded Madden also to refuse to act for Mathews. Blessington did not at all care to be responsible for either of his guests fighting a duel in which one or other might face serious injury, if not death, for he knew that d'Orsay's temper once roused would stop at nothing.

Accordingly he persuaded Madden to write d'Orsay a letter purporting to come from his principal which called forth a lengthy reply of three pages in which d'Orsay apologized for having been annoyed with Mathews (*Je suis très loin d'être fache que M. Mathews en ait choisi pour son temoin*). And he goes on to tell him which Madden (not very expert in French, especially as d'Orsay's flourishing writing was difficult to read) gathered that it was ridiculous of him (*il serait ridicule de moi*) to have spoken so strongly (*dit les paroles trop fortes*) and not to have offered him his pardon.

* R. R. Madden, biographer of Lady Blessington.

The long and the short of it – more long than short –
ended with '*cette affaire est aussi désagréable pour vous
(Madden) que pour ous*, but it would never alter the friendship of his: *Tout de voué*, Cte d'Orsay.'

On receipt of this Madden advised Mathews to shake
hands and let all be forgotten.

The next morning the two would-be duellists met and
proceeded to make peace.

'*J'espère, mon cher Mathews*,' d'Orsay told him, '*que
vous es satisfait. Je suis bien fâché pour ce que je vous ai
dit, mais j'étais en colère et —*'

To which Mathews interrupted:

'*Mon cher Comte, n'en parle plus, je vous en prie – je
l'ai tout à fait oublié.*'

Whereupon the two shook hands and d'Orsay much to
Mathews' embarrassment, flung his arms round him and
kissed him on both cheeks.

Lady Blessington, thankful that this storm in a teacup
had not led to a more serious result, felt bound to reproach
Alfred for having taken offence over so trivial a matter.
Whereupon d'Orsay burst into tears, begged her forgiveness
– and seeking Mathews made his apologies all over again
and with another more fervent embrace.

But while all seemed set for weeks of enjoyable sun-
shiny days without a care in the world, within a month
news came to the Palace Belvedere of the death of Byron at
Missolonghi.

Lady Blessington was grief-stricken, d'Orsay in floods of
tears, an ever-ready resort when required of him; Blessington subdued, and his lady writing in her diary:

> 'I can hardly bring myself to think that Byron is indeed
> gone for ever . . . I have been recalling every word, every
> look of his during our séjour at Genoa. I have been
> reading over the notes of his conversation with me and
> could almost fancy I heard his lips utter the words.'

Words that would ultimately recur when seizing the chance to recoup her fallen fortunes, she wrote the famous *Conversations of Byron*.

During these summer months, tinged with melancholy at the lamentable tidings of Byron's death, a disagreement between Blessington and the owner of the Palazzo Belvedere caused another residence to be sought and found. Since Lady Blessington rather welcomed the removal from one house to another as it gave her the opportunity to indulge her taste for interior decoration, a house less magnificent than Belvedere was chosen, and she at once began to make the necessary alterations.

Mathews, finding that Lord Blessington's interest in castle building was on the wane (in fact he seemed to have abandoned the idea of a Castle Mountjoy), the young architect returned home to spend Christmas with his parents; and in the new year Blessington also decided to return to Ireland to see his three remaining children. His wife, now having had enough of Naples, longed to see Florence again. After a few weeks at Pisa she was joined by her husband, as cheerful, as erratic and prodigal of his money as ever. While at Pisa Blessington was brought news of the illness in Florence of an old friend, Walter Savage Landor, and with his usual impulsive kindness he at once ordered his coach and drove to see him. Landor, now married, not very happily, was the father of four children.

Lady Blessington soon followed her husband to Florence with her servants, her carriages, d'Orsay and even the docile Mary Ann, now in her mid-twenties and still unmarried.

This was the beginning of one of the most intimate and sincere friendships of Margaret Blessington's life. The influence of Landor is apparent in all her published works; and although he had already published his *Imaginary Conversations*, they brought him little recognition except from the author's most selective and critical associates. Lady Blessington unlike most of the women in London had not only heard his name, but she had read and admired his book.

So now they were back again in Florence, and it was here that Blessington, having renewed acquaintance with his three children on his recent visit to Ireland, decided to send for his daughter Harriet to meet her future husband.

He had carefully considered which of his two girls would make a suitable wife for d'Orsay, and decided upon Harriet, not yet fifteen and eighteen months younger than her sister, but as she was born in wedlock her father presumed she would be more acceptable to d'Orsay.

Accordingly Harriet Gardiner was taken from her step-grandmother's indulgent guardianship, and brought from Dublin to Florence, a long and, to the child who had never before left her native Ireland, a terrifying journey. Blessington's agent in Ireland had been ordered to bring the young Lady Harriet in safety to her father. She arrived at last; pale, tearful, timid, and looked even younger than her years. Her grandmother and aunt, Blessington's sister, had dressed her in childish clothes that befitted her youth and arrested development, for she had not yet reached puberty.

While in the care of her grandmother she had known few friends of her age besides her brother Charles and her sister Mary, both slightly older than herself. Governesses had been engaged to teach the girls the rudiments of education, deemed sufficient for young ladies of the early nineteenth century: the use of the globes, a smattering of French and English grammar, music enough to play the harpsichord with as few wrong notes as could pass muster, and that was all; and Charles had a tutor.

It is certain that Margaret Blessington would have exerted all her charm when meeting her husband's daughter and d'Orsay's bride-to-be. Perhaps she remembered how at this child's age she had been forced into a marriage with a man she hardly knew. But of one thing she could be sure; that this timid little girl would never have to undergo the torture of such a marriage as she had suffered.

She who had been Margaret Farmer may have conjectured that no consummation of a forced marriage would ever be demanded by the husband of the Comtesse d'Orsay.

After fond embracing and kindly exclamations of:

'How I have looked forward to this meeting, my dear little daughter, for you are my daughter now. I want you to regard me as your mother.'

'I never had a mother,' was the answer from a drawn-in lip that opened to speak and at once closed again.

'Yes, my darling, you did have a mother, a sweet and lovely mother, but the Good God took her to Himself when you were too young to have known a mother's love. But now she has given you another mother in her stead.'

'Where is she?' Harriet gave a furtive glance around:

Margaret persevered.

'She is here, my love. I am your mother.'

'Pardon me,' Harriet made her trembling lips firm to say politely as she had been taught: 'Pardon me, madam, but you are not my mother. You are my father's wife.'

It is likely that the Dowager Lady Mountjoy and Harriet's spinster aunt Gardiner, her father's sister, had not attempted to silence their tongues in the presence of their young charges when referring to Blessington's 'disgraceful misalliance'. Harriet must have heard her stepmother reviled as 'an abandoned woman' who had contrived to marry her father for his money while she was still the mistress of another man. . . . Some of this talk had penetrated to the child's ears to be discussed with Charles and Mary, both who understood better than did their younger sister the allegations against their father's wife.

'You wait until I am old enough,' Charles had told her. 'When I'm twenty-one I'll be even with this woman who has married our father.'

Some years later he did attempt to be 'even' with the woman who had been the star-crossed Sally Power.

No wonder then that Harriet, mindful of these insinuations when confronted with the smiling lady, bejewelled and gowned in a fashion of splendour never seen in her grandmother's austere establishment, remained mistrustfully unmoved by these overtures. A child's intuition, that can be stronger than an adult's, warned her of insincerity beneath this assumption of love and motherhood. She believed herself unwanted, resented, and knew she had been brought there to marry a man she had never seen and only vaguely heard of as a 'Frenchman', synonymous with Napoleon Bonaparte, the enemy of England, as taught her by her governess.

The thought of being the wife of a man who, although he had not fought against England, being too young at the time of the Napoleonic wars, was an enemy of Britain, horrified Harriet. It left her dumb and full of hate for this smiling lady who smiled only with her teeth some of which were not entirely her own.

Said the untiring lady, her smile a little less toothsome, 'I have prepared a room for you where you can have all your books and anything you have brought with you.'

'I have brought nothing with me. We, my brother and sister, we shared a sitting-room and our books and things belong to all of us.'

'Then, my dear, you shall have more books of your very own and anything else you would like to have.'

When confronted by the pale, scared face of this child about to be sacrificed in a marriage that she must have known would prove, if not one of physical and mental torture, at least of lovelessness and neglect, did Margaret Blessington make any effort to save Harriet from any such disaster? There is no evidence that she did; but the world condemned her as an adulterous wife who had manoeuvred this marriage to secure a fortune for her lover, further to damage the already besmirched reputation of the notorious Countess of Blessington.

The meeting of Harriet with her betrothed was less of an ordeal than an agreeable surprise. She had expected to see the frightening replica of an ogreish yellow dwarf who

came down chimneys to carry children away to be eaten
alive as her nurse had told her, no matter that 'Boney' and
all Frenchmen had been beaten at Waterloo and that he, the
awful 'Boney', had died while imprisoned on an island
thousands of miles away. But in this Frenchman she was
relieved to see nothing that resembled an ogreish yellow
dwarf. Instead she saw one who might have been a fairy
prince as pictured in her story-book with his pink-and-
white face, his curly hair, his pretty clothes of colours
never seen in ordinary gentlemen's clothes before, lavender
satin, white breeches, lace ruffles and his hand extended to
her with a ring on his forefinger and one, of all things – on
his thumb! And the way he took her hand and kissed it
(leaving a slight red smudge on it), and said in French, as
she afterwards recalled it when writing to her sister and
brother:

'Ah la bonerre madamerselle Commong sa vah?'

After that he gave her no second glance but turned to
murmur in the lady's ear that to Harriet incomprehensibly
sounded like:

'Why am I given une petite lapine blanche? I am not a
fox!'

Which she judged to be something about herself that was
uncomplimentary.

The Blessingtons were of one mind to hasten the wedding
lest d'Orsay should refuse to be a party to it. He had shown
his disgust in their choice of his bride.

'Too young, too utterly naïve. I cannot bring myself to
marry a child. She looks no more than twelve.'

He was half inclined to call it off and only the induce-
ment of the 'child's' fortune urged him to call it on.

So on it went.

Arrangements were at once made for the wedding to take
place, and when d'Orsay suggested that the French Minister
should perform the ceremony, Lady Blessington agreed.
However Blessington wished to see his daughter married by

the English Minister for though born in Ireland and brought up as a Protestant by her English mother she was British. As it didn't matter to d'Orsay if he were married in a Catholic church or by a Protestant Minister or anyone else, Blessington approached the British representative in Florence, Lord Burghersh, was coldly received, and given to understand that he did not approve of the marriage. Burghersh evidently believed what he had heard from English residents in Florence, that d'Orsay and Lady Blessington were lovers, and the idea of an adulterous wife agreeing to marry her step-daughter to her lover – and a Frenchman, to boot – could not possibly be tolerated by the representative of King George IV.

Blessington thought that the reason for the refusal of Lord Burghersh to perform the marriage was the difference in religion of the bridal pair, although he may have had his suspicions as to its real cause. And if he chose to ignore the rumour that his wife and d'Orsay had been amorously intimate all this time, it suited his purpose. He was too infatuated with d'Orsay and too devoted to his wife to have attempted to investigate the *raison d'être* of such unsavoury gossip.

At this impasse in the negotiations Lady Blessington intervened. She would not accept that Burghersh could be so unreasonable as to refuse to authorize the marriage. It did not occur to her or if so she discarded any such imputation that she was suspect of promoting a marriage between her husband's daughter and her alleged lover in order to endow him with his wife's money. She therefore decided that she must persuade Lord Burghersh to reconsider his refusal, and called upon the Minister, taking the prospective child-bride with her.

This gave Burghersh the opportunity not only to repeat his refusal in such a way as to leave no doubt as to his basic intention to insult the lady whose name had become a by-word for an equivocal past and a disreputable present.

Not in so many words did the Minister state his case, yet it led to an unmistakable deduction. The lady went from him in a burning rage and determined to avenge this insult.

As Blessington did not care to take so drastic a view of Burghersh's intention, for he was always ready to follow the easiest way and avoid any unpleasantness, he attempted to make his wife take a less censorious opinion of the Minister's refusal.

'After all, my dear, he was only trying to tell you that he, as the King's Minister, did not approve of a ceremony held in the rites of the Church of England with a Frenchman of the Church of Rome. That, I am sure, is his sole reason for an objection. He is a bigot, I agree, and as such should be made to understand that he is gravely at fault but —' reverting to repetition – 'as the King's Minister, he is within his rights to object to marrying Harriet in the Church of England and also in the Church of Rome – a double ceremony as d'Orsay suggests, especially as he is French and Burghersh cannot forget that we were at war with France for fifteen years.'

'What has that got to do with it?' she demanded. 'The war is long over and forgotten and if *you* can condone an insult to your wife there are others who do not!'

Forthwith she told it all to Landor, with whom she was now on friendliest terms. Landor at once took up the cudgels on her behalf in a letter expressing his undiluted opinion of Burghersh.

'I have said on other occasions that nothing would surprise me of folly or indecorum in Lord Burghersh. I retract my words. That a man educated among the sons of gentlemen should be guilty of incivility to two ladies is inconceivable. . . . I am convinced that there is no other Minister in all the Courts of Europe who has ever been guilty of so many unbecoming and undignified actions as this man . . .'

Which was balm to Lady Blessington's wounded pride, yet she could not help but wish that Landor had written to the Minister himself accusing him of 'unbecoming and undignified actions'. However, sufficient that she had an ally and, it was hoped, an influential one, since the name of Walter Savage Landor, during his six years' residence in Florence had found favour with his fellow countrymen if not with the British Minister.

None the less it was thought to be a more 'dignified action' for Lady Blessington to ignore the insults of the Burghersh party with the contempt they deserved, and to depart from Florence for Naples via Rome.

In Naples they found the British Minister more amenable, and he, without asking embarrassing questions, agreed to marry the Lady Harriet Gardiner to the husband chosen and approved by her father. The travesty of a marriage was duly performed and, the ceremony over, the father, step-mother and bridegroom with his pale little bride departed directly for Rome. Lady Blessington's journal remains discreetly silent concerning Lord Burghersh and the unfortunate contretemps that necessitated a search for a more accommodating Minister to conduct the marriage service that transformed Harriet Gardiner into Madame la Comtesse d'Orsay.

While Madame la Comtesse de Blessington busied herself in Rome with house-hunting, a not unfamiliar occupation in these last few years, d'Orsay wrote an offensive letter to Lord Burghersh in Florence and another letter to Landor telling him he would like to cut off Burghersh's nose . . . After thus relieving his feelings on paper without assault to the Minister's nose, d'Orsay accompanied his Lady mother-in-law on her house-hunting expeditions, leaving his bride to her own lonely devices. Her father, still engaged in the writing of his novel, had nothing to say or to do with her.

So began the married life of the fifteen-year-old Harriet, Comtesse d'Orsay.

*　　*　　*

The search for a suitable house in Rome, where Lady Blessington decided to settle for the winter, occupied much of her time. Nothing it seemed would satisfy her; one was too small, another too large, the position of this unattractive, the furnishings of that appalling, until at last her diary records she had 'found an abode in the Palazzo Negroni, of which I have engaged the two principal floors at one hundred guineas a month ...'

Although the rooms were approved, the furniture was not; new curtains, table appointments, glass, cutlery, bed coverings all had to be bought regardless of expense. Mary Ann Power, who still accompanied the Blessingtons on their travels, was not yet accustomed to the lavish expenditure and grandeur of her sister's various establishments, remembering those days when Sally lived in that dirty shabby house in Clonmel and slept in an attic with Ellen.

And while Sally (as Mary Ann would often forgetfully call her) was refurbishing this, her latest palace, her domestic activities may have diverted her attention from the scared white little face of Harriet, Comtesse d'Orsay, and her part in the marriage from which, her conscience cared not to be reminded, she might have made an effort to save this victim of a fate as tragic as her own first marriage had been.

During the upheaval of moving from the hotel where they were temporarily lodged, the child bride was disregarded, hardly speaking to anyone, while her bridegroom spoke to everyone but her. Mary Ann who had been used to similar neglect while living as a dependant on her sister – 'the guest of charity', as she put it to herself – felt sympathy for this sad little Harriet and would try to make her more attuned to these unfamiliar surroundings in a city that for all its beauty had no appeal for a child pining for the home where she had been loved. None knew or cared how often, in her solitary bedroom, did she sob herself to sleep. And Mary Ann's attempt to help the neglected little bride met with no response.

'Sally, I do think,' she told her sister, 'that you might show some kindness to Harriet. No one takes any notice of her. She wanders about the house and grounds like a little lost ghost'

'If you could only know,' Sally excused herself, 'how I have tried – how her father has tried to make her happy. And as you may or may not know I, who, for my sins, agreed to this marriage, insisted that it must not be consummated until she was of an age to be a wife. She is still immature, as was I. All my efforts to bring her to me, to love her, have been repulsed. So both her father and I give up trying.'

'Yes, so much her father tries,' retorted Mary Ann, 'that he boxed her ears yesterday and called her a sulky little bitch for not having the grace to be civil to her mother – and all he got from her was: "She is not my mother." Poor little thing.'

If again the conscience of the Countess troubled her at this outspoken reminder from the retiring and equally neglected Mary Ann, she soon overcame any scruples that may have haunted her in agreeing to this marriage, by lavish entertaining so soon as her apartments in the Palazzo Negroni were ready to receive guests. In Rome she was cordially accepted by Italian society if not by the English residents. The ladies of Rome and their men – in particular the men – welcomed her with effusion, so magnificent was her establishment, so superb the food and drink, so charming the hostess (this from the men), so affable the host, so handsome the Comte d'Orsay! (this from the women). But while Roman society gladly attended her soirées, her dinners, her routs, her *conversazioni* English society in Rome and especially those of Ambassadorial circles, ostracized her as had the ladies of London. Repercussions from Florence relating to Burghersh's refusal to perform the marriage ceremony had percolated to Rome, to the delight of English gossipmongers. Also those Roman ladies who had heard of the presumed relationship between the

Contessa and the Conte to say nothing of the blind eye of the Contessa's husband who had no objection to being a . . . Hands and eyes were raised to heaven as the Italian word for the good old Anglo-Saxon 'cuckold' escaped them in shocked whispers; so that of late a noticeable reluctance to accept invitations to the Palazzo Negroni was observed by the Countess of Blessington.

As winter passed and spring danced again amid the orange-flowers in the palace gardens, and the roses were already in bloom, the lady whose diary had given but perfunctory entries all this time, suddenly announces:

'Tomorrow we leave the Eternal City.'

Why, and to where?

She does not say; but as always Blessington agreed that the choice of their next destination must be hers.

Ravenna, Ferrara, Padua, the Blessington Circus augmented by the gift from her dotingly generous husband of a *caleche* (which the Countess had coveted when in Florence, having seen Lady Burghersh driving in such a one), lumbered through northern Italy, arrived for a brief halt at Genoa and thence – to Paris.

# PART THREE

## Scandal

SIX

Paris! . . . City of enchantment, of elegance, of youth in the dawn of a new age that rebelled against the tyranny of the First Empire. This toward the end of the eighteen twenties was the order of the young Parisians' day, a day when the torch of militant idealism was lighted by Victor Hugo from the dying candles on the altars of Chateaubriand and Madame de Staël, fiercely to proclaim no other law but Nature, no other God but Art.

Yet among that army of arrogant young disciples of Hugo, some fell by the wayside, their path lost, never to be found again; while others, the more urgently progressive, ploughed onward to rank among the immortals. Alfred de Musset, publishing verses in his teens, a drunken young Dionysus snatched from his mother's apron strings to worship at the feet of Madame Aurore Dudevant, *alias* George Sand, that bizarre and brilliant *bon garçon* who wore trousers, smoked cigars, and whose works astonished *les bourgeois*. George Sand within the next three or four years would capture a greater immortal than the exquisite Vicomte de Musset: none other than the consumptive musical genius who had not yet left his native Poland to take Paris and half Europe by storm. Then there was Delacroix, a rising star in the Bohemian firmament, who swept his canvasses with a brush like a broom; and the daring and gifted Berlioz with his musical fantasies, and the very young Liszt with his Raphael-like beauty and his delirious extravaganzas. These were of the precious circle, untrammelled by tradition, that spread the budding tentacles of their 'shocking' new morality dedicated to *la vie Bohème*, from the Quartier Latin or Montmartre to the

salons of those who tenaciously clung to the remains of the
*Ancien Régime.*

This then was the Paris of contrasts, of a younger genera-
tion, striving to eject the formalities of an earlier, more
static age, and forcibly to demonstrate with clarion voice
their New Movement, their New Culture, when the Blessingtons came to town.

As the Circus rattled through the cobbled streets on their
way to the Rue de Rivoli where apartments had been
engaged for the Blessingtons and their suite, people stared
at the magnificent entourage with the Blessingtons'
appendage, the beautiful Comte d'Orsay and the shrinking
child-bride . . . '*sa fille?*' went the wide-eyed query . . . *Ou sa
femme?*' . . . *Non! Impossible! Pas cette fillette . . .*' '*et
aussi une autre timide Anglaise, la soeur de Madame la
Comtesse. . . .*' All on the right and left bank of the Seine
knew of the coming of the Comte et les Comtesses
d'Angleterre.

If the careless, spendthrift, erratic Lord Blessington saw
in these young enthusiasts from the Quartier Latin a milieu
after his own secret Bohemian heart, not so his Lady. She
would be out of her element among these progressive
youngsters bent on self-expression, who scorned *noblesse
oblige*, she who had been scorned and disobliged by the
*noblesse* that should have been hers by right of marriage to
her 'noble' Lord.

Yet here in Paris she who had been shunned, defamed
by the women of her husband's world, found herself
the centre of attention, not with the followers of Saint-
Simon, Chateaubriand and their disciples, de Musset, Liszt,
George Sand and all the rest of them, many of whom it is
doubtful she had ever heard of; not these seekers after
Truth, Regeneration, no, not they who had no entry, nor
the desire to enter the closed doors of *les aristos*, who
would despise them as the ladies of London had despised
Margaret Blessington. No doors in Paris were closed to her
who had been surrounded in St James's by the lions of

literature, art, and the great Englishmen of letters and politics; no matter that their womenfolk despised and envied her with venom in their tongues to spit. But not here in Paris. No! Here she was welcomed with open arms and open doors to receive her and her husband, and their very own Comte d'Orsay. His lovely sister Ida, Duchesse de Guiche, and his grandmother, Madame Craufurd, the leaders of *le beau monde*, were delighted that their beloved Alfred had made so excellent and profitable a match to relieve them of the anxiety of satisfying his extravagant demands. All was now satisfactorily provided by his *fillette* of a wife.

Lady Blessington's Paris journal rhapsodically extols the beauty and grace of Ida de Guiche, and, in slightly less exaggerated gush, her handsome husband, monsieur le Duc. She goes shopping with Ida as her Ciceronian guide who introduces her to M. Herboult, 'High Priest of the Temple of Fashion', as her diary records it, 'who cast an astonished eye on my bonnet'. But her confidence is restored by Ida's tactful explanation that madame la Comtesse had only just arrived from travelling in Italy where it was not possible to buy *chapeaux* adequate for Paris. Whereupon Herboult, bowing nose to knees before Madame la Comtesse, orders to be brought forth a display of *chapeaux* for Madame's approval, and to burn a large hole in the once bottomless purse of her husband.

'Three hundred and twenty francs for a crêpe hat with feathers, two hundred for a *chapeau des fleurs*, one hundred for a *chapeau negligé de matin*' are purchased to be sent to her hotel in the Rue de Rivoli. And she warns 'uxorious husbands, beware how you bring your brides to the dangerous atmosphere of Paris ere you curve your brows into a frown and your visage lengthens at the sight of a long bill ...'

Between buying *chapeaux* and *modes* and *robes*, she is again house-hunting. Their hotel, despite its elegance, is too noisy; but her search for a mansion to house herself and her

'Parisian appendage' does not interfere with her visits to the opera, the playhouse; to a military review where she is expensively seated close to King Charles, the Dauphin, the Dauphine, and their sumptuous Court, to some of whom she has already been presented. She goes to the ballet to see Taglioni make her début, and finds her 'graceful beyond all comparison. She seems to float as she bounds like a sylph across the stage.' But at the play she notes that 'the cheaper seats applaud only those scenes that refer to revolutionary implications'.

Does her 'premonition' warn her of what is to come and what she is to witness and be drawn into? Or is this an afterthought inserted when she edits her journals for publication? She is certainly writing them to be read as they will be and are to this day. Yet one cannot help but wonder that they claim so large and discerning a public, for literary style in these graphic accounts of her travels, and in her books when she turns authoress, is far from commendable.

In all these jaunts and jollities her husband has no place, or if he accompanies her he goes unnoticed as does his daughter, while his wife visits Madame Craufurd and raves about her youthful appearance at eighty, a second Ninon de l'Enclos who, when a grandmother, she recalls, fell in love with her grandson, whose amorous advances were not repulsed.

She visits and receives in her hotel apartment all the élite of Paris; the pages of her journal read like a premature Gallic Debrett. From Monsieur le Prince de . . . to Monsieur le Duc de . . . to several Vicomtes and Comtesses. Their ladies are all, or seem to be, as delighted with her as are the men. At last she finds a house that suits her overlooking the Seine and the Tuileries. It stands in large gardens surrounded by high walls and has an imposing avenue of fine trees. It was once the home of Napoleon's Marshal Ney and is named after him l'Hôtel Ney. Her journal covers pages of ecstatic descriptions of the rooms. She has taken a year's unfurnished lease for which her lord willingly dives into his fast decreasing capital to satisfy her decorative excesses that range from Corinthian columns, marble fireplaces, and a 'magician of an upholsterer' who devises a wonderful surprise for her bedroom and dressing-room fitted up 'with exquisite taste and, as usual with my most gallant of all husbands, no expense is spared'.

Almost the length of the lease had expired before the elaborate furnishings and decorations of the Hôtel Ney were completed. But no sooner is all arranged to her satisfaction and the vast reception rooms open to receive her guests than she is house-hunting again.

The mansion finally favoured is taken furnished, newly built and beautifully decorated. 'But Lord B,' her journal tells us, 'does not think it good enough . . .' An additional room was required to house d'Orsay; his wife was given a room far from his. His apartments had again to be redecorated and furnished; more 'magicians of upholsterers' were engaged at the expense of her 'most gallant of husbands'.

He missed a great deal of this removal as he was called to London to record his vote for the final passing of the Catholic Emancipation Act promoted by the Duke of Wellington.

*Carte blanche* had been left to her to secure gardeners for the neglected grounds of this mansion in the Avenue de Matignon. We are told that: 'Deep beds of earth line the sides of the terrace with an abundance of orange trees, shrubs, flowering plants . . .' There are also two aviaries, one close to her library where she can feed her favourite birds. . . .

The time for this second removal after a year of endless rounds of entertaining and being entertained, was now imminent, and Lord Blessington returned from London having recorded his vote in the Upper House.

The last finishing touches to drapery and rearrangement of furniture, the cost of which may have induced in his wife some qualms that she had taken too much for granted her 'most gallant of husband's' unlimited largesse.

While Mary Ann does most of the rearranging to satisfy her sister's exigent demands for a picture here and another there, and 'not that one here, but this one there', and furniture moved from one room to another, little Harriet d'Orsay is very much in everybody's way and told sharply by her stepmother: 'For goodness' sake go in the garden or into your own room. Don't hover about like a restless moth . . .'

And rather like a restless moth she looked, reflected in a long vista of wall mirrors in the drawing-room, where she seemed to be lost in its vastness among the quantity of knick-knacks, books piled on the Aubusson carpets and Persian rugs on the polished floors. Gowned in Quakerish grey – no *chapeaux des fleurs* nor *négligé de matin* were hers, no new clothes had been bought for her in Paris. She wore always the simple schoolgirlish dresses she had brought with her from Dublin, her Aunt Gardiner's choice. And although all her skirts had hems to let down should she grow, they were still well above her ankles with the same little frilled drawers below them as when she had been twelve, and now near to her sixteenth birthday . . .

A few days after Lord Blessington's arrival from England he expressed himself satisfied with all that had been done to the house in his absence; but it was noticed by his wife that he looked pale and exhausted . . . 'Was it very warm in London?' she asked him.

'Yes, much warmer than here.'

After luncheon served on the terrace on the afternoon of 23 May, he said he had indigestion. 'You have given me too much of your excellent chef's bouillon,' and he asked for an iced drink of orange juice.

The drink brought, he drank, felt better and ordered his horse. He would go for a ride in the Bois.

Followed by his groom he rode in the Champs-Elysées on his way to the Bois in the full heat of the afternoon sun.

146

Within an hour he was brought home on a stretcher. He had been taken with a seizure, so the servant who had ridden with him reported. All that day and the next, doctors fought to save him. He lay speechless, his face, that once rosy, genial, goodnatured face, distorted, his breath coming from lips snarled back from his teeth in a grotesque apoplectic grin. While his distracted wife watched by his bedside, d'Orsay crept in and out of the room where sunlight filtered through the slats of the closed shutters casting bars of gold across that stricken face.

His terrified young daughter knelt outside the door, her ear fastened to it, listening to the awful sounds of that dying breath within, and the tick-ticking of a long-case clock on the wall above her small bowed head; and then from that darkened room a silence, broken at last by the grave, quiet voice of the doctor:

'*C'est fini.*'

*    *    *

The first and last Earl of Blessington was taken to Dublin to lie in the tomb of his fathers. There is no record in the journal of his wife that she or his daughter went with him to his last resting place. Those who remained in the splendid house on the Avenue de Matignon waited uneasily in the freshly painted salons, their sombre garments like the wings of black hovering birds as they roamed from room to room supervising the removal of beautiful pieces of furniture, the costly decorations, pictures, objets d'art his widow had so lavishly delighted in buying; and he who had brought her from the darkness of obscurity into the light of luxury undreamed in these radiant ten years was gone! So . . . What now? The lease of this new house just entered upon, the expense of it all to be faced alone. Another epoch in her life had passed, and one still dawning on the horizon of revolutionary France. Already in the slums and alleyways around Montmartre an ominous stir was in the air, the tramp of marching feet, the waving of tri-coloured flags from windows and voices chanting *'Marchons! Marchons! . . .'* the Marseillaise first heard in those streets of blood during the Terror of five and thirty years before.

Watching from the window of her salon she saw 'some fifty or sixty persons near to the hotel of the Minister of Finance, chiefly youths crying: *"Vive le Charte! A bas les Ministres!"* '

She glanced down at the journal that lay on her knee and at a page opened with her latest entry, dated September 1829.

'A chasm of many months has passed when last I closed it. Little could I have foreseen the terrible blow that awaited me. How is my destiny changed since last I opened this book!'

Unknown to her, Destiny had already marked her for a change that would affect the whole of her future life; but the venomous breath of scandal emanating from Dublin to London had not yet drifted to her ears in Paris.

The legal negotiations dealing with her husband's Will went apace to leave d'Orsay at least forty thousand pounds in trust for the benefit of him and, in lesser degree, of his wife, besides the whole of Blessington's Dublin estates and the income of ten thousand a year from his tenants and other of his properties around Mountjoy. Yet his widow had nothing of his wealth more than the two thousand a year which he had subsequently altered from the original three thousand, and the lease of the house in St James's Square, her jewels, furniture, and her personal assets. All this would have sufficed any widow who had been unused to the fabulous luxury to which she had been accustomed, but not now when she still must pay for the upkeep of the new house in the Avenue de Matignon until its year's lease ran out.

Had current events in the City of Paris not involved her, described in her journal as 'a troubled dream', she might have disputed what seemed to be an unnatural Will. But . . . 'Would that it *were* a dream!' she cries, 'and those whom

I so much love were not exposed to pay dearly for their loyalty and fidelity to a sovereign whose misfortunes if they cannot ameliorate they can at least share....'

No dream was this; a nightmare, rather, to her alone in that great mansion, its decorations and new furnishings not yet all paid for . . . Alone except for Mary Ann, the haunted little Harriet, and the few servants who had not suddenly deserted Madame la Comtesse to join the rebels.

D'Orsay, his sister and brother-in-law de Guiche, were at St Cloud, where de Guiche had gone for the signing of the ordinances by the Council. The unpopularity of the present Ministry headed by Prince Polignac, who had been one of the prominent *invités* at the Hôtel de Ney, surprised her as she records, 'When I remember how estimable is his private character and those, too, who are responsible to the will of the Sovereign . . .'

She was torn between her own 'troubled dreams' of financial difficulties and fear of the threatening crowds that thronged the streets from the Champs-Elysées to the heights of Montmartre.

Revolution!

Within twenty-four hours a city of peace, gaiety, and opulence, 'where the butterflies of fashion expand their gay wings to the sunshine,' as she tells us, watching from her window the hideous transformation that brought confused alarm to hordes of citizens flying in terror from their homes, from their peaceable occupations: artisans, men opening their shops for their morning's trades; the butcher, the baker, the candlestick maker, men on their way to their offices; women with their baskets on their arms in the midst of their early shopping, were set upon by wild mobs of demonstrators who raided the shops of gunsmiths to seize their arms while the sound of firing boomed far and near from all quarters of the city.

D'Orsay, returned from St Cloud, brought word of huge crowds assembled in la Place de la Bourse armed with every kind of weapon they had stolen or seized by force. But her fear for d'Orsay and the de Guiches was somewhat allayed by Alfred's boast that:

'They will not attack me. My father, General d'Orsay, was a Bonapartist, et moi non plus pour la République ni pour le roi. Enfin!' He shrugged his delicate shoulders, 'they cry for me as I passed on my horse, "*Vive le Comte d'Orsay! A bas les Ministres!*" Cela je m'en fiche, alors! Mais mon beau frère, le duc, he is royalist. He will never desert the King.'

'And you?' she asked breathlessly. 'What of you? Would you desert your King?'

'Me?' Again that shrug. 'I stay with those who will be best for France, nor King, nor president . . . Ah! Ecoute!'

The shouts of the mob, the thunder of guns approaching nearer to the houses in the Avenue de Matignon, brought Harriet and Mary Ann running to the salon with white, scared faces.

D'Orsay told them:

'Do not fear. You will be safe here, isn't it? Madame la Comtesse elle est Anglaise, et aussi Marianne et Harriette.'

'I,' said Harriet in a dwindling voice, 'am Irish.'

'I must go to your grandmother.' Margaret was making for the door. 'She may be nervous alone there.'

'Alone with an army of servants? Do not you go out in this mêlée,' d'Orsay told her. 'Pour moi, I am fatigued and I have a thirst comme milles diables. Riding from St Cloud in this heat, ce n'est pas drôle, ça.'

'My poor dear!' She went to him. 'Go to your room. I will have iced drink sent to you. And you,' to the girls, 'stay away from the windows. Close all the shutters in your rooms.'

'You are never going out in all this?' exclaimed Mary Ann.

But out in all that she went, less for fear of the safety of Madame Craufurd than to satisfy her curiosity and to make notes for her journal with a view to publication. Thanks to her we have a vivid account of what she saw.

Attended by a *valet de pied* she chose to walk the short distance to the house of Madame Craufurd. But having to go along the Rue St Honoré, she found herself confronted by barricades impeding further progress. Her footman begged Madame la Comtesse not to attempt to promenade herself in this so dangerous locality for it would be impossible for Madame to mount the barricades. Would Madame not herself return?

She told him, no! She would not return. The shouts of the approaching mob along the Rue St Honoré decided her to go on and 'mount the barricades'. This with the utmost difficulty she did, clambering over the loose stones, aided by the footman whose white silk stockings and yellow plush breeches were covered in dirt and mud, as also were the lady's petticoats and shoes; but she had taken the precaution 'to attire herself,' as she recounted, 'as simply as possible.' The footman's livery, however, attracted some jeers and mud-slinging. Impatiently she urged him on and managed to climb over what she called 'a pyramid' and down on to the other side where the street, save for a few stragglers, was comparatively quiet.

At last after no further difficulty she arrived at the Craufurd mansion in the Rue d'Anjou. 'My servant,' she reports, 'knocked very loudly several times before the Swiss concierge would open the door and could hardly credit his eyes when he saw me . . .'

She was greeted by Madame Craufurd with arms outstretched to embrace her and exclaiming in voluble French:

'Marguerite! How I am rejoiced to see you! But you should not have come through the streets. My servants report already there are many killed – innocent persons. These *canaille*, they stop at nothing but they kill and kill! And they cry, these devils, they cry "*A bas le Roi!*" I suffer, *mon dieu!* How I suffer in fear for you and my dear ones. Thank God they are at St Cloud with the King. They will be safe there, one hopes. For myself, me, I fear nothing.' But the old lady's parchment white face and trembling hands as she led her visitor to a fauteuil and sank on to a sofa, gave the lie to that. Raising her eyes to the painted ceiling that depicted gods and goddesses at play surrounded by cherubs and a wine-wreathed Bacchus that might have been a portrait flamboyantly presenting the Sun King, Louis Quatorze, in a blaze of glory. 'You will comprehend,' continued Madame, 'how that I dread they will attract vengeance for their devotion to the King. They will brave death, may the good God forbid it, sooner than forsake their Sovereign, le Roi Charles Dix.'

'Have courage, Madame,' she was assured in Marguerite's execrable French. 'Ida and Monsieur le duc will be safe while they remain at St Cloud.'

'But they will not remain there for long,' sobbed Madame. 'Alfred, my grandson and his sister they will come back to Paris with de Guiche, who follows the King. And Alfred, he too will follow the King – with his life.'

The lady did not tell her that her grandson was now resting in his suite at the Hôtel Ney; nor did she give any hint regarding his safety as an avowed Bonapartist-cum-Royalist.

'You do not know, God be thanked,' Madame Craufurd removed her eyes from the ceiling to search the face of Madame la Comtesse de Blessington, 'what I know, me! of all that has arrived here in Paris during the Revolution of thirty-five years ago and now arrives here again today.' She shuddered. 'What horrors have I witnessed! Bodies hanging from the lanterns, carts taking the aristos to the guillotine where the herring women sat knitting and uttering their cries of joy as the heads fell into the basket! I am here in Paris when they took the King Louis Seize and his Queen to be murdered – Heaven help me and all of us!' She covered her face. 'And now all that I have seen will be again repeated. But you, my dear, you should not expose yourself to this danger, for the streets will be flowing with blood and ...'

At this moment: 'Monsieur le Comte Marsault,' was announced to bring Madame Craufurd once more to her feet with arms outstretched for the newcomer to kiss her little withered bejewelled hand.

'Madame! I am happy to find you here and —' he glanced aside at Lady Blessington – 'not alone.'

'Ah, yes! This dear friend – allow me to present Madame la Comtesse de Blaisenton – the Comte Marsault.'

The Comte bowed low, mumbling:

'*Enchanté, Madame la Comtesse.*'

'This dear friend,' pursued Madame Craufurd, 'has come all this way from the Hôtel New to visit me malgré the guns and those monsters out there who would kill her!'

'I am stupefied at such courage incredible!' vouchsafed the Count. 'Me, I have hastened to Madame Craufurd to be assured that she and her house are safe from these villains.'

'But yes, Monsieur le Comte, my servants are loyal. What of you and your house, my friend?'

'I too am safe so far, but there is not much left to me of my possessions of which so many were seized during the Revolution.'

'Ah yes! The Revolution which you escaped.'

'Thanks be to the Lord Jesus and la Sainte Vierge.' He crossed himself. 'Angleterre received me, an émigré, and I return to France these ten years since. But, madame, you should not remain here. Why do you not retire to Fontainebleau beyond the range of the guns?'

A distant booming was heard and Madame la Comtesse de 'Blaisenton', rising from her chair, said:

'Now that Monsieur le Comte arrives, Madame, I must go to my home.'

'No!' agitatedly cried Madame Craufurd. 'You shall not go. You must not promenade yourself through those streets alone.'

'I will escort Madame la Comtesse,' mumbled monsieur le Comte Marsault. He was a small elderly gentleman, with rouge in his wrinkles, suspiciously blond hair, and wearing clothes *à la mode* twenty years before; a corbeau coloured coat, light green kerseymeres, paste buckled shoes and an ingratiating smile, somewhat hampered by the behaviour of his teeth that had a tendency to jump from his gums as he spoke and had to be hastily readjusted.

'Veritably you will not escort her,' protested Madame, 'for she will not leave this house, nor will you, my friend. My house and my servants are at your disposal and also for Madame la Comtesse.'

In spite of her entreaties, however, and the repeated assurance of Monsieur le Comte that he would escort Madame la Comtesse to her house, that did not entirely convince he was ready to do so, for the sound of gunfire drew ominously nearer every minute, and his face under the rouge had turned quite pale – but the lady insisted she must return.

'I will send half a dozen of my men armed with pistolets to accompany you,' pleaded Madame Craufurd, 'if you insist on this so dangerous a sortie.'

'I thank you, Madame, yet so many attendants would attract attention. One servant will not. As you see I am dressed of a simplicity natural, borrowed from my maid, and if you could provide my footman with a surtout to cover his livery we will pass unobserved in a crowd.'

Thus it came about that the intrepid Countess returned through the streets not yet flowing with blood as dismally prophesied by Madame Craufurd; the crowds appeared to have slightly diminished since she had made her way through them an hour earlier.

No sooner had the door closed behind the lady than Monsieur le Comte, who had so gallantly offered to escort her, remarked:

'I have heard speak of Madame la Comtesse de Blaisenton. One says she is recently a widow, isn't it?'

'Alas, yes, but she has a sister who lives with her, and also her husband's daughter who is married with my grandson, le Comte d'Orsay.'

'So? And Madame la Comtesse de Blaisenton is very rich?'

'Not so rich as might have been, because,' confidentially Madame lowered her voice, 'because milord Blaisenton whose only son died – his heir you comprehend – left my grandson, whom he adored like his own son, almost all his money and his estates in Ireland.'

'The lady's sister, she also is married with an English nobleman?'

'No, she is not married. She is much younger than her sister, la Comtesse . . . May I offer you a glass of wine?'

While Lady Blessington was being discussed in the salon of Madame Craufurd, she had neared her house in the Avenue de Matignon without any interruption, for her clothes of a 'simplicity natural', and the livery of her footman now partially covered by a cloak did not draw attention, but when they came to the barracks in the Rue Verte, a thick rope had been drawn across the entrance to the courtyard, making it impossible for anyone to pass either forward or in or out. Some forty or fifty ruffians were there, some of whom were holding the rope at both ends, obviously to prevent the soldiers in the garrison from attempting to reach the crowds without the use of firearms, which their officers had forbidden unless in retaliation.

'The soldiers, they will shoot them and us!' cried the footman, who in his evident fright had loosened his hold of the cloak which in any case was too short for him. His hood had slipped from his head and, as he made to readjust it, the cloak slid away revealing his canary coloured livery, knee breeches and white silk stockings.

At once the rioteers spotting him in his uniform as a servant of *les aristos*, yelled a torrent of abuse demanding if he were not ashamed to wear the livery of servitude, when they and all his countrymen were fighting for Liberté, Egalité, Fraternité . . . 'Do not speak,' whispered his lady, 'I will deal with them.' And turning on those nearest her, who were thrusting their begrimed menacing faces within inches of her own, she shouted:

'You! Yes, you!' pointing a finger at the hustling crowd, 'and all of you who would prevent me and my servant from passing on my way. You abuse the laws of hospitality which France offers to England. I am an English subject —' Hoots and jeers greeted this announcement. Undaunted she went on in her lamentable broken French – 'Yes, I am an English subject and my servant, he is English. Are you not ashamed so to behave to the subjects of His Majesty, King William the Fourth, King of Great Britain and Ireland?' (I forget, she mentally reminded herself, I am not English, I am Irish but 'tis all one to them.) 'I say,' she shouted above the roars of derision and catcalls that greeted this announcement, 'that if you do not at once lower the rope to permit that I and my servant shall pass now, this instant – and do not forget' – she wheeled round savagely upon those who were attempting to press closer – 'Do not forget that it was the English who defeated your Emperor Napoleon and it is the English here in Paris who will defeat *you* if you molest *me*! I will at once inform the English Ambassador here in Paris if you attempt to molest an English woman. Lower the rope I said,' and she said it in capitals, 'LOWER THE ROPE!'

But although they had heard as much as they could understand of her French, they refused to lower the rope; and one of them, evidently their leader, a malodorous brute stinking to high heaven of garlic and drink, yelled:

'Pass then, if you can!' And raising the rope still higher, 'or leap over it!'

Whereupon she records: 'I answered, although I trembled at being exposed to their rude mirth and still more rude gaze, that I said I felt sure Frenchmen would not compel me to such an unfeminine exertion or give me cause to tell my compatriots when I return to England that deference to women no longer exists in France.'

At which tactful flattery the crowd cried: 'Let her pass!'

And others gabbling and yelling while one voice rose high above the others: *'Vive l'Anglaise! Vivent les Anglaises!'*

This was the signal for those who held the rope to lower it to the ground. She stepped across it assisted by her man, who had received a handful of mud slung at his smart yellow plush coat, and managed to gain the Rue St Honoré without further unpleasant encounter. But as she crossed the street a horde of men brandishing clubs, firearms, all kinds of weapons from kitchen utensils to pitchforks, rushed after her uttering curses and threats at her footman who was too scared to answer back at them . . . And so: 'I determined,' she says, 'never again to go out attended by this symbol of aristocracy!'

During the whole of that week conditions went from bad to worse. She spent hours of each day writing impressions in her diary of incidents brought to her from eye witnesses or that she herself had seen. She notes a striking change in the manner of her servants. 'They are more familiar, evincing veiled insolence . . . Every rumour of success for the insurgents is reported by them with ill-suppressed animation . . . Misguided men! Can they hope that servitude will be lightened as the employed of some *parvenu* elevated from the dregs of the people by revolution which sets floating to the top the ingredients of the reeking cauldron from which it is formed, instead of the more gentle and less degrading sway of those born to and accustomed to rule . . .'

These high-flown sentiments recur throughout her account of the upheaval which had its echo from England at a time when the death of George the Fourth, in the preceding January, had brought his brother William to the throne.

While Terror, a modified Terror compared with that which at the end of the preceding century murdered their king, and it looked as if another king would follow the fate of Louis Seize.

News had just been brought to her that the Tuileries and the Louvre had been taken by the people. She hears hideous reports of how they had trampled on statues, broken the busts of King Charles, and set up a dead body on his throne; one of the corpses was found lying in the streets that now did horrifically flow with blood, as Madame Craufurd had dreaded. The soldiers could not or would not repel the rioters who had seized their barracks in the Rue Verte, and rumour gave it that fifty thousand men of the army were marching on Paris to support the people.

'The People,' she tells us, 'I hear nothing but the People!'

The revolutionaries had run amok, but while there was indiscriminate shooting that killed some of their own men, the number of the dead was comparatively few.

D'Orsay heard how the insurgents had forced an entrance to the courtyard of the house where the royal pages were lodged. One of these, a protégé of the duc de Guiche and a favourite of d'Orsay, had been shot and killed.

D'Orsay did at last rouse himself from his snug retreat in his apartment at the Hôtel Ney, to make arrangements for the boy's funeral, having ascertained that the hostel of the pages was no longer surrounded. The page's parents were still with the Court at St Cloud. . . . Lady Blessington, relating the death of this boy, scarcely more than a child and with whose mother she was well acquainted, says:

'I cannot picture in my mind's eye any distinct image among the slain other than that of this poor youth. They present only a ghastly mass of gaping wounds and blood-stained garments . . .'

And then:

'D'Orsay has returned from the last duties paid to the poor young page. He brings news that the Royal Family have left St Cloud and are now at Versailles.'

The July Revolution was nearing its victorious end. The City was at the mercy of 'The People'. And while the old shattered king sat shivering at Versailles, his subjects, men, students, artisans, tradesmen, all anti-royalists, marched *en masse* in demonstrations, waving tri-coloured flags. The fleur de lys had been torn from the Tuileries and the Louvre, and on the towers of Notre Dame the tri-colours fluttered in the breeze.

'It is over,' Lady Blessington told the pale d'Orsay. 'The king will never come back to Paris.'

'Nor will I.' D'Orsay's teeth were chattering as if with cold, although the hot July sun poured through the un-shuttered windows. 'And nor will you.' He rose from his seat to close the shutters. Distant shouts and the tramping of feet could still be heard. 'Nor will you stay here.' He turned to tell her, 'We must go to London now where we belong . . .'

'Where you do *not* belong,' she retorted. 'Would you leave your sister and brother-in-law to their fate?'

'Their fate is the King's fate. They have always been royalists. Me, I am as was my father, a Bonapartist. He was general of the Emperor's army. And you yourself profess admiration for Napoleon. How often I hear you say he was the greatest military genius of all time?'

'Until the Duke of Wellington's time – greater than ever he could be and who defeated him with a handful of British against Bonaparte's thousands . . . Wellington knew it too. Didn't he tell Creevey – as I have heard it said – that when he was walking with Creevey in Brussels only a day before the battle he saw a British soldier leaning against a wall. "If I had enough of that article," he said, "I could beat him yet." And although he had not half enough of "that article" he *did* beat him.'

'Enfin, what has happened here,' said d'Orsay, 'can happen in England now. They only wait for the Coronation of the King, old William Quatre, before the people of London will break loose.'

'So you have heard that, have you?' She took a letter from her reticule. 'Or did you read this that I have received from Landor? He goes back and forth from Florence to London these days. There is much unrest there as here and perhaps London will have to go through something like we have now in Paris.'

'I know that Landor has written to you and what he thinks may happen.'

'You know, do you? So you have read this letter.'

He glanced away.

'I did look at it. Why should I not when you read mine – as you read me?' He bent over her. 'You do read me, don't you – like a book.'

'When the print,' she smiled up at him, 'is large enough, but sometimes it is too small to be read without a magnifying glass.'

'Alors! Perhaps you will not require a magnifying glass to read this.'

He dived into a pocket and produced a folded letter. 'I have received this some weeks ago but you were so bouleversée with this sacré dam' revolution that I would not worry you with these mediscence – these slander.'

She took the letter. It was an obviously disguised hand, written in large capitals. It enclosed a newspaper cutting purporting to be a letter to the editor of a scurrilous rag known as *The Age,* and headed: BLESSINGTON.

Alfred d'Orsay with his pretty pink and white face drives about in a cocked hat and on a long tailed cream coloured horse. He says he will have seventeen thousand a year to spend; others say seventeen hundred – He and my Lady go on as usual ...

She dropped the cutting as if it had stung her.

'Who wrote this abominable thing? My God! Am I always to be pilloried? My name and yours coupled to-gether! And my husband gone from me and I with no defence?'

'I am your defence, mon ange. But I do not know who send this thing to me unless it is one who has envie that I am here in Paris with you and always with you as I was with my adored friend, your husband. But he has it wrong, this canaille. I have more than seventeen thousand, isn't it?

I think whoever send it is to tell me it is the editor of this newspaper who wishes for money so not to print more scandale. What is called blacking la poste, not?'

She could not restrain a splutter of laughter in spite of her indignation at the implication of her relationship with d'Orsay.

'Blackmail? Perhaps you are right.'

'Assuredly I am right. There is more – much more of it.'

'I do not wish to see more. Burn it.'

'Non, I will not. I think you should know what mal intentions is made against you in this paper that you – that we, for I go with you as I am also diffamé – we go to London and bring against this so disgusting paper – this villainous blackposte or as we say in French this *maître chanteur* – a case for the court. We take advice of an *avocat*. Yes?'

'What,' she asked impatiently, 'are you trying to tell me?'

He moved over to a fauteuil beside her and sat with a care for his velvet coat tails.

'I try to tell you that you have ennemie in this London paper of someone who would have money from you and me. See you this.'

Another cutting was taken from his pocket.

'I am so out of myself I know not where I am. Voilà! Dieu! How I would kill this beast of hell if I could meet with him.'

She snatched the strip of paper, her eyes following the printed words as she read and re-read the slanderous Grub Street paragraph.


What a ménage is that of Lady Blessington! It would create sensations, were it not for one fair flower that still blooms under the shade of the Upas tree. Can it be conceived in England that M. Alfred d'Orsay has publicly detailed to what degree he has carried his apathy for his

pretty interesting wife, and has boasted of his contin-
ence? This young gentleman, Lady Blessington, and the
virgin-wife of sixteen all live together. You must surely
remember a lady who, some fifteen years ago, was
*acting wife* to a Captain J. of some dragoon regiment.
As he had nothing but his spurs and his whiskers, 'Mrs. J.'
used to levy taxes on her friends . . . and was introduced
to a Lord who, like a fool, married her . . .

She was white to the lips.
'This is infamous!' She crumpled the paper in her hand
preparatory to throwing it in the fireless grate.
'No, do not do that. You must keep it. Ask the advice of
the British Ambassador here in Paris. Ma grand'mère tell
me you should consult with him.'
'You have shown this to your grandmother?'
'I have. Yes. I ask her what I should do for me – for you –
and she say take it to your Ambassador.'
The advice given by his Excellency was that she should
write to her solicitor in London enclosing a copy of the
cutting.
She did so and received his answer which assured her
that there was no *prima facie* case for action against the
newspaper, but it was certainly ill-advised. She therefore
agreed to await further slanderous publications. She
realized that damage enough had already been done to her
name in the London gutter press and that a counterattack,
unless it were unavoidable, might only cause more mud-
slinging. She had ascertained that the editor of *The Age*,
one Westmacott (verified by d'Orsay who had it from one
of his previous London acquaintances) would stop at nothing. He was known to resort to this kind of poisonous
attack in his paper against any well-known name that
might be a surefire target, and be paid to keep his silence or
to publish an apology refuting the alleged libel. He would
demand a high price for it, d'Orsay had been told.
But he, having first communicated this Grub Street

malice to his Lady in the determination to return with her to London to fight Westmacott, now vacillated. Should he or should he not remain in Paris?

The convulsion that had racked the city rending it apart, with the larger faction for the People, and the lesser for the King, was now nearing its finale. Charles the Tenth had fled with his Court and the loyal de Guiches. D'Orsay, known to be the son of General d'Orsay, an avowed Bonapartist who had fought with and for Napoleon, was greeted with shouts of '*D'Orsay! Vive le Comte d'Orsay*' whenever he rode out on his cream-coloured horse; but having finally decided to accompany his Lady to London, they made the necessary arrangements for departure.

It was a very different and unfamiliar Paris from that which she had enjoyed in these last few years. The trees on the boulevards and in the Champs-Elysées showed grim signs of the devastation that brought about so drastic a change to the once joyous face of France. No longer was it the France she had known and loved but a France, trembling on the edge of a volcanic eruption, still emitted smoke from its recent activities that had won for the republicans and Bonapartists a monarch who was no longer the King of France but a King of the French, a citizen king, the Duc d'Orléans, shabby remnant of the Bourbons who had known exile and poverty. He strode about the streets with an umbrella under his arm and a genial grin on his whiskered face with a '*Bonjour, mon ami*', for all and sundry; the people were his comrades. He would appear on the balcony of the Tuileries waving a tri-coloured flag and singing, woefully out of tune, the Marseillaise accompanied by a chorus from the cheering crowds below.

Margaret Blessington, witnessing all this camaraderie, wondered what repercussions it might have upon the new King William of Great Britain and Ireland, 'the Sailor King', not yet crowned and who had had no inkling that the Throne would ever be his until the death of his brother, the Duke of York, made him heir to his elder brother, George the Fourth.

All the world knew how the Duke of Clarence lived a secluded life with his plain little Duchess, a German Princess at least thirty years his junior, whom he had married when York died childless leaving William in his later fifties to inherit the Kingdom.

He must perforce relinquish his mistress, the well-known actress Dora Jordan, who had borne him eleven illegitimate children; and at Bushey Park he had lived with the German girl he married and with whom he, surprisingly, had fallen violently in love. She, when his wife, allowed all his eleven children to live with her at Bushey.

Would London, wondered Margaret Blessington, welcome him? Or would those who for years had been fighting for Reform, not only among the down-trodden underdogs of Britain but the young pioneers who fought their campaign to right the wrongs of their brothers in harsh poverty; they of the aristocracy, the many 'Haves' who mingled with the 'Have nots', they who went in disguise to be as one of them and listen to their discontents and strive to lighten their burdens?

Would this revolution in France, she asked herself, cause a similar effect on Britain? Already she had heard of internal rumblings that might presage an upheaval. Times were changing. The old order of things had passed; what would the new order bring?

She was soon to know.

## SEVEN

She arrived in London in November 1830 with d'Orsay, her sister Mary Ann and d'Orsay's virginal wife, nondescript as ever and of less account to her husband than his unpaid tailor's bills.

Lady Blessington found London as different as the Paris she had left. The new King, not yet crowned, astonished his Ministers no less than his subjects in his capital by his unconventional and distinctly democratic, if not republican, behaviour. Accustomed as his Court and his ministers were to the dignity of the Courts of Georges Third and Fourth, that is save only when he who had been Regent was in residence at one or other of his London palaces and not disporting himself at Brighton; but during the last years of his reign as King he seldom allowed himself to be seen when he drove in his carriage. He had grown grossly fat and would insist the curtains of his coach or *caleche* be drawn that none might see how he had become a bloated grotesque. So few of his subjects had in the last ten years seen their late King.

Still less had they seen the new king, his brother, whose youth had been spent at sea, fighting in his father's warships against the French and Spanish under the command of Lord Nelson; and in later years he had lived his life of retirement, as Squire of Bushey Park.

And now – how Creevey and Greville, court gossips, giggled as they wrote in their diaries their accounts of the King's eccentricities. How he would walk the streets of London in his old country clothes, unattended; how while strolling down St James's Street in sight of Clubland, he saw an old shipmate, darted across the road to embrace him and walked arm in arm away with him roaring with laughter at their joint reminiscences of their midshipmen days. How a prostitute recognizing him had rushed up to fling her arms round his neck and kissed him, crying for all to hear: 'God bless you, Billy, my King!' to the delight of the men in the street and the hoi polloi who called him 'Our Billy' from that day.*

Great changes indeed, and for the better, one might hope, and as Margaret Blessington amusedly hoped. When Mr Greville, on his one visit to her house, told her of His Majesty's antics and wrote in his diary:

'The King is a mountebank and bids fair to be a maniac.'

'Not at all!' was her indignant reply. 'He bids fair to show some method in his madness if you think it likely he may run that way, because he chooses to live the life of a man and not a licentious overblown figurehead, who had half a dozen mistresses all old enough to be his mother and spent half the nation's money on his women and that Chinese monstrosity at Brighton. It is you and your like who make mock of King William who are maniacs, not he! . . .'

This was also the opinion of many of the lower classes who wholeheartedly welcomed the 'Sailor King' as upholder of their Rights and who saw in him their champion, with his rollicking walk that savoured of the decks in the battleships where his youth had been spent and from where he had fought with Admiral Lord Nelson; their jolly old King with his pine-apple head, his hail-fellow-well-met approach to all, from princes to beggarmen, from old shipmates to Earl Grey, who looked to be Prime Minister if the Tories should fall before or after the Coronation.

Not that this Fourth William was in favour of Parliamentary Reform, which his little Queen Adelaide nervously believed would lead to revolution like the French. 'But,' she was heard to say, 'although I could never be attractive like Marie Antoinette, I hope I would be as courageous.'

* See *Royal William*.

Lady Blessington came back to St James's Square when London was abuzz with the growing fever for Reform. The whole country bubbled over in expectation of 'The Bill, the Bill, and nothing but the Bill', which the King was to sponsor under the first Whig Ministry for half a century, with Earl Grey at its head.

In the midst of all this, the doyenne of Number 11 St James's Square set about to put her house, or at any rate the unexpired lease of it, in order.

No easy proposition to renew the elaborate running of a home that had lacked nothing of extravagant expense in the past on a fabulous income, and now must continue as before on a pittance.

Two thousand a year! How could she cope with such slender resources which would have been more than enough for a modest retirement in Tunbridge Wells or Cheltenham but never enough for the excessive luxury to which her life abroad and her first years of marriage had accustomed her.

If she at all resented her husband's Will she made no attempt to query it. When she heard that his illegitimate son, Charles Gardiner, born to his thrice-wedded wife, Mrs Brown, intended to dispute it now that he had reached the age of twenty-one, she said simply: 'So let him get on with it!' And as her husband had provided for his legitimate daughter Harriet by marrying her to d'Orsay whom he loved as his own son or, as she privately suspected, with a love less paternal than amatory, she gave no indication that she felt herself to have been wronged. Whatever her own opinion of her husband's exclusion of her right to the major portion of his wealth, she kept her silence and laid her plans for a triumphant come-back to the world of a social London whose women had spurned her.

Consultation with her husband's lawyers ascertained that for the next twelve months she could queen it as formerly at the house in St James's Square. Later she could sublet and sell any of its costly furnishings and objets d'art that were hers absolutely, and use the proceeds to buy a smaller house to meet the requirements of her reduced income.

She soon found what she sought; a house, formerly her husband's, in Seamore Place, Park Lane, which she rented, having sold the lease of the St James's Square house to the trustees of the Blessington estate. She would – she had it well planned – make an assault on London society and disdainfully ignore those ladies who scorned her as 'an abandoned woman' by irresistibly attracting their husbands.

So began the Coronation year of King William the Fourth, and Lady Blessington's revival as hostess in competition with the three principal women who received the most popular men of wit, of politics, the arts and literature. These three, her chief enemies, were Lady Holland, the Countess of Cork and Lady Charleville, a recent arrival to the haut monde of London from Ireland . . . And a formidable enemy she would prove to be.

The first of these good ladies, Lady Holland, was a divorcée and of no savoury reputation, forgotten by her marriage to Lord Holland, father of the brilliant Whig leader Charles James Fox, 'the dear James' of the late King's favour when Regent.

Lady Cork, second of the three, had known of Margaret Farmer when married to 'that dreadful Farmer man, from whom she had fled to a nobody, a Captain Jenkins who kept her in his bawdy house, and lent her round to all his disreputable associates'. So said the garbagemongers who had picked up every stray wisp of evil-minded envy concerning the notorious 'Farmer woman'. And the third of the trinity, Lady Charleville from Ireland, had been well primed by the Dowager Lady Mountjoy of her stepson's deplorable marriage to 'that creature' who had disgraced his honourable name and brought him near to bankruptcy by her wicked extravagance. A complete fabrication was this, since Lord Blessington's extravagance, shared by his lady, had always kept within his wealthy means.

The octogenarian Lady Cork, although her tongue was spiced with malice concerning any woman who might challenge her supremacy as hostess during these last sixty years, did no worse than hold Lord Blessington's widow up to ridicule. She was loud in her condemnation of the Lady's attempt to climb the social ladder on the shoulders of the Tory stronghold, and the indiscriminate reception by 'the Blessin' ', as she invariably named her, of all the younger lions of the day whether Whig, Tory, or Disraeli, who was fast becoming the darling of the ladies and the hope of the Radicals. He, having set himself up as candidate, delivered a remarkable pre-election speech from the balcony of the Red Lion Inn at High Wycombe, and electrified his gaping audience of yokels, country squires and Whiggish farmers who had expected this ringleted young fop to give them a mincing farrago of rubbish. He was now not only publishing his best selling novels, but had veered toward Whiggism; and Lady Cork, an ardent Whig, had button-holed him for her own. And here was 'the Blessin' ' snaffling her 'Dizzy'. Insufferable impudence!

In the fight for Reform Lady Cork had hung from the windows of her house in New Burlington Street, a banner proclaiming: 'The Bill, the true Bill, and down with the Rich!' And although she was one of the 'Rich' she did not scruple to possess herself of the silver spoons and other trifles from the dinner tables of her friends. But because of her high social standing, her eccentricities were leniently indulged.

This then was the hostile territory that Lady Blessington with her intrepid self-confidence determined to invade. Audaciously she flung open the doors of her house in Seamore Place in preparation for her offensive.

Her invitations were readily accepted and no expense spared in elaborate decor. She had little enough money left to her by her husband, but her stepdaughter with d'Orsay in possession of the Blessington fortune invested for his benefit, Lady Blessington felt herself to be entitled to a share of it while the d'Orsays were part of her household. Nor was Alfred disinclined to live under his lady's protection and lead his own insensate extravagant life, running up reckless accounts with tailors, bookmakers, horse-dealers, jewellers, regardless of the interest due to him, which he spent as fast as it came in. So much for his 'adorée's' reckoning on a share of the Blessington trust income.

Yet, undaunted, she entertained, having made a brilliant début receiving visitors, men only of course, except for a few of the less critical women including Rosina, wife of Bulwer Lytton, who was as extravagant with her husband's money as Margaret had been with Blessington's.

Miladi, as was said of her by one of the gossiping journalists, 'has doffed her widow's weeds, and supplied wit, fun, epigram and raillery enough to satisfy fifty county Members . . .' Yes, Members of Parliament were in full force in her smaller but still splendid house with its ruby red and gold drawing-room, and her own private sanctum where only her chosen few were admitted; a room overlooking Hyde Park, all white and gold with magnificent Sèvres vases, and exquisite knick-knacks collected in Paris and Italy and brought over to dazzle her admirers, who tactlessly retailed it to the envy of their women and their wives.

Accustomed as in the past to regale her guests with the finest food, superb wines served by footmen in canary and gold liveries, she satisfied the tastes of the gourmets who came to eat and drink as well as those who came to speechify and listen to their hostess's stimulating conversation in her seductive Irish accent and enjoy her hospitality which had all the attraction of a congenial club for which there was no subscription and the meals were all gratis.

*　　*　　*

The last few months of the year 1831 were of vital importance to Margaret Blessington and marked a turning point in her checkered career. Despite her recent widowhood, her life had seemed to promise a victory over her opponents that would raise her to the highest peak of society. She could not have foreseen that for all her determined courage to achieve her hoped-for triumph, she would be faced with a battle against heart-breaking odds and the desperate effort to maintain not only her hard won recognition as *persona grata*, but that she would fight for her very financial existence. And this must be gained solely by slavish toil at her writing desk to produce her novels and her journalism to augment the meagre two thousand a year which was all to which she could rightly lay claim.

Her invasion of London society could only be met by using the personal income of her stepdaughter doled out to Harriet by d'Orsay to whom forty thousand besides the Dublin properties were held for him in trust. This being so the question of how to meet expenses of the Seamore Place establishment had offered no difficulty, while the d'Orsays shared her house and its elaborate accessories. But she had now another problem with which to deal.

The marriage of Harriet d'Orsay had been a source of satisfaction to the Widow Blessington while the relationship between them had kept on an even keel. The child bride obscurely in the background of both her husband and her stepmother's lives had been of no account to either while she remained a child; but Harriet was no longer a child.

The emergence from a little nondescript fifteen-year-old to an attractive young woman of nineteen was so gradual as to pass unnoticed until, like Sally Power, she had suddenly become transformed. Indeed so sudden a change was this as to cause Lady Blessington a startling shock that led her to believe the child possessed, if not of the devil, of one of his imps.

Hitherto she had accepted as a foregone conclusion that Harriet, docile, submissive, would never dare to disobey an order. 'Do this. Do not do that. Leave the room and don't wander about like a miserable little ghost, you get on my nerves, child! Can you not find something to do instead of hovering around me when I am trying to concentrate on the menu for the dinner party tomorrow.'

'May I help with writing the menus?' Harriet had timidly suggested.

'No, you cannot. Your writing is deplorable and you can't spell a word of more than one syllable.'

But now, yes, now, the 'miserable little ghost' had found a voice; the voice of defiance.

It happened the morning after the dinner for which Harriet had offered to write the menus, and had been attended by several notable gentlemen and two ladies; the wife of Edward Bulwer, later to become famous as Bulwer Lytton and to end up as Lord Lytton, buried in Westminster Abbey. At present he was an ardent Whig who had seceded from radicalism to become a Member of Parliament.

His wife, a beautiful Irish girl, Rosina Wheeler, with whom he had been violently in love was the only woman in Society who accompanied her husband to Seamore Place. The marriage, however, was already on the rocks, due to Rosina's continuous extravagance to land herself and her husband deeply in debt.

Rosina, no doubt because of her Irish birth and an equally lonely and neglected childhood, had much in common with Margaret Blessington in that both desired to be a 'Somebody', not only a Somebody's wife.

There was also at that dinner the young Disraeli, Lady Cork's 'Dizzy', and a good many other young or old politicians, whether they agreed or not with this upstart Radical Jew who was for ever changing his coat from a red-hot 'Rad' to a Whig, or a true-blue Tory.

The second lady who accompanied her husband to this dinner party was the wife of a Welsh country squire of considerable means, a newcomer to London, one Wyndham Lewis, whose ambitious little wife, a Devonshire farmer's daughter, had urged him from his country seat in Wales to

172

stand for Parliament and herself manoeuvred to get him there. She who had persuaded him to take a London house in Grosvenor Gate also wished to be a 'Somebody', and triumphantly succeeded. Not only did she capture London society, but when widowed, she married Disraeli, and, even as she had persuaded her first husband, Wyndham Lewis, to embark on a political career, so was she the power behind 'Dizzy's' brilliant success. She too was honoured with a peerage and in her own right . . . But that's another story.*

Margaret Blessington was certainly a good picker in her selection of guests, for if they had not already climbed to the top of the ladder of fame, she seems to have had a sixth sense that some time or other they surely would arrive there.

Of those she selected almost all were destined to immortality in politics, literature, and the arts. And among these who attended the dinner in Seamore Place which preceded, as will be seen, Harriet d'Orsay's temerarious transformation, was little Lord John Russell, Leader of the Opposition, later to become First Lord of the Treasury and Prime Minister of England.

Disraeli, elegant as ever, was a dandiacal competitor to d'Orsay with his rings and things, his curls, his fancy waistcoat, his green velvet pantaloons and his attractive drawling voice that uttered epigrams and wit to outrival those of his hostess.

And then there was Joseph Jekyll, a journalistic snob and amusing raconteur who wrote innumerable letters to all his friends and to some who were not his friends, and whose correspondence was as catty as that of the incomparable Horace Walpole, a century before him.

And to Jekyll we owe a description of that dinner and 'the pretty melancholy Countess d'Orsay, who glided in for a few minutes and left to nurse her influenza . . .'

Yet there was no symptom of influenza when, next morning, she approached her stepmother in no 'melancholy'

* See *The Perfect Wife*.

manner but with a peremptory demand at the door of her ladyship's sanctum, where none was allowed entry without permission.

'I want to speak to you,' said Harriet. No 'please may I,' no 'Pardon me if I interrupt you.' No 'Madam', as she invariably addressed her ladyship, but inexcusably, 'I want to speak to you.'

Her ladyship was seated at her writing desk engaged on copious notes for the novel she had started and which, she prayed, would be published to augment her year's fast diminishing two thousand which had dwindled to less than two hundred, and was already bespoken in countless bills for entertainment and colourful clothes since she had now forsaken her weeds.

Raising her head, bent over a sheet of foolscap of which many other discarded sheets strewed the floor, the lady turned, her face devoid of all expression save irascible impatience:

'How dare you,' she demanded, 'come here when you know I am not to be disturbed? Go away.'

'I won't go away,' replied Harriet, with unexampled impudence, 'until I have said what I must and will say.'

'Say – *what?*' incredulously replied the lady.

'I have to say it.' Advancing into the room and carefully closing the door behind her. 'I am going away.' Harriet's eyes, beautiful, dark, long-lashed eyes that always seemed too large for her small, pale face, were fixed upon those of her stepmother that widened in something like alarm.

'Going *away!*' was repetitively italicized. 'What do you mean – going *away?*'

'What is usually meant by going away?' impudently queried this changeling of a Harriet. 'It means, if you don't understand English, having lived so long with that painted doll of a d'Orsay and speaking pidgin French with him – that I am leaving this house and you and that Thing I married, today or tonight, so soon as I can pack enough of what I want to take with me. And I am going to my grandmother and my Aunt Gardiner. They are in London now, and my brother Charles is with them and he is going to take legal advice how to obtain his rights to our father's money which you —'

'Stop!' cried the lady; she had turned white, as the pale Harriet had turned red with the enormity of her attack: 'Have you run mad?'

'No, I *have* run mad but I run sane now. I've been mad these five years since I let myself be married to your d'Orsay, but not now. No! Not now that I can see how I've been cheated of what are my rights and the rights of my brother and sister – cheated by *you* and that painted puppet all this time – yes, you!' She advanced on the dumbfounded Margaret, more than ever convinced that this devilish Harriet was possessed of the devil if not of lunacy. 'You have robbed me and Charles and our sister – all three of us,' she was shrill now, and tempestuous, stamping a sandalled foot to emphasize the torrent of words that poured from her, released in a long-stored resentment. 'You and my father between you – yes! You always had him under your thumb – you must have got at him, Charles says, to make him marry me to that Thing – God knows why, because you've had little enough out of it. My father has given it all or almost all of it to him and —'

'Will you *stop*!' agitatedly cried Margaret, white to the lips. 'I cannot know who has been telling these monstrous lies about me and your beloved father. Out! Go to your room. *Go!* You are obviously mad or – bad. How you have deceived me with your simple docile obedience, and all this time hoarding these infamous ideas against —'

'I have more infamous ideas, as you call them,' came the immense admission, with a wave of a contemptuous hand at the gilded panelling of the room, its yellow satin curtains, its console tables covered with costly objets d'art. 'All this trumpery you have bought with my father's money – *my* money! How well you have managed him and d'Orsay who is your lover – No! I *will* dare to say it —' as the dumb-founded lady endeavoured to interrupt with a frenzied, 'How dare you say —'

'I *do* dare to say what everyone knows – that he is your lover,' pursued the relentless Harriet, 'and what you have done in making my father marry me to him – yes, it was *you* who made him do this to me which is a living sin! . . . No, I *won't* stop! I'll tell you what I ought to have told you years ago. You thought me a fool, simple – an innocent half-witted fool. I was – yes, I was, and too young to understand what had been done to me – forced into this vile marriage as a child, but I'm not a child any more. I'll be nineteen in two months' time and now I know what I should have known long ago. How right my grandmother and my aunt were when they used to say of you – a nobody —' pointing a finger at the shaken Margaret, 'whose father had been in prison, and that you had been the mistress of other men before you caught my father!'

(God help me! prayed Margaret. So that is how the Mountjoy and Gardiner contingent poisoned this child's mind against me when she was in their care.) . . . But before she could deny these monstrous charges, the cruel young voice continued: 'As for the dinner party last night and your collection of nobs – because Charles says you're a *snob* for the *nobs* —'

And then the hurricane subsided, the face of this diabolical Harriet, transfigured with passionate hatred, was of a sudden becalmed as if a swiftly risen gale had been subdued after a tornado. The inarticulate submission that had shadowed the life of this 'miserable little ghost', re-turned. Not now a termagant uttering the unutterable, but the same woebegone, unhappy, and 'melancholy Countess d'Orsay', as Jekyll had seen the night before.

'I – I'm sorry,' was at last achieved in an almost inaudible whisper. 'I don't know what came over me – But,' the voice rose again in a resumption of hostility, 'Lord Tullamoore met me as I left the drawing-room last evening and he asked

why I was not at the table. And I told him I was – wasn't –'
a sob choked the words – 'wanted. That I am never wer –
wanted here. And he said others wanted me if you didn't.
And – he is Irish, too, and his mother, he said, is a friend of
my grandmamma, and so —'

'And so you tell tales and grovel for sympathy against
me, your mother – your second mother,' pronounced her
ladyship, recovering from shock even while the cataclysm
resounded in her ears. 'I know something of Tullamoore's
mother, Lady Charleville, and the poison of her tongue.
Leave me! Go to your room and pray forgiveness for your
wicked ingratitude to one who has loved and cherished you
as a daughter.'

'Daughter!' A burst of hysterical laughter preceded the
words: 'As much a daughter as Goneril and Regan were to
King Lear!'

And with this astounding reply, Harriet, sob-shaken,
tear-blinded, dashed from the room.

'God in heaven!' gasped the shattered lady, as she
gathered dignity about her as if to cloak her defeat . . .
Who, she asked herself, could have possibly imagined she
had so shocking a temper? . . . To defy me . . . to threaten
. . . Ah, yes! I see it all. A chip off the Mountjoy and
Gardiner block who had obviously spoken ill of me in the
past when this child – no child any more, indeed – had
listened, misunderstanding, until it sank in. Lord forgive
her for she knows not what she says . . .'

It was the best she could do to save her face in this most
shattering apocalypse.

Later that same afternoon, the departure of one Countess
from the house in Seamore Place was watched at the
window by another Countess, not yet recovered from the
horrifying experience she had sustained earlier that day.

With no apparent flurry nor attempt at further apology
for her outrageous rebellion, more than the sob-choked

outburst torn from her as she rushed from the room, Harriet organized her removal.

The Lady, having recounted to d'Orsay his wife's intent, he received it with remarkable *sang froid* and, apparently, with satisfaction as if Harriet had conferred on him a favour.

And he also watched from the window of Lady Blessington's sanctum where the incredible interview had taken place.

'Mon Dieu!' he exclaimed, as Harriet, cloaked and bonneted, tripped down the steps and into the carriage that awaited her, the door of which was held open by a powdered flunkey, 'it is *my* voiture she has taken and *my* pair of greys!'

'If that is all she has taken,' remarked the Lady, 'you should be thankful.'

'Comment? What you say? How more then could she take?'

'Besides French leave, you may find she has rifled your bureau where you so carelessly keep your bank notes.'

'No! She would never dare – Sacré bleu! To steal?'

'It is not stealing to take what belongs or should belong to her. And there is nothing she would not dare,' replied Margaret with the thinnest of smiles, 'now that she has broken the ice between us and would drag, not herself, but both me and you into the whirlpool.'

'Mais! Je ne comprends pas what you say. What has arrived with this personne and you that you speak of ice broken between you in a – qu'est que c'est – pool? She always so timide, why does she take this so sudden idée? Ah!' He leaned forward. 'See the voiture – it goes. Where?'

'To her grandmother to rake up more mud to throw at me,' was the inimical reply. 'Not at you, no. At me! You are the innocent victim of a wanton who has intrigued to marry her to you. And I, the faithless wife of my husband, who, having found out my iniquities, altered his Will for your benefit and Harriet's, his daughter.'

'You speak bêtise,' offendedly said d'Orsay. 'As if I – me! – should use myself to such méchanceté.' He passed a hand through his auburn curls, his face pinkening under its rouge. 'I have done nothing that could be wrong for you. How should I comprehend that mon ami, milord, would make the alteration in his testament for me?'

'Qui s'excuse, s'accuse. You lose nothing in the loss of her, for you have had the use of her money and will always have it while you live, unless,' the lady said meaningfully, 'she should bear you a child, and that, as we know, is impossible.'

Which gave d'Orsay earnestly to think.

*       *       *

The fugitive Harriet was received by her grandmother and aunt with open arms.

It is likely her flight had not been unexpected. Since their arrival in London from Dublin, Harriet had visited her step-grandmother and her aunt, Miss Gardiner, several times. And it is certain she had been closely questioned as to her married state, and they would have learned of the relationship between her husband and herself and that she was *virgo intacta*.

Further questioning and their own investigations had discovered a vital clause in Lord Blessington's Will of which Lady Blessington and d'Orsay were well aware.

In his Will Lord Blessington had bequeathed to either daughter who married d'Orsay, that if one or other of them, Harriet or her elder sister born out of wedlock to Mrs Brown, should have no child from the marriage, then the Earl's Dublin property of which d'Orsay was life tenant should revert to his illegitimate son Charles.

We know that Charles felt the injustice of his father's Will and, having reached the age of twenty-one, now prepared to dispute it.

It was therefore in the interest of the Gardiner family that Harriet's marriage should remain childless. None knew of the stipulation made by Lady Blessington in view of Harriet's extreme youth that when she became the bride of d'Orsay, there should be no marital intercourse for at least four years.

This, agreed by the father and the bridegroom, d'Orsay, served as another and entirely erroneous assumption on the part of the Dowager Lady Mountjoy and her step-daughter, Blessington's maiden sister, that the 'abandoned Farmer woman' had inveigled the unsuspecting Blessington, whose mistress they were certain she had been, into making her his wife. And her insistence that Harriet's marriage must not be consummated while she was still a child pointed to the fact that the Earl had been cuckolded by d'Orsay, obviously the lover of 'that Woman', who had manoeuvred this marriage with the child Harriet so that she and her lover should enjoy the Earl's fortune at his death. Even supposing Blessington had not predeceased her, as the Gardiner–Mountjoys saw it, 'the Woman' had provided for her lover d'Orsay after *her* death.

This would account for her passive acceptance of the Will that left her with so scanty a share of her husband's wealth and property. While she lived she would thus benefit by Harriet's marriage to d'Orsay whose mistress they fully believed her to be.

D'Orsay, who had taken with philosophical indifference Harriet's 'French leave', had time to consider how her departure would affect himself. He now realized, as Margaret had told him, that if his marriage should prove childless his life interest in Blessington's Dublin property would revert at his death to Charles Gardiner, the Earl's illegitimate son. And as there could be no possibility that Harriet would provide him with issue, he was greatly put about how to right what he took to be a wrong in respect of Blessington's 'testament'.

After anxious thought d'Orsay conceived a plan whereby he would be the sole and permanent recipient of Blessington's Dublin property. In the event of his marriage producing no heir, he could encourage Harriet to form a relationship with some other than his unproductive self, and claim the paternity of a child born to his wife; or, alternatively, if this project should fail, he would bring an action against his wife for divorce!

Having decided on this happy solution which when imparted to Lady Blessington produced another cataclysmic reaction, d'Orsay set about to find a potential deputy to perform his connubial rites.

There was no proof, he reasoned, that during the past year he and Harriet had not co-habited. Since that travesty of a wedding at Naples conducted by a more obliging Ambassador than Lord Burghersh, the d'Orsays, man and wife, had lived until now in the Blessingtons' houses. Yes, until now that Harriet had left him, presumably with a lover! What lover? Whom could d'Orsay find to act the part of father to his child?

Regarding himself in a mirror he smoothed his beautiful curls and thought whatever child he purported to beget would have to resemble him if possible, unless, of course, it entirely resembled its mother . . . With this end in view he called to mind several of his friends and acquaintances who might fulfil his requirements, and decided on one whom he knew well, a handsome young man, not so beautiful as himself, of course *that* he knew would be difficult to find, but sufficiently well-looking for the part he would be cast to play.

He had heard that Lord Tullamoore's mother, Lady Charleville, often back and forth from Ireland, was now in London full of the latest news of her son's attachment to Harriet d'Orsay. This she imparted to her dear friend, Lady Mountjoy, when visiting her at her London hotel.

Lady Charleville had never approved of her son's marriage to his wife who had been a raffish young woman, a leading light in the post-Napoleonic war years, which may have been the equivalent of the Bright Young People of a century later after the First World War.

The Countess of Charleville was taking tea with Lady Mountjoy attended by her stepdaughter, Miss Gardiner, elderly spinster sister of the late Lord Blessington. Harriet had gone out to replenish her wardrobe, having brought with her barely sufficient for her necessities when she fled from Seamore Place; so Lady Charleville was free to speak her mind.

'I am in the greatest distress,' is how her ladyship's mind spoke, 'because my son Tullamoore is always at Seamore Place and long before your granddaughter, Countess d'Orsay, left her husband.'

'I understand,' said Lady Mountjoy, 'that Lord Tullamoore is separated from his wife.'

'Yes, thank God,' was the devout reply. 'I always knew that marriage would end in disaster as Lady Harriet's has ended.'

Lady Charleville may have derived some satisfaction in dwelling upon this latest society scandal since her son had become embroiled in similar husband-and-wife trouble

She had been twice married and now in her ripe fifties had lost much of the beauty that had attracted her second husband, the Earl of Charleville, to whom she bore his heir, Lord Tullamoore.

'I cannot say,' pursued her ladyship (but she said it all the same), 'that I approve of Tullamoore's interest in Lady Harriet and, as I have heard, the poor young girl is under the pernicious influence of that Blessington creature who enticed your stepson into marrying her.'

'Harriet has been made a cat's-paw of that woman,' Lady Mountjoy energetically agreed. 'How dare she use my stepson's honoured name to dishonour it! She insisted that the marriage should not be consummated for at least four years. My poor innocent child was late in her maturity and from what she tells me she is still a virgin. It is obvious that this Farmer woman – she was a Mrs Farmer married to a man who had been in prison – and so was her father. A nice family –' said the Dowager bitterly – 'for my stepson to have married into. She deserted the scoundrel Farmer to become the mistress and later the wife of Blessington. He was always weak with women. And she who was any man's woman forced this marriage upon Harriet while for years she had been d'Orsay's mistress, so that she would enjoy the money Blessington left to Harriet by which d'Orsay benefits. The woman should be whipped at the cart's tail for a harlot from here to Newgate!'

Lady Charleville nodded sympathetic agreement and the feathers on her heavily plumed bonnet nodded with her. 'That is what I understood, and I do feel for you, my dear Lady Mountjoy, that your sweet little innocent girl should be so victimized . . .'

Meantime the sweet little innocent girl had completed her purchases in Bond Street and bought herself three new gowns, two bonnets, gloves and scarves with what was left of the quarterly allowance doled her by d'Orsay from her father's Will to him. She then ordered the carriage to drive her to Hyde Park. Arriving there she dismissed the coachman, said she would walk in the park and bade him return for her in an hour.

She walked leisurely to a seat near to the spot where the Achilles statue had recently been erected, and was greeted by a young gentleman waiting for her there.

Together they sought a seat, and he engaged her in an emotional conversation which it is not our privilege to overhear. Sufficient to say that Lady Charleville, writing to one of her numerous gossips, recounts that:

'Tullamoore staid [*sic*] with us all night and talked of Ct. d'Orsay. He seemed to think very ill of him in every way and clearly to be affected by Lady H.'s misfortune. She said she had trusted him and been most ill-used by Lady B. and d'Orsay . . . Yesterday Lady Mountjoy told me she is gone (I mean Lady Harriet) to the sea. Lady H. said Tullamoore behaved like an angel and she will always love him, for it was he who counselled her to go

to Lady Mountjoy and Miss Gardiner. She is as innocent
as an angel; yet the Will of her father is so constructed
that if she divorced this vile man he may starve her and
keep her £8000 pr. an. due to her when she comes of
age . . .'

By which it would seem that these two angelic beings to
whom Lady Charleville alluded, while engaged on celestial
talk in the shade of a tree in Hyde Park, had come to the
conclusion that it would be unwise to risk divorcing her
husband, 'that vile man', who might not only starve her but
take to himself the money left her by her father when she
should come of age.

How Lady Charleville knew of this income left to his
daughter in Blessington's Will is as much a puzzle as her
ladyship's knowledge of all to do or not to do with the
'innocent angel's' fortune or – misfortune. But after having
ascertained that Lady Charleville's beloved son Tullamoore
would not be dragged through the divorce court, her ladyship returned to Ireland leaving the Harriet débâcle to sort
itself out. As for 'Lady B.', she was left to face the storm
aroused by Harriet's brother Charles disputing his father's
Will. Yet money and her husband's incomprehensible injustice was the least of Margaret's troubles. In a note book
in which she jotted down the thoughts and ideas that had
occurred to her during the day and called her 'Night Book',
she wrote: 'We make a temple of our hearts in which we
worship an idol until we discover the object of our love is
a false god.'

By this we can assume that her 'idol' had clay feet. And
the shock of discovering his shameful intention of providing Harriet with a lover in the hope that should she bear a
child of whom he could claim paternity, thereby assuring
himself of continued wealth in the event that the lawsuit on
which Charles was bent should go against him completely
shattered his 'adorée'.

'You! How utterly contemptible —' words rushed from

her in staccato volleys like shots from a gun. 'You are lower than the lowest criminal! I trusted you – I – loved you – believed in you – was proud – as if you had been my son – and that you should think – so revolting – Oh, God!' She covered her face, tears gushed from her eyes while her body shook in a convulsion of rageful disgust. Her Irish temper and burning sense of injustice spurred her to flay him with the pain of her misjudgement and wounded pride.

'You are eaten up with your vanity – your utter selfishness – your ingratitude to me who promised your grandmother I would care for you when she begged me to look after you in London. She knew your weakness, your susceptibility to flattery which you devoured as a child devours sweets! I despise you! But I never deserted you even when I doubted your sincerity and believed that you – yes, you! – had persuaded my husband to make that infamous Will in your favour. I never would have failed you but you have failed me! You must leave my house – now, at once. I can never trust you again for I know you for what you are.'

He stood before her; his eyes wide with amaze that she who had always been so ready to grant his every wish, had enjoyed his company, his charm, that sirenic charm which men – a certain type of men – had found so irresistible, should now confront him *en colère incroyable* . . . 'No! No! You cannot mean how you say!' His self-complacency would not believe she could mean it. 'You would send me away – away from you! Never. I refuse to leave you!'

'You will go – at once.' She moved to the bell-rope. 'I will order your man to pack your things and you leave this house now. You hear me? Now!'

'Ah, I see. Mais! Naturellement. I cannot stay here with you now that Harriet has left me, yes? Personnes with big mouths, they talk. They will talk more if I stay here alone with you. But why so cruelle – so angry? Is it my faute that Harriet run away? I could divorce her, yes? And if I stay with you alone she could divorce *me*!'

Her hand was on the bell-rope. She pulled it so viciously

at this naïve interpretation of her intent to be done with him for ever, that the tassel of the rope broke off and fell to the ground. To the footman who answered her summons she bade him:

'Tell the Count's man to pack his bags. Count d'Orsay leaves for – for Paris. Tonight.'

Still convinced that his dismissal was for *les convenances*, and that Harriet's flight and his Lady's indignation at the terms of her husband's Will had caused her this *bouleversement*: 'I go,' he said. 'I think it best for you, mon adorèe, that I go. Eh well, I forgive what you say to me for you are out of yourself. Au'voir.'

He bowed and took her hand to kiss. She snatched it from him and pointed to the door.

'Go! I wish never to see or speak to you again. Never again!'

At that, with a lift of his eyebrows, a kiss blown from his fingertips and another bow, he went.

PART FOUR

*The Broken Mirror*

# EIGHT

From this time forth the protective love she had given d'Orsay, in spite of the hurt he had dealt her persisted, not wholly because of her promise to Madame Craufurd that she would never desert him. She felt herself in part to blame for his irresponsibility, his weakness and her own too ready assent to Blessington's Will.

When in a moment of anger and the heartbreak of her misplaced trust she had dismissed him – ordered him out of her house – for this she also blamed herself; and it irked her that he took his dismissal with an agreeable complacency that gave her to think he had every intention of returning to her, the same lovable exquisite boy and favourite of her husband. He was nothing but a spoiled child, so to herself she excused him, but none the less she felt it deeply that if he had failed her, she had failed him the more in the maternal devotion she had always felt for him.

These thoughts wrung from her are reflected in her 'Night Book': 'The first heavy affliction that falls on us rends the veil of life and lets us see all its darkness . . .'

In these high-flown sentiments it would seem she envisaged herself as a character in a novel she had already planned to write, rather than the 'heavy affliction' she describes and does, perhaps, masochistically enjoy.

Nor could she have failed to realize that the sadism she suffered as a child-wife rendered her more in sympathy with the fruitless marriage forced upon the child Harriet to a husband who, it had long dawned upon her, was impotent.

As for Harriet, her stepmother need have had no qualms

as to her future. Gossip brought to Lady Blessington coupled
Harriet's name with Tullamoore, and that the Comtesse
d'Orsay was madly in love with him and others with whom
Harriet was presumed to have had illicit relationships. In
fact the 'innocent angel', as rumour and Lady Charleville
gave it, was sadly fallen; a daughter not of Blessington but
of Beelzebub!

On her return to England from her travels abroad with
her stepmother and her father, Harriet had become
acquainted with the young Duc de Chartres, son and heir
of the Duc d'Orleans. He was a friend of d'Orsay who had
known him in Paris, and introduced him to Lady Blessington
when on a visit to London.

Another Parisian visitor to Seamore Place was the Count
Saint-Marsault. He had met Mary Ann Power at Madame
Craufurd's house in Paris and subsequently came to London
where he met 'Marianne' again.

Believing Mademoiselle Power to be of the wealthy
Blessington family, he paid court to her and was accepted.
Alas for Mary Ann! She took him as her last chance, being
then in her late twenties.

This elderly beau, ringed to his yellow knuckles, dressed
to kill, was apparently as rich as he had thought
Mademoiselle Marianne to be. No sooner were they married
than each discovered the other to be penniless, and both
bitterly complained how they had been deceived into
marriage.

Mary Ann returned to Seamore Place full of her grievance
against the impoverished Count, and after a month or two,
having refused to see her husband, whom she had left in
Paris where the honeymoon had been spent, she went to
live with her brother Robert and his wife in Dublin. So
much for Mary Ann, Comtesse Saint-Marsault, but not
enough yet of the Comtesse d'Orsay.

After her flight from Seamore Place and when Lady
Mountjoy and Miss Gardiner had gone back to Dublin,
Harriet remained in London, but not at Seamore Place

where her grandmother believed she had returned to 'that disreputable woman'. She never did return to Seamore Place, nor to 'that disreputable woman'; nor did she complete her love affair with Tullamoore by becoming his mistress. Instead she became the mistress of the Duc de Chartres, as desirous a young man as she was desirable. At nineteen she had developed into a very attractive young woman, and made a conquest of other desirable young Parisians while living under the luxurious protection of the Duc de Chartres, who succeeded his father as Duc d'Orléans. She lived in his royal custody for some few years until he was killed in a carriage accident.

After the death of her royal protector she was soon consoled with another French nobleman, one of the de Noailles, and, as reported in London, 'a host of others'.

Although d'Orsay had no grounds for divorce since evidence was insufficient to prove adultery with Tullamoore, he finally had to content himself with a judicial separation which would give him a share of her wealth but less than he could have had if he divorced her. Possibly had he followed her to Paris he could have obtained a divorce, although the scandal of citing as co-respondent the heir to the throne of France, the Duc de Chartres, would have dealt a death blow to his grandmother, Madame Craufurd, and the loss to d'Orsay of any intended legacy.

When banished from his lady's house d'Orsay, who may have foreseen she was bound to relent, established himself in apartments in Curzon Street. From there when Charles Gardiner, Blessington's illegitimate son, filed a suit in dispute of the late Earl's Will against his widow and Count d'Orsay, he was at her side to support her.

*　　*　　*

But in the years to come while she battled against a hostile world and struggled to keep up appearances on insufficient means, it was she who supported him; watched over him, worked for and guarded him according to her promise to his grandmother.

Following Harriet's disappearance and the dismissal of d'Orsay, the most to suffer and the least to blame in the chaos that resulted from the dispute brought by the Gardiner–Mountjoy offensive as to the validity of the late Earl's Will, was his widow.

The legal conferences and endless correspondence, the consultations with the lawyers of d'Orsay and Lady Blessington, in which she had to bear her own costs, greatly depleted her small income. Then, after some months, the case was brought into Chancery.

There ensued an interval of about three years of indecision, more costs, and anxiety for Margaret, but little to worry d'Orsay, who was still enjoying the income of Blessington's thousands and from the Dublin property. But because of the shrinkage of assets and the large sums of money involved in continuous litigation, the court decided it must take over the administration of the trust. After further conferences in and out of court, it was agreed that the Lady Harriet d'Orsay and Comte d'Orsay were to receive each the annual income of £450 to Harriet, £500 to d'Orsay, while Charles Gardiner was still in receipt of the £1000 per annum left him by his father. And nothing yet had been decisively settled.

While d'Orsay's interest in the Blessington estate was allowed and during the next decade negotiations went on and off at intervals, his debts were formidable; yet, true to his reckless extravagance he continued to live at fabulous expense.

In the meantime Margaret Blessington, while striving to adapt herself to her change of circumstances and the distasteful imbroglio of the Gardiner case and its unending litigation, had the added anxiety of monetary worries. The most immediate of these was how to find a new source of income to make her dwindling ends meet.

She still outwardly maintained a brave front; her parties

and entertainments still attracted men who shared her interests, but something was lacking.

Although d'Orsay did not return to live with her in the same house for the next few years, he was an almost daily visitor, attending her dinners, her soirées, acting host to her guests, and received as always the appreciation of men for his sense of humour, good nature and his imperishable charm. She too was thankful to have him there, yet she could no longer feel that same trust in him as before.

In the critical eyes of the world their relationship remained unaltered. She, as ever, was believed to be d'Orsay's mistress, barred from all reputable female society, while he continued to enjoy the fruits of her husband's extraordinary Will as the elegant dandy, the amusing buck, successor to Beau Brummel, but with no Prince Regent now to sponsor him. Nevertheless he pursued his haphazard career as a leader of fashionable male society. Women were not impressed by his effeminacy, his painted face, his languorous charm, even as a century before him, 'Lord Fanny', satirized by Pope, was less attractive to women than they to him.*

Denying himself no luxury, he cared nothing for an accumulation of debts entailed by his insensate extravagance. He had money enough to meet his creditors in his own good time and left all such tiresome business to his 'adorée'. She, having forgotten, or had chosen to forget, the quarrel that ended in his banishment, found on his return he was indispensable in assisting at her entertainments, while she furthered her acquaintance with men of political and literary distinction.

She would select possible aids for the exploitation of her career, if not as a novelist, as journalist for the favourite women's magazines and periodicals, believing her title would outweigh her lack of experience as a writer since her first minor successes as novelist were long forgotten.

With this decision she looked about her to choose one or

* See *A Toast to Lady Mary*.

other of the men who frequented her parties and might prove useful to her. And of the few possible she selected Edward Lytton Bulwer. He, already a popular novelist with a wife and two children, was a Member of Parliament, one of the youngest, being barely seven and twenty; an ardent Radical though with a reputation for extravagant living second only to that of d'Orsay. But the extravagance was mainly due to his wife Rosina who, for a consideration, would assist social climbers to an entrée into society. Among these was Mary Ann, wife of Wyndham Lewis. She had taken under her wing the young Disraeli and moreover induced her husband, Wyndham Lewis, Conservative M.P. for Maidstone, to promote Disraeli as co-member for Maidstone with him.

At this time the Speaker was Charles Manners Sutton, married to Ellen Power after the death of her husband Home Purves.

By reason of her influential husband, Ellen had been of no little help in securing eminent Counsel for the defence of her sister and d'Orsay during the lengthy litigation which had resulted in Lady Blessington's monetary embarrassments.

To Sally, as she always was and ever would be to Ellen, she said:

'My dear, you need have no fear that you will fail in whatever you set out to do. Imagine! Who else but you could have managed to be quit of that maniacal brute Farmer, and find so obliging a protector as Jenkins? He was glad enough to buy you as Farmer did from our cut-purse of a father! Which proves that your head is screwed on the right way. All *I* did was to extricate myself from Home Purves who cared not a jot for me. All he cared about was deer stalking and grouse shooting in the Highlands, though how he could have shot straight with that boss-eye, goodness knows! And look where I am now with no effort on my part, only luck and no exchange and bartering! How true it is that some are born great, some achieve greatness

194

(that's you!) and some have greatness thrust upon them (that's me). Sure, 'tis a miracle that our Papa, ex-jail bird, drunkard and murderer as he was . . . well, wasn't he, having just missed being hanged? And a boot-licker of titles who has two of his three daughters married to titles! You should just hear him brag about us . . . What? Oh yes, I do see him once a year, and you should hear him boasting of you and Mary Ann being married into the peerage. One an English Countess, one a French Countess, never mind that Marsault hasn't a bean and Mary Ann lives on nothing with Robert – and that *I* am married to the Prime Minister of England! Yes! That's what he, poor sot, tells his drunks who sit at, or fall under, his table. And he will have it that Charles is Prime Minister.' Ellen tapped her forehead. 'He's a bit – you know. But,' she lowered her voice, 'I'll tell you this, if you'll not breathe a word, that Charles won't be Prime Minister but he will be a peer in the House of Lords, this year, next year, sometime . . .'*

It was in this year, 1832, that Lady Blessington, in order to maintain her establishment in Seamore Place, enlisted Edward Lytton Bulwer to advise her how to embark on a literary career. We know that Byron had a poor opinion of her prowess as writer, and although she was prolific in filling pages of her diaries, she had enough critical sense to realize that her talent, unless sponsored or encouraged by a master of literature, could never be anything but mediocre. 'I am too verbose,' she told herself, and determined to overcome a lavish tendency to elaborate.

On the few occasions she had talked with Bulwer at her soirées, who with his wife, Rosina, had accepted her invitations and in return were invited to their decorative house in Hertford Street, Bulwer had recently become the editor of the *New Monthly Magazine*, and she wrote to him offering contributions to the *New Monthly*. She explained that during her visit to Genoa she had met and been on

* Charles Manners Sutton was created Viscount Canterbury in 1835.

friendliest terms with Byron and hoped that the name of him 'whose light had not been dimmed by his death' would rouse the interest of Bulwer.

It did.

Careful not to appear too eager in accepting her offer, Bulwer sent his assistant editor to interview her. He was at once impressed by her gracious personality. A priggish, sanctimonious young man was he, one Carter Hall, whose wife had made something of a hit with her sketches of Irish characters. Both were Irish, and Lady Blessington did not fail to remind him that they were compatriots, praising his wife's book (which she had never read, and only vaguely heard of it).

As a result of her persuasively engaging manner, he proposed that she should write her memoirs of Byron in a series of instalments for the *New Monthly*.

Of that first meeting Carter Hall wrote his impressions of her as '. . . having been very beautiful when young' (she was in her forties when this interview took place but she would never discuss her age unless to subtract ten or more years from it). 'Her face,' he continues, 'is peculiarly Irish, round, soft and smiling; her voice low and sweet' (she cultivated its 'sweetness' when out to attract and would enhance its 'soft' quality by slightly stressing her fascinating brogue). 'There was nothing artificial in anything she said or did and of the many persons eminent in literature and art who are her frequent visitors, all or nearly all are men . . .' He concluded his eulogy with an allusion to 'the slander that was busy with her fame,' concerning her relationship with d'Orsay, who does not appear to have discredited the allegation. As to her 'fame', if in the year that saw the passing of the Reform Bill which must have detracted interest from the social and literary activities of Lady Blessington and others of her time and age, any fame she could have acquired with the publication of the *Conversations of Byron*, may likely have been due less to her book than to her relationship, whether innocent or not, with d'Orsay.

His fame long outlived hers even to the extent of a play
written about him entitled the *'Last of the Dandies'*, and
produced in the early twentieth century.*

However, her *Conversations of Lord Byron* were published and have been printed and reprinted for the last
hundred and fifty years. The first instalment in the *New
Monthly* was eagerly read and became an instantaneous
success.

This Bulwer must certainly have foreseen since the name
of Byron would ensure an immediate response with a
feminine public who wished to know what 'that
(epithetical) Woman' had to say of him. And as each instalment appeared, so did the indignation of the ladies of
fashion, who had said their prayers to Byron, increase to
denounce her as having published a tissue of lies about her
'friendship' with the poet whose name was sacrosanct.

She was then threatened with a pamphlet written under
the pseudonym of 'The Dissector', which purported to expose the whole truth about her 'scandalous' life with
d'Orsay and prove the vast fraud she had attempted in the
falsifying of her friendship with Byron, whom it was
unlikely she could ever have known more than to exchange
a few words.

The ultimate publication of her *Idler in Italy* should have
refuted this allegation, but their exaggerated verbosity did
not tend to authenticate her *Conversations*.

The 'Dissector', who might have been anyone of her
feline enemies, never ventured beyond the boundaries of
threat, had little damaging effect upon her friendship with
Bulwer, as those who circulated the 'Dissector' menace had
possibly hoped. On the contrary it increased her intimacy
with both Edward Bulwer and Rosina, his wife.

She, who herself had suffered adverse criticism in her
marriage, was sympathetic and in return 'Marguerite' and
Rosina (they were soon on affectionate Christian names)

* Produced by the then Mr (afterwards Sir Herbert) Beerbohm
Tree at His Majesty's Theatre, London.

sympathized with Bulwer's wife when he, sick to death of their interminable rows and in one of their most bitter quarrels, took himself off to Ireland to begin the writing of his *Last Days of Pompeii* in peace.

Rosina continued to entertain as extravagantly as ever, was always in debt, but her 'darling Marguerite' could not give her anything more than sympathy for that, being in similar case herself.

It was at one of Rosina's parties following Bulwer's temporary exit, that 'Marguerite' was first presented to: 'That article over there by the mantelshelf, who is he?' she asked her hostess, indicating a young gentleman with a profusion of long curls, rings outside his white kid gloves, a canary-coloured waistcoat and green velvet trews, surrounded by a bevy of admiring women.

'Who?' Rosina paused on her way to the buffet on d'Orsay's arm.

'Permettez, madame.' D'Orsay detached himself from Rosina. 'I will present him.'

Making his way through the circle of admiring ladies, he spoke to the bejewelled and ringleted young 'article', to return with him and present:

'Madame the Countess of Blessington – Mr Benjamin Disraeli.'

This was her first meeting with the young Mr Disraeli of whom she had heard much, but had yet to read more than his latest novel *Contarini Fleming*. She had also heard of his attempt to enter Parliament as a Radical when he made a bombastic speech on the balcony of the Red Lion Inn at High Wycombe to a crowd of astonished natives who had never seen the like of this flamboyant apparition. She also heard – who had not? – how 'Dizzy', as named by the ubiquitous Lady Cork, who collected celebrities known or likely to be known as others collected butterflies, had taken him up in a big way as a promising *pièce de résistance*.

Not that there was anything of the butterfly in this very

self-assured, self-opinionated young man, unless it were
an indecisive fluttering from Radical to Whig, from Whig
to Tory, in his search for a membership of Parliament, no
matter the colour of the party he selected.

'This Disraeli,' asked Margaret of d'Orsay on the drive
back to Seamore Place after Rosina's soirée, 'what do you
know of him more than he is the *dernier cri* of the women
and that he is the writer of novels peppered with dukes,
duchesses, titles of all sorts, and himself figuring largely as
the chief character?'

'He is or will be a chief character not only in his novels
but in the eyes of the world, or is it – one should say – the
world of Parliament?' replied d'Orsay.

'I take it that 'tis part of his character to outrival you in
the fashion of his dress,' she said drily.

D'Orsay slid a arm round her somewhat ample waist.
She was putting on weight, no longer the sylph of her
'Blessing's' delight, which was an added anxiety to her
more troublous preoccupations.

'His dress does not, nor cannot compete *à la mode* with
me,' d'Orsay told her, with an offended pout. 'I am – how
you say? – *l'hôte* to myself. He is s'exposant – exhibitor –
yes?'

'Yes, I can well believe that,' she retorted.

'Also,' d'Orsay concluded, as he offered a hand to help
her out, 'he is a Jew.'

'Which,' she said as she stepped from the carriage,
'accounts for it.' And she thought: A Jew! Only a Jew could
play the showman as he does with his fantastic appearance,
and combat ridicule with that sardonic smile at himself or
at those idolatrous women he attracts as moths to his
candle – to burn their wings!

Her interest in Disraeli increased when the following
week Bulwer brought him to one of her soirées, again out-
rageously attired in a variation of the costume in which she
had first seen him. Setting aside her prejudice against his
racial ostentation, she bestowed more attention to him

than to any of her other guests. She found, despite his affectations, that the mind behind his 'coxcombery and foppishness', as she afterwards described him to Bulwer, 'was razor sharp'.

'So sharp,' replied Bulwer, elegantly reclining on a Louis Seize sofa in her ornate drawing-room, 'that he will cut through all who oppose him in his stride to the front bench.'

'He is not even a Member of Parliament yet.'

'Not yet; but when he is, you will see.'

In the spring of 1832 Lady Blessington decided that in order to maintain her establishment in the manner to which she had been accustomed she must make serious efforts to increase her diminished income.

Although the *Conversations of Lord Byron* did not appear in book form until 1834, she realized that Bulwer's cordial report of it as editor of *The New Monthly* would augur well for its continued success, and that she might turn to authorship as a means to decrease her financial embarrassments.

To this end she cultivated her friendship with Bulwer, who, young though he was, had already attracted enthusiastic attention as a writer of outstanding merit. When the *Conversations* had appeared in serial form, and despite the anonymous 'Dissector's' threat to expose her relationship with d'Orsay, she was determined to defy those who maligned her by launching out on a literary career sponsored by Bulwer and other men of distinction with whom she was acquainted.

During those 'Nine Days of May' that evoked the final crisis in the battle for Reform, she gathered to her entertainments a chosen few known to be rabid Reformers, not the least of them Lord Grey, who had badgered the King into agreeing to create more peers to ensure the passing of the Bill. The knowledge that she was ignored by her enemies, her reputation blackened by women of fashion, only urged her to further defiance. Meantime all that was talked of in those 'Nine Days of May' was 'the Bill, the Bill and nothing but the *Bill*!'

It was blared in the Press, in the streets, in Hyde Park, where demonstrators had uprooted the railings; and in Mayfair salons the chief topic of discussion was Reform, for or against – the Bill!

On an evening in those critical nine days only two women, Rosina and the octogenarian Lady Coke, were present at a dinner Lady Blessington gave to some half dozen men, including Lord Grey and her latest acquisition, Disraeli.

She was at her most sparkling, but he who engaged more of her attention than any other of her guests was Disraeli.

Greville, that cynical, sarcastic diarist who had his likes and dislikes among those he singled out for observation, held no high opinion of Lady Blessington.

'Her existence,' he notes, 'is a curiosity, her dinners frequent and good . . . D'Orsay does the honours with a frankness and cordiality' (He is obviously attracted by the lure of the fascinating d'Orsay). But the hostess he finds 'dull, her conversation uninteresting, which is never enriched by imagination . . .'

This criticism is directly opposed by Bulwer's panegyrics in a letter written at the height of their friendship in which he tells his 'Dearest Lady Blessington there is hardly any person in the world I esteem and regard so much as yourself and for whom I feel so grateful and warm an interest . . .'

Whether Rosina's interest was so warm as her husband's for his 'Dearest Lady Blessington' is not recorded, but that dinner to which Greville had *not* been invited, and in their brief acquaintance only once and never again, might have accounted for the scratch of his pen at her.

On this particular evening when the ladies had retired to the drawing-room leaving the men to their drink, Lady Cork dilated at length on 'the Bill that I —' she tapped her scanty bosom swathed in gauzy tulle from which emerged her withered neck encircled by diamonds, 'that I', she repeated gazing round at Rosina and Margaret as if to defy contradiction, 'uphold; and I feel that our dear Grey has done wonders to drive into Billy's pineapple head the necessity of filling the Upper House with more and more peers to vote for the Bill.'

'They have been rampaging up and down Hertford Street,' said Rosina who had brought with her one of her adored dogs – she had four. This was a Blenheim spaniel named Fairy. 'A whole crowd stood outside our house shouting for Edward to come and show himself because they know he is hot for Reform.'

'And what of you, my dear?' Lady Cork tapped her fan on her hostess's knee. 'Are you hot or cold, for or against, Reform?'

'I can't say I am for or against it, at all,' she replied with the softest trace of her brogue. 'Sure, hot or cold I run with the hare and hunt with the hounds in all weathers.'

'Which accounts for your success with the men who are masters of the chase.' The old lady cackled knowingly. 'And what is this I hear that you are turning authoress? It is some years since you amused us with your *Magic Lantern* and its naughty caricatures of recognizable friends – or enemies. Almack's is agog with the news that you are going to publish in book form what you know – or don't know – of Byron. Or what Byron knew of you,' she lowered a wrinkled old eyelid, 'if any man is allowed to know.'

Accustomed to Lady Cork's sly insinuations this was laughed off with:

'My friendship with Byron or any other man that I and my —' she hesitated to allow this to sink in – 'my husband had, is known to all. We met Byron in Genoa and my dear Blessington spent much of his time with him.'

'I hear,' persisted her inquisitor, 'that Lady Jersey is waiting to pounce on each instalment of your *Conversations* with claws outstretched!'

'I should be honoured if her ladyship will take so much interest in my reminiscences of the Master,' was the equable reply. 'May I take your cup? Or will you have more coffee?'

'No more. I'll not sleep a wink after this one excellent cup . . . Such pretty Dresden. But,' rendering the pretty Dresden, 'a cat will wait patiently at a mouse-hole for a mouse to come out, don't forget.'

'I never forget, nor do I regret,' was said with smiles. 'But t'would take more than one cat to seize and savage a mouse if so be it she kept out of danger.'

'I thank God,' put in Rosina, 'that no cats come prowling round our house. We can't abide cats especially those like that smirking Mr Greville, who'd have his whiskers pulled out if he came after me. You'd go for him too, wouldn't you, my precious one?' She dropped a kiss on the black muzzle of the somnolent Fairy she held in her arms. 'As for the Jersey, she is so busy excluding herself from her predecessor's reputation – the fifth Countess who was one of the late King's irregulars when he was Regent, that she adopts a Puritanical sublimity – according to Edward – that is sublimely ridiculous. You don't have to care, my love,' to Margaret, 'if the Jersey gets her claws in you.'

What her love might have had to say to that was never said, for just at this moment the men returned from the dining-room and at once severally attended on the ladies. And when all took their leave, Bulwer reluctantly at the request of Rosina, bored with d'Orsay's overladen compliments and reeking of scent, Disraeli, having bade his hostess an elaborate farewell, came back after the others had left.

'A thousand pardons, madam, but I felt it impossible to tear myself away before I could have further opportunity of enjoying your conversation which,' he laid a hand to his heart, 'I dare hope will be recorded in your memory of me – even as of Byron.'

After this grandiloquent gambit, 'I have read your *Magic Lantern*,' he mendaciously told her. 'Such a delightful humour, such delicious caricature and choice of words that I venture to prophesy your ladyship will rise, as Bulwer tells me,' (which he hadn't) 'to the highest peaks of literature.'

She flushed with pleasure. 'I am immensely flattered by your opinion. I have read your novels and can honestly say that it is *you*, not I, who are marked for the highest peak as a master of literature.'

She had read only one of his novels, *Contarini Fleming*, and didn't think much of it. But both she and Disraeli knew how and where to use tact or, as he was to put it some four decades later: 'Everyone likes flattery and when it comes to Royalty you lay it on with a trowel . . .' Nor could he know while experimenting with his trowel on a lady in a Mayfair drawing-room on a certain warm spring night that he would use these very words to his Sovereign Queen when discussing her journal written in the Highlands: 'We authors, Ma'am . . . And for Lady Blessington he added an impromptu: 'We who together share the Godsent gift of authorship.'

Nor could he have forseen how that those many years later his irresistible charm would flatter an inconsolable tear-sodden widow, magnetically to draw her from her mausoleum at Windsor and with skilful manipulation of the trowel, the brilliant cunning old statesman would name her his 'Gloriana, his Faery,' . . . But she, the future Empress of his creation, was peacefully asleep on this night of May in her small white bed in her mother's room in a country house in Kensington, a docile, obedient little girl who knew nothing of the world outside those redbricked walls any more than the world knew of her and was of the least account to the King's people as if she were non-existent. Or in her dreams, the innocent dreams of childhood, could she ever have dreamed that one day she would say: 'I can never forget what I owe to my dear, kind, considerate friend, Mr Disraeli.' . . .

And on this night in 1832 with the subdued glow of candles flickering in the light breeze that drifted through a half open window where the curtains had been left

undrawn to let in a breath of air, for those nine May days
had presaged summer's warmth, was heard a distant sound
of multitudinous cheers borne from Westminster across
the trees in Hyde Park to echo in a roar in Seamore Place. A
mob of men were waving banners, women excitedly
screaming while in lighted windows opposite heads peered,
and:

'The Bill for Reform,' murmured Mr Disraeli, 'has now
become law.'

*    *    *

Had the passing of the first Reform Bill in 1832 been
finally thrown out of the Lords, it would have plunged the
nation into anarchy. Among the Higher Whigs there was
general rejoicing, and resigned acceptance from the Higher
Tories.

Lady Blessington who had countered the challenge of
that ardent old Whig Lady Cork, with the non-committal
reply that she ran with the hare and hunted with hounds,
was still running with one of the most active Whig hounds
when the buzz of the Bill had died down.

The friendship between herself and Edward Bulwer had
ripened, and with each issue of the much discussed *Conversations* that appeared in his *New Monthly Magazine* the
lash of tongues took up the accusation that 'the Blessington
Woman' had disgracefully maligned and falsified the name
of Byron.

Jekyll, second only to Greville as an equally catty arch
gossip, while professing disgust at the 'horrible attacks on
Lady Blessingon, and that former associates of Byron were
frightened to death' . . . followed hounds in the chase with
the reminder: 'The conversations of a dead man cannot be
contradicted, so if Miladi is not scrupulous on the score of
varacity she can report as she pleases.'

The noise of the 'Dissector's' threat publicly to expose
her relationship with d'Orsay in his (or her?) pamphlet
never went beyond a threat for fear of counterattack from

Miladi in an action for libel; and the belief that the whole thing was a forgery assured the success of the *Conversations*.

Bulwer's encouragement decided her to enlist his help and influence to attain further entry into the world of literature. Their friendship, if not on Bulwer's part that of a lover (for he seems to have been one of the few men who were more desirous of her mind than her body), linked them in a bond of sympathy and understanding. She had the gift, rare in Bulwer's women, of being a good listener and would draw from him confidences he would divulge to none other.

'There is nothing,' she told her sister Ellen, 'that a man wants more from a woman than to reveal himself, his thoughts, his aspirations and above all – his marital problems. I have listened for hours to Bulwer's complaints against Rosina, their incessant quarrels, her extravagance, although he is as much a spendthrift as she. Both are to blame, both entirely self-centred, and each thinks the other is at fault. And so it is with Disraeli. He, of course, isn't married – yet, but I have been regaled with his tormented love for that girl – Henrietta – he was so mad about, and now it is all over and forgotten. Neither Dizzy nor Bulwer is capable of loving deeply anyone but himself. I feed their ego, that is my attraction for these two and that is why they both love me – not with the snatch-and-grab love of the he-male for the she-male – all response to their snatch-and-grab, or to be more realistic, the lust of man – was killed in me by Farmer. As for d'Orsay and our supposed relationship, whatever is said of that and will be said long after both of us are dust – although,' she added with a sparkle of that humour which was not her least engaging charm – ' 'tis sure *he* won't be dust! He'll see to it his corpse is embalmed like that of the Pharaohs and perfumed with attar of roses. But whatever the mud-slingers who choose me for their target may say, I have never been more to d'Orsay than guide, philosopher and *dis*passionate friend.

206

And until Blessington – bless him – made that unaccountable Will I was his banker. He's another who will always
be the lover of himself rather than of any . . . man.'

'Talking of Blessington's Will, has Charles Gardiner,'
asked Ellen, 'got any further with his attempt to disprove
it?'

'They don't seem able to prove or disprove anything in
the Court of Chancery. It will take years to make up its
mind, even though the Will says in black and white that
d'Orsay is to have the whole of it except —'

'Except,' Ellen finished for her as she paused with a
crooked smile on her lips, 'tuppence-ha'penny for you –
Well,' again forestalling Margaret, 'isn't that miserable two
thousand a year your Blessing let you have, about tuppence
ha'penny compared to d'Orsay's forty thousand and the
whole of his Irish estates?'

'He will only get the income from forty thousand when
all is settled – if ever.'

'Only!' Ellen puckered her pretty nose, 'and I'll wager
he'll squander the lot of it in half a year and he'll be living
on you for the rest of his life. You'll see.'

'Not yet, and he can't touch the capital while it remains
in trust. He married Harriet for her money or rather the
money her father promised *him*, and now the marriage is
broken up he is only waiting until he can find grounds for
divorce, and then he will have all that Blessington allowed
her when she came of age, if he hasn't had it already.'

'I don't think he will ever find grounds for divorce.'
Ellen, never backward in gleaning contemporary chatter
recounted, 'When Charles and I were in Paris last year talk
was rampant round Harriet d'Orsay and the duc de
Chartres. He will be duc d'Orléans when his father dies.
D'Orsay can hardly cite royalty, even French royalty, in a
divorce case.' Ellen chuckled softly. 'Just imagine that little
milk and water Miss fooling you as well as that painted
pimp of a d'Orsay, she with not a word to say for herself to
run off into the arms – or the bed – of a prince who may

one day be King of France. She will be another Pompadour or a de Maintenon, I shouldn't wonder. But so long as d'Orsay can lay his hands on all her money I don't suppose,' Ellen said obscurely, 'that he cares whether he can or he can't.'

'Can't what?'

Margaret allowed Ellen the indulgent smile she kept for her alone. She would always be the little sister of their shared attic days.

'Can't get her with child or take on some other man's child. Charles says he could claim parentage of it and so keep all the Blessington money now and for ever and after death when you tell me he'll be mummified.'

'How macabre can we get!' laughed Sally (as she would always be to Ellen).

'Well, you said that is how he will end – like an Egyptian Pharaoh. As for you, everyone thinks you have made a fortune out of your talks with Byron even if not two words of them are true.'

'I can show them my diary where I have written down every word he said, if they believe I have made fiction out of fact.'

'Or,' Ellen teased her, 'that you made *believe* was fact.'

'*Et tu, Brute?* No, I may have embroidered fact with fiction in the *Magic Lantern*, but I could never have invented Byron's brilliant perception of human nature and his sympathy with his fellow creatures. Nor could I have thought up his many contradictions in pages and pages of those series that have left such a deep impression on my mind. He, the spoiled child of genius, is – was – a sentimentalist, and, *au fond*, a romantic. Yet he will point ridicule and sarcasm at himself whom he loved more than any love of his life. As to making a fortune out of Byron, all I have had from the *Conversations* is the sale of the copyright for the series which is a quarter of what the *New Monthly* makes on the sale of each issue. How right Byron was to say that Barrabas was a publisher! Bulwer must have

208

guessed the magazine would sell like hot cakes – although he doesn't own the *New Monthly* he gets better paid as editor than I for even all my issues – and it is selling in thousands on Byron's name, not mine.'

'Yet you are still sending money over to Ireland to help Robert and his family and our precious old drunk of a father,' said Ellen, 'to say nothing of Mary Ann.'

'Poor Mary Ann.' Margaret sighed. 'How she, and we too, were deceived into thinking Saint-Marsault was so wealthy – always bragging of his ancestral châeaux which may or may not have belonged to his ancestors or his father who he says was guillotined during the Terror, but he hasn't a sou now. And he thought Mary Ann was an heiress, living with us and seeing how we lived – and how I for one,' she added dolefully, 'can never live again. I will *have* to earn money, especially since Robert lost the Mountjoy agency and hasn't enough to keep his wife and family as well as Papa and Mary Ann. I can't let them starve.'

'They don't do so badly,' Ellen reminded her, 'what with you handing out to them more than half you have, and Charles helping Papa, who in his turn is for ever passing round his hat – as if we hadn't enough to do with our two lots of children, Charles's and mine, and only one of my girls, Louisa, of marriageable age.'

Ellen got up and went to a wall mirror to adjust her bonnet, the latest thing in broad-brimmed pokes. Her gown of blue tarlatan flounced to the pointed waist and worn over half a dozen petticoats, was a forerunner of the crinoline.

'I suppose,' she added returning from the mirror to bestow a kiss on Sally's cheek, 'that you will go on writing now not only to keep yourself but to keep all the Powers that be, including the Prince of Dandies, as Charles calls him ... Goodbye.'

'Goodbye, darling' ...

She stood at the window to watch her sister enter her carriage and drive away, then going to her bureau she wrote a note to Bulwer inviting him to dinner 'for a tête-à-tête', to ask his advice.

The 'tête-à-tête' resulted in an introduction to his publisher, Richard Bentley, who, Bulwer told her, had been much impressed by her Byronic conversations.

At a meeting with Bentley in his office a few days later, the copyright for a three-volume novel was offered to her for the sum of four hundred pounds. So handsome an offer for a book not yet written by an unknown author was doubtless due to the influence of Bentley's most popular writer who had engaged his publisher's interest in Lady Blessington's first venture into fiction.

'If,' he told Bulwer, 'it *is* her first venture into fiction. I still cannot believe that those remarkable *Conversations* were ever remembered verbatim. If they were ever remembered at all.'

'Her memory,' Bulwer replied drily, 'is equally remarkable.'

It required all her determination and arduous labour to complete a three-volume novel in four weeks from March, so that Bentley could publish it, in the following June.

Day in, day out and half the night she sat at her desk covering page after page with scarcely any alteration, until six hundred of the nine hundred and eighty pages were ready for the printers.

*The Repealers*, her first attempt at serious fiction, brought nothing like the success of her *Conversation* series. Although it aroused universal indignation, purporting to deal with Irish politics, it was in fact a satire on the vanities and follies of Irish and English social life, with particularly clever and easily recognizable sketches of London hostesses. It is obvious that 'the Blessington woman' was taking a mischievous revenge on those good ladies who had systematically denigrated, ignored her and virulently attacked her reputation.

Lady Charleville (Lady Abbeville) features in a pastiche that presents her as : 'A woman of fashion in Ireland and a

complaisant follower of women of fashion in England . . .
She knew everything that was going on everywhere and
possessed a power of ubiquity as extraordinary as her
loquacity . . .'

Those who were victimized could not answer back since
there was no obvious derogation in the thinly disguised
characters. If Lady Charleville recognized herself she may
have been uncomfortably reminded how she brought to old
Lady Mountjoy the news that embroiled her son, Tullamoore, with Harriet d'Orsay and stirred up scandal enough
to keep tongues wagging for a month. Contrary to the
wicked little caricatures that pricked but did not draw
blood at which her pen was adept, the author of *The
Repealers* goes to the other extreme in fulsome flattery of
well-known men who were her frequent visitors at Seamore Place, and of her personal friends. Among them
Bulwer figures largely; and Disraeli, who had already made
a hit with his novels, but had yet to become a shining star
in the political galaxy.

Bulwer's wife, Rosina, is described by Lady Oriel (Blessington) as 'The wife of our most popular writer and one of
the very few perfect specimens of Irish beauty . . . Hair like
the wing of a raven with the sun's rays full on it, skin white
as the driven snow and with eyes of heaven's own blue . . .'

It is not surprising that rodomontade such as this should
have earned her condemnatory reviews. Madden, her
biographer, and one of the visitors at the Blessingtons in
Genoa, calls it cuttingly 'her first and worst novel . . '

Writing at such high speed she could scarcely have
expected more or even as much recognition; and if it had
not been for her name that, since her marriage, had always
attracted attention whether favourable or not, she might
have begun and ended her career with her 'first and worst'.
But there were others than Madden who recognized the
book as one that might be followed by possible money-
spinners, despite the small sales of this one. However, the
four hundred pounds she had received for *The Repealers*

recompensed her for its tepid reception; and when the publicity it had gained and the continued popularity of her *Conversations* brought her the offer of an editorship on a recently published annual, *The Book of Beauty*, she believed herself set fair for success in her chosen career.

The fashion for annuals had started about ten years before; they were presented as gift books, richly bound in morocco and sold in thousands at Christmas. Large sums were paid to the contributors, most of whom, writers and illustrators, bore well-known names.

The second volume of the *Book of Beauty* made its appearance in the autumn of 1833 with Lady Blessington established as editress.

At once she took upon herself complete control with boundless energy and determination to make a success of herself as a writer. She knew that publication of this kind depended partly on attractive production but chiefly on a judicious selection of contributors who would appeal both to a feminine public and to more erudite readers.

This hardy annual, the *Book of Beauty*, which was to flourish for several years, had been promoted and financed by one Charles Heath, a notable engraver. In appointing the Countess of Blessington as editress, Heath must have realized not only the snob value of a title, but that her many female detractors would buy copies solely out of curiosity to see what 'the Blessington' had to say in her 'vicious caricatures', as they described the portraiture of some of them in *The Repealers*.

But she had no intention of carrying into her editorial pages her revenge against those who had so long maligned her. Heath, having chosen her as commander-in-chief of his annual, left her to deal with it. He had complete confidence in her ability to draw contributors into her net – which he described as 'your elegant spider's web to entice large or small flies into your parlour' – her 'parlour' being her red-and-gold drawing-room at Seamore Place. One of the most important of these 'flies' was Landor, who on a visit to

London had been lured into allowing two of his *Imaginary Conversations* to be included in the *Book of Beauty*. Edward Bulwer was another whose name alone would have ensured large sales. She also included a few carefully selected illustrators as well as some items of her own verse and prose signed in her name but not necessarily her own, having possibly been found in dead and gone editions of unknown authors of the past, elaborated by herself.

The gathering of material for the first annual combined with her own prolific output began to tell on her health. More than ever she must exert herself as the hostess *par excellence* to arrange her dinners, her soirées, and to select guests as likely contributors. There must be no falling off of the reputation for good dinners and good wine which Greville had so grudgingly allowed her; and with d'Orsay to charm and assist as host there was no lack of an appreciative attendance at her dinners, conversazioni and soirées for which she had made her name among men of distinction. All these were invited to her editorial 'web'.

Long after her entertainments were over and the last guests gone, she would return to her work. In order to avoid distraction she had removed her writing-desk to a remote room at the back of the house that had been used for storage.

Because of her limited income and the necessity of supplying her Power dependants in Ireland with enough to live on in comfort, she had been forced greatly to reduce her domestic staff but she retained her personal maid Anne Cooper. Anne, who had been with her for years and was devoted to her, told Madden in later years:

'She would labour day and night for money to meet her expenses and maintain her establishment and how she was called on to assist her family nobody knew but me! . . . No woman was ever so loaded with such as called themselves her friends and so many being hypocrites! No woman was so wickedly abused . . .'

After one long night's session at her work and proof

reading for the forthcoming issue of the *Book of Beauty* in the November of that year, 1833, when, exhausted with the effort to appear at dinner her gay and lively self, and forced to hear Bulwer's whispered confidences about his misery with Rosina; of the pending separation which always discussed between them, had not yet been finalized; had listened to Disraeli's flattery and braggadocio and how he had told Lord Melbourne, who asked him what he wanted to be, and had answered him: 'I want to be Prime Minister . . . He didn't think I meant it!' drawled Disraeli, but I did, and – I will! . . .' How tired she was, how utterly wearied of having to keep the social ball rolling, to engage the interest of those she wished to ensnare for contribution to the annual in the coming year; how to fulfil Heath's expectations of her should this year's annual prove a success, to give her a rise in salary. And while concentrating on the proofs before her and correcting printers' errors, her head nodded, she dozed . . . and dreamed, or did she? What was that shattering of glass, the creaking of footsteps, that stealthy silence and then a night bird's cry – or what?

She started up, awake, alert . . . Instinctively she went to pull the bell-rope forgetting that this sparsely furnished room, unused until lately, had no bell. The servants slept in their own attic quarters. The night was moonless, dark; no sound more than that distant bird's cry and the far-off voice of the watchman calling the hour: 'Half past two o' the clock in the morning . . .'

Something, some inner sense told her to go downstairs to the corridor that led to the ground floor rooms and her own sitting-room. The doors of both were open, but the butler always closed the doors at night.

Entering her sitting-room she saw that the curtains at one of the tall windows had been ripped from its pelmet; a pane of glass lay shattered on the carpet, pictures had been torn from the walls, occasional tables overturned, bereft of priceless objects d'art and bric-à-brac. The communicating

214

door of the drawing-room also was open, and here the same upheaval told its tale . . . Burglars! A robbery! . . . Everything portable had been stolen, exquisite pieces that Blessington had collected and given her, gone! . . . And, she suddenly remembered, all was uninsured! Not that intrinsic loss mattered compared to this cruel blow, depriving her of all she had held dear in memory of him she had been used to call her 'Blessing'. But that for some unfathomable reason he had bestowed on d'Orsay all that should rightly have been hers she felt no resentment; yet she often asked herself: Where did I fail him? Why am I doomed to fail those I love and in what way? If fail I did, or if they did, or do not, fail me . . .

A small object caught her eye half hidden in the fold of a rug that had been thrown aside by the thieves. She knelt and lifted it. A gold snuff box, his favourite. Some few grains of bergamot still lingered there. Then tears smarted and fell. So small a token left to her . . . of him.

## NINE

The first *Book of Beauty* met with an immediate success selling thousands of copies, to the delight of Charles Heath, who at once raised the salary of his editress. Her *Conversations of Bryon* were equally successful, notwithstanding the chorus of repetition concerning its doubtful authenticity from those who would seize on any chance to malign her, saying she never had more to do with Byron than a passing word or two, if indeed she had ever met him – all the same snarling litany slung at her as before. Yet the *Conversations* when published in book form became a best-seller. The sales were redoubled, reprinted and devoured by a public who would seize on any account of him who had been and still was their idol.

At last the harassed Lady of Seamore Place could relax from the ever present anxiety of making frayed ends meet. But there could be no cessation of work, for she must fulfil her contract with Heath and show him that his faith in her as his money-spinner was justified. None the less she could now enter upon a period of tranquility. Her entertainments were no longer snares to entrap possible contributors for her annuals. Nor was she now entirely unaided in the exigent demands of editorship, of ceaseless correspondence and continuous research for adequate material. She invited her brother Robert's daughter Ellen to give her some secretarial assistance and live with her at Seamore Place, an arrangement that resulted in the life-long devotion of her niece.

Her friendship with Bulwer had intermittently progressed since their first meeting two years before and was now cemented by their mutual sympathy, for both suffered from the bitter stabs of jealousy. And when in June 1833 Bulwer's novel *Godolphin*, published anonymously, only Lady Blessington was allowed to know the identity of the author, until its dedication to d'Orsay in a reprint declared: 'When the parentage of Godolphin was still unknown and unconfessed you were pleased to encourage his first struggles with the world . . .' Why Bulwer should have dedicated the book to d'Orsay is inexplicable, for he was surely the last person to have encouraged the world-famous Bulwer with his 'first struggles', if he ever did struggle, born to wealth with success destined to him. The only explanation that could reasonably account for this choice of dedication was that Bulwer wished to avoid any connection with Lady Blessington in those chapters of the novel that deal with the fashionable life of social London.

She was now set fair to becoming a celebrity, not as the mistress of d'Orsay nor as the unfaithful wife of the defunct Blessington, nor as the woman whose equivocal past and notorious present barred her from decent society, but as a novelist of literary merit. Whether a century later any such distinction would be attributed to her is doubtful, for even her closest adherents could not allow her more than to damn with faintest praise her *Repealers*.

During this period of comparative calm after the storms and uncertainties of the previous years she was engaged on writing a successor to *The Repealers*. Again Bulwer's influence served to obtain with Saunders and Otlay, a new firm of publishers, the production of this second novel, entitled *The Two Friends*. There was no necessity now for her to rush through hundreds of pages in a few weeks. She could take her time between the onerous duties of editorship and her more leisurely hours of entertaining; nor were her invitations extended chiefly to possible contributors to her *Book of Beauty;* her doors were open to newcomers other than those who might be of use to her professionally. Among these, with a letter of introduction from Landor while on a visit to Florence, was a young American journalist, one Nathaniel Parker Willis.

He had been sending reports on his European travels to his paper, the *New York Mirror*, giving lively accounts of the places and people he had met; and as the names of Lady Blessington and d'Orsay had already reached America to be seized by avid newsmongers, he readily accepted an invitation to call on her ladyship at Seamore Place which followed his note enclosing Landor's letter of introduction.

He was a self-possessed, self-satisfied young man, with a round cherubic face, a mouthful of smiling teeth, and an observant eye for impressions to be mentally inscribed for his weekly reports to the *Mirror*.

He arrived at Seamore Place on an afternoon which was not one of the lady's days for entertaining, and found her alone. Because she saw at once that the young American had come neither to criticize nor to condemn her, she could meet him without reserve or suspicion of what he might relay to his editor concerning her and d'Orsay. And so with this bland, forthcoming American she could be her natural, friendly, uninhibited self. When d'Orsay arrived at the same time as the butler with tea, Willis was at once only slightly less enslaved by the Frenchman's charm than by that of his hostess.

In his account of this first meeting with her he wrote: 'My eyes were busy finishing for memory a portrait of the celebrated and beautiful woman before me . . .' A memory that served to portray her more favourably than have her various biographers, who may not have had the advantage of seeing her described by Willis as: 'A merry, captivating Irish woman who frankly confessing to forty, looks something on the sunny side of thirty . . .'

His memorizing eye noting a portrait of her by Sir Thomas Lawrence, 'which is' (he grows lyrical) 'a representation full of loveliness and love, the kind of creature with whose divine sweetness the gazer's heart aches . . .'

218

gives evidence that Willis, as others before him, had lost
*his* heart to her 'who had never a heart to return' . . .

His rhapsodies are inexhaustible. 'Her person is full,'
(she was inclined now to embonpoint and suffered a strict
diet) but according to Willis, 'she preserves all the fineness
of an admirable shape; her foot in a satin slipper a Cinderella might look for in vain; her complexion is of a girlish
delicacy and freshness. Her dress of blue satin, cut low and
folded across her bosom, shows to advantage the round and
sculpturelike curve and whiteness of a pair of exquisite
shoulders . . . Her features are regular and her mouth, the
most expressive of them, has a ripe fullness and freedom of
play peculiar to the Irish physiognomy. Add to all this a
voice merry and sad by turns and you have the prominent
traits of the most lovely and fascinating women I have ever
seen.'

When this flamboyant account of his first meeting with
Lady Blessington reached the gossip columns of London
magazines, Willis was attacked as having made copy out of
a social and private encounter. And she in turn was
criticized by her feminine rivals in having used the American for her own 'vulgar publicity'.

She must have laughed with d'Orsay over the extravagant hyperbole of Willis and named him the 'Yankee
Noodle'; but although she could never surrender herself to
the men she victimized, she would not discourage their
admiration, however blatantly exaggerated it might have
been.

When, after his first visit to Seamore Place Willis called
again the next day, he found her surrounded by several
men, no women; and these, as he at once realized, would
offer more copy for his London and New York papers.

There was Bulwer's brother Henry, future chargé
d'affaires at the British Embassy in Paris, already *persona
grata* in diplomatic circles and greatly disapproving of his
famous brother's radicalism. There was also Albany

Fonblanque, editor of the *Examiner*, but Willis was naturally more interested in the brother of Edward.

He gives a more pleasing impression of Henry than of the famous Edward who came in later. Henry he describes as 'small, very slight and gentlemanlike, a little pitted with the small-pox and of very winning and pleasing manners'.

When Edward arrived he was effusively welcomed by 'the splendid person of Count d'Orsay'. Willis found him to be something of a disappointment. He tells us: 'I had made up my mind how he should look, but no two things could be more unlike than the real Mr Bulwer . . . *Imprimis*, the gentleman who entered was not handsome . . . He is short, very much bent in the back, slightly knock-kneed and as ill-dressed a man for a gentleman as you will find in London. His figure is slight and very badly put together. His nose is aquiline and far too large for proportion though he conceals its prominence by an immense pair of red whiskers . . .'

This description of Bulwer contradicts the various reports of his dandiacal tastes, and more particularly the drawing of him by d'Orsay, who gives him a handsome profile and a nose that does not appear to be 'far too large'. But Willis admits that he 'liked his manners extremely, a more good-natured habitually smiling expression could hardly be imagined.' This belies the moody, irritable Bulwer who poured his marital grievances into the sympathetic ear of his 'Dearest Lady Blessington'.

The evening passed well into the early hours of the morning and the talk, as is habitual with literary folk, was centred on the writing of their books, of publishers, and of reviewers of whom Bulwer said he 'would rather go in disguise than hear the opinion of people who judged him neither as a Member of Parliament nor a dandy – simply a book-maker'.

Asked if he kept an amanuensis, 'No,' he said, 'I scribble it all out myself and send it to the press, half print and half hieroglyphic, and correct the proofs much to the dissatisfaction of my publisher, who sends me a bill of sixteen pounds six shillings and fourpence for extra corrections . . . Then I am free to confess I don't know grammar. Lady Blessington, do you know grammar? *I detest grammar . . .*'

Whether Lady Blessington also detested grammar is not recorded, nor if she would answer that question was she given a chance to do so, for Bulwer, always more interested in the sound of his own voice than in another's, went rattling on.

'I wonder what they did for grammar before Lindley Murray.' (Nobody commented on that one because it is unlikely any of them had heard of Lindley Murray, even had they the opportunity to admit it.) 'Oh, the delicious blunders one sees when they are irretrievable! Thank heaven for second editions that one may scratch out his blots and go down clean to posterity.'

One of the company inquired if he ever reviewed his own books, to which he answered emphatically: 'No. But I could! And then *how* I should like to recriminate and defend myself indignantly!'

To which Lady Blessington may have silently agreed since, despite the good sales, her work had not been so well reviewed. Willis too was less impressed with her latest book *The Two Friends* than with her 'divine sweetness that had made his heart ache'.

Of *The Two Friends*, just published, he said: 'It has made a great noise. Living as she does in the midst of the most brilliant and mind-exhausting circles in London I wonder how she finds the time . . . Her novels sell for a hundred pounds more than any other author's except Bulwer's . . .'

His travel letters to the *New York Mirror* were so peppered with references to Lady Blessington and in such glowing terms of her personality, her beauty, her charm and her 'assemblage of men of genius, the only Republic of letters in the world', that he had qualms as to how the more puritanical of his readers in the United States would regard his panegyrics of London society; also her ladyship's intimacy with Bulwer and other 'men of genius'.

Willis therefore made copious cuts for the American edition of what he called his *Pencillings by the Way*. Unfortunately one of the more popular national British Press had read the articles when they were issued in three-volume book form in England before any abridgements had been made. Its appearance created a stir of indignation among the most prominent of Lady Blessington's 'Republic of letters'.

If d'Orsay could never have enough publicity whether eulogistic or not, Bulwer took great exception to having his name bandied in the gossip columns of the American newsheets. The frequent allusions to Lady Blessington she also found embarrassing, but was not disposed to protest against them, for she had no wish to draw further attention to herself and her friendship with d'Orsay, Bulwer and others, already so often misconstrued.

But Bulwer, in a lengthy and verbose letter to Willis, was at pains to express his disgust at the liberties taken with his name, in that he was, as he wrathfully asserted: 'A very fair subject for public exhibition, and that he looked with reprehension upon the principle of feeding frivolous and unworthy persons of the public from the sources which the privilege of hospitality opens to us in private life . . .'

There are three pages more of it couched in mounting exacerbation and concluding with 'the great disservice you [Willis] have done to your countrymen in this visit to England, and that in future we shall shrink from any claimants on our hospitality'. But in more concise and unrestrained indignation he relieved himself to Lady Blessington.

'Of all damnable impertinence that this Yankee should come here and write about all of us – you, I, and others. D'Orsay, of course, laps it all up as he always does if there is any reference to him in the press here, there or anywhere, but you may not have seen what he – this Yank – wrote to me when we first met him here, describing me more or less as a hump-back with a monumental nose —'

'No,' she interrupted stifling laughter, 'he was warm in praise of you, er, your good looks and you – um – your genius and —'

'He said I had red hair,' cut in the irate Bulwer, 'red whiskers he called them.' He stroked the auburn decoration he had cultivated on either side of his face; 'and he said I had the manners of a schoolboy.'

'No, he said you greeted us all with the joyous heartiness of a boy let out of school . . .'

'I don't care what he said of my manners, but I do object to his unwarrantable invasion – as I wrote to him – of the inviolable decorum of London Society which must render us more than ever on our guard against acquaintances from the other side of the Atlantic who return courtesies of our country with caricatures in another.'

To which she told him equably: 'Don't make mountains out of journalistic molehills.'

Unappeased, he tramped about her drawing-room in anything but the cool and calculated ominously polite Bulwer who had written a three-page letter to Willis.

'I told him,' Bulwer swung round on her as she still struggled against inward laughter, 'that is I *wrote* it, that in future I'd see him in hell before I would see him in *my* house!'

'You didn't write that, of course,' he was reminded by her to whom a contrite and apologetic Willis had shown Bulwer's letter.

She had all to do to prevent him from falling abjectly at her feet as he had fallen abjectly in love with her: 'The most lovely fascinating and exquisite etc' whom he had so rhapsodically depicted her in his letters to New York.

But as to his estimate of her sales which far exceeded those of other authors with exception of Bulwer, this was a great exaggeration. That her novels sold well but not to much profit, as she had sold the copyrights, was due to her notorious name rather than to her merit as a writer. However she was content to earn the salary Bentley now gave her for editing the *Book of Beauty*, and enjoyed her elevation to the ranks of authorship. If not regarded as a leading light in literature at least, as Charles Greville spitefully recorded, 'She provides us with those gorgeous inanities called the "Books of Beauty" and other trashy things of the same description. And so, by all this puffing and stuffing and practising on the vanities of some, the end is attained . . .'

To console her for this and similar disparagement she was thankful for Bulwer's confidence in her and in her work and also for Disraeli's friendship. That d'Orsay had now returned to her as if there had been no breach between them was further compensation. He could never see himself in the wrong nor could he believe he had been directly responsible for their separation. The lawsuit, still undecided, concerning Gardiner's dispute over Blessington's Will, did not at all affect d'Orsay. He lived as extravagantly as ever, belonged to all the best clubs, was continually at Crockford's playing deep and losing high. It was said that on one occasion he borrowed ten pounds from a friend as he had been played out, and the next day accosted him at Crockford's and thrust several hundred pounds' worth of notes at him, saying: 'Prenez, mon ami. These are yours — what I win with the ten pounds you lend me! . . .'

His dress became more than ever remarkable and was emulated by all his younger followers. He lived far beyond his income until the final settlement by the Court of Chancery should prove Blessington's Will valid and he the rightful legatee.

But on the assumption that all would be decided in his favour he mortgaged his inheritance up to the hilt, ignoring his lady's warning of the consequences that might result from such reckless expenditure.

His establishment in Curzon Street was on a par with the fabulous luxury of the Blessington household during the late Earl's lifetime, while his widow, striving to keep

224

up appearances, 'slaved away', as she put it, at her desk from midnight till after her guests had gone.

Her 'slavery' brought enough financial reward to enable her to tide d'Orsay over his more immediate debts; and in the summer of 1834 she was completing her next annual *Book of Beauty* to be shipped to America, India and the colonies. With the British sales Heath was again enabled to increase her salary, but her success as journalist and novelist gained her less monetary advantage than feminine envy. Her intimacy with men of literary and political distinction, and the consistent avoidance by their women of 'that Blessington creature' who because of her piquant language the more correct ladies of fashion were pleased to call her 'the Countess of Cursington'. Greville's persistent attacks, for his knife – or rather his pen – could dig deep, described her as 'ignorant, vulgar and commonplace'; and her work as 'this trash that goes down in America because it is written by a Countess', probably helped more to increase the sales of her work than any warm praise from her would-be – and always frustrated – lovers.

It is possible, as his letters written to her from Ireland bear witness, that Bulwer was one of these. He had recently fled from Rosina since their latest and most shattering brawl after the publication of the *Last Days of Pompeii*.

'I cannot tell you what pleasure I felt in my solitude first at the sight of your handwriting, next at the praise, and above all at the sympathy of a friend.'

He goes on to tell her of how he has suffered, presumably from marital rows, . . . 'So that I feel at times thoroughly overpowered not by any ordinary melancholy but by a profound dejection which leaves me literally crushed and helpless . . . This letter, my dear friend, is for your eyes only. There is a grand and true saying of yours, "There are a few before whom one would condescend to appear anything but happy" . . .'

This correspondence between them continued for several

weeks while he sought her sympathy and, without absolutely committing himself, he wrote:

'I have to thank you for the most beautiful snuff-box I have ever seen . . .' She has evidently sent him her husband's snuff-box that the thieves who burgled her room had dropped in their hurry to escape. Yes, she cared enough for him to give him that treasured memento of which he tells her: 'I shall bequeath it to my boy as a token of the pride and affection his father has felt in one of the few friendships he ever permitted himself to form . . . unbroken by a single shade of insincerity or wrong.'

His criticism on publication of *The Two Friends* which to a less infatuated critic may have been less deserving of his praise. He finds her novel, 'most charming, it cannot fail to please universally. It is written in a thoroughly good tone and spirit; very elegant and sustained . . .'

For him it could have been not so much 'sustained' as 'restrained', for in another letter he tells her: 'You do not like to paint the passion of love . . . In writing we should see nothing before us but our own wild hearts . . .'

If this declaration offered her his 'own wild heart', it failed to induce in her a 'passion of love' that, had such passion not been destroyed in her young girlhood, might have stirred her to a late awakening.

Having been advised by her doctor to take a rest from overwork, for she was feeling the effects of those late nights, 'burning my candle at both ends', as she told her niece Ellen Power, who promised to look after all her correspondence while she was away, she took a short holiday in Hampshire. But although only a few miles from the house of her former protector Jenkins she made certain that in her walks and drives she would avoid his estate. However, for all her care, on one occasion when driving through the New Forest she told her coachman to stop, having seen a mist of bluebells, and went to gather some. The sound of a horse's hooves muffled on the moss caught her ear. She looked up.

It was Jenkins, whom she had not seen for these . . . how long . . . fifteen years?

He recognized her at once, and dismounting raised his hat and came to greet her.

'History repeats itself.' He took her hand that held a bunch of wild flowers. 'This is the second time I have come upon you in a wood.'

'Only it wasn't a wood. It was a wayside.'

'Where you had fallen?'

'Yes. I had – fallen by the wayside, all those years ago and you – you raised me up from where I fell.'

Loosening her hand he turned to hitch his horse's bridle to his arm and said:

'Do you walk here? I see your carriage waiting.'

'I – yes.' She looked at him sideways, a small smile on her lips. 'My carriage can wait. It is seldom we are given a backward glimpse at our lives that have come to us out of the past.'

He looked down at her who was looking up at him. She saw that his hair, uncovered by his hat before he had replaced it, had greyed. The once firmly articulated line of jaw and cheekbone had been somewhat lost in a thickness half hidden in his high cravat; but his eyes showed no trace of time in their unfaded blue. She remembered him as if forgetfulness had not eclipsed the years.

'What do you here in this remote part of the world?' he asked her. 'When you left me – how long ago? Was it ten – twenty years – or yesterday, for you are unchanged as the day I saw you leave me with Blessington.'

'Why am I here?' She answered him. 'It just happened that I chose to take a breathing space away from my work. And Hampshire holds nostalgic memories and so I – I came.'

'But not to see me. You stayed away from me?'

'I did so.' She lifted the nosegay of bluebells, violets and late primroses to her lips. 'I did not care to force open a closed window.'

'Closed?' he echoed, nodding. 'It is always difficult to open a window that has remained closed year in, year out, all weathers. Its frame will become swollen in rain or wintry frosts and warped by summer's heat . . . So best not to force it.'

Pacing beside her, his steps slowed to keep time with hers and leading his horse, he continued after a pause: 'My window was never shut. I saw you always through its glass – not darkly – all these years. I followed your life without me, I applauded your success and grieved with you when you were widowed. I read – and with what pride – of your achievements. It was when I had the – the care of you I dared believe that I – or the contents of my library – helped you to find yourself.'

'Oh, yes!' Impulsively; and slid her hand in his as she was used to do when they walked through his woods together. 'You did – you *did* help me. Had I never known you nor read with you the works of masters past and present, I might not have become what I am – nor would I have married Blessington.'

'If not him, perhaps —' he hesitated, '– perhaps you would have married me?'

She shook her head. 'If you hadn't taken me away from my father and my hateful life, for it was in your house I met Blessington, I could never have known you as I – as I did come to know you. I think that destiny *does* shape our ends. I believe all that happens to us is ordained.'

'You are a fatalist?'

'I may be – No, not in the sense that Fate, or accident, controls our lives. We have been given our own will to choose the way that God – or whoever it is – dominates us from our birth to death. And I believe that our lives here on earth are but a trial, a test of our weakness or our strength to prove ourselves worthy of death.'

'Worthy of – death?' he repeated, half questioning, half meditatively. 'Is death for you worth while? Do you not

feel it is an end to all that our lives have shaped? An end –
or a beginning?'

'Yes, sure 'tis a beginning. I read somewhere, or I may
have thought it, but it is a lovelier thought than I could
have imagined – that death is our birthday in heaven.'

He turned the hand he held upward to drop a kiss in its
palm.

'You have not changed. The same soft warm little trace
of the Irish in your voice, and the mist of Ireland's blue in
your eyes, that are neither blue nor grey but the colour
mistakenly called violet – and you are ever as young as
you were, to speak of life and death with the ripple of a
laugh. You were always on the verge of a laugh even when
most serious.'

She said, with a catch in her voice:

'You have made an image of me that I could not have
been. I was, as I remember – always rather uncertain, never
sure of myself. I had so much to have made me – afraid of –
of life and —'

'Not afraid of me?' he broke in quickly. 'Were you afraid
of me?'

'No! Oh no, not of you but of men – not *you*, but just
because you were a man.'

'Yes,' he said quietly. 'I understand. And you have never
lost that fear?'

She hesitated before replying:

'Not the fear of man but of what he might – want of me.'

'And which,' he told her, 'is what all men want of you
and that you can never give.' He stayed his walk. The horse
stopped too. He mounted and leaned from the saddle to
brush her forehead with his lips.

'You are and always will be a riddle – an unsolved riddle
of a woman. A sleeping beauty who has never been
awakened.'

She looked up at him.

'You could not have spoken like that to me in the old
days.'

'I have had a wife since then.'

'I heard that too. Are you happy?'

'What is happiness? A vapour, a passing whim, or a whimsy – or a wishful thought? Yes, I had a modicum of happiness. She died. And I am alone again – and childless.'

She had nothing to say to that, and stood watching him ride away until he was lost between the green aisles of the forest; then she walked slowly back to her waiting carriage at the entrance of the wood thinking: I too am alone and childless. Had I known him as he is or seems to be now, would I have been different, or would I have remained always . . . a riddle of a woman? . . .

*　　*　　*

On her return to London she began to write her third novel, *Confessions of an Elderly Gentleman* and was in haste to complete it before the lease of the house in Seamore Place should terminate, for she decided she would not renew it. Its situation in the heart of fashionable London had been chosen by her when she had contemplated leading the life of a lady of leisure as Margaret, Countess of Blessington, widow of a wealthy Member of the House of Lords. But as the ostracism she endured from the women of society had increased since her husband's death so did her income greatly decrease. Moreover, as Seamore Place with the comings and goings of carriages to Hyde Park, did not give her the quiet she desired she felt she should remove herself to a more rural neighbourhood without a complete withdrawal to the country.

There was also d'Orsay to be considered. She must persuade him to live less extravagantly until he could be certain that Gardiner's suit should fail to prove Blessington's Will invalid, for she could not continue to reimburse him as she had been doing on the strength of his plea for a loan lost and seldom won on the green baize at Crockford's. His grandmother, at last aware of his profligacy, was disinclined to give him more money to fritter away. He had of late been exploiting his talent for portraiture as a lucrative concern and now charged fees to his friends who asked him to draw or paint them. He was thus enabled to pay off the least of his debts. But the greater part of these were still accumulating and he was hard put to it to keep at bay the most pressing of his creditors. They all knew the extent of his inheritance should Blessington's Will be proved valid, and he borrowed from the bearded gentlemen of St Mary Axe at a golden interest.

Besides his portraits that were gaining popularity, he had developed a taste for sculpture. He made a bust of the Duke of Wellington and a drawing of the Iron Duke on horseback giving him an enormous nose and a remarkable and unlikely horse that evoked much comment, mostly unfavourable, explained by d'Orsay as the 'last t'ing in modern sculpture that give the spirit – voyez-vous – of the model, more than the exact likeness, isn't it?'

None the less those men who were not enamoured of him did in fact detest him, libelled his efforts as 'fakes and not his own work but that of a mendicant who was on his beam ends and to whom d'Orsay paid a pittance to do what he was unable to do himself'.

But he continued to excite the interest not only of the *ton*, but others of more importance with whom he had come in contact and who amusingly wrote their accounts and reminiscences of him, which may have gone far to make of him a legend. Among these was Captain Gronow, who said his artistic talent although undeniable, was 'somewhat too gaudy . . . When I used to see him driving in his tilbury I fancied he looked like some gorgeous dragon-fly skimming through the air . . . All his imitators fell between the Scylla and Charybdis of tigerism and charlatanism.'

And Carlyle, to whom he was introduced by a mutual friend, said: 'This Phoebus Apollo of dandyism came whirling hither in a chariot that struck all Chelsea into mute admiration with its splendour.'

Of d'Orsay's splendour, 'Poor d'Orsay!' as Mrs Carlyle

recalls him, 'he was born to be something better than the King of the Dandies. His wit, I suppose, is of the sort that belongs more to animal spirit than to real genius . . .'

None could have thought him a genius, unless it were that he contrived to live in 'splendour' without paying for it. The tradition of his promiscuous gallantries was circulated by disappointed women and perhaps by those of his favourite men who insinuated if he were not hermaphroditic he preferred their intimate friendship rather than that of any woman unless it were Lady Blessington, of whom they spoke as his 'mother'. Indeed some did actually believe him to be her son as the result of a youthful indiscretion. This is an absurdity promulgated by the scandalmongers who would seize on any malicious inference to besmirch her name.

The withdrawal from Seamore Place to the comparative isolation of a village on the outskirts of London was not wholly due to the desire for peace and quiet that she might work uninterruptedly at 'my scribbles', as she called her writing, but because her ostracism from feminine society made it difficult to ignore her defeat. As the wife of Lord Blessington she had been sheltered by his name and lawful protection; as his widow and the prey of all men whether or not she responded to a capture, condemned her in the eyes of the Ladies Jersey, Charleville, Mountjoy and others as a 'wanton'. Therefore, flaunting her indifference to slander she avoided all encounter with those who would malign her.

The house she chose in Kensington, for which negotiations were completed in 1835, had been the residence of Wilberforce for several years until he died three weeks before his campaign against slavery had become law. It stood behind high walls in three acres of grounds well back from the road and occupied the site on which eventually the Albert Hall would be built.

Although the hostess of Seamore Place had let it be known she was forced, for reasons of economy, to leave

232

London, there were no signs of economy in the expenditure lavished on the redecorations as befitted a country mansion in contrast to the smaller house in Mayfair.

She had a gift for interior decoration, and because of her continued editorship of *The Book of Beauty* and the sales, although moderate, of her novels, she felt justified in launching out on this new project.

The furnishings and colour schemes of Gore House were similar to those of Seamore Place except in the rooms that overlooked the beautiful gardens. With these she attempted to capture a rural aspect in starry-blossomed chintzes and apple-green curtains, while her writing-room, on an upstairs floor facing the road, captured the effect of sunlight to a north aspect with an old-gold carpet, yellow curtains and chair covers.

Her greatest satisfaction in this secluded retreat was her garden. Here she could indulge her love of flowers to her heart's content. The terrace along the south bank was planted with lilac and hydrangeas; roses were profuse in the numerous flower beds. On the lawns enclosed in high red-brick walls she could walk undisturbed, and followed by the dogs which London traffic had denied her, she also adopted various other pets including a talking crow that lived in a portable cage indoors and could be moved from room to room. He would shriek 'Up boys and at 'em!' to the delight of the Duke of Wellington, one of her many admirers, who would drive out from his house at the gates of Hyde Park to enjoy tea in her library with its white-painted book shelves.

But her chief hobby was the keeping of a variety of birds in an aviary, and provided one of the great attractions for visitors to Gore House which she would display with pride; and to Wellington, one of her most frequent visitors, she said:

'I abhor the caging of wild birds, as when a young girl, I saw in our market place at Clonmel a pedlar selling caged songsters – a lark and a robin. I rescued the robin, but the lark died. All these you see here were bred in captivity.'

'A splendid home for them,' remarked the hero of Waterloo, inclining an ear to her, for in his late sixties he was growing deaf, though he would never admit it. 'Clonmel did ye say?'

She nodded. 'I was born at Knockbrit and we moved to Clonmel when I was about seven.'

'Clonmel,' he repeated. 'Born there were ye?'

'No,' repeating it louder. 'I was born at Knockbrit in County Tipperary.'

'So ye're Irish! So'm I – born in County Meath. 'Tis a good island is the Emerald Isle and it breeds a good run of soldiers – also Peel's Peelers. D'ye know half of them are Irish? . . . That's a fine pair o' gold and silver pheasants ye have there.'

'This one —' She opened a door in the aviary and holding out her hand called softly: 'Goldy, come.'

A magnificent golden pheasant flew to perch on her wrist. She offered him a biscuit from her reticule. He gently took it from her. 'Tame as you please,' she told the Duke, 'and so is this falcon. I named her Perdita because we found her lost – my gardener and I, flown from – goodness knows where, maybe the woods of Highgate. She was but a chicken then and we reared her.'

It is presumed that her house move aroused current comment, as did all her activities, mostly insulting as was this from Grantley Berkley, a well known journalist.

'In the year 1836 Gore House, previously the residence of the pious William Wilberforce, became the headquarters of the demi-monde with the Countess Blessington as their Queen.'

Bulwer, in a letter to one of his political sponsors, the radical Lord Durham who had first met him under the auspices of Lady Blessington at Seamore Place, wrote:

'She has moved into Wilberforce's old house in Kensington. It has cost her a thousand pounds in repairs, another

thousand in furniture, gardeners, two cows, and declares
with the gravest possible face that she only does it for
economy . . .' A criticism that might have been induced to
allay suspicion of a warmer interest.

No sooner had she finished with refurbishing the house
and gardens and the installation of the two cows (perhaps
another attempt at economy which, however, failed its
purpose for she found herself more than ever harassed with
tradesmen's bills), than d'Orsay, enticed by the two cows
and prospect of fresh cream daily, also foresook Mayfair
for 'the country' of Kensington Gore.

He installed himself in a house close to the entrance
gates and 'set up an aviary', as Bulwer reported, 'of the best
dressed birds in ornithology'. This was not d'Orsay's aviary
but his lady's who allowed him to believe it his, and laughed
at Bulwer's description of the pigeons 'who followed
d'Orsay's dandiacal fashion by wearing trousers down to
their claws! . . .'

Her salon at Gore House was now more than ever the
haunt of the famous or perhaps the infamous, and as always
her visitors were men.

Disraeli, a firm favourite, was much in evidence
especially when Savage Landor arrived, invited by the
Lady of Gore House to spend a few weeks or months or
whatever length of time he could spare from his family in
Florence.

Contrary to 'Dizzy's' usual conversational powers he
would sit silently listening to the exchange of talk between
Landor and his hostess on the terrace and making mental
notes of all that was said for his next novel. Among other
notabilities who enjoyed the hospitality of Gore House was
John Varley, famous in his day for watercolours. He was a
bulky giant of a man with a face described as 'shattered
rock', and had been a habitué of the Blessingtons' house in
St James's Square. More than fifteen years had passed since
Blessington's young countess had taken London's male
company by storm. Since then she had lost sight of Varley.

Now, however, he reappeared, no stranger to the hostess of Gore House, although she greeted him in her slight brogue as:

'Sure, stranger! After all these years. Where have you been that you did not come to see me for – how long is it?'

'I lose count of time,' he replied, gallantly bowing over her hand, 'when I look at you and can only see that time has passed you by. Fifteen years as if it were yesterday, for there is no sign that you are more than one day older.'

'Flatterer!' She laughed and introduced him to the circle of guests and – 'Do you know Mr Disraeli?'

'I have had that pleasure,' Varley heartily replied.

'And I too,' Disraeli offered him his jewelled fingers, 'I was one of your honoured *invités* to your private view at your exhibition at the Society of Painters.'

'And I, also,' Bulwer edged his way between them. 'I was greatly impressed with your stories of William Blake. An extraordinary man of parts, and a mystic whose death has left the world lost of a poet and artist unequalled in the past and present century.'

'That we may well believe,' chimed in Disraeli. 'I am tremendously interested in your and Blake's astrological findings.'

This opened a discussion on Varley's latest craze for the occult.

To the men who now crowded round him he discoursed at loud and gesticulatory length, his huge bulk and height towering above them while he told of marvels he had witnessed and which had been practised by those of the ancient world hundreds of years before the coming of Christ.

'Do we not learn of the Witch of Endor?' he thundered. 'And what of the prophets of the Old Testament? What did they not foresee, and tell of the Redemption?'

'But we of my religion, as a Catholic,' said d'Orsay, 'I do not believe in these spirits who do speak to us from the dead.'

'But there are no dead,' was Varley's objection to that. 'Those who speak to us are the living. Only a veil separates us from them who have passed over to the Other Side.'

There was a buzz of interest from all, including Disraeli who enjoined Varley to give some instances of 'this science you have resurrected from ancient times'.

Whereupon the company, escorted by their hostess, trooped to the library. There, seated at a round table, Varley recounted in particular to Bulwer for whom mysticism held a peculiar fascination, how he had foretold the date of a friend's death on the very day he died without any symptom of previous illness. 'As for Blake,' continued Varley, eyes upraised as if in communion with a lurking emanation, 'he would summon to his presence the very persons of Moses, David, Mark Antony and Julius Caesar and would at once proceed to draw their portraits.'

'Remarkable!' breathed Bulwer; echoed by Disraeli with a twist of his lips and a slanting smile at his hostess who sat, hands folded under a chin that showed the slightest inclination to duplicate itself despite the daily care for her diet. 'Truly remarkable,' repeated Disraeli. 'Do you resort to a crystal in order to foresee – whatever is unforeseeable to lesser visionaries?'

'No. I am privileged to investigate the truth of my visions without the aid of a crystal, as did Blake who executed some fifty such drawings for my interest, especially the most curious of any, which was the ghost,' said Varley gazing round upon his listeners with eyes that looked to be protruding from their sockets, 'the ghost,' he repeated, 'of a flea!'

A silence followed this singular pronouncement broken by a sound from Disraeli as of a hiccup which was hastily smothered in a handkerchief.

'I can see him now,' proceeded Varley, 'as though he were before me —' Everyone looked round and about in some trepidation as if to see a spectral Blake glide through the closed door. 'While immersed in his drawing of a flea,' proceeded Varley, 'he explained to me that the apparition of the flea had told him that all fleas were bloodthirsty beings reincarnated in the size and shape of insects. This is the theosophical belief that the eternal spirit can be manifest through an evolutionary process in various forms according to the manner of its life, good or bad, until eventually it becomes one with the universal brotherhood of man, perfected.'

'Which is to say,' Bulwer was tremendously impressed, 'that this flea Blake drew for you was passing through a form of expiation for the sins of its previous existence.'

'Yes, that would seem to be so,' agreed Varley.

'Incroyable!' exclaimed d'Orsay. 'I am glad that in this life in which I now am – what do you call it – a reincarnation – is not so bad or so sanguinaire as to make of me a flea revenant in my next life!'

'But why,' put in Disraeli, 'is a flea manifest as of a bloodthirsty being? Why not a tiger reincarnated, since a tiger – or some of its species – is bloodthirstily man-eating and would surely drink more human blood than would be possible for the expiation of a sinful flea?'

To this Varley was not prepared to answer. He evidently resented Disraeli's flippant reaction to his mystic revelations. But Bulwer, turning to Lady Blessington, asked:

'Did you not own or have lent to you a crystal ball at one time, as I remember you told me?'

'Yes,' she assented, a trifle pale, 'I still have it. 'Twas given me by an Indian Pascha – Pascha Nazim whose family had owned it for generations. I looked in it once but —' she shuddered, 'never again.'

'Can we – can I —' urged Bulwer. 'Will you show it to me?'

Somewhat unwillingly the magic crystal was produced from a drawer in the lady's bureau.

'Let me see.' Bulwer took the crystal into his hands and gazed into it, his face darkening. 'It is cloudy. I see only –

No! I see a storm – a flash of – it might be fire – or lightning!'

'Or a reflection from the candelabra,' murmured Disraeli.

'Don't look in it,' cried Margaret. 'Give it to me – I don't like it.'

'I will take it.' Varley took the crystal that Bulwer had uneasily rendered.

'It will only offer that which is ordained,' Varley said in a deep hollow voice, 'and only those who are privileged to have the sight allowed them, may perceive what is their ultimate Karma . . .'

From Disraeli came a muttered monosyllable unheard by any save d'Orsay standing next to him. Although the word was not in common use among gentlefolk or in the presence of a lady, he had heard it many times before among Englishmen, and hearing it now *sotto voce*, he broke into a smothered laugh.

Soon after that the company left, but Bulwer lingered.

'What I saw,' said he solemnly, taking Margaret's hand in farewell, 'was an indication of what I know to be the destruction of my marriage – the last and fatal storm. It is coming.'

Within a few weeks it came. . . . The complete breach of the marriage between Bulwer and Rosina finalized in a deed of separation. They had been man and wife for nine years, were still in their early thirties and she had borne him two children. Her life took a downhill path, his ascended to heights of fame as Lord Lytton, novelist, politician, even as did Disraeli's. Both ardent radicals in their youth they became Conservative Members of Parliament; yet neither could have known as they took their leave of the Lady of Gore House on a summer's evening many years before, that they were each destined for immortality.

'Why then,' asked d'Orsay, when Bulwer had gone and he was alone with her in the library, 'why were you afraid to look into the ball of glass? Surely you do not believe in

this blague Varley speak – Mon Dieu! A flea! – quelle
bêtise; and Bulwer so big a fool as Varley. Tiens! Ils sont
sots, les deux!'

'Not such fools,' she said, 'as those who don't believe. I
saw what I fear I will live to see —' again a shiver passed
through her – 'here in this house before I ever knew of its
existence or that I should ever come to be here, I saw this
room, this very room – all bare and broken, desolate —'

'Non!' he put his arm round her, 'it is all in your imagination. We are not meant to see into the future. Ma
grand'mère she would often say to me – les choses secrètes
– the secret t'ings they belong to le bon dieu, not for us
to see ...'

It was as well that in the years to come he could not see
'the secret things' he was not meant to see.

*　　*　　*

No sooner had Lady Blessington been installed in Gore
House than she became as always the cynosure of comment, chiefly unfavourable, from those men and women
with no access to her circle. Grantley Berkely, who had
already had a snipe at her as 'Queen of the demi-monde',
followed it up with an equally insulting reference to 'the
Queen of a certain male society at Gore House lauded and
toadied by her admirers'; while another journalist, also one
of her unfavoured, put her into verse.

> Mild Wilberforce, by all beloved
> Once owned this brilliant spot
> Whose zealous eloquence improved
> The fettered negro's lot.
>
> Yet here still slavery attacks
> When Blessington invites
> The chains from which he freed the blacks
> She rivets on the whites.

As the months and years slipped by we find her more than ever immersed in her literary work and the endeavour to meet her commitments, both in the production of the *Book of Beauty* and the search for eminent contributors so that the standard she sought might be maintained and also her loans to d'Orsay.

For he still spent as recklessly as ever. He borrowed from Jews, tradesmen who sent in their quarterly bills, although content to wait in the hope that in due course the hundreds or thousands owing them would have to be paid.

Within a year or two of the removal to Gore House the formal separation between d'Orsay and his wife was completed. This meant, or so d'Orsay optimistically saw it, an end to his financial embarrassments and the ceaseless borrowings on reversions of interest from the Blessington estate.

For several years he had been living at a fabulous rate of expenditure until with a sudden hideous shock it was brought home to him that he had not the means to continue his happy-go-lucky pursuit of life. If no way out of the impasse with which he was confronted could be found, he must be thrown into bankruptcy or imprisonment – for debt!

'Quelle horreur!' To his lady he came, pale, distraught from the shattering news that Harriet – 'cette chienne! What she do to me – écoute! Read this.' He flung at her a document in which Harriet's advisers, the lawyers and trustees of her father's settlement, offered d'Orsay an ultimatum to the effect that:

'The Lady Harriet d'Orsay should buy her husband's claim on the Blessington estate for a hundred thousand pounds together with that of her brother, Charles Gardiner's income of £1000 per annum.

'To buy – me! Mon héritage! To steal from me what is mine – my right! They cannot do this to me!' Up and down her room he raged, his hair dishevelled, tears falling in mascaraed trickles from his lashes down cheeks that under the rouge were pallid. 'How can she take from me – *buy* from me! She has no money more than her income allows her – unless – ah, yes! I see it! Le Duc – c'est d'Orléans! She is his maîtresse – he give her all the money to buy from me! Nom de Nom! How am I trahi – deceived by this traitresse!'

'Calm yourself, my love,' she made attempt to soothe him. 'If this reads aright, you are offered at least a hundred – yes, a hundred thousand pounds for the estate and lands —'

'That!' He turned savagely upon her. 'That is not *mine*! I owe – with what I have borrowed from the Jews and what I have bought – or been lent in annuities on what I am to have – all gone! I will have not'ing – not'ing . . . Ruiné!'

Nothing in truth when the sum total of his debts were realized at fifty thousand more than the hundred thousand offered him by his wife.

The gutter press gave headlined news of the d'Orsay débâcle, and the most scurrilous of weeklies, *The Town*, that specialized in the intrigues of any man or woman of fashion, swooped down on d'Orsay's latest disaster. . . . 'He, having let his house and lost all of Lord Blessington's money, has gone to live with his mother, the Countess of Blessington'.

'His mother!' A deliberate jibe at the ageing mistress of a lover young enough to be her son. He, at her advice, had let his rented house and moved to her establishment nearby that he might reduce his current expenses and manage to exist at *her* expense on the £500 a year which was still his due, and had been paid to him during the long litigation of the Court of Chancery's inquiries.

With the transfer to Gore House he was relieved of the immediate anxiety of debts that must be met by the hundred thousand paid to him for relinquishing his inheritance; and he took up residence under his Lady's roof with no fear of arrest even though his income of five hundred pounds would not keep him in gloves. His fears dissolved by his 'mother', as *The Town* suggested, he went his own careless way as before the bolt from a cloudless blue had fallen upon him.

He attended race meetings, lost far more than he won, and his gambling debts at Crockford's mounted rapidly. Yet no trivia of money or the lack of it troubled him. The lady's visitors at Gore House were, as always, enchanted with the glamorous d'Orsay who did the honours to the habitués and to all newcomers of importance who now included Charles Dickens. The famous author of *Pickwick, Oliver Twist, Nicholas Nickleby* and others of his works that like Bulwer's successes would live for ever, was a welcome guest at Gore House; and became one of 'the Blessington's' most intimate friends. In one of the letters exchanged between them: 'The year goes round so fast,' he tells her, 'that when anything occurs to remind me of its whirling I lose my breath and am bewildered. So your handwriting last night had as startling an effect upon me as though you had sealed your note with one of your eyes . . .'

The note from her which had so startling an effect upon Dickens was a reminder of his promise to contribute to *The Keepsake*. She had lately become editress of this, another hardy annual in line with her *Book of Beauty*; and these together with churning out two novels a year, 'my potboilers', she called them, that must never boil over if she sought to keep d'Orsay's wolves from her door, were causing her to feel the strain of continuous work day in, night out, till dawning.

D'Orsay, as always, despite his debts, continued to bask in the comfort and care of her whom he 'adored', as he never ceased to tell her. He charmed Dickens as he had charmed Bulwer and all who came to wait upon the fascinating, witty and still beautiful Lady Blessington.

'My goodness, Sally, I never cease to wonder how you do it!' remarked Ellen, now Lady Canterbury, for her husband had recently received a viscountcy on his retirement as Speaker of the House of Commons.

'Do what?' inquired her sister looking up from a sheet of proofs she was correcting for a forthcoming novel, *The Confessions of an Elderly Lady*, a companion to her previous *Confessions of an Elderly Gentleman*.

Ellen had called at an awkward time and notwithstanding the butler's murmur: 'Her ladyship is not at home,' had rustled past him into her sister's sanctum. Useless to hold Ellen out if she insisted on coming in.

'How you keep going at it hammer and tongs,' was Ellen's answer to Sally's question. 'Not only do you publish two books a year – three-volume novels and those annuals too, but you still have time for men to swarm around you in flocks.'

' 'Tis the drones that swarm. Sheep follow each other in flocks,' smiled Sally.

'Those who come here,' Ellen said, 'are bees – or drones if you like, for the others are the dilettantes, the sheep who herd together.'

'But the majority, if sheep, are prize exhibits and if drones, one or other will capture the Queen and be killed by her.'

'Which one have you killed? Disraeli, Bulwer – or is it your latest, a royal one now and he *is* a drone if you like, kicking his heels here while he waits to take France by storm.'

'If you mean Nap he is not yet acknowledged royal.'

'Nap? Is that what you call him. I thought Nap was a game of cards!'

Resignedly the proofs were laid aside while she thought: She will stay here for dinner and keep on and on – no work for me till midnight . . . And she said:

'I allude to Louis Napoleon whose mother Hortense – I met her in Rome – is the daughter of Josephine, the great Napoleon's wife. He is an exile from France

244

after his attempt to seize the throne of Louis Philippe, but he is only here on a brief visit. He intends to come back next year.'

'So he's your latest catch, is he?'

'I don't catch anyone – they all attempt to catch me, but they never do.'

'Greville dined with us the other night,' Ellen was enjoying herself retailing the newest gossip, 'and he said that the Prince – that's to say "The Pretender" to the throne of France, as Greville called him, was wearing an enormous ornament, a spread eagle in diamonds clutching what looked to be a cannon ball of rubies.'

'Yes, he wears that as his badge of office.'

'Talking of a badge of office,' Ellen dropped her voice; a small worried crease between her delicate eyebrows. 'Fairlie, my son-in-law, has no office now. He never seems able to keep any position he is offered and what with the anxiety over that lovely child of theirs – none of the specialists Louisa consults can offer any hope that she will regain her speech let alone her hearing – I am quite distracted. Charles's peerage has brought him nothing – only more expense to keep up appearances. And Louisa isn't at all well either. She has been ordered a change of air for herself and Isabella. The doctors say London life is all wrong for her. There might be a faint chance that she would be able to hear however slightly if she lived out of London. I suppose you, Sally, would – would you?'

Sally finished that hinting pause:

'Of course. Let the darling come here. I'd adore to have her. She is such a lovely intelligent child to be so cruelly afflicted. Bring her to me as soon as you can, if Louisa can spare her.'

Louisa, Ellen's daughter, Mrs Fairlie, could willingly spare her. Unable to afford a long sojourn out of London or a permanent removal with the rest of her family, she welcomed her aunt's offer to take under her care the child whom Disraeli, enraptured at sight of the lovely little

creature, deaf and dumb from birth, described as 'the
'Beautiful Mute'.

The arrival of little Isabella, great-niece of Lady Blessington, offered the childless woman whose youth had been
deprived of her womanhood's fulfilment, a new resilience
in her frustrated middle age. This 'Beautiful Mute' now
compensated for the loss of much that Margaret Farmer
had missed.

In those summer months of 1837 Sunday was the one
day in the week she could devote herself entirely to Isabella.
With her visitors, Disraeli, Bulwer (who had just returned
to London after his separation from Rosina) she, seated
with them on the terrace would watch Isabella at play or
feeding the white fantail pigeons that came to take from
her hand while the golden pheasant would perch on her
shoulder. That she could not hear the soft coo of the pigeons
nor the hum of the bees in the herbaceous borders, nor
could she call to the dogs who followed her wherever she
went, was no loss to her who had known only silence in all
her short life.

Then, when the sun sank behind the trees and gilded the
roof of a house in Kensington, Isabella would curtsy to her
aunt's guests holding up her face to be kissed by the gentlemen, and would be taken to her little white bed in a room
that overlooked the gardens of the great red-bricked house,
a mere bird's flight from Kensington Gore.

On an early June morning Isabella stirred in her sleep
and woke. Yet she could not have heard the galloping of
hooves and wheels clattering post-haste along the King's
highway, nor the bustle and hurry at the gates to those
acres of tree-timbered gardens flung open to admit the
carriage, unless it were the vibrations of this noisy approach
in the stillness of that summer morning that caused her, for
an instant, to wake from her dreams, and turn on her
pillow to sleep and dream again.

And while the child slept, another child, or one just out

of childhood, was awakened by her mother whose bedroom in that country house in a Kensington village she shared.

'Drina! Drina!' she was breathlessly told. 'Vake! Get up at vonce! The Archbishop of Canterbury and Lord Conyngham haf komm to see you! . . .'

Wrapped in her dressing-gown she went slowly down the stairs, not a little scared – for why should the Archbishop wish to see her so early in the morning? . . . A long-case clock in the hall struck five sonorous notes.

Pale, clutching her dressing-gown closely about her, the fair-haired young girl with blue eyes, widely wondering, her mouth slightly open over a small receding chin, saw, as she entered the room, Lord Conyngham kneel to her, the Archbishop bow low to her and, as from a far distance, heard him say:

'His Majesty the King is dead. Long live . . . the Queen!'

## TEN

The Coronation year of the young Queen Victoria, although she was almost entirely unknown to the vast majority of her subjects, brought a great wave of rejoicing in Britain. It was as if a dead orchard, barren of fruit, had suddenly burgeoned with blossom overnight. Vanished as the snows of winter in spring's warmth was the memory of a series of bloated, dissipated and ridiculous old men with exception of the last of them, this girl's late uncle, considered to be 'the best of a bad lot'.

And she who had stepped from a schoolroom to a throne was given an unprecedented welcome from the crowds that lined the shouting streets of her capital as she drove in her state coach to Westminster Abbey for her crowning.

With the child Isabella beside her the Lady of Gore House had taken the day from her literary work to watch the procession from a window in Piccadilly and lend to the excited little one a glimpse of the girl Queen with her pink cheeks and fair hair seated in her robes of splendour, happily acknowledging the resounding cheers accompanied by the peal of bells from every church steeple.

And while the child in her shroud of silence heard no sound, she saw and seeing thought, but could not say, that a princess from a fairy tale had come to life.

Yet this year of rejoicing for England, that began so auspiciously for the little girl Queen, did not augur so well for the Blessington–d'Orsay ménage. Not that anything so tiresome as debts and clamorous creditors could trouble Carlyle's 'Phoebus Apollo of dandyism', however much it may have harassed his 'adorée'.

Striving to keep up appearances, to be always the

gracious hostess, she received with every evidence of partisanship the claimant to the throne of France, Louis Napoleon Bonaparte when he returned to London in that same Coronation year.

That d'Orsay at once presented himself to the exiled prince at his house in Carlton House Terrace gladdened the heart of Lady Blessington. She was thankful to see he had found an interest beyond his own supreme ego and self-indulgence in support of this scion of the Bonapartes. But for all her 'pot-boiling' efforts to maintain her position as editress of two annuals and the author of a twice-yearly production of three-volume novels, she could still help those of her relatives dependent upon her assistance.

Her father had recently died aged seventy. She had regularly sent him the quarterly allowance made him by Blessington, which he as regularly drank away, eventually to kill him. There were countless others, both relatives and even casual acquaintances, whose hard-up tales reached her ears and to whom, whether deserving or not, she would always be generous with largesse she could ill afford.

As for d'Orsay, she must now give all she could scrape together to ward off the insistent demands of his creditors. Not that she had ever refused to subsidize him when he was continually overdrawn with his bank; but as his debts alarmingly increased she, in her turn, was discredited by those who, having failed to gain satisfaction from d'Orsay, would threateningly approach her, since d'Orsay had given them to understand she would stand security for him.

Yet all these difficulties were but minor trials compared to the more personal misfortunes that dogged her during the three years following the Queen's accession.

In her unending toil at her desk, interspersed with the entertainment of notabilities who might prove to be sub-scribers to her annuals, the one joy and compensation for her wearisome work was the lovely child whose frail body sustained so uncomplainingly the affliction with which she had been born. But those few years while she had Isabella in her care passed too swiftly for the woman who had never known or been given love as she knew it now.

The child's delicate fingers had been taught to voice her silent speech; and because of nature's deficiencies she had developed an intelligence beyond her years. A voracious reader, she delighted in signed copies of Bulwer's or Disraeli's works presented to her by the authors. But most of all did she enjoy reading the Bible and devoured chapters from Genesis to the Gospels, missing out many that were too dull and difficult to understand. Some which she did read she could not understand either, and would write questions to her aunt in round, clear letters.

Seated on the terrace with the white poodle, her aunt's favourite dog at her feet, she watched the reddening sky where the sun's journey westward tinged the clouds with gold and saffron; and the thought may have formed in that young too speculative mind: Did God, perhaps, dress the clouds in those pretty colours for the death of the sun? No, it couldn't be, for the sun never died. It rose again in the morning – as the Bible said Jesus had risen in three days. For a wedding, maybe. Whose wedding? God's wedding? . . . And taking from her knee the note book in which she wrote her questions and their answers: 'Please,' she asked in large round careful letters, 'is God married?'

And she watched her aunt's lips form the reply:

'No, darling, God is a spirit. There is no marriage or giving in marriage in Heaven with God the Father.'

'But,' the pencil wrote again the words: 'If God is a spirit and not married how can he have a son? Jesus is his son isn't he?'

'Yes, my love, as you are God's dear little daughter, for we are all God's children,' was the answer to the child's lovely face upturned to her, the golden hair like a halo round her head in the last of the sun's rays.

'But,' persisted the written unpunctuated question, 'it is in the Gospel that Jesus is God at least he does not say so himself not eggzackly –' (carefully altered to exsackly) – 'he says I am does not he so how can he be both and as it says he has a mother Mary is his mother isn't she?' Laboriously the words were spelled out. 'So why if he had a mother and is God as well as a man who has a son why is he not married to Mary. It is all very puzz —'

It was here, and something to the relief of her aunt, the point of the pencil broke so that the puzzle which has puzzled more sophisticated inquirers than a seven-year-old 'Beautiful Mute' was evasively answered, still more to puzzle Isabella, with:

'Try to tell yourself, dearest, that "I believe, help thou my unbelief".'

Having recovered from her surprise, to say nothing of her alarm at these written questions, Lady Blessington was still more watchful in her guardianship of the child entrusted to her care. And as two years slid by from summer to harsh winter months, she saw, and hardly dared to see, the slow relentless pursuit of the enemy drawing near and ever nearer to its innocent victim who had weathered the storms of whooping cough, measles and the like infantile illnesses, always to recover and to grow more frail and frailer still, while the doctor pronounced with hearty cheer that she would grow out of it. . . .

What she would grow out of was not medically defined, and did not altogether assuage the fear that watched those delicate fingers, so like the fallen petals of a rose, spell as she had been taught, to voice her silent speech.

The woman in her care of this beloved child had given up all thought of work, heard the grave-faced specialist called in for his further opinion pronounce his doubtful verdict. Those small deaf ears could not hear, but seeing her aunt's tears that followed the doctor's departure, she stretched out a hand in comfort and to ask for her 'book'.

And when brought to her she wrote:

'Do not cry dear Aunt the doctor does not know that I know I will be well again soon and Gods son he told me so I dreamed he said that I am to go to another house more in

the country than this is and where I will be able to speak
with my voice I dream that very often . . .'

Her room overlooking Kensington Gore had been
changed so that she could see the spacious grounds of Gore
House and the birds for her delight; and when she was
lifted to the open window the white fantails would flutter
down to feed from her hand.

She wrote a letter to her 'Dear Aunt' to thank her in the
words she could not speak for:

'. . . a barley sugar and large cake. I am writing in bed,
at night. I have a pain and cough a deal. How kind you are
to bring me what I want. Give my love to Alfred . . .'

This note Isabella wrote was treasured by her 'Dear
Aunt' and endorsed:

'From my Blessed grand-niece written on Saturday night
January 28, 1843 . . . She expired on 31st January at twenty
minutes before eight in the evening when she resigned her
pure spirit without a struggle . . .'

But not without a struggle did her grand-aunt resign herself to this bitter loss of the child who had replaced the
daughter never born to her, and in her thwarted womanhood could never have been conceived . . .

It was a melancholy year for her to whom 'this blow has
fallen so heavily upon me', as she wrote to Henry Bulwer,
Edward's brother, now Chargé d'Affaires at the Embassy in
Paris. Then, within two months of Isabella's death, her
mother, Louisa Fairlie collapsed suddenly and died, her
heart and strength worn out with grief and the long painful
illness of her child. The husband of Mrs Fairlie had been
incapable of earning a living and had been helped by his
mother-in-law; but since the death of his wife he could no
longer look for assistance from Lady Canterbury or her
husband who, himself in receipt of a handsome pension of
four thousand a year since his retirement as Speaker of the
House of Commons and his elevation to the peerage,
systematically lived beyond his means; so Lady Blessington
was called upon to help her niece's widower, John Fairlie.

And all this besides her other dependants in Ireland, her sister Mary Ann, Countess Marsault, her two nieces, the daughters of Robert Power, and always – Alfred.

Then, a year after the passing of Isabella, Lord Canterbury died as suddenly of a heart attack as had his stepdaughter, Louisa. From the severe shock of these treble deaths within so short a time, Ellen Canterbury suffered a severe breakdown of health, and she too died within four months of her husband while staying with her sister at Gore House.

The pressure of financial embarrassments, the deaths of those dear to her, the gradual estrangement from her friends, since she could no longer afford the lavish entertainments of the past, told upon Margaret's health; and as time slipped by, so did those men who had thronged her salon also leave her, either for marriage or other claims upon them. They no longer required her influence to procure them literary appointments.

Disraeli, one of her most loyal adherents, wrote to her from Bradenham, his father's house, to congratulate her on her latest book of essays, *Desultory Thoughts and Reflections*; and to inform her of his intended marriage to the widow of his Conservative co-candidate for Maidstone, Wyndham Lewis . . . 'I assure you,' he wrote, 'that a day seldom passes that I do not think or speak of you, and I hope I shall always be allowed by you to count the Lady of Gore House among my dearest and most valued of friends . . .'

Whether his future bride, Mary Anne Wyndham Lewis, some twelve years his senior, was equally hopeful of counting her future husband among Lady Blessington's dearest and most valued of friends is not known, but after his marriage he wrote again from Bradenham to say:

'I propose calling at Gore House tomorrow with my dear Mary Anne who I am sure will be delighted at finding herself under a roof that has proved to me at all times so hospitable and devoted . . . From ever your Dis.'

If 'ever her Dis' found the lady's hospitable roof as devoted to his Mary Anne as it was to him, it is likely that Mrs Disraeli had been at pains to confide in her hostess as she told her husband after his several proposals of marriage had been rejected: that the disparity of their ages could not make for happiness. 'But,' said Mary Anne who still retained the faint Devonshire burr in her voice with which she had been born and brought up on her grandfather's Devonshire farm before her apprenticeship to a milliner in Exeter – 'I did tell him that 'tis better to be twelve years younger as was I to my late departed, than to be twelve years older as I am to Dizzy. And he said – quite hurt he was too – "You think I am too young for you" – No, I said, "I am too old for you . . ." '

But it turned out to be one of the most successful and happiest marriages of any politician in the nineteenth century; and when in his later years Queen Victoria offered her great statesman a peerage, he begged to be allowed to refuse it, 'Because, your Majesty,' he said, 'there is one far more deserving than am I of such an honour, since I owe all that I was and all that I am to her . . .'*

So that Mary Anne was honoured with a Viscountcy in her own right; and not until her death did Disraeli in his old age accept from his Sovereign Queen, whom he had created Empress of India, the Earldom of Beaconsfield.

Yet despite the few faithful friends left to the Queen of Gore House, fate had more cruel blows with which to buffet her.

She found a temporary respite from a succession of misfortunes when Dickens, editor of *The Daily News*, offered her the post of society correspondent in its columns for a provisional six months. The salary of £250 gave her an interim surcease from incessant debts incurred not only by d'Orsay whom she must always assist, but also her own liabilities . . . But not for long.

* See *The Perfect Wife. Life of Mary Anne, Viscountess Beaconsfield.*

254

Dickens renounced his editorship before the provisional six months had ended, and the new editor had no further use for her services. Again must she take up the burden of her two annuals and the onerous work of producing her twice-yearly novels, yet the income earned from these had considerably decreased. No longer was she a popular novelist both here and in America where the 'Works of Lady Blessington' (much was made of her title in the States) had been published in two large octavo volumes. These contained five of her novels and *The Conversations of Byron*, yet their sales were far less than the praise offered them from the reviewers.

There was still another blow – a thunderbolt – to fall upon her: this an act of God as she was forced to accept it.

The winter of 1845 had brought to Ireland a severe potato blight, followed by famine to render the peasantry and others destitute. Particularly did these dire happenings affect Margaret Blessington whose income of two thousand derived solely from her husband's Irish property. The trustees of her jointure now wrote to inform her that owing to the present disastrous conditions in Ireland the income therefrom could not be paid.

In desperation she wrote to Bulwer, her staunch support in any difficulty. His ascendance rose high as hers sank low. He had been created a baronet in the Melbourne Ministry in token of his literary achievements and now Sir Edward Bulwer-Lytton (he had taken his mother's maiden name when he received his honour) replied to his 'Dearest Lady Blessington' that he 'had none but pleasurable recollections unbroken by a single shred of insincerity or wrong . . .' Which was balm to her who ever since her tormented childhood had been accused and defamed of both . . . And Bulwer – she could never think of or call him anything but the name by which she had always known him – advised her to consult her lawyer and insist he claim for her absolute priority of all to which she was entitled. But this sound advice only succeeded in her lawyer obtaining a meagre portion of her income and the pledge that she make up the deficit with the sale of her jewellery, much of which had already been sold to pay for the more immediate of d'Orsay's debts, besides almost all the silver stolen in the burglary at Seamore Place.

Yet there was worse to come than this latest misfortune. Her two annuals, *The Keepsake* and *The Book of Beauty* were now her chief source of revenue since the sales of her novels had brought her too little to maintain her many commitments — and d'Orsay. Then came the shattering news that Charles Heath, her one anchorage on whom she had relied as a safe harbour in her perilous literary voyage, was declared bankrupt!

Among his numerous liabilities there were seven hundred pounds owing to Lady Blessington for the editorship of her two annuals of which he had been the sole proprietor.

Now was she lost indeed. Seven hundred pounds owing to her never to be paid!

At the end of her tether, her resources dwindled while daily d'Orsay's debts mounted to formidable heights, since for the past two years, he had been living a life of evasion from duns, never daring to venture out of the grounds of Gore House until after dark lest he be met with a bombardment of writs.

And still in his carefree optimism and unbounded faith in himself and his universal popularity with men, he refused to face reality. Despite that each day brought ominous reminders of his financial collapse, he, always delighting in the spectacular, saw himself as a crusader quixotically supporting Prince Louis Napoleon Bonaparte whose abortive attempts to seize the throne of France had landed him in gaol.

During his imprisonment, d'Orsay exploited him in numerous letters to France and excitable oratory in England to all who would indulgently listen. When the Prince escaped from prison and reappeared in London, d'Orsay paid far less attention to his own difficulties than to those of the heir presumptive to the Throne of France who had suffered such malicious degradation, as d'Orsay loyally regarded it. While he and the supporters of this Bonaparte were fighting to restore him to the throne, d'Orsay may have seen himself as a future king's favourite.

When he slunk behind bushes in the gardens of Gore House hiding from bailiffs, or walking arm in arm with his prince, he heard from the royal refugee of his sufferings during the revolution of 1848: how he had been spat upon, despised by the royalists who denied *him*, Louis-Philippe, his right to the Kingdom of France or, as self-styled, King of the French, finally to be driven from his throne to flee the city sobbing: *'Comme Charles le dix, absolument comme Charles le dix.'* . . . And then – Paris, under mob rule in the government of France, miraculously elected him – yes, him, *'Moi! le President . . . Président de la République Française!'*

So immersed was d'Orsay in the astonishing reversal from rags to riches of the Republican President that he gave no thought to the sinister threats that pursued him. His aim and purpose now was to follow the Prince President and place himself at his elbow with the reminder that, as his father before him, he had always been loyal to the Bonapartes and if this Bonaparte were not the King of France, he was of equal power or even more power than that of the ex-monarch, for did he not represent the People of France? '. . . Sûrement?' he railed at his lady, having broken in upon her at her work, 'Mais sûrement Napoléon will not forget me-Me!' he thumped his chest. 'I was always his support – his beaux ami in the days of his malheures and now he has not'ing for me, not'ing! I had thought for au moins un ministre des beaux arts – but no! Is zis the reward for my fidélité?' . . . And so on and on while she sat, pen in hand, a blot upon the sheet of paper where she had been interrupted in the middle of a sentence.

Just as she was about to offer words of consolation, he tempestuously continued, a hand ruffling his auburn curls:

'Everyone here, mais *everyone* from the Duke of Wellington to the cab-men – le cocher – believe he will do somet'ing for me now he is in power – le Président. Mais non! He must – vraiment he must – *now*!'

And now his valet was at the door.

'Pardon, Miladi, M'sieur le Comte . . .'

D'Orsay rounded on him savagely. *'Diable! Qu'est ce que vous voulez? Allez donc!'*

A man from the pastrycook had arrived, he was informed by the apologetic valet, daring his master's wrath to remind him that M'sieur le Comte had expressly commanded the pastrycook to bring the cakes and pâtés and all he had ordered for dinner that evening for Monsieur le Comte to see if he approved . . .

'Now de nom sacré! I forget – le dîner! I must dress for le dîner. Tell this bête to leave his *gâteaux – mon dieu! Gâteaux!* At a time like this!'

He rushed from the room and up the stairs to his own apartment followed by his valet whom he bade:

'Le vert. I wear the green and the new pantaloons – les jaunes.' While the man went into an inner closet where his suits hung in cupboards ranged along the walls, he sat before his dressing-glass to examine his face . . . too pale. A good impression must be given to the Chargé d'Affaires of the Embassy here in Londres. No longer pour le roi mais pour la République, le Président . . . 'Hélas!' the exclamation broke from him as he turned to see, not his valet but a man in a white cap and apron carrying a tray and on it a long envelope; no gâteaux.

'You are the Count Dawsay?'

The astonished Count rose from his seat before the looking-glass, his face bereft of every expression save that of wrathful amaze as the man handed him the envelope.

D'Orsay, controlling his horror at what he divined the

packet contained, the intruder produced his bailiff's badge of office. . . . 'Sacré Bleu! Un appel!'

The furtive hiding and slinking evasion from behind bushes in the walled gardens of Gore House was over. The enemy – this *sacré favori de la loi* had stormed the gates. He was a prisoner unless – But no! Not yet!

The evening sun lowering to light the tree-tops with fiery shafts, cast swords of gold through the window across the Persian rug at his feet.

'*S'il vous plaît*,' politely he waved the officer to a chair. 'Asseyez-vous – be seated if you please. That you have the avantage de moi is to your credit . . . I will be happy to oblige you and the gentleman you serve who have give me the honeure of your visit. But if you will please to sit —' he pointed to the ottoman, 'for I must finish my toilette before my guests arrive who will dine with – Pierre!' To his man who, standing agape, he gestured to disrobe him and then dress him in the dinner suit – *le vert* – *et les pantalons jaunes*. Then his shoes must be replaced for shining black pumps with paste buckles, his cravat adjusted, his hair curled and the final touches from the hare's foot to cheeks somewhat too pale, and:

'Voilà! I am at your service, monsieur.' Gracefully he bowed to the sheriff's white aproned emissary who rose holding out the envelope which d'Orsay had refused to take – 'but not tonight. It is no longer the day, and your – what is it you call zis t'ing?' Always, when it suited him he would exaggerate his French accent. 'It is too late to gif to me.'

'It is a summons, which in England,' the messenger of the law stonily explained, 'is called a writ, and if not replied to within seven days you will be arrested. You are warned.'

Saying so, he again handed him the writ, and head high, the tray under his arm, he went.

No sooner was he gone than d'Orsay tore open the packet and after one glance at its contents, rushed from the room.

He burst in on Margaret. She had risen from her desk

where he had left her an hour before, and stood by the empty fireplace. She too held a document but was not looking at it. Her eyes, wide, startled, stared into space; her face was drained of all colour.

D'Orsay, disregardful of her pallor and her evident distress, for she shivered as if with cold although the evening was warm, poured out his tale. 'It is the end for me!' he cried. 'I have put him off for tonight – he cannot – what is it? – serve me the t'ing after the sun is down but tomorrow when the sun is up he will be here again! Crois tu – cette manière infâme – to come to me déguisé comme chef – I have not see what the t'ing it say —' he held it out to her. 'You read it – what it say.'

She smoothed the crumpled sheet of paper. The summons stated that he was being sued for two thousand pounds owing to – the name of the firm was unknown to her but she realized it had long been owing – an accumulation of three or four years' debts.

'You will be safe tomorrow,' she told him, 'as it is Sunday, but you cannot stay here another night. Gore House cannot guard you any longer. Nor can I because,' she looked down at the paper she held, 'because I too have been served with – this.' She showed him the writ which had been brought to her during the hour or so since he had left her.

It was an execution for a considerable sum, about fifteen thousand pounds owed to a firm that had supplied her with much of the equipment of Gore House when she moved there from Seamore Place. The firm, Howell and James, a year or two before, had taken out a policy on the life of Lady Blessington as security for her debt. To this on the advice of her solicitor she had agreed; but the firm, having heard the gossip that ran round the town concerning her straitened circumstances at Gore House and how a guard had been placed upon the gates, barred and locked against intrusion from d'Orsay's creditors and, as it was assumed, from her own, had decided not to wait for a future and

uncertain date to take their money. That both she and
d'Orsay were served on the same day and within the same
hour looked to be more than coincidental. It may have been
from one mutual source, if Howell and James were in
collusion with one or more of d'Orsay's many creditors.

It is characteristic of her who had always taken to herself his problems and difficulties that she did not complain
to him of this her latest calamity; for although she was not
– for the moment – in danger of imprisonment which certainly would be the fate of d'Orsay unless he left England
immediately, she knew she must at all costs devise means to
save herself from a similar disaster.

Again she urged him:

'You must go. You are safe until sundown, but there is
no time to be lost. You must leave now – at once – for
Paris.'

'Mais! Parbleu!' he cried frantically. 'How can I go now?
I have invitès for dinner. All is preparing. There is no *time*
to make the excuse – that I am ill – or dead – Dieu! I wish
I am —'

'Listen to me.' Forgetful of her own trouble, she insisted.
'You must leave here early in the morning. You can still
have your dinner. Your friends need know nothing of your
plans. Tell Pierre to pack you a bag and order a post-chaise.
You can be in France by the afternoon if you leave early
enough before sunrise.'

'My dinner!' he clutched her arm. 'What of my dinner?
I have mes amis – le chargé d'affaires from the Embassy, he
will arrange a ministre – I cannot leave my dinner.'

'I tell you that you will *have* your dinner! Your guests
shall come and you will be your own good self to amuse
them and give them those excellent pastries and *le pâté de
foie gras* – mind you send Pierre with some for me that the
pastrycook has brought.'

'How did he know I give un dîner tonight – le canaille?
And to bring a tray wiz him – ma foi! And the man – the

real pâtisserie man he came also at the same time probablement – and my chef he t'ink they are both together!'

She did not require to remind him of the sleuth-like prowlings in taverns of the Kensington and Brompton villages to glean gossip over the tankards concerning the strong guard put upon the gates of Gore House; nor the reason for it. The whole town knew of Comte d'Orsay's debts, and the servants of his 'amis' would have frequented the inns nearby in company with his own staff and stablemen.

'No!' he sank on his knees before her. 'I will not go wizout you to Paris – you must not let me go alone – how can I be wizout you in all zis miserable —' he buried his face in her skirts – 'siz so terrible t'ing that has come to me if you are not with me – and to leave you alone here?'

'I shall not be alone. I have half a dozen servants, my maid Anne and Ellen. As for this,' she disengaged from him who was sobbing. Whether his tears were real or not did nothing to alter her decision that he must be out of England on the morrow. 'This summons – is of no use to you or the law.' She tore it into shreds and flung the pieces in a wastepaperbasket by her desk. 'So when they repeat their writ and come here to arrest you,' she returned to him who still knelt, his face uplifted, his eyelashes smudged, 'there will be no d'Orsay to be dragged off to prison.'

'Prison! What you say?' He scrambled to his feet. 'I will not to be taken to – Sacré Bleu! prison! Jamais de la vie! .. I go. Yes, I go now.' He dashed to a bell-rope and pulled. To the footman who answered it – 'Tell my valet Pierre – to come to me.' And as the man bowed and withdrew: 'I will order Pierre to take messages – I will write to mes amis to say I go to Paris to ma grand'mère who is ill – See, I write the notes now.' He went to her desk, she followed him.

'You will tell Pierre,' she said calmly, 'to pack you a bag, only one, the rest can be sent off later, and you will receive your guests as if nothing has happened.' She arranged his cravat. 'You must put yourself to rights. Grovelling on the floor will not improve your appearance nor your nice new pantaloons.' And to Pierre who had entered, she gave him hurried directions in French and added that on no account was he to tell any of the other servants that his master was going to Paris tomorrow.


In the misty dawn of the next morning, he crept out of the house, cloaked and muffled, carrying a jewelled-headed swordstick; and with Pierre similarly cloaked and bearing a portmanteau, they gained the gates and unlocked them with a duplicate key. There was never any need to guard the doors or gates at night for no arrest could be made after sundown. A post-chaise with horses and postilions waited in the lane that led from the highway.

'Allez!' cried d'Orsay. And to the postilion on the nearest horse, 'Quick! I must be at Dover wiz'in four hours! . . .'

*     *     *

She had bidden him goodbye and Godspeed when he came to her bedroom, promised she would come to Paris so soon as she could deal with her own difficulties here. She had told him nothing much of these difficulties, that must entail, as she realized, her own removal from Gore House. Because apart from her own debt to Howell and James, she owed little more, since she had always striven to stay clear of any outstanding commitments. But from time to time she had subsidized d'Orsay; and her own tradespeople, knowing the straits he was in, had seen to it that either he or she must defray his accumulation of unpaid bills, so that she was confronted with debts of thousands of pounds not her own, but his.

She knew she could have asked and received help from Bulwer and others who would be only too willing to assist her; but pride forbade that. There was nothing else for her to do but to extricate herself and save her honour from an even worse scandal than any which for years had attacked her name. She would have to raise enough money somehow by selling the lease of her house and all its contents.

She consulted a well known auctioneer, one Phillips of New Bond Street. He went carefully through her assets. She had pictures and furniture, objets d'arts of considerable value; and when he had catalogued her effects, she found that with the lease of the house the total would realize something well above twelve thousand pounds. This would repay Howell and James and some of d'Orsay's immediate debts.

The date of the sale was scheduled for the first week in May. She, with her niece Ellen and her personal maid Anne Cooper, left Gore House for a quiet hotel in Mayfair. She deliberately avoided meeting any of her friends; she knew they would have tried to persuade her to cancel the sale and allow them to take over her liabilities. She held herself aloof from them, did not even allow them to know where she was staying.

An immense crowd of women from all ranks of Londoners, but particularly from Mayfair and Belgravia, thronged the rooms during the twelve days of the auction. It had been well advertised by Phillips to view 'the costly and elegant effects of the Rt. Hon. The Countess of Blessington retiring to the Continent'. Many of the women who had refused to know her, defamed her and spread scandalous reports of her association with d'Orsay, now flocked to see and gloat over her misfortune, to take up and finger with contemptuous shrugs and amused whispered asides the various articles to be sold, and such of her jewellery that had not already gone to defray the worst of d'Orsay's previous debts.

'She must have been a godsend to *les oncles*,' sniggered Lady Jersey, the doyenne of Almack's, 'this woman taken in adultery.'

'No,' corrected another of the ladies who had refused to

recognize her. '*Not* taken in adultery. Blessington was too engrossed with d'Orsay to care that she had been "taken" with him.'

'Or with Bulwer?' smiled another.

'Is he here?'

'I don't see him. Too busy, perhaps, consoling her, wherever she may be.'

But if Bulwer were not there that day he certainly attended the sale on one of the subsequent days, and bought a set of Byron's works in three volumes bound in morocco and inscribed with the Blessington arms; this he ordered to be sent to her, for she had promised to let him know her address in Paris.

Almost all her old friends and her subsequent biographer, Madden, were there and he reported: 'It was the most signal ruin of an establishment I ever witnessed . . . a crash on a grand scale, a sweeping clearance of all the house's treasures . . . The armchair, where the lady was wont to sit,' he sadly records, 'was occupied by a stout, coarse gentleman of the Jewish persuasion examining a marble hand extended on a book . . .'

Among the numerous people who came to look if not to buy was Thackeray, who had occasionally visited the Lady of Gore House in her happier days, but had been more interested in d'Orsay than in her. He visited d'Orsay in Paris shortly after he left Kensington, and wrote that he was 'mad with vanity'. He had shown Thackeray his poems which he declared were the best verses ever written, 'verses so fatuous and crazy as ever I saw . . .'

Nothing of d'Orsay's was on view at the sale; she could have included them and they would likely have fetched a considerable sum, but she had them all packed and stowed away to be taken to Paris for him with her own belongings, such as were left to her.

Disraeli was there but does not appear to have bought anything. The lovely portrait of Lady Blessington by

Lawrence went to Lord Hertford for well over three hundred pounds.*

The lease of Gore House with its contents was likely to fetch about £15,000 and that, with what had been allowed her by the trustees from her depleted jointure of two thousand, would enable her to live, if not in the luxury to which she had been accustomed, at least in a modest apartment in Paris.

Before she left London, when the sale was over, the house dismantled, the servants dismissed each with a grateful remuneration, she told Ellen Power, her niece, who had been with her through all her later trials, that she wished to go to the house and see it once more.

'May I go with you?' Ellen asked.

No, she wished to go alone . . .

She had a key to the front entrance; the gates were unlocked and gardeners still at work among the flower beds. She went up to one of them. She had paid their wages until such time as the lease of the house with its grounds should be sold, and to the head gardener she gave instructions.

'I am sure, according to my agent, that this house will be sold in the near future, but until then you will take care of the aviary and dovecote pending a new purchaser of the lease who will, of course, wish to retain your services.'

The man who was, as were all her staff, devoted, assured her that the birds would be well cared for, and the dogs, but if he might be allowed to keep the spaniel —

'Certainly. I shall take Blanche' (the white poodle bitch) 'with me to Paris when I go, but if the purchaser of Gore House should not want the birds, Mr Disraeli and Sir Edward Bulwer-Lytton will share them.'

She had arranged with both 'Dizzy' and Bulwer to take the birds in the event of a purchaser not wanting them, to which they both agreed. Disraeli said his father would be

* Now in the Wallace Collection.

delighted to have the white fantails at Bradenham, and Bulwer had told her that any birds or dogs she wished to dispose of would be welcome at Knebworth, his mother's house.

She walked slowly across the smooth-shaven lawns, heard with failing heart the soft coo-coo of the fantails whose door to the dovecote had been closed while the gardeners were at work. But in the aviary where the golden pheasant lodged, the door had been left ajar; he swooped down to her shoulder. She caressed his satin yellow head, remembering how Isabella had loved him.

Swallowing tears, she reminded herself that Marcus Aurelius had said self-pity is the greatest form of cowardice – but she thought, I am at heart a coward for I have never been able to confront life without a grudge and the desire never to have been born.

And as she inserted her key into the door of her empty hall she saw that the walls, panelled in pastel shades, showed spaces where pictures had hung, now festooned with cobwebs. Wisps of straw and footprints in the dust denoted the carting away of all that had been sold. She would have to tell her agent who was selling the lease that he must send servants to clean up the rooms where the auction had been held.

So on into the library connected with her own sanctum, her writing-room. The scenes of desolation struck her with a sense of recurrence . . . I have seen all this before! The thought swept down upon her in a sudden blinding flash . . . the crystal! She had seen all this emptiness, the grave of her past life in that ball of glass she had gazed into so long ago . . . Those who had sat at the round table in this empty forsaken room were here again with the memory of how Bulwer had hung on the words of Varley, who had known Blake and discoursed on the marvels of mystical science . . And how Disraeli, in apparent wrapt attention with tongue in cheek, had professed himself an ardent disciple . . .

As a drowning person is supposed to see his or her whole

life pass before him in a kaleidoscopic series of impressions, so, standing solitary there in her desolate library, its shelves bereft of their books some of which she had written, so did she see her life from its earliest years spread before her, as in a tapestry, scenes that had long lain dormant in a corridor of her mind, resurrected and relived . . .

Shadows of the past were retraced in fleeting but vital glimpses through clouds of years; her father, red of face, in a drunken rage – the day he threw at her a goblet of wine that spilled on her dress; her mother, a small angry ghost, her hair in wisps, scolding her for the mess on the dress cut down from one of her own – 'You clumsy brat! Upsetting your father's wine.' Useless to deny it. She would often be scolded for what was none of her fault. So it had been all her life, wrongfully accused that she must carry with her the stigma of adultery and – worse, because of the marriage with d'Orsay of Blessington's daughter . . . The rowdy dinner table and her father's guests from the barracks making merry, and Captain Jenkins glancing across at her where she sat, downcast and hating it all, and Captain Farmer leering at her when she got up to go, and her father saying between hiccups 'No! You stay . . .' The agony of her wedding night and her husband – O God, her husband! And the ache and torment of her shocked mind and body and she not yet fifteen . . .

Shuddering she sank on to a window seat. Dust had collected where she had been used to sit and watch Isabella at play with the dogs . . . All gone. All I have loved have left me. If I could only have lived a normal life as a woman, wife, and mother! Why should I have been denied what should have been my birthright? Success? . . . Mirage!

She dug her nails into a palm of her hand. What has been my success? Journalistic patter. Trashy novels, the only work I have ever done that could be worthwhile is my Conversations, and those are only what I have remembered from my talks with him and much of it – the worst of it –

invented . . . My 'Idlers' in France and Italy, more journalistic, half-invented jargon. And those few years of respite
in rural Hampshire with Jenkins . . . I owe all of my knowledge of literature to Jenkins, not that he cared for as did I,
the masters of literature, but I could make free of his
library . . . And the day Lord Mountjoy came to dine . . .
'I think we have met some time ago at your father's house
in Ireland . . .' And again a bargain struck for her, twice sold
as if I were up for sale in a slave market. Ten thousand
pounds' worth of me! . . .

A bitter laugh escaped her. Jenkins, for all his wish to
make me his wife were I divorced from Farmer, was not
above striking a bargain for the price of the jewels he had
given me and all else I had cost him as his mistress, which
I never was – not in actuality. Neither his nor any other
man's mistress, come to that . . . Then at last a second
marriage, Countess of Blessington, luxury, wealth and . . .
emptiness. Why was my life with him so empty? Unreal. A
puppet of a woman acting a part. Despite a spurious success
as author, and the splendour of my salons, I was never more
than a puppet pulled by a string dancing to the tunes
expected of me before an audience of men, some destined to
greatness, who wanted from me all I could not give . . .
Warped. I have been warped from my childhood. Dis-
dained, discarded. The Ugly Duckling, unloved and unlov-
ing, robbed of any love I could have had to offer . . . The
poor solace of my maternal instinct that showered its
longing for a son upon him for whom I sacrificed myself,
leaving behind my name a trail of slime as if I were a slug
crawling in the mire of scandal, to lose me all that could
have made life bearable . . . *Damn* Marcus Aurelius! I *am*
full of self-pity, a pitiable coward sitting here to bemoan all
that I was and all that I was not or might have been. And
now nothing . . . Nothing left to me but a broken life.

On the wall opposite where she sat a cracked mirror
hung askew. One of the chains supporting it had been
loosened. She got up to examine it thinking it might have

been knocked in the removal of a tallboy that had stood beside it.

And as she gazed at her reflection, distorted in the mirror that bore a deep gash across its splintered glass, she recalled, among the drifting debris of her memories, a verse from Byron's *Childe Harold*.

> Even as a broken mirror, which the glass
> In every fragment multiplies and makes,
> A thousand images of one that was,
> The same and still the same, the more it breaks
> And thus the heart will do which not forsakes
> Living in sheltered guise and still and cold . . .
> Yet withers on till all without is old.

*    *    *

A slight breeze stirred the calm waters of the Channel as the boat moved slowly from the quayside. Leaning on the rail she saw the white cliffs recede until a dim blur on the horizon melted to a shadow between the sea and sky, while her lips framed whispered words remembered . . . 'As of a song unsung'.

AFTERWORD

She was never to return to the England she had left and held such poignant memories. Her englamoured life had been a bizarre contradiction, a picaresque so fair in promise, so unfulfilled.

In her years of marriage, of widowhood and success — that she had always belittled — or, knowing her limitations she concealed behind a mask of gaiety and humour, her life's bitter disillusionment.

Modern psychologists might have attributed her abnormal revulsion to the sexual act as resultant on the horrific initiation of her wedding night while yet an undeveloped child, and the three months of bestial sadism that preceded her escape from a husband who must have been deranged.

Her love for d'Orsay as misjudged by her enemies was, so she herself admitted, the thwarted love of a mother for a son. That her name has excited so much interest and speculation, for the most part equivocal, during the past hundred and fifty years is possibly due less to her contribution to literature than her attraction for men, her intimate friends, whose names have become immortalized.

After she left England for Paris in her fifty-ninth year we know little of her life more than the renewed friendship with Ida de Guiche and her husband, and that she took upon herself the continued care of d'Orsay and his debts. Although he had by this time regained his full legacy it had been mortgaged up to the hilt, but he still managed to present to an admiring audience, including Rachel, the famous Parisienne actress, 'the Phoebus Apollo of dandyism'. Yet beneath this legendary façade a more realistic image emerged when he was bereft of the woman who had sacrificed herself for him.

From the wretched childhood of Sally Power and such obscure beginnings, few have scaled the heights of social brilliance, favoured and disfavoured, to die a lonely and frustrated death in Paris where she had once been received with homage from the British Ambassador, the Court of King Charles X and lesser mortals. And it was in this Paris where she enjoyed to entertain in the magnificent salon of the mansion which had once belonged to Napoleon's Marshal Ney, that she became the widow of the first and last Earl of Blessington.

On her retirement to Paris the sale of Gore House provided her with sufficient means to live in a modest apartment in the Rue du Cirque near to the Champs-Elysée, but within four days of her removal there she was taken with a seizure and beyond all medical aid her heart refused to rally.

She died more peacefully than she had lived.


Not until he had irrevocably lost her did d'Orsay realize all she had suffered in her ceaseless care of him, had endured infamy and disgrace for her association with one whose narcissistic egomania had caused her crucifixion.

When at last he saw himself for what he was, the utterly selfish child of a would-be mother's love, he confessed to Madden who visited him in Paris and found him completely shattered by her death. 'In losing her,' he said, 'I have lost everything in the world that mattered to me . . .'

Too late he strove to make amends by causing a monument to be built on the fringe of St Germain where she had always wished to lie rather than in the Blessington vault in the Ireland that held such grievous memories for her.

On a hillside above the village of Chambourcy overlooking the distant green and gracious valley, and the far distant waters of the Seine, d'Orsay bought a plot of land.

There stands the tomb, a pyramid of granite, in the shade

of an old chestnut tree. And there to this day can be seen the last resting place of her who as Blake might have called her the 'little girl lost', Sally Power, remembered in a few simple lines composed in verse by Walter Savage Landor to which he adds an epitaph to Margaret, Countess of Blessington.

> Thou sleepest, not forgotten nor unmourned
> Beneath the chestnut shade by St Germain

And three years later d'Orsay was brought to lie beside her.

# AUTHORITIES CONSULTED


*Blessington–D'Orsay: A Masquerade*. Michael Sadleir
*Bulwer: A Panorama: Edward & Rosina*. Michael Sadleir
*The Most Gorgeous Lady Blessington* (2 Vols). J. Fitzgerald Molloy
*D'Orsay, The Complete Dandy*. W. Teignmouth Shore
*The Idler in France* (2 Vols). Countess of Blessington
*The Idler in Italy* (2 Vols). Countess of Blessington
*A History of France*. André Maurois
*Lady Blessington's Conversations of Lord Byron* edited by E. J. Lovell Jr.
*Reminiscences & Recollections (1810–1860)*. Captain Gronow
*Literary Life & Correspondence of the Countess of Blessington* (3 Vols). R. R. Madden
Extracts from Greville's *Diary*, *Ladies' Magazine*, Blessington Papers, *etc.*

Also available by
DORIS LESLIE

## THE MARRIAGE OF MARTHA TODD

'Miss Leslie is one of those women authors who have an almost psychic contact with their characters . . . brilliantly portrays the Victorian double-attitude to sex.' *Sunday Express*

## THE REBEL PRINCESS

'Doris Leslie . . . plunges the reader right into the intrigue and debaucheries of a court dedicated, it seemed, to anything rather than ruling the country.' *Books and Bookmen*

## A YOUNG WIVES' TALE

(A sequel to *Folly's End* and *The Peverills*)

'Miss Leslie has given to her story a certain political seasoning; there is reference to the unrest – industrial and social – that was so marked a feature of life both in Britain and elsewhere during the early years of the last century.' *Guardian Journal*

## THE DESERT QUEEN

'Colourful mixture of T. E. Lawrence and Elinor Glyn.' *The Sunday Times*

## THE DRAGON'S HEAD

'An accomplished romance.' *Books and Bookmen*

## THE  INCREDIBLE DUCHESS

'It's all full of colour and drama, from Elizabeth's early life at court, to her final days in France, where she died "unmourned in England, but loved to the last by the great European women of her time." ' *The Oxford Times*

## CALL BACK YESTERDAY

'Noel's marriage founders when her selfish young husband turns to other women . . . All this and the wartime blitz as well.' *Evening Despatch*